THE SIALKOT SAGA

About the Author

Ashwin Sanghi is among India's highest-selling English fiction authors. He has written several bestsellers in the Bharat Series (*The Rozabal Line, Chanakya's Chant, The Krishna Key, The Sialkot Saga, Keepers of the Kalachakra, The Vault of Vishnu*) and two *New York Times* bestselling crime thrillers with James Patterson, *Private India* (sold in the US as *City on Fire*) and *Private Delhi* (sold in the US as *Count to Ten*). He has also co-authored several non-fiction titles in the 13 Steps Series on Luck, Wealth, Marks, Health and Parenting.

Ashwin has been included by *Forbes India* in their Celebrity 100 and by *The New Indian Express* in their Culture Power List. He is a winner of the Crossword Popular Choice Award 2012, Atta Galatta Popular Choice Award 2018, WBR Iconic Achievers Award 2018, the Lit-O-Fest Literature Legend Award 2018 and the Kalinga Popular Choice Award 2021.

He was educated at Cathedral and John Connon School, Mumbai, and St Xavier's College, Mumbai. He holds an MBA from Yale University. Ashwin lives in Mumbai with his wife, Anushika, and son, Raghuvir.

You can connect with Ashwin via the following channels:Website www.sanghi.in

Twitter @ashwinsanghi
Instagram @ashwin.sanghi
Koo @ashwinsanghi
Clubhouse @ashwinsanghi
Facebook fb.com/ashwinsanghi
YouTube youtube.com/ashwinsanghi
LinkedIn linkedin.com/in/ashwinsanghi

Acknowledgements

It would be impossible to write the books that I do without the assistance, input, guidance, love and support of so many. Here are some of those without whom these books in the *Bharat Series* may not have happened.

My publishers, HarperCollins *Publishers* India—in particular, Ananth Padmanabhan and Udayan Mitra—who always ensure that my books reach my readers quickly and efficiently.

Prita Maitra, my primary editor, who continues to be indispensable in editing the series in addition to several other individuals including Karthika VK, Deepthi Talwar, Ashok Rajani, Aparna Gupta, Karthik Venkatesh and Swati Daftuar whose edits, inputs and guidance have been invaluable in various books of the series from time to time.

Rupesh Talaskar, my talented illustrator, who has meticulously executed maps and internal illustrations in various books of the series, and Semy Haitenlo, who has designed stunning book covers for each of them.

Ameya Naik, the versatile composer who has composed the haunting tracks used in the trailers of these books, and the teams at TwistStudio and Oktobuzz for their video trailers and social media support from time to time.

Deepshikha Kumar and Nijansh Verma of SpeakIn for their advice and input on my speaking tours and events. Also, Ashoo Naik and Chirag Nihalani of Collective for their efforts towards bringing my stories to a wider audience through cinema, television and OTT.

My parents, Mahendra and Manju Sanghi, and my siblings, Vidhi and Vaibhav, who have always encouraged me to follow my dreams. My wife, Anushika, and son, Raghuvir, who have been my constant support in my writing endeavours. Had it not been for their unconditional love, none of my books would have been possible. My little rakhi-sister Farah, who has taught me that not everything in life can be explained and that some things are better left unexplained.

Gautam Padmanabhan, my friend, philosopher and guide who gave me my first publishing break and has encouraged me through several stories of the series.

The late Ramprasad and Ramgopal Gupta, my maternal grandfather and maternal granduncle, who inspired me with their stories and books. Their blessings prevent the ink in my pen from running dry.

Finally, Ma Shakti, the One who puts power in my pen. I thank you, Ma, for your abundant blessings—forever.

Praise for the Bharat Series

The Rozabal Line (2008)

'In *The Rozabal Line,* Ashwin Sanghi does a Dan Brown by mixing all the ingredients of a thriller—crusades, action, adventure, suspense—and pulling off, with dexterity and ease, a narrative that careens through cultures and continents, religions and cults.' ~*The Asian Age*

'*The Rozabal Line* by Ashwin Sanghi is a kickass thriller that forces you to re-examine our histories, our faiths.' ~Pritish Nandy

'Sanghi's flair for religion, history and politics is clearly visible as he takes the reader across the world spanning different decades. A mixture of comparative religion, dangerous secrets, and a thrilling plot makes for an esoteric read.' ~*The Statesman*

'Sanghi has got the sure-fire formula right.' ~ *The Times of India*

'A provocative, clever and radiant line of theology, Sanghi suggests that the cult of Mary Magdalene has its true inspiration in the trinity of the Indian sacred feminine, thereby out-thinking and out-conspiring Dan Brown.' ~*The Hindu*

Chanakya's Chant (2010)

'With internal monologues and descriptions as taut as a-held-by-the-thumb sacred thread, we have Ashwin Sanghi's cracker of a page-turner, *Chanakya's Chant*. Two narratives flow like the Ganga and Yamuna ... a brisk technicoloured thriller.' ~*Hindustan Times*

'I'm utterly enthralled. A delightfully interesting and gripping read. The historical research is deeply impressive ...' ~Shashi Tharoor

'A gripping, fast-paced read, the novel is a true thriller in the tradition set by Dan Brown.' ~*People Magazine*

'Political grooming and conspiracy remain at the core of Ashwin Sanghi's historical thriller. Bloodshed, legal trials, betrayals, murders, assassination attempts and all that which make this into a page-turner.' ~*Sakaal Times*

'Released in India to wide acclaim, *Chanakya's Chant* is a political page-turner.' ~*Business India*

***The Krishna Key* (2012)**

'Why should racy historical thrillers or meaty fantasy sagas come only from the minds of Western writers? Ashwin Sanghi spins his yarns well and leaves you breathless at every cliff-hanger. No wonder his books are bestsellers!' ~*Hindustan Times*

'While the plot is set in today's world, one can expect to travel back and forth in time with generous chunks of history and nail-biting fiction.' ~*The Telegraph*

'An alternative interpretation of the Vedic Age that will be relished by conspiracy buffs and addicts of thrillers alike.' ~*The Hindu*

'Just finished *The Krishna Key* by Ashwin Sanghi. Rocking story and incredible research. Loved it!' ~Amish Tripathi

'Sanghi manages to blur the line between fact and fiction and give a whole new perspective to history and the Vedic Age.' ~*DNA*

***The Sialkot Saga* (2016)**

'*The Sialkot Saga* moves at a breakneck pace hurtling through time and space uncovering ancient secrets and burying modern ones.' ~*The Hindu*

'The book spreads across decades and centuries, till it reaches present day India and will sure have both historic and thriller readers in for a treat.' ~ *The Times of India*

'There are books that take time to develop an interest and then there are books that grip you from the very first page. *The Sialkot Saga* is one such book that hooks you from the start.' ~*Hindustan Times*

'There's never a dull moment in the book. In fact, the story takes on such a pace that the overwhelmed reader is compelled to put the book down and take a deep breath on many an occasion.' ~ *The Financial Express*

'Sanghi weaves a masterpiece building up the readers' involvement in the novel with every turn of the page.' ~ *The Pioneer*

***Keepers of the Kalachakra* (2018)**

'The book can't be put down till all pieces of the jigsaw puzzle are put together.' ~*The Financial Express*

'The author packs a powerful punch ... spicy and saucy, a survey of the past and the present ... without a dull moment, without a dull page.' *~The Sunday Standard*

'Science and spirituality collide in Ashwin Sanghi's latest thriller.' *~India Today*

'Spread over a vast canvas, the novel has an engaging plot laced with mythology, history and legends.' *~The Hindu*

'Ashwin Sanghi's *Keepers of the Kalachakra* is as explosive as a time bomb ticking in your hand. Every chapter springs an unpredictable surprise.' *~Deccan Chronicle*

'*Keepers of the Kalachakra* has it all: political characters that remind you of real-life politicians, a racy, complex plot and enough improbable twists to keep you hooked.' *~Hindustan Times Brunch*

***The Vault of Vishnu* (2020)**

'In an enthralling alchemy of myth and science, Ashwin Sanghi gives us the sixth book in his Bharat Series. As with all Ashwin's books, the research is meticulous and the technical(ese) leaves one gasping as *The Vault of Vishnu* takes the reader through the highs and lows of history, myth, physics, warfare technology, AI and biochemistry.' *~The Times of India*

'*The Vault of Vishnu*, like all of Ashwin's books, is a heady mix of history, myth, science and thrills.' *~The Hindu*

'A very interesting and intriguing thriller, thanks to the author's storytelling gift and painstaking research on Hindu metaphysics.' ~*The New Indian Express*

'Sanghi's latest work uses his favourite tool—mythology—and blends it with history to deliver some edge-of-the-seat action.' ~*Hindustan Times*

THE SIALKOT SAGA

Ashwin Sanghi

HarperCollins *Publishers* India

First published in 2016

This edition published in India by HarperCollins *Publishers* in 2022
4th Floor, Tower A, Building No. 10, Phase II, DLF Cyber City,
Gurugram, Haryana – 122002
www.harpercollins.co.in

2 4 6 8 10 9 7 5 3 1

P-ISBN: 978-93-5629-243-7
E-ISBN: 978-93-5629-246-8

Typeset by Art Works, Chennai

Printed and bound at
Thomson Press (India) Ltd

Disclaimer

This is a work of fiction set in a background of history. Public personages, both living and dead, may appear in the story under their given names. Scenes and dialogue involving them are invented. Any other usage of real people's names is coincidental. Any resemblance of the fictional characters to actual persons, living or dead, is entirely coincidental. No claim regarding historical accuracy is either made or implied. Historical, religious or mythological characters, events or places, are always used fictitiously.

Asato mā sad gamaya
From the unreal lead me to the real

Tamaso mā jyotir gamaya
From darkness lead me to light

Mrtyor māmrtam gamaya
From death lead me to immortality

—Pavamana Mantra, *Brihadaranyaka Upanishad*

1947

Prologue

The train arrived in Amritsar leaking blood. It had started its journey crammed with Hindu and Sikh refugees in Sialkot on the Pakistani side of the border. It had rumbled into Amritsar Junction three hours later.

Railway Constable Sukhbir Singh boarded the train with an impending sense of dread. There were no waving hands, nodding heads, wailing babies or excited shouts. In fact, there was no sound at all. The eerie silence was the first sign of things to come. The second indication of what lay within was the swarm of buzzing flies.

Inside compartment after compartment lay slaughtered bodies tangled together grotesquely, almost like a tossed salad of human corpses. Bodies hanging out of windows, piled upon each other, stabbed, decapitated, mutilated or with throats slashed. Men, women and children—no one had been spared.

When the train departed from Sialkot Junction, the people on board had foolishly heaved a sigh of relief. They were blissfully unaware that a hastily formed battalion of avengers was awaiting the train's arrival at the bridge over the River Ravi. By the time the train rolled off the bridge, it carried a cargo of human death. The river beneath the bridge had turned pink with bleeding corpses that had rained into it from the train above.

On both sides of the hastily drawn-up border, there had been ruthlessness and depravity by all communities—Hindus, Muslims and Sikhs. Shooting and stabbing of victims seemed almost humane when one considered the ghastly catalogue of other horrors that had been perpetrated. Previous communal riots paled in comparison to the unprecedented brutality that India's Partition had thrown up. Over fifteen million people had been left homeless, with Muslims fleeing India for Pakistan, and Hindus and Sikhs abandoning Pakistan for India. The eventual death toll of India's Partition would exceed a million souls.

Constable Sukhbir Singh entered the death train in Amritsar, calling out to his colleagues for help. He began the process of looking for survivors although his instincts told him that no one had been left alive.

Luckily, Sukhbir Singh's instincts were often wrong.

Within a few minutes he struck gold. *What was that sound? Was it someone sobbing?* Sukhbir began shoving aside corpses like a man possessed. If there was even one survivor left on this train Sukhbir would find him.

A few minutes later he pulled out a small, frightened boy from underneath a bench seat. The boy's kurta was stained with blood from a corpse that had fallen on him. His cheeks were stained with tears and soot. The boy trembled as Sukhbir reached for him.

'Hush, little one, I'm not going to hurt you,' whispered Sukhbir as he lifted the whimpering boy into his arms. He hugged him gently, attempting to drive away the memory of the demons that the boy had witnessed and been possessed by.

Unfortunately, he knew that the demons would plague him for the rest of his life.

Drenched in sweat and blood, Sukhbir Singh was about to exit the train with the child when he heard a groan. Were his ears deceiving him? Was it yet another human voice? And then it came again.

Sukhbir called out to his colleague Chandprakash. 'Chand, I need you to take this boy to the retiring room. Find him something to eat and drink. I have to find the other voice.'

ॐ त्रियम्बकं यजामहे
सुगन्धिं पुष्टिवर्धनं ।

250 BCE, Pataliputra

उर्वारुकमिव वन्धनान्
मृत्योर्मोक्षिय मामृतात् ।।

The streets of Pataliputra lay quiet. Even the late-night taverns had packed off their last customers.

The sixty-four gates built into the massive walls that surrounded the city had been shuttered for the night. Five hundred and seventy sentries stationed in individual towers along the perimeter maintained vigil for intruders from across the surrounding moat.

In the centre of town stood the magnificent royal palace nestled in a bed of splendid gardens and lakes. The massive doors to the palace lay locked, having been secured by the royal guards. But a secret entrance remained open. It was used only once every full-moon night.

By nine specially chosen men.

Inside the palace, the emperor was still at work. He barely ever slept. It meant that everyone else around him also remained sleep-deprived. He sat at the head of the meeting chamber. Floor-mounted flaming torches threw dancing shadows that bounced off the walls as the monarch deliberated with the nine men.

Ashoka was not a handsome man. In fact, most people found him rather unattractive. In the past, though, he had always exuded a spirit of unbounded energy, which seemed to have entirely vanished these days.

Kalinga had changed him.

Kalinga had been the proverbial thorn in Ashoka's side and he had finally succeeded in plucking the federal republic out several years ago. Ashoka's great triumph at Kalinga had eluded even his father and grandfather. The victory should have been cause for grand celebration.

So why had it felt so hollow?

Ashoka had conquered Kalinga by sending 100,000 of his own warriors to their deaths. Twice that number of Kalingans had died. The River Daya that bordered the battlefield had turned red for several months after the gruesome war.

And then, there had been a transformation in the emperor. *Ashoka the Wicked* had morphed into *Ashoka the Righteous*.

The emperor looked at the nine men in the room. Each one of them was seated on a throne that was identical to that of Ashoka. No single man was greater than the other inside this chamber. Ashoka was lost in thought. Could he trust them to do what was required? Would they honour their word to him? Realizing that he had no alternative, Ashoka took a deep breath and spoke.

'I have called you here because I am very worried,' he began. The oldest among them, the Preserver of the Secret, knew better than to show any reaction. He awaited his instructions while holding his bulky folder. The folder was stitched from fabric and had a jellyfish-like emblem embroidered on the cover.

'Over the years, we have almost perfected our research,' continued Ashoka. 'The voluminous folder before you contains a body of inquiry that is pathbreaking. Emperors would willingly give up their kingdoms to acquire such incredibly empowering knowledge. Your research has helped make the Mauryan Empire prosperous. It has enabled us to win wars, subdue our enemies and provide a better life to our people.'

He paused. His mind was struggling to find appropriate words for the occasion.

'But look at what I did with your work! I annihilated a third of a million people in my lust for power! I am wracked by shame, guilt and remorse. And you know what? There is nothing inside your folder that has a solution for my condition.' Ashoka dropped his gaze to the floor.

'Your highness, the Kalinga War was a decade ago. In subsequent years you have done much to play the role of father to your people,' said the Preserver of the Secret. He was the oldest among them. His name was Kalapasika. Ashoka looked up as Kalapasika spoke.

'You have established free hospitals; you have supported universities and monasteries; you have built rest-houses; you have planted thousands of trees; you have kept taxes low; you have ensured that government officials deal with citizens in a caring manner. No emperor has ever done so much for his people in such a short span of time,' said Kalapasika—without a hint of flattery in his voice.

Everything that Kalapasika had said was absolutely true. Ashoka smiled a weary smile. 'Thank you for trying to cheer me up, Kalapasika,' he said. 'Try as I may to bribe my way out of karmic damnation, I shall not succeed. Eventually, I too shall have to the pay the price for my sins!'

He paused yet again.

'As you know, knowledge is power,' he said. 'Power can be used for good. It can also be used for evil. Under no circumstances can we afford to let our knowledge fall into the wrong hands.'

'What are you suggesting, *Devanampiya*?' asked Kalapasika using Ashoka's preferred title—Beloved of the Gods.

'We need to ensure that your scholarship is preserved for generations to come without ever allowing it to be wrongly used,' replied the emperor.

The thoughts running through the minds of the nine men were almost identical. How do we bury such powerful knowledge? Almost as though he was reading their minds, Ashoka asked, 'So how does one bury such powerful knowledge? I suggest that our wisdom should be vested in a single person. Who could that person be?'

Ashoka looked at each of the nine men before he spoke. 'Kalapasika, would you be willing to take up this onerous responsibility? After all, you are the Preserver of the Secret as also the oldest in this group. You would need to guard this knowledge with your life. You must not let the outside world know anything about what you possess.'

'But I am mortal,' said Kalapasika. 'How shall I preserve the information for posterity? How will we improve upon the research? What will happen when I die?'

'When death is near, you shall choose an appropriate successor to preserve the material,' replied Ashoka. 'Your successor does not have to be your blood relative although you may choose to appoint one. Merit, honesty, loyalty and strength should be the key criteria in choosing your successor. Your knowledge shall be passed down to your successor accompanied by an oath of complete secrecy.'

Kalapasika nodded.

'As you can see, Kalapasika, your role is particularly critical. Greed is a terrible motivator of men. You shall have to take extraordinary precautions. It is vital that the information in your safe custody should only be used to benefit mankind, not to further the aims of individuals. We have jointly perfected our research up to the seventeenth step. We must reach the eighteenth.'

'Devanampiya, as suggested by you a year ago, I have entirely memorized the notes—like a student in a gurukul. Every successor of mine shall do the same.'

Ashoka nodded. 'Good. Can you recite all eighteen steps?'

Kalapasika began reciting.

*'Svedana… Mardana… Murchana… Uthapana… Patana…
Rodhana… Niyamana… Sandipana…'*

Ashoka closed his eyes, almost meditating on the words.

*'Gaganagrass… Carana… Garbhadruti… Bahyadruti…
Jarana… Ranjana… Sarana… Kramana…
Vedhana… Bhaksana.'*

Ashoka opened his eyes. 'Please recite the mantra,' requested the emperor.

Kalapasika folded his hands in mental supplication to Shiva and began chanting in Sanskrit.

*'Om tryambakam yajaamahe
sugandhim pushti-vardhanam,
Urvaarukam-iva bandhanaan
mrityormuksheeya maamrataat!'*

The ancient passage from the *Rig-Veda* was an exceptionally powerful mantra. Kalapasika paused.

'Now the conclusion,' instructed Ashoka.

Kalapasika began in Prakrit, the preferred language of the Mauryan court.

*'All that is gold does not glitter,
Not all those who wander are lost.
Food that is sweet can be bitter
Eyes meant to see can be glossed.
Seeing eyes are children two,
But the discerning eye is the mother.
Potions and chants, it is true,
Are complemented by another.'*

Ashoka then spoke to Kalapasika and the eight remaining men for the final time that night. 'Until today, I used to refer to you as my Nine Special Men. Henceforth, you shall be called the Nine Unknowns. This is our last and final meeting. It is now time for you to disband and return to the far-flung places whence I had requested you to come. I am thankful for your time and efforts. May God be with you.'

Book One
1950–1960

Bombay lay inundated with refugees in 1950. Over a million people displaced from Sindh and Punjab were now sleeping on the city's streets. Shivaji Park, the nucleus of Marathi-speaking, middle-class Bombay, was densely packed. More than half a million souls had gathered to hear Jawaharlal Nehru speak.

Hours before his plane arrived at Santa Cruz airport, shops had downed their shutters and people had started lining the streets hoping to catch a glimpse of their living deity. The police had a difficult time keeping the throngs in control as Panditji's open maroon car drove by.

The government had set up five refugee camps in Bombay but they were hellish places. Each family had to live within thirty-six square feet of space. There was no electricity. Twelve water taps were allocated to serve 10,000 people.

A young Muslim couple, Ayub and Shabana Sheikh, with their son in tow, had begun their trek from the Dongri area of the city. It had taken them several hours to reach Shivaji Park. They had jostled their way into the venue to hear the man who was no less than a god to them. Ayub, a dockworker, had hoisted his son, Arbaaz, on his shoulders so that he would have a better view.

Panditji began speaking. 'Since I first unfurled the national flag on the Red Fort, three years have been added to India's long history, which began thousands of years ago. During these years, we have seen achievements and failures, we have experienced joy and sorrow. The good work we have done will remain even though we pass away. So will India, though generations come and go.' The tumultuous crowds were enthusiastic in their response.

'We must constantly remind ourselves that whatever our religion or creed, we are all one people,' said Panditji. To the young Muslim couple, Ayub and Shabana Sheikh, Panditji's words gave them hope for Indian Muslims.

Ayub looked up at little Arbaaz who sat on his shoulders. He seemed entirely oblivious to the importance of Jawaharlal Nehru. The boy was busy surveying the crowds around him, almost imperiously.

It was probably a sign of things to come.

Kurukshetra.

For most people, the name conjured up visions of the epic battle between the Kauravas and Pandavas. For the moment, though, the ill-fated plains of Kurukshetra had been converted into a huge refugee camp, the largest among the 200 that had been established to accommodate the flood of humanity from Pakistan.

The Bagadias were not refugees. Brijmohanlal Bagadia was from Calcutta, where he ran a small jute trading operation. The family had been attending a wedding in Delhi that winter of 1950 and had heard that Mahashiva Baba was visiting the nearby Kurukshetra camp.

Mahashiva Baba was a sadhu from Varanasi whose devotees believed that he had been alive for over 300 years. Brijmohanlal's mother had received *darshan* of the holy man many years ago and she had always kept his photograph in her prayer corner.

'If only we could meet him once and seek his blessings for Arvind,' said Brijmohanlal to his wife, Shakuntala. The poor woman was valiantly attempting to keep up with Brijmohanlal while firmly dragging Arvind by his hand.

While claims of the baba's immortality could be doubted, his ability to organize relief work could not. Mahashiva Baba had created an organization of thousands of devoted followers which came to be known as 'Jeevan Prakash'. Besides operating universities, schools and hospitals, Jeevan Prakash also took up relief work wherever it was needed. The camp at Kurukshetra consumed hundreds of tons of flour, lentils, rice and cooking oil. The refugees had to be fed, clothed, housed and provided medical facilities. People like the baba were saviours. The armed forces were working overtime at the camps but they needed all the help that they could get. Mahashiva Baba and his devotees had been welcomed with open arms.

The Bagadias wandered through the camp at Kurukshetra and were stunned by its size. Over 300,000 souls inhabited the camp, many of them having travelled in long caravans on foot or bullock cart from Pakistan. More than ten million people had fled their homes, a migration that reduced the exodus of the Jews from Egypt to a minority.

After an hour of wandering in the hot sun, the Bagadias finally reached the tent occupied by the baba. The baba wore only a loincloth and sported thick matted hair above his ash-smeared forehead. He sat on a square piece of cloth that was little bigger than a kerchief. No one knew his age but he looked like a man of forty. There was a glow on his face and the muscles of his chest and arms rippled as though he had worked out for every day of his life. His face was accentuated by a prominent jaw. Next to him was a smoking chillum made of clay and a copper pot filled with *bhasma*—holy ash. A musky-sweet smell permeated the air. The baba rarely ate. His energy came from meditation and weed.

His eyes picked out the Bagadia family instantly. He asked one of his followers to guide them to him. 'How is your mother? Does she still keep my photograph in her prayer corner?' he asked Brijmohanlal. Brijmohanlal stared at the baba with his mouth agape. The baba had never seen him before and yet seemed to know everything about him. Both husband and wife prostrated themselves before him.

'Place the boy in front of me,' instructed the baba softly as they got up. Shakuntala placed the eight-year-old in front of the sadhu. Arvind sat cross-legged before the baba, playing with a toy soldier. He was oblivious to the holy man.

The baba smiled at the boy. Arvind did not return the favour. The baba then took some ash from his copper pot and smeared it lightly on the boy's forehead as he chanted:

'Om tryambakam yajaamahe
sugandhim pushti-vardhanam,
Urvaarukam-iva bandhanaan
mrityormuksheeya maamrataat!'

Looking up at the parents, he said 'Take care of this boy. He is destined for many big things in life.' The parents stepped forward and touched the baba's feet, grateful for his blessing.

As the Bagadias walked out of the baba's tent, they noticed a pervasive air of gloom. 'What's the matter?' asked Brijmohanlal of one of the baba's disciples. The man had tears in his eyes.

'Sardar has passed away,' he said softly. The iron man of India, Sardar Vallabhbhai Patel, had died following a heart attack. Patel had gifted 565 princely states to the Indian union.

Earlier that year Babasaheb Ambedkar had gifted 395 Articles to make up the Constitution of India. Probably the longest in the world.

Key moments in Indian history were being created. The moment passed was history, the unborn moment a mystery.

Dusk had descended on the congested streets of Dongri. On the pavements, steaming hot kebabs freshly grilled or pulled out of bubbling oil were the main attraction for those who were breaking their fast for Ramadan.

The house that Ayub and Shabana occupied with little Arbaaz was certainly not a house. It was more of a room on the second floor of a decrepit building that overlooked Hazrat Abbas Dargah on Palla Gully.

From dozens of matchbox windows, families peered out to catch the spectacle of the mohalla below. One of the faces peering out was that of the ravenous nine-year-old Arbaaz. It was his very first Ramadan fast.

On the street below, the situation was chaotic. The country's first general elections had been announced for October 1951 and Chief Election Commissioner Sukumar Sen had the unenviable task of getting 175 million adult Indians to cast their votes in the biggest experiment in democracy. Politicians of all hues were busy holding iftar parties to woo the Muslim electorate of the area that sweltering June.

Inside the ten-by-ten room, Shabana tried her best to make their home look presentable. Ayub would be home soon.

She felt terrible for him—having to labour in the docks while fasting.

She placed the earthen water pot on the corner stool and carefully arranged a few dates that would be needed for *iftar*. She had not cooked. Ayub would be taking them out to the streets to sample the delectable fare on offer.

She looked inside the pot and checked the copper wristlet at the bottom. Little Arbaaz would often ask what it was there for. She would simply tell him that copper was good for the health.

'Come on, Arbaaz, wipe your hands and face,' she said, handing a small damp towel to him. 'You got into so much trouble at school for being dirty.'

Arbaaz obediently started scrubbing away the sweat and soot from his face, neck, arms and hands. It had been an exceptionally hot and muggy day. Arbaaz looked at the grimy towel as he handed it back to his mother. 'It's not worth the effort,' he said to her.

'What's not worth the effort?' asked Shabana.

'Cleaning up,' replied Arbaaz.

'Why?' asked Shabana, indulging him.

'Now I'm clean but the towel's dirty. There's simply no way to get something clean without getting something else dirty.'

Calcutta wasn't a city. It was a story. In 1690, Job Charnock, an agent of the East India Company, had carefully chosen the place for a British trade settlement. It was a good choice. It was protected by the Hooghly River on the west, a creek to the north, and by salt lakes about two-and-a-half miles to the east. On 24 August, 1690, Charnock had made a generous offering at an old Kali temple and had then pitched his tent on the site of the charred ruins of an old factory. At that time there had been three substantial villages along the east bank of the River Ganges—Sutanuti, Gobindapur and Kalikata. These three villages were bought by the British from the local landlords. Then the Mughal emperor granted East India Company freedom of trade in return for a yearly payment of 3,000 rupees. Calcutta was born.

Brijmohanlal, Shakuntala and the now nine-year-old Arvind were seated at a table in the Waldorf restaurant on Calcutta's Park Street. It was a Sunday ritual for the Bagadia family. The parents would take their son to the Waldorf for a Chinese meal followed by cassata ice cream. Being vegetarians, the lunch order remained fixed: sweet corn soup, vegetable spring rolls, fried rice and chop suey.

Brijmohanlal was short, plump and dark. His black hair was pasted together in place with a generous topping of Brylcreem. Shakuntala was petite and fair. Her long hair was neatly braided and she was always dressed elegantly in Banarasi sarees. On her slim hands were bangles that were perfectly colour-coordinated with her saree. Arvind seemed to have taken after his mother more than his father.

In this little haven called Waldorf there was no sign that the American Congress was debating a food request from India; nor any sign that the Soviet Union was in the process of sending 50,000 tons of wheat to meet the country's food shortage. There was no shortage at the Waldorf in 1951.

Father, mother and son sat at their usual table surrounded by the rich red interiors of the restaurant. Their favoured waiter, Liang, was on holiday that day. He had been a permanent fixture with the restaurant from the time that it had moved from Tangra, Calcutta's Chinatown, to Park Street.

The new waiter took their order without the usual flair and familiarity of Liang, and disappeared. Thirty minutes later, their food had still not arrived.

'Where is that bumbling waiter?' fretted Brijmohanlal, tapping his fingers impatiently on the linen-covered table.

'Papa, I don't understand something,' perked up Arvind suddenly.

'What is that, *beta*?' asked Brijmohanlal.

'Why are these people called waiters, when we are the ones who wait?'

In 1951, a man called Acharya Vinoba Bhave had started travelling across India asking wealthy landlords to voluntarily give up a piece of their land to the landless labourers of the country. It was known as *Bhoodan*. Sharing was caring.

Downstairs on Palla Gully, the proud father Ayub was holding forth with his dockyard friends. They were huddled together in a circle, puffing from a single cigarette that was being passed around after each puff. Sharing was caring in their world too.

One of them, a jocular Hindu called Raju, narrated a joke while exhaling smoke through his nose.

'The Mughal emperor announced that he needed a new bodyguard,' began Raju. 'Three swordsmen applied: a Hindu, a Christian and a Muslim.'

Ayub rarely had time for frivolities. He was usually overworked trying to eke out an honest living. Raju, though, was a friend, who managed to get him to laugh.

'To test them, the emperor let loose a fly in the room,' continued Raju. 'He turned to the Hindu swordsman and asked him to kill it. The swordsman effortlessly swept his sword in the air and the fly fell to the floor, cleanly dissected into two.'

'Hindus rule!' commented Shinde, another dockhand. 'Then what?'

'The Christian swordsman was given the same test. He swung his sword twice and managed to cut the fly into quarters before it hit the ground.'

'Must be our fascination with the cross,' commented Lewis, a dock foreman gratefully accepting the cigarette from Raju. 'In any case, more power to Christ!'

'The Muslim swordsman was then administered the test,' continued Raju. 'He chased the fly around the room and swung his sword a few times. He then sat down with the fly still buzzing around his head. The emperor asked the Muslim swordsman why he had stopped. After all, the fly was still alive.'

'So what was the deal?' asked Shinde, chuckling.

Raju looked at the men with a deadpan expression before delivering the punchline.

'The Muslim swordsman looked at the emperor seriously and said: 'Yes, it's alive, your highness. But now it's circumcized.'

The men burst into guffaws and were about to light another cigarette when Shabana's voice from above said, 'Are you going to stay there all night or will you come up? Maulvi Saheb and Doctor Saheb are ready.'

The men quickly went up to the second floor. The cramped quarters of Ayub and Shabana Sheikh sported a festive air. Little Arbaaz was to undergo his *Khitan*—or ritual circumcision. Islam did not prescribe a specific age for circumcision but their maulvi was of the view that they ought to get their son circumcised before the age of ten.

A kind doctor from St George Hospital had agreed to carry out the procedure for free. Behind a temporary curtain, Arbaaz was administered a local anaesthetic. He started wailing piteously when the needle touched the base of his male member. Shabana was driven to tears seeing him like that. 'Do we really need to do this to him?' she asked. She backed off when she saw Ayub getting irritated.

But a few minutes later the procedure was over, the foreskin having been snipped off cleanly. Arbaaz hadn't felt a thing once the local anaesthetic had taken effect. He was the hero of the day.

Maulvi Saheb called the gathering to prayer. 'God is great, there is no God but Allah. Muhammad is the messenger of Allah,' he intoned. He then made Ayub whisper the words into Arbaaz's right ear.

'Now for the pudding,' said the maulvi. 'The child's first taste after circumcision should be something sweet. What do we have?'

Shabana had made extra-sweet *kheer* for Arbaaz. She fed him, delighted by the twinkle that returned to his eyes. He enjoyed the kheer with relish until the discomfort of the surgery began setting in. He started crying once again and Shabana went scurrying for the painkillers that the doctor had left behind.

Brijmohanlal and Arvind were in the living room of the Bagadia family home on Alipore Road. A 78-rpm record-player was playing a song of Kundan Lal Saigal and Arvind was wondering how he could convince his father to turn it off.

'What will I be when I grow up, Papa?' asked Arvind innocently.

'You are the son of a businessman,' replied Brijmohanlal. 'You shall also be a businessman. A great one.'

'Will I become as big a businessman as you, Papa?'

'You will become even bigger,' replied Brijmohanlal, smiling. 'I placed foolish limitations on myself.' He walked over to the record-player and lifted the needle off the vinyl. Mission accomplished for Arvind.

'What do you mean, Papa?' continued the boy, savouring the silence.

Brijmohanlal wondered how to explain the difficulties of life to a ten-year-old boy. He picked up an empty jar from the dining table and headed outside to the garden. 'Come with me,' he instructed Arvind. They walked over to the kennel that housed Sultan, their Alsatian. The dog wagged his tail happily as he saw father and son approach. After a few minutes of play, Brijmohanlal knelt on the grass and opened the glass jar that he had carried into the garden and held it up in the air, close to the large dog's massive head. He waited for a few minutes before shutting the lid. Arvind watched the mysterious ritual, utterly bewildered by his father's actions.

'Can you see what's inside?' asked Brijmohanlal.

'Fleas,' answered Arvind.

'Fleas love jumping,' replied Brijmohanlal. 'Can you see them jumping around inside? They're hitting the lid of the jar each time they jump.'

Arvind nodded, but wondered again what the point of this discussion was. He made a mental note to never ask questions like 'What will I be when I grow up?' ever again.

Brijmohanlal placed the jar in a corner of the garden. 'Leave them alone for a day,' said Brijmohanlal. 'We'll complete our discussion tomorrow.'

The next day father and son were back in the garden. 'They're still jumping,' observed Arvind.

'Yes,' agreed Brijmohanlal. 'But do you notice that they are no longer jumping high enough to hit the lid?'

Arvind peered inside the jar. His father was absolutely right.

'Now observe, Arvind,' he said. Brijmohanlal twisted off the lid. 'When I remove the lid, the fleas continue to jump, but they're not jumping out of the jar. They won't jump out because they've conditioned themselves to jump only so high. They have set limits on themselves.'

Arvind looked closely. The fleas continued jumping, but within the jar.

'That's me—jumping only as high as I have been conditioned to. And that's precisely what I want you to avoid, Arvind,' said his father. 'Your future is limitless!'

Arbaaz was seated in the back row of the classroom of Rosary High School on Dockyard Road. It was stiflingly hot. The single creaking fan was struggling to circulate air but all that it did was make a racket.

Arbaaz's father, Ayub, earned around thirty rupees per month as a coolie at the docks but still managed to send his son to school. A kind priest at the Church of Our Lady of the Rosary had managed to secure admission for Arbaaz in its parish school in the charity quota.

'You will not grow up to be a coolie,' said Ayub to Arbaaz. 'Concentrate on your studies so that you never have to lead the slavish existence that I do.'

Arbaaz was bright but lazy. As usual, his homework had not been done. It was a repeat offence that attracted a swift stroke of the cane on the right hand.

His closest friend at school was a boy called Murali Iyer. Murali's family had migrated from Madras to Bombay to seek a better life. Little did they know that they would be derided as *lungiwala*s in the city of dreams.

Murali hurriedly passed his own notebook with the cover ripped off to Arbaaz. 'Take it,' he said. Arbaaz looked at the homework and smiled. Murali was the smartest kid in the class but handing in Murali's homework as his own would not be an option. Mr D'Souza would pick up on it instantly.

'Come to the front of the class to receive your punishment,' said Mr D'Souza, the class teacher, a man who was exceptionally particular about cleanliness and grooming.

Arbaaz had been digging a pit in the playground before class. Conscious of how dirty his hands were, Arbaaz tried his best to rub his palms against his shorts on his way to the front. But it was of no use. The right hand that he eventually held out to Mr D'Souza was filthy.

Mr D'Souza looked at it. It seemed as though Arbaaz hadn't washed all day. 'Turn over your hand,' instructed Mr D'Souza. The boy's nails were equally grubby.

'Arbaaz, if you can find me another hand as dirty as this one in this classroom, I'll spare you the cane,' said Mr D'Souza in mock exasperation.

In less than a second, Arbaaz whipped out his left hand from behind his back to submit it for inspection.

'See, sir? Just as dirty,' he said innocently.

There were giggles from the benches. Mr D'Souza tried hard to retain his scowl but eventually gave up.

After class, Arbaaz went over to Murali's desk.

'Thanks for trying to help me,' he said. 'I shall not forget it.'

'Will you give me a job one day?' asked Murali.

'Maybe I'll be coming to *you* for a job,' replied Arbaaz.

'Unlikely,' said Murali. 'You see, I'm intelligent but you're smart. Generally, the intelligent land up in the employment of the smart.'

Houseboats on the Dal Lake were made from cedar wood and were usually furnished with intricately carved furniture and Kashmiri carpets. But this houseboat was one of the cheaper ones that had seen better days. The view, though, was stunning. From the balcony of the floating home one could see the vast, mirror-flat sheet of water reflecting the misty peaks of the Pir Panjal mountains. Brijmohanlal Bagadia, his wife Shakuntala and eleven-year old son Arvind had spent two weeks in paradise. It was now time to head home to Calcutta.

The family emerged from within and sat in a brightly painted shikara to reach the bank. From there they got into a car that would take them to Lakhenpur on the Punjab border. One of Brijmohanlal's friends was a senior army officer there and they would spend a couple of days with his family before heading back to the drudgery of Calcutta.

After a rather long road trip they reached Lakhenpur in the Kathua district. Lakhenpur was the gateway to Jammu and Kashmir from Punjab and the rest of India. That day Lakhenpur seemed exceptionally busy. Long traffic snarls prevented their movement for several hours.

'What's causing the rush?' Brijmohanlal irritably asked the driver.

'Dr Shyama Prasad Mukherjee is here,' the man replied.

Dr Mukherjee was the founder of the Bharatiya Jana Sangh, which would evolve into the Bharatiya Janata Party, the BJP, in later years. He was in direct conflict with Jawaharlal Nehru on the government's Kashmir policy and had decided to visit the state to protest against Sheikh Abdullah's permit policy, a system that required ordinary Indians to obtain a visa to visit the state. Upon reaching Lakhenpur he had been arrested by the Kashmir police. It was widely believed that the arrest strategy had been privately decided upon by Jawaharlal Nehru and Sheikh Abdullah.

'If he is here, I would love to meet him,' said Brijmohanlal. Dr Mukherjee had been born to a high court judge in Calcutta, Sir Ashutosh Mukherjee who was also Vice-Chancellor of University of Calcutta. Brijmohanlal's family had known the Mukherjee family well.

'I doubt we'll be able to make it in the car,' advised the driver. 'You're probably better off walking.'

Without waiting for even a moment, Brijmohanlal got out of the car and began briskly walking towards the epicentre of the action. Shakuntala and Arvind followed.

They saw a police vehicle disappearing from the scene. Dr Mukherjee was in it and was shouting out to a young man, 'Go back and tell the whole country that I have entered Jammu without a permit but as a prisoner.'

Brijmohanlal hurried up to the young man and asked him where they were taking Dr Mukherjee. 'Srinagar,' he replied. 'Why do you want to know?'

'We've just come from there. Dr Mukherjee's family was known to my family in Calcutta,' said Brijmohanlal.

'Why have they arrested him?' asked Arvind.

The young man, in his late twenties or early thirties, looked at Arvind. 'A single country can't have two Constitutions, two Prime Ministers, and two national emblems. What do you think?'

Arvind thought about it for a moment and then spoke. 'Roses are red, violets are blue, we have one problem, who needs two?'

The young man laughed and patted Arvind on his head. 'I too love poetry but mostly in Hindi. What's your name?'

'Arvind Bagadia. And yours?'

'Atal Bihari Vajpayee.'

Arvind trudged along Loudon Street as he made his way towards La Martiniere, one of Calcutta's finest schools. On the eleven-year old boy's back was a heavy knapsack, ostensibly filled with books.

Brijmohanlal was not counted among the city's super-rich but had made enough money to ensure a comfortable life for his wife and son. The family lived on Alipore Road, a street famous for the swanky residences of the rich and powerful, but theirs was one of the smallest houses, modestly furnished and scantily staffed. That particular dichotomy was to be found in almost everything about the Bagadia family. They would take holidays in fashionable destinations but stay in the cheaper hotels. They owned a car but would invariably use public transport. The Bagadias seemed to be keeping up appearances of an alternate kind.

Brijmohanlal had one particular quality, though, that distinguished him from his ilk: contentment. Among Marwaris, that particular word was anathema. One was never meant to be content. Contentment squeezed the brakes on progress and wealth accumulation. But that was Brijmohanlal. Content. Like the fleas.

Arvind, however, was a different kettle of fish. Arvind always wondered why his father chose to remain at the bottom of the top. Or the top of the bottom.

The Marwaris of Calcutta were the city's economic elite, having established dominance in the areas of banking, jute and tea, but Brijmohanlal had remained a fringe-player. The truth was that by the end of 1953, many Marwaris like him were not sure how long the newly independent India would last.

In the north, Shyama Prasad Mukherjee had died after forty-three days in the Srinagar prison. He had been jailed like a common criminal even though the authorities knew that he had coronary troubles. Despite having informed the doctor that he was allergic to penicillin, the doctor had injected him with precisely that. The country would have spiralled out of control if Nehru had not placed Sheikh Abdullah under arrest.

In the south, a man called Potti Sriramulu had died on the fifty-eighth day of a fast unto death in a demand for a Telugu-speaking state. In the Punjab, someone called Master Tara Singh had begun demanding an independent country called Khalistan. It was not unreasonable to wonder whether the idea and notion of a united India would survive.

Arvind sighed as he walked towards school. It was a bloody waste of time. School never made anyone smart, he reasoned. How many millionaires had wasted their time over William Shakespeare or the Battle of Plassey?

At five feet, Arvind was rather tall for his age of eleven. He was an unusually good-looking boy. But then, the looks of a Marwari man rarely mattered. What usually mattered was the thickness of his wallet.

Arvind was dressed in his winter uniform: grey worsted trousers, white half-sleeved shirt, regulation school tie, a webbed belt with the school colours, two-button school blazer, white socks and laced black leather shoes. Students were required to line up for inspection in the morning and would be sent home if anything was out of place.

Arvind's walk to school always took an exceptionally long time. Not because of the distance but because of the frequent stops that he made along the way.

'Good morning, Debashis,' said Arvind, as a man in tattered clothes and unkempt beard approached him. 'How much do you have for me today?'

'Fourteen annas,' said the tramp, handing over a small brown paper bag to Arvind. The boy took the bag and carefully counted the coins. Pulling out a small notebook from the pocket of his shirt he made a note of the transaction in pencil.

'Ten per cent is the premium,' said Arvind, handing over a rupee in exchange. 'I have given you two pice more than the agreed premium. I'm noting it down and will deduct it the next time, fine?'

'Sure, boss,' grinned the vagabond, giving the boy a mock salute. 'I have no idea how or why you do it, but I'm happy to switch my annas into rupees with you while the party lasts!'

Arvind tucked away the coins into his knapsack and walked on. There were fifteen minutes left before school started. He waited for another couple of minutes at the street corner and his patience was rewarded. Another drifter emerged, his breath heavy with cheap hooch.

He wordlessly handed over a crumpled ball of newspaper to the boy. Arvind carefully opened the grimy container and looked inside. Twenty-two annas and five pice. It had obviously been a good day for the bum. Which explained the hooch.

He pulled out the five pice and handed it back to the man. 'You know I can't take these. Only half-anna bits, one-anna pieces, or two-anna coins,' he said.

Arvind quickly did the sums in his head. 'Sixteen annas to a rupee. You gave me twenty-two annas. That's one rupee and six annas. Add a premium of 10 per cent and I owe you one rupee, eight annas and one pice.'

Handing over the exchange value to the drunk, Arvind placed the coins in his bag and made his way to school. He would meet the other drifters, bums and vagabonds of Loudon Street on his way back in the afternoon.

He sighed contentedly.

These days he was growing convinced that business was simply a name given to the art of taking money from others without using force.

'Mr Bagadia, I would be most grateful if you could answer my question,' said Mrs Fonseca, the English teacher, glaring at Arvind through her horn-rimmed spectacles. When she used his surname it usually meant he was in trouble.

'I'm sorry, ma'am, could you repeat the question?' requested Arvind, hastily tucking away his notebook listing the transactions he'd made and his pencil. English literature was usually the ideal class for catching up on his accounts.

'Perhaps if you concentrated a little more on my class and a little less on doodling, you would not need to have questions repeated,' snapped Mrs Fonseca.

'I'm very sorry, ma'am,' said Arvind, putting on the most apologetic face that he could summon. It always helped to let people feel that they had been able to have their way. It softened them up for a fall.

'The question,' sighed Mrs Fonseca, 'was this. Which was the last play that Oscar Wilde wrote?'

Arvind scratched his head before he answered. 'The Importance of Being a Genius,' he said confidently.

'The Importance of Being a Genius?' asked Mrs Fonseca incredulously. 'You have not done any preparation at all, Mr Bagadia! There is no drama by that name. The last play that Oscar Wilde wrote was *The Importance of Being Earnest*.'

'But ma'am, I remember reading about Oscar Wilde's arrival in the United States,' said Arvind, who effortlessly recalled everything that interested him and discarded anything that did not.

'What does that have to do with my question?' asked a visibly irritated Mrs Fonseca.

Other students in the class were snickering. Arvind had painted himself into a tight corner. As usual, it would be pure entertainment to observe him extricate himself.

'It's just that when Oscar Wilde arrived in New York Harbour in 1882, he was asked by an American customs official if he had anything to declare,' replied Arvind.

'Is there a point to your story, Mr Bagadia?' asked Mrs Fonseca, on the verge of throwing a fit.

Arvind resumed.

'Apparently, Oscar Wilde replied: *I have nothing to declare but my genius,*' continued Arvind. 'Wouldn't you agree that it's more important to be a genius than earnest, ma'am?'

'I simply do not understand why you collect these coins from beggars, paying them a premium,' muttered Joydeep, one of Arvind's classmates. The boys were headed back home after school.

While Arvind was tall and fair, Joydeep was short and dark. They made for an odd couple.

'My father gives me a measly allowance,' replied Arvind. 'He says that learning Gandhian frugality will help me in life! So I usually have to find ways of supplementing my income.'

'But I never see you spending on anything except those lemon sweets,' argued Joydeep. 'What do you do with the coins that you collect?'

'I pass them on to Mr Bhattacharjee,' replied Arvind, sucking on one of the aforementioned sweets.

'Who?'

'Mr Bhattacharjee. He's the brother of our school's canteen operator and he works for a company called Bengal Alloys,' replied Arvind confidently.

'And what does this Bhattacharjee do with the coins you give him? Is he a coin-collector?' asked Joydeep curiously.

Arvind laughed. 'What lies behind you and what lies in front of you, pales in comparison to what lies inside of you,' he said cryptically.

'What?'

'Tsk. You've forgotten Fonseca's English lit. class this morning! Ralph Waldo Emerson said that,' replied Arvind, rolling the sweet from one side of his mouth to the other.

Most of the time, Arvind was a royal pain in the ass. 'What's your point?' asked an exasperated Joydeep.

'The Indian one-anna coin has the lion capital of the Ashoka pillar on one face and a bull on the other face. Heads and tails,' replied Arvind.

'So?'

'What lies behind and what lies in front—the two faces of the coin—are irrelevant. What lies between the two faces—metal—is important, though,' replied Arvind.

'So why do you collect them?' demanded Joydeep impatiently.

Arvind looked at his friend seriously. 'The metal used for the anna coin is cupro-nickel, comprised of 75 per cent copper, and 25 per cent nickel. The weight of an anna coin is around 3.88 grams.'

'Why do you collect them?' persisted Joydeep.

'The demand for copper and nickel have grown tremendously in recent times,' replied Arvind, ignoring Joydeep's irritation. 'Copper-nickel alloys are being used for marine applications due to their resistance to seawater corrosion. Even my mother has a copper kada among her things. I have tried convincing her to give it to me but she refuses. She says that it has antique value that I will understand only when I grow up.'

'That still does not answer my question. Why do you collect them?' asked Joydeep.

'With most military vessels having been bombed during the last world war, there is renewed ship-building activity and hence higher demand for copper and nickel,' replied Arvind finally. 'The reason that I collect them is because the higher demand has made the metal used in some coins worth more than their face value.'

Joydeep scratched his head, attempting to digest what his friend was telling him.

'This is true for the half-anna, one-anna and two-anna coins which are now worth 40 per cent more than their face value! Even if I give the street bums a 10 per cent premium and Mr Bhattacharjee keeps another 10 per cent for himself, I still make a cool 20 per cent off every coin that I trade!'

Much planning had gone into this excursion. Money had been saved over several weeks to make it happen. Ever since the movie had been released Ayub had been wanting to go and see it. But a coolie's salary meant restraint and patience.

Little Arbaaz looked up at his parents as they walked towards Pila House. The British authorities had closed all the cemeteries in the area in 1830 to build gaming clubs and theatres called Play Houses. Locals who couldn't pronounce the term 'Play House' ended up referring to the area as *Pila House*. The name had stuck.

'This is where we turn,' said Ayub, firmly pulling Arbaaz along with him. The signboard outside said 'Royal Talkies'.

They walked through an arched doorway under a hand-painted poster that depicted Pradeep Kumar, Bina Rai and Noor Jehan, the stars of the movie. The film was called *Anarkali* and had been produced by Filmistan.

The Royal Talkies too had originally staged plays but eventually the stage had given way to a cinema screen. With a seating capacity of 600, the crowds outside were staggering. Bombay simply couldn't get enough of Bollywood. Not only the Royal Talkies, but also the other cinemas, such as the Edward, New Roshan Talkies, Alfred, Nishat, Gulshan, Imperial and Capitol, were always to be found running house full.

A large blackboard displaying show times written in chalk hid most of the booking clerk as Ayub bent down to pay. There were four screenings that day—at 12.30, 3.30, 6.30 and 9.30. The Sheikh family bought three tickets at the box office at four annas per ticket.

They walked in, crossed a lobby floor done up in a monochrome chessboard pattern and avoided the counter groaning under the weight of fried snacks and a soda fountain. Arbaaz was firmly pulled away from those delights. The family could just about afford the tickets.

The Sheikhs sat inside for the next two hours and fifty-five minutes, utterly captivated by the images on the screen. They laughed when Akbar gave Nadira the name Anarkali when she asked for a pomegranate flower. They cried when Akbar had her imprisoned for dancing intoxicated in his court. They sang along with Lata Mangeshkar's voice in '*Yeh Zindagi Usi Ki Hai*'. They gasped when the conflict between Akbar and Salim reached its climax.

Emerging from the dark and cool interiors into the street, Arbaaz asked his father, 'Why did Akbar behave so badly with his son?'

Ayub thought about the question for a moment before replying. 'Unfortunately, in the conflict between power and love, power usually wins, my son,' he said.

Arbaaz sighed as he walked down the street in Bombay's searing summer heat. Another long walk to the grocer's. His mother always seemed to have a perennial demand of errands for him.

Arbaaz wondered whether Javed and his band of thugs would be waiting for him at the Dongri street corner. The last time that he had passed by, they had caught hold of him by the scruff of his neck and taken turns in using him as a punching-bag.

The tall but skinny lad had long limbs and drooping eyes. His hair was jet-black but a touch of henna applied by his mother made it appear brownish. His fair complexion was blemished by mild eruptions of acne that always embarrassed him. Arbaaz was an easy target.

Arbaaz stuck his hands into his coarse and thick twill-weave cotton pants. It was the same cloth that went into making the dungarees of British workmen. In fact, the word 'dungaree' was simply an English bastardization of *Dongri*.

Dungarees hadn't changed but Dongri had. It was now the hotbed of Bombay's underworld.

The name that brought on an instant feeling of fear was that of Abdul Dada. His writ ran large in the areas stretching from Crawford Market to JJ Hospital. No ordinary citizen who lived in Umerkhadi, Chakala Market, Null Bazaar, Kamathipura or Chor Bazaar could do so without keeping on the right side of Abdul Dada.

The street-corner teenage bully—Javed—was small fry but seemed mightier than Abdul Dada in Arbaaz's eyes. Javed's gang of delinquents was bad news for everyone in the neighbourhood. A couple of weeks ago, they had bashed up the local hooch shop-owner because he had refused to give them their usual supply without payment. On another occasion, they had held the postman at knifepoint and forced him to part with all the money orders that were in his bag. Arbaaz turned the corner only to find that his worst fears had come true.

Javed stood menacingly, leaning against a lamp-post, surrounded by his tribe of yes-men. 'Well, well... what have we here?' said Javed loudly. 'It seems that little Arbaaz is on another errand for poor Shabana. I wonder how much he has in his pockets. Pick him up, Rashid, let's see what he's worth.'

A hulk of a boy stepped up and knocked Arbaaz to the ground. Catching hold of Arbaaz's ankles, he held him upside down and shook him vigorously until a few coins tumbled out of his pockets. 'Not very much, I see,' said Javed. He paused for a moment, surveying an upside-down Arbaaz.

'Put him down, Rashid,' said Javed contemptuously. The hulk dumped Arbaaz unceremoniously on the pavement.

'Now strip him of his clothes,' instructed Javed.

'But—but…' stammered Arbaaz.

'It is your duty to carry sufficient money in your pockets. Whenever you carry less, we shall also take your clothes. We're not a charity!'

Javed crossed his arms and smugly watched his thugs strip off Arbaaz's clothes as the frail boy pleaded to be spared the ignominy. A few minutes later, Arbaaz was entirely alone and entirely naked. They had taken his underpants too. Tears rolled down his cheeks but he could not wipe them away. He needed his hands to cover his privates.

And then something snapped inside him and Arbaaz would never be the same boy again. Mahatma Gandhi had once said that an eye for an eye would end up making the whole world blind.

It was time for the world to go blind.

Arbaaz sat at his desk. In front of him was a 9p postcard issued by the Department of Posts.

Also in front of him was an Urdu book. It was titled *The Urdu Letters of Mirza Asadu'llah Khan Ghalib*. Books were an odd sight in the Sheikh household. Arbaaz had borrowed it from his teacher at school.

'*As-Salaam-Alaikum…*' he wrote carefully, ensuring that the spellings and script were perfect.

'By the grace of Allah, may I humbly request you…' he wrote, referring to the Ghalib book for appropriate phrases. One had to keep the tone mature yet reverential.

Once he was done, he surveyed his work proudly. He hurried to the post box down the street to drop off the postcard. Having dropped it into the red cylinder, he took a deep breath.

The real challenge would be tonight.

The house on Sandhurst Road was quiet, with all the residents fast asleep. Arbaaz had been squatting across the railway tracks for over two hours. He had reviewed the plan several times in his head. He knew that he would be in big trouble if the strategy backfired.

He got up and stretched himself. He felt inside his right trouser pocket. It was there. It had meant months of saving to buy it. He was reassured when his fingers touched the plastic. He hesitated for a moment, wondering whether he was doing the right thing. Then he remembered reaching home naked and being called filthy names by the street urchins who had followed him. He made up his mind.

He nimbly crossed the railway tracks and reached the double-storeyed house. A sign outside the gate read *M.J. Rehman, Advocate*. Arbaaz swung open the gate and his heart fluttered as the hinges squeaked in the stillness of the night.

Nerving himself, he walked cautiously to the house, avoiding the twigs that lay scattered on the ground. He looked up towards the window that he had been observing all night. It was wide open.

He quickly shinned up the drainpipe, as nimble as a coconut-harvester in Kerala. Devoid of friends, Arbaaz had spent days climbing trees and hiding in them. His lack of strength was balanced by his agility and speed.

Some animals hunt. Others hide.

He reached the window and peered inside. He could discern a figure on the bed. Its open mouth was snoring, expanding and contracting rhythmically to the pattern of the snores. Arbaaz pulled himself over the window ledge and gingerly stepped inside the room.

He stood motionless for a minute, allowing his eyes to adjust to the darkness. He then walked over to the desk and opened one of the drawers. The Bombay humidity had swollen the wood and the drawer squeaked. The figure on the bed stopped snoring. Arbaaz froze in fear.

He remained frozen for over a minute and almost magically, the snoring resumed. Arbaaz heaved a sigh of relief as he set about completing his task.

'Please, I beg you to stop hitting him!' pleaded the mother as Mohammad Jaafar Rehman, Advocate, swung his leather belt yet again to deliver swift justice.

'I've tolerated his unruly ways a thousand times!' shouted Mr Rehman, quite beside himself with fury. 'Dodging classes and failing exams, playing gang-leader to a bunch of retards, harassing the neighbours… but this is the last straw!'

Thwack! The leather belt struck Javed yet again, this time on his thighs. Deep red welts had formed on his back and legs at places where his father's belt had struck. The boy yelled in pain as he attempted to stay on his feet.

'It is your pampering that has created this mess,' said the lawyer to his wife as he got ready to swing the belt yet again, wielding it like a crime-fighter in a Bollywood movie.

'Will you please stop trying to kill our son and tell me what he has done that is so terrible?' asked the agitated mother.

'See this?' asked Mr Rehman, holding up a plastic packet containing a beige-coloured powder. 'This was inside his desk drawer. It's heroin! Our son is now a professional drug-dealer!'

'Where did you get this, Javed?' asked his distraught mother in tears.

'I honestly have no clue, Mother,' replied Javed feebly.

'Liar!' shouted Mr Rehman as he swung the belt yet again, the leather smacking Javed on his upper back. Javed lost his balance and fell to the ground.

'How do you know that these drugs belong to Javed?' asked Mrs Rehman, hoping that the question would cause the beating to cease.

'A poor, pitiful mother like you wrote to me,' replied Mr Rehman. 'She sent me this postcard. Read it and tell me if I should show mercy to this pathetic specimen that we call our son!'

Javed's mother took the postcard from her husband's hand and read it.

As-Salaam-Alaikum Rehman Saheb. I can turn to no one else for help. My son is addicted to the drugs that your boy sells. I have tried my best to help him stop the habit but to no avail. Your son ensures that his customers remain addicted. I cannot go to the police because they will arrest my son first. I know that you are a respected lawyer and a good man. By the grace of Allah, may I humbly request you to get rid of this scourge? I shall be forever in your debt.

— A mother who wants her son back.

'How could you do this, Javed?' asked Mrs Rehman, her face turning red with anger. 'I protected you when you failed each year, shielded you from your father when you were up to mischief, made excuses for you when your teachers called me to school…'

'Mother, I swear… this stuff is not mine!' pleaded Javed, furiously racking his brains to figure out who had set him up.

'Stop it!' snapped his mother. 'Your father is right. I have been far too lenient with you. From this day onwards things will change.'

Turning to her husband she said, 'I think he needs a few more.' She then turned and walked out of the room.

Atop a tree that bordered the Rehman home, Arbaaz watched events unfold with a quiet smile of satisfaction.

Some animals hunt. Others hide. And a few hunt while they hide.

Iqbal and Arbaaz looked odd standing next to each other. Iqbal had broad shoulders, muscular arms and wrestler's thighs. Arbaaz, on the other hand, was tall and skinny. Iqbal looked at the scrawny lad once again.

'You want me to train you?' he asked. 'Why?'

'Because I'm tired of being picked on,' replied Arbaaz. He was at the local *taleemkhana* which was not very different from the local Hindu *akhada*. The only real difference was that there were no idols of Hindu gods on the walls. Instead there was an *ayat* from the Qur'an. Iqbal was the local *pehelwan* who ran it.

'Your training starts now,' said Iqbal. 'Stand on that cot.'

Arbaaz followed his trainer's instructions. Iqbal pulled out a hen from a cage in the corner of the room and pushed it under the cot. He handed Arbaaz a *lathi*. 'Your job is to prevent the hen from getting out from under the cot. Remember that you cannot touch the hen. Simply move the lathi on all four sides of the bed fast enough and you will achieve this.'

It took the hen less than ten seconds to escape.

Iqbal laughed. He took the *lathi* from Arbaaz and got one of his students to catch the flapping bird and put it back under the cot. 'Now observe,' he said as he effortlessly swung the *lathi* on all four sides of the bed without touching the bird. 'What we do is create an artificial barrier. The bird thinks that there is a wall on all four sides of the bed. This is the sort of speed at which I expect you to move the *lathi*. Clear?'

Arbaaz nodded.

'What are you wearing underneath those baggy pants?' asked Iqbal abruptly.

'Underwear,' said Arbaaz.

'Here, put this on before coming back tomorrow,' said Iqbal handing him a *langot* and a bottle of oil. 'You will need it for the wrestling bout. And also apply this all over your body when you get here.'

'What is it?' asked Arbaaz.

'Sesame oil,' said Iqbal. 'Ever heard about *baana, banethi, binnaut* and *khari gatka*?'

'No,' admitted Arbaaz.

'They are various forms of Indian self-defence. I am going to teach you all of them. By the time I am done with you, even a simple coin tied in a piece of cloth will become a deadly weapon in your hands.'

'What time should I come each day?' asked Arbaaz.

'Come here after saying your prayers at dawn. You need Allah's blessings to achieve this miracle. Your training will last for two hours daily. Here, drink this.'

A boy holding a glass offered it to Arbaaz.

'What is this?' asked Arbaaz.

'Milk with crushed almonds,' replied Iqbal. 'You will drink a glass of this after your training each day. At home, I want you to consume dal and mutton. The protein will fill you out. See you tomorrow.'

Arvind noticed her from across Rawdon Street. While the boys' school had its main gate opening on Loudon Street, the girls' school had its main entrance from Rawdon Street. The two La Martiniere schools, one for boys and the other for girls, faced each other across Rawdon Street.

She was a delightful creature. She was a dusky Bengali beauty with deep eyes and dimples that appeared whenever she smiled, which was often. He had been on one of his coin-collecting rounds when she entered the school gate along with her friend, and he had been unable to take his eyes off her. He had never experienced anything like that before. The worst part was that he couldn't discuss it with anyone. Certainly not his parents. And his friend Joydeep was entirely inept in such matters.

Too shy to introduce himself and too scared to find out her name from anyone else, Arvind resigned himself to waiting on Rawdon Street to surreptitiously steal glimpses of her. A few days later he saw her friend walk out from the school gate alone. It was now or never.

His heart was beating wildly as he walked up to her. 'Excuse m—m—me, c—c—could I ask you a question?' he stammered.

The girl was heading towards a private car but she stopped for a moment and looked at him enquiringly.

'I was wondering whether you could tell me the name of your friend,' babbled Arvind nervously. 'You know, the one that you're usually with.'

'Why should I tell you?' asked the girl almost dismissively.

Arvind's mind froze. He had not anticipated the question. He could feel his pulse quicken as he struggled to offer an explanation.

'I th—think,' he stammered timidly. 'I think I—I—'

'Well, get on with it,' said the girl. 'What do you think?'

'I think… that I'm in love with her.'

There. He had said it. And it had come out just fine, initial stammering aside.

The girl smiled. 'Her name is Paromita.'

'I'm so sorry for not introducing myself,' said Arvind, his stammer having disappeared after receiving a smile from the girl. 'I'm Arvind. What's your name?'

'Shreya,' replied the girl. 'Nice to meet you, Arvind.'

'Do you know what her favourite subject is?' asked Arvind, his courage building up further.

'Chemistry, I think,' said Shreya. 'Why?'

'Could I pass on a note to Paromita through you? I could give it to you first thing tomorrow evening.'

'Why not in the morning?' asked Shreya.

'Because she's always with you in the mornings,' said Arvind, his face blushing red.

'You've been watching us?' asked Shreya.

Arvind nodded awkwardly. He wondered whether she was thought that he was creepy.

Shreya giggled. 'That's sweet. Sure, give me the note tomorrow after school. We come together in the mornings but she usually has extra classes in the evening so we leave separately. I'll pass on your note to her,' said Shreya, moving towards the car that was waiting for her.

'Er, Shreya, one more thing… ' said Arvind.

'Yes?'

'Does she already have a boyfriend?'

The next day Arvind was waiting on Rawdon Street when Shreya emerged after school. He quickly crossed the street and passed the note to his courier-cum-accomplice.

He had considered using his classroom French to woo Paromita but had decided against it. *Too cheesy*, he thought. In any case, in that year, 1954, the French had only just vacated Pondicherry, handing it back to India. In Arvind's mind it seemed foolish to use the language of a quitter. He settled for the language of chemistry instead.

Shreya read the note.

Dear Paromita. You don't know me but I know you. My name is Arvind and I was hoping that we could be friends. I think that you are a compound of copper and tellurium. I can best be described as an unstable mixture of carbon, ruthenium, sulphur and hydrogen. Do you think that our chemistry could work?

— Arvind

That day, *Filmfare* magazine had announced the winners of their cinema awards. At a ceremony held at the Metro cinema in Bombay, *Do Bigha Zameen* had won in the Best Film category, Bimal Roy had been named Best Director for it, Dilip Kumar had bagged the Best Actor award for *Daag,* Meena Kumari had won Best Actress for *Baiju Bawra,* and Naushad had won the Best Music accolade for it. Arvind, too, was hoping that he would be a winner that day—in a different sense.

'I'm confused,' said Shreya to Arvind. 'This note hardly sounds romantic at all. Are you sure you want me to give this to her? Will it work?'

Arvind nodded. 'Yes. I'll take my chances. I owe you a favour for this, Shreya,' he said as he walked away thinking of Paromita.

Arvind wondered whether Shreya had passed on his note to Paromita. It had been two days. The longest two days of his young and impatient life. Had he made a fool of himself? Was she laughing at his note?

He kicked a pebble on the pavement as he trudged towards the gate. 'Ouch!' said a female voice as the pebble hit her. Arvind looked up and realized that his pebble had struck Paromita's ankle.

'I'm *so, so…* sorry,' he stammered, not knowing how to frame an adequate apology. All he wanted to do was to bend down and massage her ankle for her.

'It's fine,' said Paromita. 'It was a small pebble.'

There was an uncomfortable silence.

'Er, I got your note from Shreya. Thanks,' she said.

'I hope I didn't say something foolish,' said Arvind. 'I wasn't sure how you would react. You don't even know me… '

Arvind realized that he was gushing. Why couldn't he stop the absurd flow of hastily formed sentences?

'No, no… I think you're sweet,' she said.

Sweet? What did that mean? Sweet like a kid brother? Sweet like a puppy?

'I, too, have a note for you,' she said, handing over a small piece of paper to Arvind. She quickly turned away in embarrassment.

'See you later,' she said, running towards her own school.

Arvind's heart was thumping as he sat down on a fire hydrant and read the note. It said:

Dearest Arvind. Thanks for calling me a compound of copper and tellurium. I sympathize with you for your unstable mixture of carbon, ruthenium, sulphur and hydrogen. To me, you are a combination of hydrogen, erbium and oxygen. Just remember that I'm not and will never be a compound of helium, argon, thallium, einsteinium and sulphur.

— Love, Paromita.

He quickly pulled out his chemistry textbook and referred to the periodic table. He laughed ecstatically.

Copper and tellurium were represented by the symbols Cu and Te. A compound of copper and tellurium would read as CuTe. He'd used that to describe her in his note.

Carbon, ruthenium, sulphur and hydrogen had the symbols C, Ru, S and H. In his note he had told her that he had a CRuSH on her.

Hydrogen, erbium and oxygen had the symbols H, Er and O. She was calling him her HErO!

And helium, argon, thallium, einsteinium and sulphur had the symbols He, Ar, Tl, Es and S. Paromita was telling him that she certainly wasn't HeArTlEsS.

The spanking new Indian Institute of Technology at Kharagpur would hold its very first convocation ceremony two years later. They would have been proud of the scientific prowess of a schoolboy and girl. At the convocation, Nehru would announce, 'Here stands a fine monument of India, representing India's urges…'

At that moment all that Arvind wanted was to deal with his own urges.

Arbaaz took out a cigarette, lit it and allowed his mind to wander. The gentle breeze was comforting as it dried the sweat on his muscular back. As his trainer had predicted, Arbaaz had morphed from a scrawny kid into a muscled hunk. His face retained its innocence, though. His short hair, chiselled jawline, aquiline nose and big brown eyes were enough to set feminine hearts aflutter.

Arbaaz had no time for love, however. His father, who had been a coolie for many years, had passed away a couple of months ago. It had been a painful death. Blood cancer. Luckily, the end had come quickly. Arbaaz had aged ten years during those ten months of 1956. Financial pressures had forced him, barely fifteen, to approach his father's supervisor at the docks for a job. Mr D'Souza, his fourth grade teacher, had attempted to help him get a clerk's job at the newly created Life Insurance Corporation but it had been in vain.

'You will not grow up to become a coolie,' Ayub used to say to little Arbaaz. 'Concentrate on your studies so that you never have to lead the slavish existence that I do.' Arbaaz wondered what had been the use of his school education. It still only qualified him to be a coolie. Albeit a fluent English-speaking one at that.

'Forty rupees per month,' the supervisor had said, a cigarette dangling from the corner of his mouth. Ten rupees more than what his father's salary had been. It was not negotiable. Arbaaz had simply signed along the dotted line.

The next few days had been backbreaking. Massive crates containing tape-recorders, cigarettes and automatic watches from Dubai, textiles and garments from Aden, and cans of beer and vials of perfumes from Singapore needed to be physically—and carefully—hauled off the ships that docked.

Payday had soon arrived. As the coolies lined up to receive their weekly pay, a local thug by the name of Yusuf stood watching, swiftly taking a percentage from each dockhand.

When Arbaaz had received his money, he walked on, ignoring Yusuf. Suddenly, he received a painful kick up his rear. 'Pay up, motherfucker,' said Yusuf angrily.

'Why?' asked Arbaaz innocently.

'Why? He has the temerity to ask me why!' shouted Yusuf to his band of thugs. 'This entire city jumps when I snap my fingers and this asshole asks me why!'

Before Arbaaz could use his fists, five of Yusuf's men had surrounded him and whipped out their Rampuris, long foldable knives with a razor-sharp edge. 'Pay up or get sliced up!' they barked.

Arbaaz had reluctantly paid up, even though he could have given them a tough fight. Some animals hunt. Others hide. And a few hunt while they hide.

'Half your salary because of your insolence,' said Yusuf laughing. 'Pay *haftaa* obediently next time and it will only be 20 per cent.'

The wedding at Burdwan Palace in 1957 was a grand affair. The richest and most powerful business magnates of Calcutta—the Birlas, Jalans, Khaitans, Dalmias, Goenkas, Singhanias, Bangars, Bajorias and many others—were fully represented. Rajaji had flown from Delhi to Calcutta and was expected to put in an appearance later that evening.

C. Rajagopalachari, or Rajaji as he was known to most, had held many posts including Governor of West Bengal, Governor-General of India, Union Home Minister and Madras Chief Minister. But Rajaji was getting fed up of Nehru's socialism. Rumours were rife that Rajaji was likely to quit the Indian National Congress and establish a new outfit called the Swatantra Party. Many industrialists and traders of Calcutta and Bombay were supporting him.

Brijmohanlal Bagadia was inconsequential among the moneyed Marwari lot but had been invited nonetheless. He detested these events. He ended up meeting people who made him feel small. Nevertheless, he was expected to keep up appearances, smile and bow down in servility to Marwari aristocracy.

Arvind, however, was excited. Not because of the event but because they were getting a new car. After much thought and discussion, Brijmohanlal had placed an order for a vehicle produced by a company called Hindustan Motors. Modelled on the Oxford Morris Series III, it was called the Ambassador. There was a waiting list of three years for delivery but Arvind had already started making plans around it.

Most of the guests, though, couldn't care less about the Ambassador car. Most of them were interested in a man attending the wedding. It wasn't Rajaji. The man's name was Haridas Mundhra.

Brijmohanlal pointed him out to Arvind. Mundhra had started his career as a light-bulb salesman and had risen to dizzying heights through swift deals, stock-juggling and flexible ethics. He had even been indicted by the Bombay Stock Exchange for selling forged shares. But that hardly mattered here. No one cared how you got your money so long as you had it. The news was that a week ago Mundhra had managed to get the government-owned Life Insurance Corporation to invest millions into six of his ailing companies, effortlessly bypassing all committees. Arvind stared at him from a safe distance. *Why can't I become like Mundhra one day?*

Seated on a throne-like wheelchair was the grandfather of the groom, Sir Gyanchand Seksaria, who was chatting with Mundhra. As Mundhra moved on to meet the next admirer, Brijmohanlal nudged his wife and son, and they made their way to Sir Gyanchand. Brijmohanlal bent down to touch the old man's feet and then prompted Arvind to do the same.

The old man looked at Arvind. 'Are you married yet?' he gruffly asked the boy, ignoring Brijmohanlal.

'He's only sixteen,' answered Brijmohanlal hastily. 'Better that he settles down in business first… with your abundant blessings, of course.'

'Harrumph!' offered Sir Gyanchand, clearing his throat. The old man had a permanent scowl on his face, more particularly during celebrations. Men like Sir Gyanchand were happiest when transacting business. Celebrations like these were pure irritants.

'This new-fangled notion of boys getting married after eighteen is bunkum,' opined Sir Gyanchand. 'Better that they get married early, have children in good time and then get down to making money.' Brijmohanlal nodded in pretended agreement. *Which world are you living in, old man? The Hindu Marriage Act passed by Parliament makes it illegal for a boy less than eighteen to marry.*

Turning to Arvind, Sir Gyanchand said, 'It shall be your turn next time!' He then folded his hands to greet the next guest in line. It was a not-so-subtle indication to the Bagadia family to move on.

Suddenly, Arvind saw a familiar face. It was the man they had met in Srinagar—Atal Bihari Vajpayee. Arvind rushed over to him to shake his hand. Vajpayee remembered the boy who had expressed his views in a poem.

'How are you?' he asked Arvind, affectionately ruffling the boy's hair.

'The family keeps talking about me getting married,' said Arvind. 'It's rather irritating.'

'Tell them you spoke to me,' said Vajpayee. 'I'm thirty-three and am still unmarried.'

'Do you plan to get married?' asked Arvind.

'Not if I can help it,' said Vajpayee.

That year, the thirty-three-year-old had been elected to the Lok Sabha from Balrampur. His oratory had so impressed Prime Minister Nehru that he had predicted that the young man would some day become India's Prime Minister.

A few months later, an equally posh event took place at a magnificent art deco house on Alipore Road. It had been acquired by a Marwari family that had taken over one of the prominent British managing agencies of the time. A son—an heir—had been born and a grand *nahaan* ceremony was being held to thank the gods for the blessing. Cooks had been flown in from various cities so that the finest variety of cuisine would be served at the banquet. The dinner service would constitute gold platters.

It seemed so foolish. Why was the birth of a child endowed with a penis more important than the birth of one missing the aforesaid appendage? Fed up with the inequalities of Hindu society, Ambedkar had converted to Buddhism the previous year.

Wearing an uncomfortable bandhgala suit, Arvind tried to kill time by estimating the value of the diamonds that the ladies were wearing that day. A friend whose father was a jeweller had explained the four Cs of diamonds to him—cut, clarity, colour and carat. *No jeweller ever talks about the fifth and most important C—cost,* thought Arvind. Arvind was using his newly acquired knowledge to good use when he heard another 'Harrumph'.

Turning around he noticed that he was blocking the passage of Sir Gyanchand's magnificent wheelchair. He hastily stepped aside and then bent down to touch the old man's feet. The baron scrutinized him. 'You are the Bagadia boy, aren't you?' he asked grumpily. It was almost an accusation rather than a question.

'Yes, sir,' replied Arvind.

'Have you produced any children yet?' asked the patriarch.

'No, sir,' he replied respectfully. 'I'm not yet married.'

'Don't worry. It shall be your turn next time!' repeated Sir Gyanchand as he thumped his walking cane on the ground to signal for his attendants to push his wheelchair forward.

The old man's lost it, thought an irritated Arvind to himself. *He really gets my goat.*

Towards the end of the year there was a tragedy in the Chamaria family. The Chamarias had made their fortune through moneylending. Mourners had gathered at the burning ghat for the cremation. Only men were allowed in. Arvind accompanied his father. Attendees showed customary sorrow while they continued to wonder what would be a respectable time to leave the cremation ground.

Sir Gyanchand's wheelchair rolled up next to Arvind. The old man cleared his throat noisily as he watched the smoke rise from the pyre. His eyes were watering from the fumes and he coughed. Arvind bent down, touched the old man's feet and graciously offered his kerchief to Sir Gyanchand.

As the octogenarian took the kerchief, Arvind quietly whispered to him, 'Don't worry, sir, it shall be your turn next time.'

At the end of the day, coolies would converge at various eateries and hooch dens that operated in Carnac Bunder. One day Arbaaz met a man at one of these. His name was Raju. He was much older than Arbaaz, his sideburns having turned grey.

'You're Ayub's son?' asked Raju, gulping down the remnants of his coarse drink.

'Yes,' replied Arbaaz. 'Father died. I took his place.'

'I liked your old man. He was a good friend. I even attended your snip-snip ceremony,' offered Raju matter-of-factly. 'He was straight as a rod. That's why you're stuck doing this backbreaking work. I hear you had a run-in with Yusuf.'

'I will set him right one day.'

'Revenge is delicious but can sometimes cause indigestion. Tread carefully,' advised Raju.

'What did you mean about my father being upright?' asked Arbaaz.

'I offered him lucrative opportunities but he never agreed,' replied Raju.

'Like what?'

'To become part of the Crescent House gang.'

'What's that?' asked Arbaaz.

'Can you keep your mouth shut?' asked Raju, breathing into Arbaaz's ear. Arbaaz nodded.

'Meet me outside this joint at midnight,' said Raju, winking at Arbaaz. 'Bring a gunny bag with you.'

A couple of hours later, Arbaaz waited for Raju outside the watering hole. At a little after 12 o'clock, Raju appeared along with five other men. All of them carried heavy gunny bags. Arbaaz's gunny was empty while the others' bags were stuffed. *What the hell are they carrying?* wondered Arbaaz. One of the men had a mooring rope looped around his shoulder.

They headed to Alexandra Dock, avoiding the main gate. A few hundred yards away from the gate, they scaled the wall using the mooring rope. They then used the rope to haul up their gunnies.

'Follow me,' hissed Raju as they headed towards a bunch of crates that had been offloaded during the day. 'Aslam, did you make sure that those carts were placed in the zone where the searchlights don't reach?'

'Yes, boss,' replied a beefy man who seemed to have muscles rippling on every inch of his body. 'You had marked an X at the spot where you wanted them kept. They are exactly there.'

As they reached the spot, Raju took over. 'Ignore the big crates. They contain heavy cargo. The smaller ones contain the stuff that we're interested in,' said Raju. The others watched as he used an iron spike to pry open a wooden crate.

Arbaaz saw the beam of a searchlight heading towards them. He nervously watched as it came nearer but overshot the spot where they were. He relaxed and took a deep breath.

Looking down at the crate that Raju had opened, he saw yellow tins of State Express 555 cigarettes. *The House of State Express, 210 Piccadilly, London,* they proudly displayed on their glossy surfaces. *By Appointment to Her Majesty.*

Each of the men took several tins and placed them in the empty gunny bag that Arbaaz had brought along. After many tins had been removed, they emptied out dried grass and sand from one of the stuffed gunny bags, filling it into the empty spaces of the crate.

'Supervisors become suspicious if the crate is too light or if the contents are moving around inside,' explained Raju as he directed another man, Paul, to use a hammer and nails to seal off the crate.

Raju pried open another crate. It contained Schlitz beer cans—sixteen-ounce flat-tops. 'Bingo!' exclaimed Raju as he began stuffing the cans into the sack that had now been emptied of sand and grass. When the bag was three-quarters full he stopped. 'Can't be too greedy. Each of us has to scale that damn wall along with the cargo.' The process was repeated—sand and dried grass emptied from a sack and stuffed into the empty spaces of the crate with the purged gunny being used to store the contraband.

The next half-hour was spent pilfering watches, lighters, audio-players and perfumes. The seven men hauled the gunny bags to the wall. The beefy Aslam went first, followed by Paul and the others. Raju and Arbaaz stayed on the inside of the wall, tying each gunny bag to the mooring rope as the five men on the other side pulled up the haul.

Suddenly a searchlight illuminated the two men for a brief moment. 'Run away from me,' hissed Raju, heading right while Arbaaz headed left. 'Crouch down and wait for a few minutes,' he heard Raju say. 'They alter the angle of the light every thirty minutes so the radius will change.' They remained crouched for the next thirty minutes. It was past 2 am when Raju and Arbaaz pulled themselves over the wall and joined the other men.

'Where to next?' asked Arbaaz.

'Next stop is that cluster of buildings you can see from here,' said Raju, pointing to a few decrepit structures. One of them had a board that said 'Crescent House'. It actually read *Cr scent Ho se* because a couple of the letters had fallen off.

A truck was waiting in the courtyard. The men silently placed their takings in the truck while Raju negotiated the final price with a seedy looking man. There came a moment when Raju ordered the men to unload the stuff because the price wasn't right. Mr Seedy relented.

'Where will it go?' asked Arbaaz as the truck departed.

'Carnac Bridge,' replied Raju, counting the money. 'From there it will be distributed to places like Musafirkhana that specialize in selling this stuff.'

'Seven of us. Thirty per cent for me as your leader. Fifteen per cent each to Aslam and Paul for coordination. Ten per cent each to the remaining four.'

Raju handed over some money to Arbaaz. 'Count it,' he instructed.

'It doesn't matter, Raju Bhai,' replied Arbaaz. 'Whatever you give me is fine.'

'Count it,' repeated Raju, more firmly this time. 'In business, there are no friends. *Dhanda* is dhanda.'

Arbaaz counted the cash. A hundred rupees. A little over two months' pay for a single night's effort. He was suddenly wracked with guilt.

Raju sensed it instantly. 'Don't worry,' he said. 'The guilt passes. In my world, there is only one motto that you need to remember.'

'What is that?' asked Arbaaz as he placed the money in his pocket.

'If you do not get caught, you deserve to keep it!'

Bagadia & Co was located in Burrabazar, the commercial hub of Calcutta. Burrabazar had no beginning, middle or end. It was like a living organism that kept growing through the subdivision of its own cells. Burrabazar was divided into twenty-five chaotic *katra*s or markets, each one being home to the traders of a specific commodity.

Bagadia & Co was a *gaddi*—or office—located in Mullick Street, at the heart of this hodgepodge. The building was known as Kaligodam and the Bagadia office occupied two rooms on the third floor. Located close by were the offices of the Bangars, the Jalans and the Bajorias, wealthy Marwari families who owned the biggest jute mills.

It was a Sunday but the Bagadia office remained open all seven days. Brijmohanlal would often say that weekends were meant for the white-skinned only. Brown skins needed to work all seven days to stay in business.

Arvind had enrolled at St Xavier's College on Park Street. St Xavier's was the popular choice for children from business families while kids of professionals and government servants usually chose Presidency College on College Street. Each day, after lectures ended, Arvind was required to report to his father's office. Brijmohanlal had decided that his son needed to get some business training at the age of seventeen. These were troubled times and it was better that Arvind learnt the ropes quickly, reasoned his father.

Earlier that year in 1959, the Dalai Lama had crossed the McMahon line and entered Indian territory. All-India Radio's Akashvani service was saying that His Holiness had disguised himself as a common soldier in order to reach the Indian border. The Chinese were irked that the Dalai Lama was provided asylum by the Indian government. The prospect of war with the Chinese was a grim possibility but Nehru brushed it aside with his *Hindi—Chini Bhai Bhai* exhortations.

Indeed, troubled times did lie ahead, but troubled times usually meant opportunities too. A company called Bajaj Auto had just been granted a licence to manufacture scooters in India. Brijmohanlal Bagadia had made up his mind that his son's training would have to be swift so that he would be able to exploit business opportunities as they arose.

Inside the Bagadia office, Tarachand Agarwal, a *munim* dressed in his traditional dhoti, black coat and accountant's cap, watched Arvind carefully as he wrote the numbers into the red fabric-covered *bahikhata*. Both were seated on white cotton-covered mattresses. Next to the munim sat his most prized possession, his cashbox. In front of the munim was a small teakwood desk that contained a lockable compartment for papers as well as an inkpot. Arvind turned up his tongue against the corner of mouth in concentration. He had to get it right.

'Actually, the bahikhata system is a perfect double-entry system,' explained Tarachand Agarwal. 'It records all transactions that involve real, nominal or personal accounts.'

'But they say that double-entry was invented by the Europeans,' argued Arvind.

'Nonsense,' scoffed Tarachandji. 'In our system, all transactions are first entered in the *rokadabahi*—or cash book. They are then posted into the *khatabahi*—or ledger. A *nakalbahi* serves as the journal. Finally you prepare a *kacha-ankada*—or trial balance. How is this not double-entry?'

'But Munimji, where is the debit and credit in this?' asked Arvind.

'In our system we simply call it *naam* and *jamaa,* but the principle is the same, that of debit and credit. This system allows us adequate accuracy while providing us with room to be creative when needed.'

'But...' began Arvind in his usual argumentative tone. A look from Tarachand silenced him.

'To become a master of accounting, Arvind Babu, all you need to remember are two fundamental rules,' said the munim.

'What are those, Munimji?' asked Arvind.

'Rule number one: your accounts must always present a true and factual picture of your business operations.'

'And what's the other rule?' asked Arvind.

'Rule number two is to occasionally forget rule number one.'

'Take it easy, Arbaaz,' said Raju soothingly. 'If you can perform on the docks, there's no reason why you can't in bed.'

Arbaaz looked at Raju as they walked towards Safed Gully. Safed Gully used to be home to zari workers, brothels for exotic escort services, dentists, skin clinics, and theatres like the Royal and Alfred. Prostitutes from Europe and Japan used to be trafficked into this area for the recreation of British soldiers. It was the reason why the area was called Safed Gully, or White Man's Street.

Of course, these days there were no Europeans in this locality of Kamathipura. Their place had been occupied by Indians. It was one of the lesser discussed outcomes of Indian independence.

They reached another dilapidated building. 'This is where we get off,' said Raju. 'Pun entirely intended!'

'Where are we?' asked Arbaaz.

'Bachchuseth ki Wadi,' explained Raju. 'It's famous for its *kothewalis*, *tawaif*s and *mujra*s. I have a thing going with Ameena. She can seduce any man merely with her looks. But we're not going to waste your time with all that stuff.'

The brothel was humming with activity at this late hour. They began climbing the precarious staircase of the rather derelict building. Each step seemed to creak as they climbed. 'Don't be fooled by the packaging. The material inside is top quality,' assured Raju.

They briskly strode into a room that was empty except for a large maroon velvet sofa placed on a woven carpet. Bilqis Begum, the queen bee of the brothel, sat alone on the sofa surrounded by several ladies of varying ages. Bilqis was busy stuffing a paan into her mouth but stopped when she saw Raju enter.

'Ah! My favourite customer,' she cried out cheerfully. 'And I see that you've brought along a friend. Does he have a name?'

Raju and Arbaaz sat down next to her on the sofa. 'His name is Arbaaz, and he needs gentle handling,' explained Raju softly to Bilqis Begum. It seemed rather ironical that a hunk of a man needed gentle handling.

Bilqis Begum nodded knowingly. 'Ah! I love cherries. I have just the right girl. Where is Faiza?' The madam clapped her hands to punctuate her question thrown out to the ladies.

From amongst the girls who were standing there, a petite lady with the complexion of polished rice stepped forward. She had dark brown hair that fell to her hips, twinkling eyes, a pert nose and full lips that were deep red with lipstick. Her near hourglass figure was accentuated by the clinging pink saree that was draped around her. Unlike the others, she wasn't a girl. She was a woman.

Without a word, she held Arbaaz's hand and led him out of the room and up a further flight of stairs. Inside the bedroom, she made him sit on the bed as she seductively removed her clothes. Arbaaz nervously watched as she removed her saree, blouse, petticoat and undergarments.

Now resplendent in her complete nakedness, Faiza smiled at him and sat by his feet. She placed her hands on his thighs and Arbaaz felt an electric current surge through his body. She began unbuckling his belt. He flinched. 'Don't worry,' she soothed. 'I will take care of everything. Just enjoy your trip to heaven and back.'

Arbaaz was in a daze.

His mother had always said that the way to a man's heart was through his stomach. That day Arbaaz realized that the access point was far lower.

'Take me to Number Seven Lyons Range,' said Arvind, getting into the *tana* rickshaw.

Accompanying Arvind was a clerk from his father's office. The clerk wondered why he had been assigned this task.

'Where are we going?' asked the clerk.

'There is a neem tree. I go and water it each month and watch it grow,' replied Arvind. The clerk cursed his luck. At this time he could have been sipping sweet, scented tea in Burrabazar.

Arvind ignored the exertions of the sweat-soaked barefoot man who huffed and puffed as he pulled the rickshaw through the narrow streets. It was quite remarkable that the humble rickshaw could access nooks and crannies that the carriages belonging to the Calcutta Tramways Company could not. But Arvind was oblivious to the world around him. He was busy studying a page in the *Statesman*.

'What are you reading?' asked the curious clerk.

'Oh, this and that about Bombay; about happenings in this century; about the allure of the Kohinoor; about dying… '

The clerk shut up. He was more interested in the rising price of *roshogolla* at K.C. Das than the philosophical questions of life and death.

As they reached their destination, they were met by a dhoti-clad gentleman with a waxed moustache and oiled hair who was waiting for them at the street corner. The clerk started to dismount but Arvind held him back.

'Nice to see you, Arvind Babu,' said the dhoti-clad man, walking up to the rickshaw.

'I hope that my neem tree is growing, Dipankar Da,' said Arvind, remaining seated. It was an old joke between them.

Way back in the 1830s, a group of brokers used to meet under a neem tree on Clive Street. They would trade loans of the East India Company and shares of the Bank of Bengal. Unfortunately, in 1905, the Chartered Bank began constructing an office building where the neem tree once stood. It had forced the brokers to relocate to 2 China Bazaar Street. Eventually, they had got their own building at 7 Lyons Range. Arvind still chose to refer to his stock market investments as his neem tree.

'Oh, absolutely,' said the oil slick. 'Your investments in Bombay Dyeing, Century Textiles and Kohinoor Mills have all done well.'

Oh, this and that about Bombay; about happenings in this century; about the allure of the Kohinoor; about dying…

'Good. I need you to liquidate them all,' said Arvind.

'All of them?' asked Dipankar Da.

'Yes, all.'

'What about the liquidity that will come from the sales? Where do I park it?'

'Invest in Tata Steel and the new offering by Bajaj Auto. Textiles are old hat. Steel and automobiles are the new frontier. By the way, here's some more money from my weekly earnings,' said Arvind, handing over cash. 'You may send me the receipt at my house by post.'

'Are you sure that you want to exit Bombay Dyeing, Century Textiles and Kohinoor Mills? Prices are still going up, Arvind Babu. Brokers are eagerly lapping up the stocks.'

'In the few years that I have been playing the markets, I have learnt only one thing, Dipankar Da.'

'And what is that?' asked the broker, who often planned his own investment strategies according to the ideas of the boy.

'I have learnt that one should be cautious when others are eager and be eager when others are cautious.'

Arbaaz sat inside Napoli for the first time after his newly discovered fortune. It was a popular open café where one could consume a hot dog and an espresso for a rupee. Arbaaz was sipping a Coke as he attempted to appreciate the loud music. The owner had a huge collection of the latest vinyls in the jukebox. Four annas was all it took to pick a song from them.

Fed up of the noise, Arbaaz walked to a saree store. 'Show me something in blue,' said Arbaaz, as the shopkeeper unfurled yet another saree before him. Arbaaz bought it without any haggling.

He then headed over to Patel's. Seth Shyamjibhai Patel was the local grocer with whom their family had a running account that was always overdue.

Sethji scowled when Arbaaz walked in and was all smiles by the time Arbaaz cleared all his old dues.

The grocer had turned serious after counting the cash, though.

'Why the glum face, Sethji?' asked Arbaaz.

'They've split Bombay state into two new states—Gujarat and Maharashtra,' said Sethji.

'How does that concern you?' asked Arbaaz.

'They're saying that Bombay will be the capital of Maharashtra. I am Gujarati but my family has lived in this city for generations. Where does that leave me?'

Arbaaz digested the information. What Patel was saying made sense but Arbaaz had more pressing matters to attend to.

'Relax, Sethji,' said Arbaaz. 'The world is growing smaller. One of the loaders at Santa Cruz airport says that Air-India will soon be starting flights to New York. Can you imagine that? Where one lives will soon become irrelevant. Twenty years in the future, no one will bother about whether your kids are Gujarati- or Marathi-speakers.' Arbaaz secretly wondered if what he himself had said was true. Sethji, too, gave him an uncertain look.

Arbaaz walked briskly home to his mother and handed over the saree and forty rupees—a full month's wages. He would have liked to give her more but she would have become suspicious.

'If you do not get caught, you deserve to keep it,' reiterated Arbaaz to himself as he hugged his mother, at the same time feeling a little guilty. Guilty about his double life as a dock thief. Guilty about his nocturnal adventures with Faiza. That woman had taught him more in a few months than he had learned during his lifetime.

His thoughts then went back to the comment by Patel. Who cared whether Bombay was part of Maharashtra or Gujarat? One day he, Arbaaz Sheikh, would control Bombay. Then none of this would matter.

But first he needed to sort out that rascal, Yusuf.

Arbaaz kept watch over Yusuf's house for the next couple of days, making notes of the times at which people came and left.

'I need your help,' said Arbaaz to Raju a few days later.

'Tell me,' said Raju, stuffing a paan into his mouth.

'I need to straighten out Yusuf,' said Arbaaz.

'Have you lost it? No one messes with Yusuf. Better to pay him his haftaa and stay clear. His niece is married to Abdul Dada's nephew. I'm sure you know who Abdul Dada is—or has your penis switched places with your brain?'

'I can bet you that Abdul Dada doesn't know of the extortion racket at the docks,' said Arbaaz. 'The last thing he would do is to take money from poor labourers. Yusuf only throws about Abdul Dada's name. I'm certain that he's on his own in this dirty little scheme.'

'Be careful, whatever you do,' advised Raju.

'I shall take your advice seriously, Raju Bhai. In any case, all I need is for one of your chaps to pickpocket a man who prays each day at the Jama Masjid on Sheikh Memon Street.'

'Who is he?' asked Raju, a trickle of red paan juice escaping from a corner of his mouth.

'His name is Kareem. He runs the eatery on Carnac Road.'

'Why the fuck do you want my chap to pickpocket a cook?' asked Raju incredulously.

'Because I need to get into his good books,' replied Arbaaz.

'What was that? Are you saying you want to loot someone in order to become their friend? You are one crazy bastard,' said Raju, masticating his paan vigorously.

'That I am,' agreed Arbaaz with a sly smile. 'There's one more thing, though.'

'Now what?'

'One of your friends is a chap called Tawade. He is a foreman at Jai Jagdish Oil Mills.'

'What about him?'

'I need an introduction.'

'That can be done. *Now* may I get on with my life?' asked Raju sardonically.

'Just one final request, Raju Bhai,' said Arbaaz, mustering up his courage to make the request.

'And what might that be?'

'The chap who pickpockets Kareem… I need your permission to beat him up.'

Arbaaz watched the man as he trained his students. From a hook in the ceiling hung a rope. Suspended from the rope was a clothes hanger at average shoulder-height. From the hanger dangled a shirt and a pair of trousers—the poor pickpocket's practice scarecrow. On each of the pockets as well as the rope were sewn little bells that would tinkle when the suspended scarecrow moved.

Around six boys were present in the room. Each one was called up individually to tackle the scarecrow. There were items in all the pockets—sunglasses, pen, wallet, change, kerchief. The objective was to retrieve all the items without any of the bells tinkling.

It was obvious that the boys were novices. Most of them were unable to achieve any results without the accompaniment of several bells. But then a young man stepped forward. The trainer called him Chhotu. Chhotu cleaned out the dummy in a matter of minutes. Not a single bell sounded. His movements were fluid and graceful, almost like a dancer's. The other boys clapped and Chhotu took a little bow.

'He's the one,' said Arbaaz to the trainer. 'I need him.'

Arvind looked at Paromita wistfully. The past few months had been the best ones of his life.

Paromita was so damn beautiful! She was almost angelic, with a flawless complexion, sharp features, full lips, cute dimples and brown eyes with a hint of naughtiness in them. Arvind still found it hard to believe that she had chosen him for a boyfriend.

They were comfortably ensconced at a table inside India Coffee House on College Street. A waiter sporting a white turban had served them several cups of coffee through the afternoon but neither Arvind nor Paromita had bothered to consume them. Love seemed to offer an endless supply of nourishment.

She had brought along her dog-eared copy of the *Rubaiyat* of Omar Khayyam and was reading out her favourite quatrains. '*A book of verses underneath the bough, a jug of wine, a loaf of bread—and thou beside me…*'

'I already have thou beside me,' joked Arvind.

'Oh, hush. Listen to these words, Arvind… '*Ah make the most of what yet we may spend, before we too into dust descend!*'

'Mercifully, we're not spending much, particularly at this place,' said Arvind, deliberately oblique. Paromita gave up.

Arvind suddenly asked, 'May I tell you something?'

'Sure,' said Paromita.

'You have the prettiest smile I've ever seen,' he said earnestly.

Paromita blushed. She knew it was true but still loved hearing it from Arvind.

'Now may *I* tell *you* something?' she asked.

'Go ahead,' said Arvind.

'The smile on my face mostly happens because of you.'

The Jama Masjid near Crawford Market was a rectangular building of brick and stone surrounded by a band of double-storeyed buildings. The eastern gate of the mosque led to an ancient tank that held around ten feet of water. Steps and embankments allowed the faithful to cleanse themselves before performing *namaaz* in the central courtyard.

Arbaaz watched as Kareem prepared himself for namaaz. He first washed his hands and arms up to his elbows. He then gathered water from the tank in his cupped hands and washed his face. He joined his fingers together and ran his hands over his hair from his forehead to the back of his neck. He then brought his hands to the front while wiping the side of his head. Finally, he bent down to wash his feet up to his ankles while making sure that water passed between his toes.

Kareem walked up the steps oblivious of Chhotu, who was tailing him. Just as Kareem crossed the sixteen black stone arches that supported the mosque, Chhotu inserted his index and middle finger ever so lightly into Kareem's pocket. Like a true artiste, he snagged and jerked out the wallet.

Immediately, a commotion arose as Arbaaz shouted, 'Stop! Thief!'

Kareem halted in his tracks and felt for his wallet. Realizing that it was missing, he looked in the direction of the fleeing Chhotu. The young pickpocket would have liked to make a quick exit but knew the script. He was, as expected, caught by Arbaaz, who delivered a couple of resounding slaps on his face. 'How dare you steal inside the house of Allah?' he thundered as he prised the wallet out of Chhotu's hands and deliberately allowed him to flee.

Arbaaz walked up to Kareem and handed over the wallet. 'I believe it's yours, *Bhaijaan*,' he said, as he handed it over to the grateful Kareem. The old cook, mostly whiskers and wrinkles, smiled gratefully as he patted Arbaaz on his head affectionately. 'Thank you, my son. May Allah always look after you. Let me know if there is some way in which I can repay you for your kindness.'

'Now that you mention it, I am told that you make the best *paya nihari* in town,' began Arbaaz.

Arvind and Paromita snuggled up as they sat on the bench overlooking Rabindra Sarobar. It was a wintry evening, peaceful except for the chirping of the migratory birds that flocked to the lake from colder climes.

Paromita tucked her head into Arvind's shoulder as he pulled her tightly into his embrace. Time seemed to stand still as they savoured their rare moment of physical closeness.

Arvind cupped his free hand under Paromita's chin and lifted her head to face him. She was so utterly captivating. There was no girl prettier than her.

Arvind looked into her eyes and asked, 'May I tell you something?'

'Sure,' said Paromita, smiling.

'You have the prettiest smile I've ever seen,' he said earnestly, looking at her kissable lips.

Paromita knew what should follow. Her eyes shone as she asked, in her turn, 'Now may *I* tell *you* something?'

'Go ahead,' said Arvind, staring at her lips.

Paromita reached up and kissed him. It was a tender kiss that had him gasping for more.

'What did you want to ask me?' he said between kisses.

'Shut up and keep kissing me,' said Paromita.

They were inside the hot kitchen of the eatery and Kareem was showing Arbaaz the essentials of his most famous dish. Kareem's restaurant was famous for its paya nihari—goat's hooves in a soupy curry. The dish had its origins in Old Delhi during the last years of the Mughal Empire. Nihari was usually cooked overnight in massive quantities to be served to labourers for breakfast.

Arbaaz watched Kareem as he roasted the trotters over an open fire to burn off any bristle. He then proceeded to cut the hooves into smaller pieces with a heavy meat chopper. He placed the chopped trotters along with bay leaves and peppercorns into a stockpot and added lots of water.

'This will boil and then simmer for several hours,' explained Kareem as though he were on a cookery show. 'Letting the meat cook through, fall off the bone and almost melt in your mouth is the key to good paya nihari. The gelatinous fat, juicy bones and marrow will melt together to form the rich, meaty gravy.'

'That still doesn't explain why your paya tastes so good,' said Arbaaz. 'I have heard so many people say that there is something that is unique in the taste of Kareem's paya nihari.'

Kareem smiled, baring his yellowed and crooked teeth in the process. 'Here's the secret,' he said, pointing to another pot that was sitting in the corner of the kitchen.

'What's that? Some secret masala?' asked Arbaaz.

'Yesterday's leftovers,' replied Kareem. 'I add a kilo from each day's leftovers to the next day's cooking. This reused nihari is known as *taar* and it's this taar that provides the distinctive flavour that my eatery is famous for.'

'So every dish has a little bit of the past?' asked Arbaaz.

'Precisely. My kitchen has an unbroken taar chain going back a couple of decades!'

'And that's why there are so many regulars like Yusuf Miyan who come here each day,' offered Arbaaz semi-casually.

'Yes, my son,' said Kareem. 'Yusuf Miyan not only drops in but also calls for it at home. His servant picks it up from me each morning at 7 am sharp.'

'He likes it that much?' asked Arbaaz.

'He even asks his servant to pick up a separate pouch of taar,' replied a beaming Kareem. 'The paya is shared but the extra taar is only for him. That's the sort of fan following this dish has!'

Arbaaz spent the better part of the day visiting Jagdish Oil Mills at Sitafalwadi along with his friend Murali. The foreman, Tawade, was happy to sell him a tub of pulp left over after all the oil had been squeezed out from the castor beans. He would have been happy to sell it even if Raju Bhai hadn't asked.

Arbaaz headed over to the room that Raju had provided at the rear of Crescent House.

'Do you know how this process works?' asked Arbaaz. Murali nodded.

Murali transferred the pulp into a pot and added benzene to it. Using a spatula he mixed the material and then added water. Magically, the mixture separated into two distinct layers—one aqueous and the other organic.

'See? It is this aqueous layer that we're interested in,' said Murali.

He looked at the chemical bottles that he had procured from Kalbadevi. Hydrochloric acid and sodium carbonate. He would need gloves and a mask to carry out the next part of the filtration.

Murali was putting his school education to good use.

You murder my dog? thought Arbaaz to himself. *You had better guard your cat!*

Somewhere along the stretch from Bhendi Bazaar to Mohammed Ali Road was a small workshop. Arbaaz stood inside, watching the blacksmith work. The thin, wiry man fired up his welding torch, the rosebud tip glowing incandescently as he worked on the hammer.

'Let me see, you want a hook just below the hammerhead and you want the base of the handle to be sharp, like a skewer?' he asked, clamping the hammer with tongs over his anvil in order to strike it.

'Yes, Bhaijaan,' replied Arbaaz. 'I need a dozen of them—identical.'

Nodding, the blacksmith continued his work, hammering, heating and polishing until he was satisfied. Every now and then he would clean the anvil before resuming his painstaking work.

There was something magical about hammering hot metal into submission. If only Arbaaz could do that to men.

Arbaaz walked up three flights of stairs to reach the terrace of the building. He was alone. In his hand he clutched a book that Murali had passed on to him. Clotheslines criss-crossed the area with all manner of garments flapping in the wind. He ducked below several dangling clothes until he reached the ledge. The view into Yusuf's living room across the street was perfect from here. It left Arbaaz comfortably hidden behind the ledge.

Some animals hunt. Others hide. And a few hunt while they hide.

Arbaaz watched the group of men as they sat on the floor in Yusuf's room. Plates of kheema and paya nihari accompanied by naans lay inside the circle. Yusuf sat, lording over his men. He ate sloppily, slurping the marrow from his bowl with relish. Arbaaz could see Yusuf jazzing up his paya with the special pouch of taar.

Hope it tastes good, thought Arbaaz. *I made it specially for you.*

Arbaaz kept staring for another twenty minutes, lighting up a cigarette as he sat behind the ledge and waited. The men had finished their breakfast and the servant was clearing the dishes.

Arbaaz opened the book to the page that Murali had marked when questioned by Arbaaz.

Ricin is extracted from the seed of the castor plant. The castor plant is extremely common: it's used as an ornamental plant and is also an important cash crop. The seeds are heavy with oil and castor oil is used for varied purposes. It's a fairly common laxative. Also, because it's more capable of withstanding high temperatures, it's a good alternative to petroleum oil in motor engines.

Castor oil is absolutely safe to ingest because castor oil does not contain ricin. It's the castor bean mash that is left behind after oil extraction that contains ricin. All one needs to do is to place the mash in a solvent to break down the oils and fats, filter the mixture and allow it to form a powder.

The average adult only requires 1.78 mg of ricin to die. That is about the size of a few grains of table salt, which is what colourless and odourless ricin looks like.

Ricin is a toxic protein that attacks cells and prevents them from synthesizing their own protein. Without protein production, key functions in the body begin shutting down. Even in survivors, permanent organ damage is caused. Often there aren't any instant symptoms. There can often be a significant delay before symptoms begin manifesting, even up to a day or two.

Is there an antidote? Unfortunately not. Many governments have been working on an antidote but nothing has come of the research as yet.

Arbaaz silently thanked his parents for having insisted on providing him with a school education. He then thanked God for giving him a Tamil friend who knew how to put that education to use.

Payday arrived.

Arbaaz lined up for his wages. Yusuf wasn't there but the news about him was everywhere.

Late in the previous night, Yusuf had begun to feel gastrointestinal effects like violent vomiting and diarrhoea. This had lead to severe dehydration. By the time he had reached the hospital, his kidneys, liver and pancreas had failed.

An hour later, Yusuf was dead.

The paya nihari was never even suspected because seven others had eaten along with Yusuf and they were all fine.

One of Yusuf's henchmen, a dirty one-eyed man called Bilal, strolled in confidently along with a diminished band of thugs. Most of the other men were busy with Yusuf's funeral arrangements.

Bilal was bad news. He was a street fighter who had lost his eye to an ice pick during the gang war between Abdul Dada and Rangarajan Pillai.

'Pay up,' said Bilal as Arbaaz emerged from the line.

'Fuck you,' said Arbaaz, walking on.

Bilal went hopping mad. 'Kill the *madarchod*!' he yelled to his men who immediately flicked open their Rampuris.

But before they could attack Arbaaz, Raju's men swiftly descended on them. Aslam and Paul were in the lead. A dozen coolies pulled out hammers that they had hooked into the sides of their trousers, safely tucked out of sight under their shirts. Each hammer had an extra large hammering head and an iron spike affixed to the handle. It was a deadly weapon.

It was a ghastly sight. Bilal's men were left with cracked skulls and broken limbs. Bilal lost the one good eye he had come with. It was the last time that any of Yusuf's men would set foot in the docks.

Arbaaz's ingenuity had not escaped the attention of others. One of the important people who had noticed was Abdul Dada.

Arvind watched the machine spitting out the papers. It was past 10 pm and he was the only one inside the college premises besides an extremely nervous Joydeep.

Joydeep's father was headmaster of the college. Arvind had convinced Joydeep to allow him to use the cyclostyling machine of the establishment.

The office of the headmaster usually resonated with an ominous thwacking sound most afternoons. It was the sound of metal meeting paper as the cyclostyling machine spewed out examination papers. But the sound of the same machine at night was eerie. And it wasn't examination papers that were being produced here on this occasion.

This was the fifth time that Arvind was using the machine in four months. Usually, Joydeep would first say no and then Arvind would find some way to bribe him. 'Use it carefully, else I'll be in big trouble,' Joydeep would plead each time, nervously keeping a lookout for the watchman who was invariably to be found asleep at his station. Joydeep's concern was not unfounded. Arvind had nothing to lose because he was not a student at this college!

As on the past occasions, Arvind had patiently created the master stencil using the special typewriter that made small holes beneath the text. He had then filled the cyclostyle machine with printer's ink, attached the master stencil and started cranking. Soon the machine had started spinning out his documents by forcing ink through the stencil onto paper. Arvind was getting rather good at this. He picked up one of the cyclostyled letters and checked it for legibility. It was perfect. It read:

B. Ravi and I. Daga
Investment Advisors

1 December, 1960

Dear Sir,

Over the past few months I have been regularly sending you investment advice and share market tips absolutely free of charge. You will recall that:

On 1 August, I advised you to sell your shares of Century Textiles. I believed that the prices had reached a peak. I was proved right.

On 1 September, I advised you to buy shares of National Rayon. I saw them as good value. Those who took my advice have registered 26 per cent appreciation in the value of those shares.

On 1 October, I advised you to sell your shares of Bombay Dyeing. I thought that prices would head downwards. They did.

On 1 November, I advised you to buy shares of Tata Steel. I was certain that they would do well. Those who acted on my advice have seen 15 per cent appreciation in the value of those shares.

I now have a very special tip to offer you. Ignore it at your own peril…

Joydeep looked at the printed letter. 'Who exactly are B. Ravi and I. Daga?' he asked.

'You really want to know?' asked Arvind.

'Do I have an option?' asked Joydeep. 'I'm up to my neck in it with you.'

'*B. Ravi and I. Daga* is simply an anagram of *Arvind Bagadia*,' admitted Arvind with a glint in his eyes.

'How have you managed to be right four consecutive times?' asked Joydeep curiously.

'How many letters are we putting through the cyclostyling machine tonight?' asked Arvind in reply.

'One hundred and twenty-five,' answered Joydeep.

'Do you recall how many we cyclostyled the first time—in August?' asked Arvind.

'That was a crazy night,' remembered Joydeep. 'Probably around 2,000. The next day, my father was convinced that one of the peons was stealing ink.'

'Exactly. It *was* 2,000. But we printed two different letters. A thousand letters told people to sell Century Textiles but another thousand told people to buy Century Textiles.'

'I can't remember the details,' admitted Joydeep. His brain was usually exhausted by Arvind's schemes before they bore fruit.

'Obviously, my advice turned out right for a thousand people,' said Arvind.

'So what's the catch?' asked Joydeep.

'The next month—in September—I only wrote to the thousand who had received the right advice from me. Once again, I sent out two letters. I told 500 people to buy National Rayon and another 500 to sell National Rayon. In the process I was left with 500 people who had received perfect guidance from me twice.'

'So?'

'So I took it a step further. I sent out letters in October to those 500. I told 250 people to sell Bombay Dyeing and an equal number to buy Bombay Dyeing. This left me with 250 people who had received excellent advice from me on three consecutive occasions.'

'Hmm. Where are you going with this, Arvind?' asked Joydeep.

'In November I sent out letters to the 250 people who had seen my suggestions turn out absolutely right on three occasions. I told 125 people to buy Tata Steel and another 125 to sell Tata Steel. This database is my pot of gold. It comprises 125 people who think that I can never go wrong!'

'What are you now suggesting to them?' asked Joydeep.

'To make an investment of a lifetime. And to do it quickly and quietly before anyone else gets wind of it,' replied Arvind.

350 CE, Kosambi

ॐ त्रियम्बकं यजामहे
सुगन्धिं पुष्टिवर्धनं ।
उर्वारुकमिव बन्धनान्
मृत्योर्मोक्षिय मामृतात् ॥

Samudragupta watched the Kushan craftsman carefully weigh and place a gold blank on the anvil. An assistant cautiously placed the punch-die on top of the blank. Lifting his gigantic hammer, the goldsmith struck the punch die with a single forceful blow.

The Brahmins began chanting hymns. It was a proud moment.

'It's ready, sire,' said the goldsmith, moving aside. Samudragupta stepped forward to look at the newly minted gold coin that lay on the anvil.

The courtiers watched their handsome ruler examine the coin. Samudragupta was a sight to behold and appreciate. There was scarcely a hint of fat on his muscular frame. A richly beaded skullcap studded with gems sat on his head. He was clad in a soft tunic with its pointed ends secured by a maroon cummerbund. His muscular legs were encased in loose but tapering trousers. By his side hung a long jewel-encrusted sword that had vanquished many powerful kings. It was the very sword that had made the Gupta Empire vast and prosperous.

Over the years, Samudragupta had minted many coins. Some of them depicted him as an archer; in others he was shown slaying a tiger; in one he wielded a battle-axe. But this particular coin was special. It depicted a horse. It was no ordinary horse. It was the animal that had been used for the king's *Ashwamedha Yajna,* or horse sacrifice. This coin had been minted to mark the successful conclusion of that sacrifice.

Samudragupta had revived an ancient Vedic tradition by undertaking the Ashwamedha Yajna. A white horse had been left free to wander through various lands. Wherever the horse went, Samudragupta's army followed. Kings who tried to stop the horse ended up fighting Samudragupta's forces. Those who didn't were forced to accept his suzerainty.

By the time Samudragupta was done, his empire was almost as enormous as that of Ashoka. In the east, it included almost the whole of Bengal; in the north the empire ran along the Himalayas; in the west it extended up to Punjab; in the south it encompassed most of the peninsula. Samudragupta was now officially Emperor of Aryavarta and Overlord of Dakshinapatha. He was *Raja Chakravarti.*

The emperor called out to his court poet, Harisena. 'Is the inscription for the pillar ready?' he asked.

'Yes, your majesty,' replied Harisena. 'The town of Kosambi, established on the sacred hermitage of Sage Kusumba, awaits the stories of your deeds.'

'Ah, so you do not believe in the tale that Kosambi got its name from the trees that dotted the area?' asked Samudragupta slyly.

'Kosambi usually conjures up visions of a sacred hermitage on the banks of the Yamuna, sire, but we can certainly accommodate your views in the historical records,' replied Harisena smoothly.

Samudragupta laughed, the muscles of his chest rippling as he did. 'Your chisel is a dangerous tool, Harisena,' he said. 'You can use it to alter the historical narrative at will! Where do you plan to place the inscription?'

'I can show you the exact spot where we plan to inscribe your achievements when you visit the site,' replied Harisena glibly. 'The inscription will be executed later, only when your highness attains *moksha*.'

The emperor laughed yet again. 'Moksha? My body lies covered with a hundred marks caused by the blows of swords, battle-axes, arrows and spears! There is no moksha for ruthless warriors like me, Harisena!'

'Aren't you forgetting that you permitted King Meghavana of Sinhala to build a grand monastery in Sambodhi?' asked Harisena. 'That was an act of religious tolerance, wasn't it? A Hindu king being benevolent to Buddhists. Doesn't the great Buddhist scholar Vasubandhu adorn your court?'

'And that will get me moksha?' asked Samudragupta incredulously. 'A monastery in Bodh Gaya will get me deliverance? Impossible! By the way, where is Vasubandhu?'

Born a Brahmin, Vasubandhu had embraced Buddhism many years ago. His insightful commentaries had resulted in an entirely new school of Buddhist thought known as *Yogacara*.

Vasubandhu stepped forward. In his hand he held a folder bearing a jellyfish symbol on the cover. Vasubandhu's presence at the court of a Hindu monarch was testament to the secularism of Samudragupta. The emperor was a man of outstanding abilities and effortlessly played many roles—monarch, soldier, statesman, poet, musician and philanthropist. When not wielding a sword, he was to be found playing a lyre. He had transformed the empire into one that was not only economically strong but also one that was a hub of learning, art, religion and culture.

The enlightened policies of Samudragupta and his successors would give birth to several greats: Aryabhata, who theorized the concept of zero; Kalidasa, who wrote the beautiful play *Shakuntala*; and Vatsyayana, who wrote the *Kama Sutra*. The Gupta Empire would invent *Chaturanga*, the original form of chess, and compile the *Sushruta Samhita*, a comprehensive guide to Ayurveda and surgery. This was undoubtedly a golden age, both literally and figuratively.

Vasubandhu spoke softly. 'The monastery built by King Meghavana is indeed grand, your majesty, but the great Bodhi tree that was once the centre of attention now feels neglected. Maybe if you were to get a railing constructed around it…'

'Say no more,' said Samudragupta. 'I shall provide a railing around the Bodhi tree. That shall be my contribution. Vasubandhu, you know what needs to be done. We shall need gold… lots of it. This railing shall be in solid gold. A gift from Samudragupta can be no less.'

'We may have to seek permission from the monks, your majesty. They have monastic rules,' began Vasubandhu.

'They will be delighted,' declared Samudragupta dismissively. 'In any case, there is only one rule that applies here.'

'And what rule is that, your majesty?' asked Vasubandhu.

'It's called the golden rule. He who has the gold, makes the rules.'

Book Two

1960–1970

Arvind looked at the bank statement once again. He simply couldn't believe how well his scheme had worked. His company—a firm with no staff, assets, customers, turnover or track record—had collected one lakh rupees from interested investors.

A small room had been procured on a nominal rent at Burrabazar, just a short walk from the Bagadia gaddi. His father had wondered why a separate office was necessary. 'You could continue to run your new business from right here,' Brijmohanlal had suggested, but Arvind had turned down the offer. 'I don't want you to be affected by the risks that I may take,' he had wisely explained to his father.

Standing inside the office that was empty save for two steel desks, two chairs and a steel cupboard, Arvind still felt like a king.

He looked at the magazine on the table. The cover story was about the twenty-seven-year-old heir to a Madras-based conglomerate. His empire included textile mills, hotels, tea and tobacco. The young man had just returned from Eton and Oxford and was being groomed to take over the reins of the business. Eager to prove himself, the scion was getting into all sorts of deals.

Taking his gaze off the article, Arvind looked at Joydeep. 'I used a trick to get my investors to invest but now I'll use every trick in the book to give them returns,' he said to Joydeep who was the company's second employee at a monthly salary of 300 rupees.

'What do you plan to do with the money?' asked Joydeep.

'I plan to travel,' answered Arvind.

'Travel?' asked Joydeep incredulously. 'You just said that you want to get extraordinary returns for your shareholders. How can you blow it up on personal expenses like travel?'

'Not just any travel. Very specific travel.'

'Where to?'

'That's irrelevant. Ah! I see my travel agent has arrived. Come in, Mr Mitra. Have you done what I asked?'

The man who had walked in was a short and chubby, bespectacled man, eager to please. 'Oh yes, Mr Bagadia, I have the information right here. On the 19th of this month, Mr Deshmukh will be travelling from Bombay to Delhi.'

'Excellent. In that case, I shall go to Bombay on the 18th and fly from there to Delhi on the 19th.'

'Yes, sir, I shall make the bookings. Also, as you asked, Mrs Sharma will be flying from Delhi to Calcutta on the 25th.'

'Good. That will bring me back home to Calcutta on the 25th. Any news on Mr Rao?'

'Yes, sir. He will be going from Madras to Calcutta on the 28th.'

'Which means that I shall have to go to Madras on the 27th,' said Arvind.

'But there is no flight to Madras from Calcutta on the 27th so I'll have to put you on a flight on the 26th. You will have to spend an extra day in Madras.'

'That's fine,' said Arvind. 'Any idea about Mr Rao's return to Madras?'

'He's here in Calcutta for a full month. He's in talks to acquire tea plantations.'

'Good work, Mr Mitra. I hope you have taken care of the Airport Station Managers of Indian Airlines?' asked Arvind.

'Yes, Mr Bagadia,' replied the travel agent. 'All the concerned managers are aware of your special needs.'

'I'm happy with your efforts, Mr Mitra. Going forward, I shall pay you an extra two-per-cent bonus over and above the usual agency commission that you earn from the airline.'

'I am most grateful, Mr Bagadia. You are very kind,' said the rotund little travel agent as he waddled from the office.

'Arvind, are you crazy? Why are you travelling to Bombay, Delhi and Madras? We don't even have a business plan as yet,' said Joydeep.

'I may not have a business but I do have a plan,' replied Arvind cryptically.

The blindfold was removed and Arbaaz squinted his eyes. He had been on his weekly sojourn to the paradise of Faiza's body in Safed Gully when he had suddenly been surrounded by four burly men. It had taken them less than a minute to overpower him, tie his hands and blindfold him. They had unceremoniously dumped him into the backseat of a Studebaker Commander and had deposited him thirty minutes later on a cool marble floor. It was Abdul Dada's house.

'So you're the chap who bumped off my dear little niece's husband,' said Abdul Dada. It was a statement, not a question. Arbaaz looked at Abdul Dada.

The tall and handsome Pathan was dressed in a perfectly tailored white safari suit. Next to him was a box of State Express 555 cigarettes. He picked up the box, took out a cigarette and tapped the end lightly against the box. Lifting a heavy gold-plated lighter in the shape of a naked nymph that required either of her tits to be pressed for the flame, he lit up. He took a long drag, allowing the nicotine to hit his lungs.

His style statement was powerful enough to be imitated by Bollywood but the gang lord's white clothes did not match his deeds. Dada sported black sunglasses, rode a black Mercedes-Benz and enjoyed his Black Label scotch. Those elements were much more synchronized with his black deeds.

Flanked by two beefy bodyguards, Abdul Dada sat inside his Bandra house on a throne-like seat covered with a faux tiger-print fabric. He had shifted to Bandra from Dongri a few years ago. The news was that he wanted to be close to his latest mistress, a leading Bollywood heroine who was down on her luck these days. Equally, he wished to place a safe distance between himself and the wife who was famous for throwing heavy vases and ashtrays in his direction.

Ruthless to foes and generous to friends, Abdul Dada was not a man one took lightly. Despite being a Muslim, Abdul Dada would spend crazy amounts on the annual Ganeshotsav in Lalbaug. Bollywood heroes were always there in attendance to draw the crowds. He would also sponsor thousands of Muslims who were too poor to get to Mecca for Hajj each year. If one asked residents of Umerkhadi, Chakala Market, Null Bazaar, Kamathipura or Chor Bazaar, they would confidentially reveal that Abdul Dada was a menace, a megalomaniac and a messiah, all rolled into one package, a rather sophisticated one at that.

'Whenever blood is spilt, mother earth cries out for more. So tell me, my boy, why shouldn't I listen to mother earth?' asked Abdul Dada, silkily.

'I poisoned him. No blood was spilt,' said Arbaaz.

The bodyguards flinched. One of them gasped. No one ever spoke like that to Abdul Dada. It was obvious that this halfwit had a death wish.

Abdul Dada stubbed out his cigarette into a Baccarat crystal ashtray, looked at Arbaaz and then burst out laughing. It was a deep and throaty laugh that made his bodyguards smile.

'I never could stand the bastard,' said Abdul. 'I tolerated him because he was family. I should be thanking you for ridding the world of a pest.'

'I'm sorry, Dada,' said Arbaaz. 'He was extorting poor labourers in your name. It was evident to me that the instructions did not come from you.'

'I know,' said Abdul. 'Allah has given me enough. I take from the rich but give to the poor.'

'You are a saviour to all of us,' flattered Arbaaz.

'I like your spunk,' said Abdul. 'If I wanted, you would have been dead by now. Your mother would have had her head bashed in. Your sweetheart at Safed Gully would have had her pretty face slashed. Your dockside friends would be getting sodomized in jail. Your house would be a pile of smouldering rubble and I would be jerking off on the embers. You get that?'

Arbaaz nodded penitently. 'I'm very sorry, Dada. I should have come to you rather than doing what I did,' he said.

'Let me tell you something, son,' said Abdul Dada. 'There's no fucking dignity in complaining. Sometimes one's got to show the world that one has a big fat dick! You did that.' Abruptly, he added, 'You want to come and work for me?'

'Yes, Dada,' replied Arbaaz. 'There's nothing I want more.'

'Call Hameed and Mustafa,' said Abdul Dada to one of his bodyguards. Within a few minutes the two were before him.

'These are my most trusted men,' said Dada. 'Give them your respect and they will teach you everything that there is to know.'

'Yes, Dada,' said Arbaaz as he looked at the two men who were responsible for the city's illicit liquor trade, gambling, smuggling, land encroachment, narcotics, extortion, prostitution and contract killings.

Hameed was a beefy man in his forties. On one side of his face was a white scar. The story was that his face had been slashed by a whore hired to kill him. Hameed managed Dada's smuggling, land encroachment and extortion businesses. Fiercely loyal to his boss and quick-tempered, he sported a thick moustache that quivered when he got angry because of a twitch in his upper lip. Addicted to Charminar cigarettes, Hameed had teeth which were a dirty brown.

Mustafa was younger—around thirty-five. He was a tall, thin fellow who had balded early. To prevent snide remarks about his hair growth he had shaved his head entirely. Mustafa managed Dada's gambling and illicit liquor businesses.

'This is Mustafa,' said Abdul Dada to Arbaaz. 'He handles our *matka* operations. Go with him and learn the ropes.'

'Yes, Dada,' replied Arbaaz as he followed Mustafa out.

'If you are done with travelling around India for no apparent reason, can we get down to finalizing the business plan?' asked an exasperated Joydeep a month later.

Arvind put away his copy of the *Tintin* adventure comic book. It was called *King Ottokar's Sceptre*. Arvind had never been much of a reader, but comic books were different. If his English literature teacher, Mrs Fonseca, were to see him now, she would probably throw a fit.

'Certainly,' replied a beaming Arvind. 'Here's the plan. We shall be prospecting for gold in India.'

'A goldmine? We don't have the money for that!' spluttered Joydeep.

'Of course we do,' replied Arvind. 'The chairman of the United Federation Bank has assured me of the required financial resources.'

'But… but… why mining?'

'You see, Joydeep, India has substantial gold resources but our country is nowhere in the list of major gold-mining nations. We shall change all that.'

'But aren't mining concessions expensive?'

'True. That's why we shall need some assistance from the Minister of Mines.'

'What s—sort of h—help?' stuttered Joydeep.

'The minister will help issue us an RP—a Reconnaissance Permit—for three years. We would apply for RPs based on a recent study by the Geological Society of India. The RP would give us the right to explore the concerned areas.'

'And then?' asked Joydeep, nonplussed.

'If, after basic exploration, we discover that the area has potential, we apply for a prospecting licence. This allows for full drilling in that area,' explained Arvind.

'And then?' asked Joydeep, falling into a pattern.

'The rock samples we obtain from drilling would be analysed to identify areas where gold potential is high. We would, accordingly, then apply for a mining licence.'

'But all of this could take years! Think about the manpower, technology and capital costs,' argued Joydeep.

'Absolutely,' concurred Arvind. 'That's why we need a potential buyer for the mine. Someone who will buy us out well in advance.'

'Are mining licences transferrable?' asked Joydeep.

'No,' replied Arvind. 'That's why the RP will be issued in the name of a shell company. We will transfer the shares of that company to the buyer later.'

'How do you know all these people?' asked a bewildered Joydeep. 'You seem to have discussed bank loans with the chairman of the United Federation Bank. You have sought approval for RPs from the Minister of Mines. You have even identified a potential buyer for the shell company. How, Arvind? *How*?'

'By running up travel expenses that you were against,' replied Arvind. Arvind looked at his friend and smiled.

Joydeep looked bewildered. Arvind explained.

'Actually, I had told the travel agent to find out when Mr Deshmukh, the chairman of the United Federation Bank, would be travelling from Bombay. I had also told him to find out when Mrs Sharma, the Minister of Mines, would be travelling out of Delhi. Finally, I asked him to find out when Mr Rao, the maverick scion of Rao Enterprises of Madras, would be travelling from Madras.'

Joydeep attempted to digest the information.

'I knew that I would never be able to get appointments to meet with any of them,' continued Arvind. 'So I did the next best thing I could. I ensured that I occupied the seat next to them on flights that they took. Luckily, all domestic airlines, including Airways India, Bharat Airways, Himalayan Aviation, Kalinga Airlines, Indian National Airways and Air Services, have been merged into a single entity—Indian Airlines. All that my travel agent needed to do was to monitor the bookings of Indian Airlines.'

'You asked the travel agent to ensure that the Airport Station Managers were taken care of. What was that all about?' asked Joydeep.

'The Station Managers of Indian Airlines decide the seat allocations on the day of the flight,' answered Arvind. 'It was critical that I be given the seat next to my target. Hence the extra 2 per cent to my agent! Now did you find out about that court case that went against Mr Rao?'

'Yes,' replied Joydeep. 'I did some research. He lost the case because the other side hired an incredibly capable law firm based right here in Calcutta.'

'What is the law firm's name?' asked Arvind.

'Don't you want to know about the case that he lost?' asked Joydeep.

'No. It's irrelevant. I simply want to know the name of the firm that made him lose,' replied Arvind.

'Digby & Dastur,' replied Joydeep. Arvind made a mental note.

'So you're serious about acquiring goldmines?' asked Joydeep.

'That's why it's called a mine. Because it must be mine,' laughed Arvind.

Abdul Dada looked at the man who stood before him. He was trembling slightly and his lips seemed parched. Dada immediately asked Arbaaz to seat him on one of the several visitors' chairs in front of his desk.

'Arrange for some chilled Rooh Afza, Hameed,' said Dada, as the man sat down, staring saucer-eyed at the two burly bodyguards who stood behind Dada.

'Don't be nervous,' Dada said softly to him as the man gratefully sipped the sweet sherbet. 'I am here to help.'

Arbaaz and Hameed stood to one side while Dada put the visitor at his ease. A few minutes of silence later, the old man spoke with a quiver in his voice. 'Dada, I have come to you because I have no one else I can turn to.'

Abdul Dada nodded. 'I am here to solve your problems,' said Dada. 'Speak.'

'My son established a small shop in Lalbaug selling mithai,' began the man. 'I was in no condition to assist him financially and my son went to a loan shark for help. The terms were extortionate but my son had no alternative.'

'Go on,' soothed Dada.

'When he was unable to pay up, they began threatening him. They even roughed him up on two occasions. I am a retired magistrate and I have many friends who are still in positions of power. I approached them.'

'And?' asked Dada.

'They got the cops to question the loan shark. It only aggravated the matter. Yesterday, my ten-year-old grandson, Prasad, went missing from school. The police are helpless and clueless,' said the old man, tears streaming down his cheeks.

'Did you tell the police whom you suspected?' asked Dada.

'Yes, but they said that Bombay is a big city,' said the helpless man. 'Many policemen are on his payroll. Please, Dada, by Allah, please help. That little boy has done nothing wrong. Why should he pay for the errors of his father?'

'Hameed, take down the name of the loan shark from this gentleman,' said Dada. Hameed immediately did so.

'Don't worry, your problem shall be solved,' said Dada.

'I'm indebted to you forever, Dada,' said the visitor.

'Yes, you are,' said Dada simply.

Hameed brought a finger to his lips, signalling for silence as he observed the two men leaving the warehouse. They took extra care to padlock the door as they left. In all probability this was where the little boy would be. Hameed gave a signal to the two men picked for this job—Arbaaz along with an old battle-hardened hand nicknamed Chikna.

Chikna leapt out from the shadows, a heavy country revolver in hand, and smashed it into the loan shark's head. The loan shark's accomplice reached for his gun but before he could draw it, Arbaaz delivered a resounding frontal blow to his mouth. He fell unconscious to the ground, blood trickling from the corner of his lips.

Chikna held his gun to the loan shark's head while Hameed whispered. 'Dada has sent me for the boy. Don't fuck with me. Where is Prasad?'

'I don't know what you're talking about,' said the loan shark, seemingly unaffected by the events that had just transpired.

Hameed nodded to Arbaaz. Arbaaz took out his custom-designed hammer with the iron-spike at the base of the handle and pushed the man against the warehouse door.

Holding up the man's left hand against the door, he brought down the hammer with bone-shattering force on the man's forefinger. The man screamed in agony.

'I have just started with one finger of your left hand,' said Arbaaz. 'I will smash all five and will enjoy the sound of your bones cracking. I will then repeat the process with your right hand. C'mon, make my day, *benchod*.'

Exactly half an hour later, the kidnapped Prasad was in the arms of his parents and his grandfather.

That day Arbaaz understood what it meant to be Abdul Dada.

'I need to withdraw our entire balance in cash,' said Arvind. 'I believe we have 94,516 rupees in our current account.'

The teller almost fell off her chair. The spectacles on her nose certainly did. Luckily, her glasses were tethered to a chain around her neck.

'But—but—you need to maintain a minimum balance in your current account, sir,' she argued.

'What's the minimum balance required?' asked Arvind.

'A thousand rupees,' answered the teller.

'Fine. Leave a thousand rupees in the account and give me 93,516 rupees,' said Arvind.

The visibly upset teller counted the cash and handed it over to Arvind after obtaining his signature on the passbook.

Arvind looked at the wall calendar behind the teller once again. Mr Rao would still be in Calcutta. One month was still not up.

Arvind placed the cash in his briefcase, rejoined Joydeep who was waiting at the entrance and walked to a shop across the street.

The dealer was waiting for him. 'The price of gold today is 111.87 rupees per ten grams. How much money do you have?' asked the man.

'I have 93,516 rupees,' replied Arvind.

'Which means that you can get 8,359 grams of gold,' said the man, whistling under his breath. 'Are you sure you don't want it in biscuits or bars?'

'No. I would like raw nuggets. Preferably four-mesh in size. What's the premium?'

'Twenty per cent over spot prices,' answered the man shiftily, handing over three nuggets for Arvind's inspection.

'We had agreed on 10 per cent,' said Arvind examining the weight, shape and colour and handing back the nuggets.

'True, but I had thought that the purity level was less. These are all in the twenty-to-twenty-two karat range.'

'Ten per cent—or else I walk back to the bank and redeposit my money,' said Arvind, without flinching.

'Fifteen per cent. You don't want me to lose money do you?' asked the gold dealer.

'Because I like you, I'll give you 11 per cent. Nothing more,' said Arvind.

Eleven minutes and 12 per cent later, Arvind and Joydeep left the shop with a briefcase containing more than eight kilos of gold nuggets.

The suitcase gave way as they were crossing the intersection of Nehru Road and Esplande Row. Eight kilos' worth of gold nuggets poured out of the suitcase and onto the road.

Joydeep frantically waved for the traffic to stop as Arvind attempted to gather the nuggets on the road and place them back in the suitcase.

But it was too late. Every passer-by was attempting to pick up some of the scattered gold.

Calcutta's gold rush had commenced.

Mustafa operated the business, seven days a week, from a tiny office in Sewri. His men ran matka dens in mill areas like Tardeo, Byculla, Mazgaon, Reay Road, Lalbaug, Parel, Naigaum, Sewri, Worli and Prabhadevi, thus making it easy for mill-workers living in the nearby chawls to place bets easily.

Mustafa's journey had been an interesting one. Born to a fisherman in Kutch, he had arrived as a migrant to Bombay, and joined the ranks of the city's quarter-million textile mill-labourers. He had begun accepting bets on the opening and closing rates of cotton as a mere hobby. He had never thought that it would ever catch on in the way that it did.

The opening and closing rates of cotton would usually be transmitted to the Bombay Cotton Exchange in Sewree via telegraph from the New York Cotton Exchange twice daily five days a week. For Mustafa, this schedule meant that betting carried on Monday through Friday.

Mustafa's little office in Sewree would be overcrowded with mill-workers at 9 pm and midnight, when cotton prices from New York would be announced and bets would be settled, many of the men having walked great distances to get there.

Then one day, Abdul Dada had paid Mustafa a visit. Dada had heard about the new craze from his men and had decided that he wanted in on the action. He made Mustafa the proverbial offer that could not be refused.

He advised Mustafa to revamp the operation so that bets would be made on playing cards randomly drawn from a pitcher—a *matka*—instead of using cotton prices. By this one simple change, it would now become possible to carry on betting seven days a week. It would increase business by 40 per cent.

Abdul Dada had offered Mustafa his shops, warehouses and men so that his betting footprint would be across 200 locations. This extended reach would make it extremely convenient for men to place bets near their homes or factories. It would increase business by a multiple of ten. Mustafa would be required to keep a 10 per cent commission on all bets and share 65 per cent of that with Abdul Dada. Mustafa knew that Abdul Dada was not someone with whom one could negotiate.

Mustafa sat down to explain to Arbaaz how matka-betting worked. A tea boy placed two *cutting-chai* glasses of copper-coloured sugary tea in front of them. Mustafa slurped his tea loudly and then began the lecture.

'Pick any three numbers from zero to nine,' he said.

Arbaaz thought about it and said, 'Five—nine—three.'

'Good. Now add up the three numbers. What do you get?' asked Mustafa.

'Seventeen.'

'What's the last digit of that number?'

'Seven.'

'So the first draw would be expressed as 593 and represented by seven. This is the opening draw. Now pick another three numbers from zero to nine,' said Mustafa.

'Seven—one—eight,' answered Arbaaz.

'Now add up the three numbers. What do you get?'

'Sixteen.'

'What's the last digit of that number?'

'Six.'

'So the second draw would be expressed as 718 represented by six. This is the closing draw,' explained Mustafa.

Arbaaz made notes as Mustafa spoke.

'People bet on all of these outcomes at various odds. People bet on the opening or closing three-digit numbers, in this case 593 and 718. They bet on the opening and closing representative numbers, in this case seven and six. They also bet on the opening and closing representative numbers combined, in this case, seventy-six. Finally, they bet on the sums of the opening and closing draws, in this case, seventeen and sixteen. So you have odds that vary from 9:1 to 999:1.'

Arbaaz listened, wishing that he had paid more attention to the mathematics taught by Mr D'Souza in school.

Class over, he got up and went in search of a Tamil Brahmin who would understand it all.

'Mustafa Bhai, I'd like you to meet Murali,' said Arbaaz.

Mustafa nodded cursorily as he continued writing the books. The previous day's bets, takings, pay-outs and profits had to reach Abdul Dada by noon.

'I'm in a hurry,' said Mustafa. 'Dada wants to meet both of us today.'

'May I bring Murali along?' asked Arbaaz. 'He's an old school friend of mine. We studied together at Rosary High School.'

Mustafa looked at Murali. He was a thin, scrawny Tamilian with a sandalwood paste mark on his forehead.

'Dada does not like meeting strangers,' said Mustafa gruffly.

'Please, Mustafa Bhai,' pleaded Arbaaz. 'Just for a few minutes. This could be very important.'

Mustafa relented. He knew that Dada would be pissed off to see a newcomer. *Why am I protecting Arbaaz's ass?* he asked himself.

The three of them got into a beat-up Austin A40. The car sputtered to life after several unsuccessful attempts in getting the engine to turn.

Upon reaching Abdul Dada's Bandra home, the men were ushered into the don's massive bathroom. He was inside a sunken marble bathtub, smoking a 555 cigarette while bubbles from a fragrant foam bath floated up into the air. A young woman in pink bell-bottoms and matching top sat on a stool at his feet buffing his toenails.

'Who is this boy?' Dada asked Mustafa upon seeing Murali.

'Dada, his name is Murali, and he is a mathematical genius—a prodigy,' replied Arbaaz. 'I insisted on bringing him to meet you. He was in school with me.'

'And why would I be interested in meeting him? Have you no fucking sense?' asked Abdul Dada, gesturing for the pink lady to disappear.

'Because I think that we can triple our daily matka profits while leaving the turnover untouched,' replied Arbaaz, ignoring Abdul Dada's anger.

'You say he is a wizard, huh?' asked Abdul, softening a little upon hearing that profits could be tripled. 'What is 9867 divided by thirty-four?' he barked.

'290.2058… up to what decimal place do you want the answer?'

Then Dada rattled off a series of numbers for Murali to multiply. 'What is 7,686,369,774,870 multiplied by 2,465,099,745,779?'

Murali noted down the numbers but did the calculation in his head. 'The answer is 18,947,668,177,995,400,000,000, 000,' replied Murali in thirty-two seconds.

'That's nothing, Dada,' said Arbaaz. 'I could never do square roots while this chap does seventeen roots in his head!'

'So how does your friend think that we can triple our profits?' asked Abdul Dada.

Arbaaz nodded at Murali. The young man took out a folded sheet of paper from his shirt pocket and began reading.

'Presently, a single digit predicted correctly gets a ten-to-one pay-out,' began Murali hesitantly. 'Considering that the probability of predicting a single digit correctly is one in ten, we should keep the pay-out eight to the rupee. Over the long term we will make extra money by doing this.'

'Go on,' said Abdul Dada, his ears perking up at the suggestion of increased profits.

'A double-digit prediction should have a return of seventy to the rupee versus the one-in-hundred probability of correct prediction. We could make a killing by progressively lowering the pay-outs against riskier odds,' continued Murali.

'I like the sound of this boy,' said Abdul Dada, grimly pleased.

'Even within single, double and triple digits, let's lower the pay-outs for numbers that are predicted with higher frequency. For example seven, eleven, 108 and 786 are regularly chosen by punters as per the frequency distribution. These are considered as lucky or sacred numbers. Let's lower the pay-out on these.'

'What happens for a triple?' asked Mustafa, now beginning to grow irritated by Murali's know-it-all attitude.

'A triple digit has a one-in-a-thousand chance of winning. The return should be significantly less, say 250 per rupee.'

'And a full forecast?' asked Abdul.

'The odds here are one in a million. So a pay-out of 10,000 per rupee should be fine,' replied Murali. 'When the pay-out sounds big, the odds really don't matter.'

'Thanks, Murali, could you wait for me outside?' asked Arbaaz. Murali left the marble bathroom.

'I am proud of you, Arbaaz,' said Abdul Dada. 'Barely a couple of days into the business and you are already finding ways to make me richer. Mustafa, let's do what that Madrasi *lungiwala* says. Pay him a salary so that he can continuously tweak the pay-outs for you.'

'Yes, Dada,' said Mustafa, surprised by the turn of events. 'Come on, Arbaaz, let's go back to Sewri.'

'Wait,' said Abdul Dada. 'Mustafa, *you* go. Take the lungi-wala with you. Arbaaz will stay here. I need to give him a piece of my mind.'

Mustafa left the two men alone. He looked displeased.

Abdul Dada spoke softly. 'It's always better to let your enemies overestimate your stupidity than your cleverness. In future, never allow any of the men, including Mustafa or Hameed, to feel threatened by you. When you have an idea, meet me separately about it.'

'I'm sorry, Dada,' replied Arbaaz.

'After a victory, it's a good idea to sharpen one's knife,' replied the don, getting out of the tub and calling for the lady in pink. 'But good show, nonetheless. From today onwards, you will report directly to me and shall remain by my side.'

The *Statesman* carried an article about the gold nugget episode.

A large quantity of gold nuggets accidentally fell on the road at the busy intersection of Nehru Road and Esplanade Row. The owner of the nuggets, Mr Arvind Bagadia, said to this reporter that he had been on his way to his safe deposit vault when his suitcase gave way. Sources indicate that Mr Bagadia is involved in gold exploration and currently has six sites under investigation. Although Mr Bagadia was able to recover half his material, he says that the other half got stolen by passers-by.

Brijmohanlal went ballistic.

'Do you realize the loss you have incurred? Have you lost your mind? Is this what I taught you about business? Can you even fathom what the Income Tax authorities will do to us?'

Arvind listened to his father's tirade patiently but kept staring at the black rotary telephone on his desk.

'Why aren't you listening to me?' demanded his father. 'What's so interesting about that telephone?'

Arvind stayed calm and quiet. He started counting backwards softly to himself from one hundred. The phone rang when he reached seventy-three.

'B. Ravi and I. Daga,' he announced, picking up the call as though he were the company's switchboard operator. 'Mr Bagadia? I think he has stepped out for a meeting but should be back in ten minutes. Would you like me to give him a message, sir?' continued Arvind. 'Uh-huh, Great

Eastern Hotel, yes. What time? Noon? Certainly, sir. I shall convey the message.'

'What was *that* all about?' asked Brijmohanlal, still visibly upset.

'I'll tell you later,' said Arvind as he dashed to the exit. He reached the Great Eastern Hotel on Dalhousie Square twenty-two minutes later on foot. 12 pm. He was dot on time.

Arvind waited until his watch showed five minutes past noon. He then walked in.

Established in 1840, the Great Eastern Hotel was known as the Jewel of the East. Englishmen quipped that a man could walk in at one end of the hotel, buy a complete outfit, a wedding present, or seeds for the garden, have an excellent meal, a *burra* peg and, if the barmaid was agreeable, walk out at the other end engaged to be married.

Arvind wasn't there for marriage, though. Money took precedence.

As he settled down into a comfortable leather armchair, a young and dapper south Indian gentleman in a perfectly pressed suit walked up to him. 'Nice to meet you once again, Mr Bagadia. Thanks for dropping by at short notice,' he said.

'Likewise, Mr Rao,' said Arvind, getting up to shake the immaculately manicured hand. 'It was good chatting with you on the flight from Madras.'

'You are in the news today, I see,' said the young tycoon in a perfectly clipped accent. Eton and Oxford had done their work.

'I was foolish,' began Arvind.

'So tell me more about your mining business,' asked Mr Vijay Rao.

'We are prospecting in many regions—around six places. We are fairly optimistic that half of these will yield grades of three to four grams per tonne,' explained Arvind.

'Come now, don't be modest,' laughed Mr Rao. 'As we speak there are only two operational goldmines in India—Hutti and Kolar. And judging by what you spilled on the road, I'd say that your business is fully operational.'

Arvind made as if to fidget nervously. He leaned over conspiratorially. 'The find was just a fluke. It takes almost a decade to strike gold from the time that one starts exploring, Mr Rao. The exploration cost is staggering. It involves geological surveys, sampling, assessing and drilling. Frankly, I'm in over my head, sir.'

'That's why I telephoned,' said Mr Rao. 'If you like, I could solve your financial problems in one stroke.'

'Really? How?' asked Arvind innocently.

'I am willing to buy all six mines from you at a negotiated price,' answered the young businessman.

'But we still do not have mining rights. All we have are Reconnaissance Permits for the six sites. There is no guarantee that these sites will produce anything. It seems unfair to be selling you rights that we do not have.'

'Let me decide that,' said Vijay Rao. 'I am willing to offer you a cheque of five lakh rupees for all six sites. I assume that you have a shell company and that the shares of the shell company can be sold?'

'Oh yes, sir. And your offer is most generous. It's just that—'

'What's the matter? Isn't it a great offer?' asked Mr Rao, lifting his eyebrows.

'Oh, absolutely. It's just that my solicitors think that they have offers in the vicinity of fifteen lakh. I feel embarrassed to be mentioning this given how kind you have been to me.'

'What do lawyers know? If they were so clever they would be in business,' said Vijay Rao angrily. 'Who are your solicitors?'

'Digby & Dastur,' replied Arvind smoothly.

Arvind saw Mr Rao flinch. It was evident that he was uncomfortable hearing that name. Digby & Dastur was one of Calcutta's oldest law firms, having been established in 1893 as a partnership between an Englishman, Mr J.L. Digby, and a Parsi gentleman, Mr G.C. Dastur. The brand equity was substantial. Most importantly, the firm had recently beaten the pants off Rao's lawyers in court.

'I am willing to pay you ten lakh by cheque at this very instant if you promise me that we will not go to lawyers to negotiate terms,' said Mr Rao.

'Could I please request you to consider improving the offer?' asked Arvind.

'Here's what I can do. I will pay you ten lakh by cheque. In addition, I shall give you my shares of a company called Albert Mills. It's a textile manufacturing unit in Bombay but is of little use to me.'

'But...' began Arvind.

'But me no buts, Mr Bagadia. Do we have a deal or not?'

Arvind screwed up his face as he thought about the proposal. Even if the shares of Albert Mills were worthless, he would still have ten lakh. Two minutes later he looked the young Rao in the eye and said, 'You drive a hard bargain, sir, and my father will be livid with me for doing this, but my gut tells me to go with you. So the answer is, "Yes".'

Mr Rao took out a chequebook from the inside pocket of jacket and scribbled on a page. He then asked the waiter to bring him a sheet of paper. He wrote down a simple one-page agreement in longhand, reviewed it and passed it on to Arvind for his approval.

Arvind signed off and gratefully accepted Mr Rao's cheque.

'The shares of Albert Mills will reach you by post from my Madras office,' said Mr Rao, getting up.

Arvind forced himself to breathe normally while shaking the man's hand. He continued with his deep breathing until he had exited the hotel.

Only when he was at a safe distance from the hotel did he let out a whoop of joy.

The waiter watched the two young men as they sat in the Udupi joint. Plates of dosas, idlis, medu vadas and steaming *sambhar* accompanied by filter *kaapi* sat on the table.

Both of them were attacking the food ravenously.

'Why did you get me that job, Arbaaz?' asked Murali as he dipped a piece of dosa into the sambhar.

'Simple, Murali. I take care of my friends. I knew you needed a job,' replied Arbaaz, slurping sambhar directly from the bowl in front of him.

'Was that the only reason?' asked Murali.

Arbaaz laughed. 'The deal between Mustafa and Abdul Dada is that Mustafa should take a 10 per cent commission on all bets and share 65 per cent of that with Abdul Dada. I think he is skimming some more off the top. I need you to keep me informed,' he said.

The two friends clinked their steel coffee tumblers. It was to be the beginning of a long and fruitful partnership.

'I need to deposit this cheque of ten lakh,' said Arvind. 'I think we have only a thousand rupees in our current account.'

The teller almost fell off her chair yet again. Luckily, the spectacles on her nose did not require the safety harness on this occasion.

This man was crazy. Withdrawing his entire balance a day ago and depositing over ten times that the very next day.

'Yes, sir,' she said. 'Let me get the branch manager for you. Would you care for a cup of tea?'

Money changes everyone and everything, thought Arvind.

Job done, Arvind walked up to Joydeep who was seated in the reception area. 'Not bad for a day's work, right?' he asked Joydeep with a twinkle in his eyes. 'I think our investors should be pretty happy with a 1,000-per-cent return on their money, what say you?'

Joydeep laughed. 'I had no idea that you planned to drop that gold deliberately on the street, Arvind. I was in panic!'

'I ensured that we dropped it at the intersection of Nehru Road and Esplanade Row because the editorial office of The *Statesman* is right there. I knew that there would be a reporter lurking around. Turns out I was right.'

'I'm glad you sold the goldmines, Arvind,' said Joydeep softly.

'Why?' asked Arvind.

'Because you should be making steel, not gold,' answered Joydeep.

'Why?' asked Arvind.

'Because you have balls of steel, my friend.'

She had asked to meet him rather suddenly. Arvind had been so completely caught up with the goldmine business that he had hardly spent any time with Paromita for the past few weeks.

Given his recent success, Arvind had decided to splurge. 'Let's go for dinner to Mocambo,' he said to Paromita. Mocambo was located on Calcutta's Free School Street, just off the famous Park Street, a fashionable kilometre-long stretch that hosted several restaurants and nightclubs known by exotic names such as Trinca's, Sky Room, Blue Fox and Moulin Rouge. By nightfall, expensive cars would line the street and elegantly dressed gentlemen in dinner jackets, and ladies carrying expensive handbags would head to one of the many clubs to spend the evening doing the foxtrot or cha cha to music and crooning by live bands, mostly manned by white Anglo-Indians.

Paromita didn't seem too excited by the idea. 'I'd rather we just met casually,' she began before Arvind cut her off. Eventually, she went along with his plan.

'Did you hear the news?' asked Paromita once they were seated. 'The Indian army liberated Goa today. They called it Operation Vijay. As of 1961 we have ended 450 years of Portuguese rule.'

'Why should I care?' asked Arvind. 'Let foreign powers surrender to the Indian army. At the moment all I can think about is surrendering to you.'

The stunningly beautiful Paromita smiled her usual angelic smile. Arvind pretended to have been hit by an arrow in the heart. They laughed.

A husky-voiced chanteuse was singing some wonderful songs backed by a five-piece ensemble and the restaurant was buzzing. A German architect had executed the interiors, an Italian chef had created the menu, and a British fashion designer had designed the dresses that the singers wore. The dance floor was made from reinforced glass imported from Belgium, engineered with coloured psychedelic lights below. The only thing Indian about the restaurant was the people inside it.

Arvind took a sip of his whisky and asked, 'May I tell you something?'

'Sure,' said Paromita, sipping her wine.

'You have the prettiest smile I've ever seen,' he said as part of their ritual.

'Now may I tell you something?' she asked, suddenly serious.

'Go ahead,' said Arvind.

'I'm shifting to Bombay, Arvind.'

'Why are you leaving me?' asked Arvind, the joy having entirely drained from his voice.

'I'm not leaving *you*, Arvind,' Paromita reassured him patiently. 'I'm simply leaving Calcutta. I have no option—my father has been transferred to Bombay. My parents are relocating.'

'But why do you need to go with them?' asked Arvind unreasonably.

'And where would I stay?' asked Paromita. 'You are nineteen, Arvind. Yes, you've made a ton of money but that's not my situation. I'm from a conservative Bengali family and will stay with my parents until the day that I'm married.'

'But we could get married,' argued Arvind. 'I'll come over to your house right now and ask your father for your hand in marriage. We could move into my house thereafter. Problem solved!'

Paromita looked at Arvind with moist eyes and shook her head. 'That won't happen, Arvind,' she said.

'Why? Tell me what I can do to keep you here,' urged Arvind desperately. 'I'll do anything and everything I can to make you stay.'

There was an uncomfortable silence. She then began hesitantly. 'My maternal uncle in Bombay is the famous movie director Pinakin Deb. He spoke to my mother… '

'About what?' demanded Arvind.

'He's making a movie and needs a fresh face,' said Paromita. 'He has offered to give me a screen test for the role.'

'So you would leave me for a stupid movie?' Arvind asked, hurt.

'Try to understand Arvind. I love you and you're not making it easy for me…'

Arvind stood up, took out his wallet and left a generous amount to cover the bill.

'Where are you going?' asked Paromita, tears running down her cheeks.

'You know what's worse than loving someone, Paromita?' asked Arvind, each word leaving his lips with a mixture of love, rage, petulance and regret.

'What?' asked Paromita.

'Knowing that the other person never loved you to begin with,' said Arvind as he turned around to walk out of Mocambo while the crooner in the mermaid-like dress continued to sing '*Will You Still Love Me Tomorrow*?' by The Shirelles.

The only weekly indulgence of Abdul Dada was a customary visit to the Ambassador Hotel in Churchgate.

Abdul Dada's men smuggled the supplies that the establishment needed from time to time and Jack Voyantzis, the hotel's Greek owner, had become a friend of his. Jack was always to be seen with a stunning woman by his side and a massive Havana cigar firmly clenched between his teeth. Earlier in the year he had been spotted raising a toast to two exceptionally beautiful women, Maharani Gayatri Devi of Jaipur, and Jackie Kennedy, who had been on a visit to India.

The Ambassador boasted a restaurant that was the definitive go-to place for the well-heeled. It was called The Other Room. One had to be in black tie to get inside. That was the necessary condition. The other condition was that Jack Voyantzis had to like you. Abdul was always at the top of Jack's list.

A jazz quartet managed by Toni Pinto provided impeccably smooth arrangements while diners dug into sirloin steak, lamb chops or braised ox tongue. There were other equally good Bombay establishments such as Bombelli's, the Rendezvous, Astoria's Venice and Little Hut at the Ritz but the only one that Abdul frequented was The Other Room.

That evening Abdul headed to the Ambassador in his black Mercedes-Benz Ponton W128. One of his bodyguards sat in front while the don and his mistress sat at the back. She was dressed in a black saree accentuated by a solitaire diamond necklace. Her hair was done up in a bouffant that made her look almost as tall as Abdul. She had a face that had captured the hearts of many men during her Bollywood glory days.

A beat-up Baby Hindustan followed Dada's Mercedes-Benz. This second car contained another bodyguard along with Arbaaz.

As the car approached Churchgate, Abdul Dada's driver honked because his access was cut off by a victoria, one of Bombay's ubiquitous horse-drawn carriages. Suddenly, there was a barrage of bullets as two men seated inside the horse carriage began firing into Abdul's car. The windscreen exploded into thousands of shards as bullets hit the car. The driver and the bodyguard, who were seated in the front seat of the Mercedes-Benz, died instantly, their *kattas* not having been fired even once that night.

Arbaaz and the second bodyguard who were in the following car got out and crept up to the Mercedes. Arbaaz was holding his revolver, something that Abdul Dada had insisted that he must carry at all times. He reached the left door of Abdul's car and opened it. Inside the car was a gory mess of blood and glass. Dada's beautiful mistress had taken a direct hit to her chest and was slumped over and very dead. Dada had sensibly crouched into the leg space between the front and rear seats. A bullet had grazed his right shoulder and the blood was running down the front of his starched white shirt to merge with his crimson cummerbund.

The shooters reloaded and began targeting Arbaaz and the second bodyguard. Arbaaz used the door as a shield to pull out Dada. 'Don't worry about me, son,' said Dada. 'Get me their balls. I want them served to me on toast for breakfast tomorrow morning.'

Arbaaz called out to the second bodyguard. 'Pull out Dada and put him in our car. Let me go and get Dada's breakfast while you keep the *bhadwa*s busy.'

Arbaaz quickly slipped under the Merc and began pulling himself forward on the road. The shooters were now targeting the bodyguard and Abdul Dada. The bodyguard wrapped himself around Dada while continuing to fire shots from his *do-naliya,* a double-barrelled shotgun.

Arbaaz pulled himself to the front of the car and quickly slipped under the victoria, the rear of which was almost touching the front bumper of the Merc. He prayed that the men in the victoria had not seen him and that he would have the advantage of surprise.

Emerging behind the rear legs of the horse, he took a clean shot at the driver who crumpled over with a large red hole in his forehead. All at once, the horse whinnied and went into a frenzied gallop. The victoria lurched forward and Arbaaz quickly grabbed the platform that usually displayed the badge number of the carriage. He pulled himself up into the driver's seat, narrowly missing being kicked by the horse's rear legs.

Inside the victoria were two men and several guns. They turned around when the carriage started moving but Arbaaz was able to deliver a clean bullet into one man's throat. The man lurched backwards from the impact of the shot. The other man, a short and stocky fellow with dark lips and tattooed arms, took aim at Arbaaz but was swayed by the moving carriage that was now out of control. The extra few seconds allowed Arbaaz to jump into the carriage. The gun in the fat man's hand fired but the bullet went astray. By then Arbaaz had fired his own gun. It shattered the man's right hand and he yelled in agony.

Arbaaz smashed his gun into the man's head but was unprepared for the uppercut that was delivered to him by the fat man's left hand. Arbaaz felt woozy but forced himself to concentrate. He fired his gun a second time. It was a deliberately aimed shot. The man's left hand shattered. *Look, Ma, no hands!*

Utterly incapacitated, the man attempted to head-butt Arbaaz but Arbaaz brought down the handle of his revolver on the man's head. He then pushed the barrel of the gun into the man's mouth and said, 'You have three seconds in which to tell me who sent you.'

Arbaaz began counting aloud. 'One… two… thr—' but a muffled voice emerged from the man. 'Please don't sh—sh—shoot!'

Arbaaz took the barrel out of the man's mouth. 'It was Rangarajan P—P—Pillai,' said the fat man.

'Rangarajan Pillai ordered the hit?' asked Arbaaz. Pillai was Bombay's Hindu don. In the underworld, too, there were divisions along lines of caste and religion. Abdul Dada was the city's Muslim don so there had to be a counter-weight from the Hindu side. That counterweight was Rangarajan Pillai.

'Y—y—yes,' stammered the fat man.

'Why?' demanded Arbaaz. 'I will not hesitate to blow your *bheja* to bits if you do not tell me everything.'

'Yusuf's wife went and pleaded with him after Abdul Dada spared you. She was very angry that Yusuf's murder went unavenged.'

'I'm sparing your life,' said Arbaaz as he took aim at the horse that was now beyond control. The tug buckle had lodged itself into the animal's skin and it was quite obviously in agonizing pain. The horse crumpled in a heap on the road, causing the carriage to lift off the ground.

Arbaaz jumped off the carriage. 'Hope you enjoy your stay in Arthur Road Jail. Our friends in khaki are almost here.'

'What the fuck just happened?' asked Arbaaz as he stood in front of Abdul Dada. Both of Dada's bodyguards were gone—killed in the shootout.

Dada's personal physician, who lived on Warden Road, had been called in. He had administered a tetanus shot and cleaned and bandaged the wound on Dada's shoulder. Dada's key men, Hameed and Mustafa, had been called in too.

'It's an old story,' replied Dada. 'A drama in several acts. Tell him, Hameed.'

'Pillai is from Madras and moved to Bombay around a decade ago,' said Hameed to Arbaaz, his moustache quivering in anger. 'He started out as a coolie in the railway station but then came into contact with the hooch gang. He began distributing hooch, and later narcotics, to areas in Matunga and Chembur. These were areas that were dominated by south Indian immigrants. This obviously put him in conflict with us.'

'I put out a hit on him,' explained Abdul Dada, nursing his whisky. 'It resulted in a bitter gang war that lasted over two years.'

'Then what happened?' asked Arbaaz.

'Both sides realized that the other could not be wished away,' replied Hameed. 'We met and divided up the geography as well as the sectors. The areas in which we were strong were illicit liquor, gambling, smuggling, land encroachment and contract killings. Our writ ran large in Umerkhadi, Chakala Market, Null Bazaar, Kamathipura and Chor Bazaar. Pillai's strength lay in narcotics, extortion and prostitution and, in geographical terms, his constituencies were Matunga, Chembur, Dharavi and Mulund. We agreed to live side by side. A truce was arrived at.'

'But then why this attack?' asked Mustafa. 'Why would Pillai risk destroying the truce in Bombay by acting on the complaint of Yusuf's wife?'

'Bombay is not ruled by any government these days. The damned war with China has placed severe limitations on government machinery,' said Abdul Dada. 'Sometimes

I feel like going to the front and shooting the Chinese myself. We're being drubbed by them so badly!'

'The result,' explained Hameed, getting back to the topic, 'is that half of Bombay runs under Abdul Dada's command and the other half under the directions of Pillai. Dada's word is law among Muslims and Pillai's word is law among Hindus although both gangs have a mix of both communities in them. Just like Dada sponsors the Ganesh mandal, Pillai feeds thousands at the Mahim dargah every day. This attack is a clear indication that Pillai no longer wants to be don of half the city. He wants it all.'

'I suggest that we hunt them down and finish off Pillai and his henchmen once and for all,' said Mustafa. 'Give me the nod, Dada, and we'll go rip their balls off.'

'Learn to control your temper, Mustafa,' remonstrated Abdul Dada. Turning to Arbaaz he asked, 'What do you think?'

'Given that the attempt on your life has failed, they will be on their guard,' replied Arbaaz. 'This is not the time to go after Pillai.'

Abdul Dada smiled. He saw in this young man a quality that his other men did not have. The ability to think, reason and analyze.

'Why are we listening to this nonsense?' asked Hameed. 'Arbaaz knows nothing about the way our world operates. Dada, if you don't retaliate, you will lose respect. People will think we are scared of Pillai!'

Abdul Dada was quiet. He took another gulp of his whisky, emptying his glass. He then looked at his men.

'We will not do anything for a couple of days. I need time to mourn the woman I lost. She was a good woman. She took care of my needs unlike that ungrateful wretched wife of mine. I also need time to think,' he said as he dismissed everyone.

Arbaaz was called back after everyone was gone. 'Can you handle the assignment on your own?' asked Abdul Dada.

Arbaaz did not hesitate. 'Yes, I can. I am convinced that we will not need to let this escalate into an all-out war.'

'Don't ever let me regret this decision,' said Abdul Dada. 'You will share your plans with no one but me.'

Arbaaz nodded.

Arbaaz scanned the restaurants once again. He noticed cars pulling up, the windows rolling down and cash being dispensed to restaurant managers who waited at the kerb. In front of each restaurant sat a double or triple line of starving men waiting for their next meal. Without exception, each man was dirty, hungry and pitiful. Perfect living advertisements for the cause of charity. Inside the restaurants, vats of yellow mutton curry bubbled while the hungry men's stomachs growled as they waited for the next donation that would feed them.

The Wardhi restaurants of Mahim were truly unique. Nowhere in the world could one find restaurants that were targeted at the malnourished. These restaurants were profit-making businesses even though the end result was charity. They were *hunger eateries* that stood on the short stretch of the main road leading up to the turn for the tomb of Makhdoom Ali Mahimi. In fact, the entire area of Mahim owed its name to that particular fourteenth-century saint.

Mahim was being decked out for a rather important annual event as Arbaaz wandered about. During the annual ten-day Mahim fair that was just a week away, millions of devotees would visit the tomb. A huge procession would kick off from Mahim police station, which was believed to be the actual site of Makhdoom Ali Mahimi's home. Two police officers would be drawn from each of Bombay's police stations. This group of officers would then offer a *chador*, the customary sheet of flowers, at the tomb of the saint.

During the fair, all the Wardhi restaurants were funded by Rangarajan Pillai. No hungry man, woman or child was to be turned away. For ten days any hungry person could get a meal without having to stretch his hand out for a donation from a passing car.

In a surprising act of mutual tolerance, Pillai would also provide a chador at the tomb while the cops, supposedly his sworn enemies, looked on. It had been wryly commented by an observer that the fight between cops and gangsters was only a choreographed drama for the poor suffering masses; behind the scenes they were all in it together.

Arbaaz lit up his Four Square cigarette as he walked towards Mahim Bazaar. He visited the shops that supplied the meat to the restaurants of the area. While the shops received their supplies from the Deonar abattoir on larger trucks, they employed small three-wheeled delivery vehicles to drop off the meat at the restaurants.

A plan began to emerge in Arbaaz's head. He smiled as he hitched a cab. His next destination was K. Rustom's for an ice cream sandwich. Then, some quality time at the People's Free Library at Dhobi Talao.

The qawwali singers were rendering their respect to God and Mahimi Baba at full throttle. Mahim beach had been converted into a fairground with a Ferris wheel and a toy train. Onlookers watched youngsters performing acrobatic stunts as balloon-hawkers, toy-sellers and kulfi-vendors attempted to entice the kids and their parents.

It had taken seven hours for the sandalwood paste and chador meant for Mahimi Baba's tomb to reach its destination. The tomb of Makhdoom Ali Mahimi was located in the most congested area of Mahim. On this particular day it was impossible for an individual to move unless the crowd surrounding him willed it. Accompanied by a police band and hundreds of people, a Sub-Inspector of Mahim police station applied sandalwood paste on the saint's grave and, along with other officers, placed the chador.

The crowds in attendance debated over why the police had such an important role to play in the rituals. Some claimed that a sepoy had offered water to the saint while he lay dying. Others claimed that Mahimi Baba had helped the police solve a very tricky case and the long arm of the law had been indebted to him ever since.

The next high-profile visitor was Rangarajan Pillai. Wearing a crisp white half-sleeved shirt and spotless white *dhoti,* the gangster sported a sandalwood mark between his eyebrows, just above the bridge of his nose. Around his neck was a thick solid gold chain with a locket of Venkateswara. Even though his security was not apparent, there were several tough men in the crowd sporting revolvers and pistols. They maintained a discreet distance from Pillai because of the heavy police presence.

Behind Pillai stood a fakir. On his head he wore a green turban. A short white beard reached his neck. He wore a dirty white kurta, black waistcoat and brown lungi. Around his shoulders was a green wrap that had the first line from the Qur'an embroidered on it. Around his neck hung chains with an assortment of beads and *taweez* lockets. In one hand he held a pan containing hot embers and leaves that created a sweet smoke around him and in his other hand he held a soft broom.

Pillai's presence was almost magnetic. It was a well-known fact that police officers, customs officials and municipal authorities were on his payroll. Unlike Abdul Dada's smuggling operations that were centred around the city's official docks, Pillai's narcotics team operated from landing sites in the mangroves of Sewri-Wadala, Versova, Worli, Gorai, Mahim and even distant Ratnagiri. There was no dispute that could not be settled once Rangarajan Pillai became arbitrator. There was no parcel of land that could not be developed once Rangarajan Pillai decided that it needed developing. There was no police officer that could not be transferred if Rangarajan Pillai wanted it.

After Pillai had placed the chador, he folded his hands and bowed in obeisance, first to the tomb and then to the fakir. The holy man blessed him by tapping his shoulders with the soft broom.

Turning around, Pillai snapped his fingers. It was a directive that feeding of the thousands of poor and downtrodden should commence. Pillai walked out of the tomb and headed to the designated restaurant where he would symbolically serve a few meals himself by ladling out portions of the mutton curry to the hungry-eyed assembly. The fakir followed him. *This persistent fakir wants to extract some more money from me,* thought Pillai to himself. *Religion has become a business these days.*

'A thousand blessings be upon you,' said an old toothless man as he received the first meal from Pillai. Pillai smiled benevolently and replied, 'I live for your blessings, sir.' The fakir also blessed the toothless man who scurried away with his plate.

The next person was a skeleton of a man, his ribs jutting out grotesquely under his skin. Pillai served up another portion of rice and curry to him. The man looked at the steaming food, almost incapable of recognizing it. He hadn't had a square meal in days. He dug in with his face, like an animal. The fakir blessed the skeletal man although he was oblivious to the blessing.

The line waiting to be served was a long one. Suddenly, there was a shout. It was the toothless man who had been served first. 'This is not mutton! It's pork! It's *haram*!' The skeleton-man also stopped eating. He looked at Pillai accusingly. He suddenly threw the plate at Pillai angrily, staining Pillai's starched white shirt with oily curry. 'What can we expect from a Hindu? You come here to pollute us rather than feed us!'

The crowd gathered around Pillai. His men attempted to reach him but because they had been asked to maintain a distance, they were caught unawares. One of them fired a gun to disperse the crowd but it had the opposite effect. 'Hindu pig!' shouted one man. 'He purposely feeds us in order to defile us,' shouted another. Within a few seconds the crowd had turned nasty and Pillai, the all-powerful don, was suddenly at the receiving end of blows. The fakir held on to Pillai, shielding him from the blows.

The police also tried their best to reach Pillai. They wielded their lathis and cleared a passage but by the time that they got there, Pillai was dead from a stab wound to his heart.

The fakir was missing.

'What a plan, and executed with such finesse! I'm proud of you, my boy,' said Abdul Dada as Hameed and Mustafa looked on. 'Most rookies start with small targets and here we have a rookie who went after the biggest of them all!'

'We could have done it the old-fashioned way and still been successful,' said Mustafa resentfully. 'Why did we need to go through this drama?'

Fuck you, chutiya… I did your job and now you want to fuck me for having done it well, thought Arbaaz to himself but he kept quiet.

'Pillai's men are livid,' said Hameed. 'We should be prepared for severe retaliation.'

'When the head is chopped off the body dies,' replied Abdul Dada. 'Instead of finding fault with this lad, let's congratulate him for a job well done. Come on, Arbaaz. Tell us once again how you killed him.'

Arbaaz was uncomfortable. He knew that neither Hameed nor Mustafa were happy with his sudden elevation in Dada's esteem. He maintained his silence but was prodded repeatedly by Abdul Dada.

Eventually he spoke. 'I knew that the only way we could get Pillai was when his guard was down. The Mahim fair was the perfect opportunity. I bribed the cook at the restaurant to change suppliers. Once this was done, it was easy to substitute pork for mutton. All I needed was a three-wheeler that could pick up the meat from Deonar and deliver it to the restaurant. The cooks have no way of telling one cut of meat from the next because these are the worst cuts—the ones that no one else will take. They just simply shove whatever they get into their vats.'

'That was a capital idea,' guffawed Dada.

'I also knew that the only man who could get near Pillai would be a fakir,' continued Arbaaz. 'I wore a waistcoat on purpose as part of the fakir dress code. It was needed so that I could tuck away a Rampuri knife. Pillai is extremely conscious of his secular image and is particularly respectful when approached by religious people.'

'How did you know that?' asked Dada.

'I spent several hours at the People's Free Library at Dhobi Talao, scanning the newspapers for articles about Pillai. There were several details about Pillai in them.'

Dada laughed even louder. 'I never thought that I would ever have a lieutenant who actually knows how to read! Make sure that you get me the *Times of India* tomorrow morning,' said Dada to Arbaaz.

'Why, Dada? You never read the newspapers,' said Arbaaz.

'Yes. But I shall relish reading that *madarchod* Pillai's obituary.'

Arbaaz entered his home—a cosy little two-bedroom apartment in Colaba—using his keys. His progress socially upward had been steady but certainly not slow. First, it had been a used Bajaj scooter, then a ramshackle Morris Minor, and then a Dodge Kingsway—and then the new flat. Abdul Dada was happy to indulge him, giving him extra pocket money to enjoy himself. Arbaaz's Four Square cigarettes had made way for Dunhill.

He could smell something cooking. It was his mother's famous chicken biryani. He tiptoed to the kitchen where she was busy browning the onions and grabbed her from behind. He had surprised the old woman. She turned around and slapped Arbaaz playfully. 'I could have ended up with a nasty burn,' said Shabana crossly.

'But you didn't,' said Arbaaz, his stomach growling. 'I'm hungry, Mother!'

'Go wash your hands and sit down at the dining table,' said Shabana. 'I'll get you your food shortly.'

Arbaaz put his gun on the kitchen counter and impatiently picked up a spoon with which he scooped out some steaming biryani from the cooking pot.

'I don't want that thing in my kitchen,' said his mother firmly. Arbaaz quickly put the gun back in the holster and gave his mother a peck on her forehead.

'This is part of my life now, Mother,' he said. 'Abdul Dada does not allow me to go anywhere without it.'

'I hope that Allah protects you, my dearest Arbaaz,' said Shabana. 'I worry about you all the time. I lost your father. I don't want to lose you too.'

Getting his mother to accept his new role in Abdul Dada's team had been exceedingly difficult. Arbaaz's father, Ayub, had always been morally ramrod-straight and Shabana had loved that quality of his even though it had meant them living near poverty-level.

In order to convince her, Arbaaz had slyly arranged for them to visit Haji Ali Dargah. A bribed holy man—the same one who later provided Arbaaz with his fakir costume—had met them and 'predicted' that Arbaaz would rise to dizzying heights if he worked alongside any man called Abdul. The rest had been easy.

Shabana walked over to the water pot and took off the cover. Peering inside it, she pulled out the copper wristlet that remained at the bottom as an ionizer.

'Keep this with you,' she said, handing over the kada that now bore a green layer of patina around it.

'Why?' asked Arbaaz.

'It may protect you more than that gun of yours,' she said. 'Next time you may possibly not need that fake holy man to convince me either.'

They were in their new office on Chowringhee Road. The goldmine deal had helped them go upmarket. Besides Arvind and Joydeep, now there were three more employees on the payroll—an accountant, a receptionist and a typist.

The typist was a young lady by the name of Hilda Fonseca. She was his old English teacher's daughter. Mrs Fonseca had spoken to Arvind on the phone, a tad embarrassed to be asking for a favour. Arvind had immediately put her at ease.

'When I would complete my accounts in your class, did you ever confiscate my notes?' he asked her.

'No,' said his teacher.

'Hopefully, your daughter will be just as understanding,' joked Arvind. 'And I hope she won't scold me!'

'Arvind, did you hear the news?' asked Joydeep, breaking Arvind's reverie.

'What?' asked Arvind.

'Nehru has died,' said Joydeep glumly.

Arvind was saddened but not surprised. The Prime Minister's health had been declining since the debacle in the Sino-Indian war. He had spent the better part of 1963 recuperating in Kashmir.

'How did he die?' asked Arvind.

'Apparently, he had returned to Delhi from Dehra Dun. He had a full night's sleep but complained of intense back pain in the morning. The doctor arrived but Nehru collapsed. He died shortly thereafter. It was a heart attack.'

The next day, the body of Jawaharlal Nehru, draped in the tricolour, and with chants of *Raghupati Raghava Rajaram* in the background, was placed for people to pay their last respects. Later that day, Nehru was cremated in accordance with Hindu rites at Shantivan on the banks of the River Yamuna. It was the end of an era.

'There will be a change of guard,' said Arvind softly as he read the newspapers.

'You mean Indira Gandhi?' asked Joydeep.

'Unlikely,' said Arvind. 'Kamaraj is the power behind the throne. My guess is that he will prop up Lal Bahadur Shastri in order to neutralize Morarji Desai, the real contender.'

'How does this concern us?' asked Joydeep.

'This is a moment of profound change. Great political transformations also bring about economic transformations. We must seize the moment.'

Arvind was lost in thought for a few minutes. He then picked up the phone to speak to Dipankar Da, his old and trusted stockbroker.

'*Nomoshkar*, Dipanka Da,' said Arvind. 'Which are the best fertilizer and pesticide companies in India currently?'

Ten minutes later, he was off the phone. 'What are you thinking?' asked Joydeep.

'Shastri is very different to Nehru,' replied Arvind. 'He is a socialist but is not dogmatic about it. This man will bring about substantive changes in India's food production, you watch. All inputs needed for agriculture will be in demand. This is the time to start investing in those companies.'

'Arvind, Dipankar Da had called,' said Joydeep. 'While he was investing in various pesticide and fertilizer companies on your behalf, he came across an edible oil unit. The unit is up for sale in entirety.'

'Why?' asked Arvind.

'Apparently the management siphoned off cash. The banks are refusing to lend them working capital. They have no stock on hand as collateral.'

Arvind telephoned someone. Joydeep could only catch snatches of the conversation. 'Mr Sampat Tejpal… export commitments… edible oil prices… '

Arvind got off the phone and turned to Joydeep. 'Where is the factory located? Get Dipankar Da to meet us there.'

An hour later, Arvind, Joydeep and Dipankar Da were at the factory premises of Bharat Edible Oils. The factory manager took them around the premises.

The company had started as an edible oil trading company and had grown to an oilseed crushing company and eventually morphed into an integrated edible oil manufacturing unit. Under the guidance of its founder, the company had commissioned an ultra-modern plant for crushing various kinds of oil seeds such as coconut, soya bean, groundnut, mustard, sesame and cottonseed. Most visible in the sprawling factory premises were the endless rows of storage tanks. The finished products were stored in those massive structures.

'The plant is quite modern,' commented Arvind. 'So what happened? Why is the company in financial difficulty?'

Dipankar Da spoke. 'The company was established by the father but the sons were least interested. After his passing away, they sucked out the cash, thus causing a mismatch between loans and collateral. The banks are refusing to extend credit. The company needs someone to infuse cash. Simple as that.'

The factory manager took them up a ladder to one of the tanks. Opening the submarine-like hatch on top, they peered inside. The tank was empty.

'According to the bank's records, this tank should have a thousand kilolitres of groundnut oil inside it,' said Dipankar Da. 'As you can see, there is nothing inside it except for a few inches of oil at the bottom.'

'What if I can get the banks to extend credit?' asked Arvind.

'You can buy this factory for next to nothing owing to the unserviced bank loans,' said Dipankar Da. 'And if you can get the banks to start pumping in money, everything else will fall into place.'

'Tell the owners that I will buy it,' said Arvind. 'Draw up the papers. One more thing…'

'Yes?' asked Dipankar Da.

'The machines. Can they be made to run without any raw material?'

'Which bank provides working capital to Bharat Edible Oils?' asked Arvind, studying the balance sheet.

'Central Commercial Bank,' replied Joydeep.

'Didn't they carry out stock audits from time to time?' asked Arvind.

'My enquiries tell me that the bank manager was on the take,' said Joydeep. 'He looked the other way while the spendthrift sons sold the stock but never bothered to repay the bank.'

Arvind put aside the balance sheets and picked up a book entitled *Encyclopaedia of Chemical Processing and Design*.

'What are you looking at?' asked Joydeep.

'Which oils does the company produce?' asked Arvind, ignoring Joydeep's question.

Joydeep sighed. 'Coconut, soya bean, groundnut, mustard, sesame and cotton seed.'

'Make a few notes for me, Joydeep,' urged Arvind, reading from the book. 'The specific gravity of coconut oil at thirty degrees Celsius is between 0.915 and 0.920.'

Joydeep dutifully jotted the figures down.

'The specific gravity of soya bean oil at thirty degrees Celsius is between 0.915 and 0.920.'

More notes were scribbled by Joydeep.

'The specific gravity of groundnut oil at thirty degrees Celsius is between 0.909 and 0.913.'

Yet more notes.

'And the specific gravity of cotton seed oil at thirty degrees Celsius is between 0.910 and 0.920.'

'Arvind, what is this about?' asked an exasperated Joydeep, putting down his pen and pad.

'The matter is of some gravity,' replied Arvind, smiling slyly. 'You want me to be specific?'

'Is the bank following up for an audit?' asked Arvind, putting away the *Indrajal* comic book that he was reading. He had ditched *Tintin* for *Indrajal* these days. Ever since he had put in an annual subscription to *Indrajal* for sixty-four rupees, he received a weekly comic that contained stories of *The Phantom*, a mysterious character created by Lee Falk. In the background, a vinyl of the Beatles was playing '*A Hard Day's Night*'.

Joydeep nodded. 'They know that you are in the saddle. The expectation that their bad loans may suddenly turn good is exciting them no end.'

'Good. What is the storage capacity of the tanks at the factory?' asked Arvind.

'Around one thousand tonnes,' said Joydeep. 'It's one of the largest storage capacities in our country.'

'Is there a regular supply of water to the factory?' asked Arvind.

'Yes,' answered Joydeep. 'The factory is on the banks of the Hooghly. Water isn't a problem.'

'Fine, Joydeep. What is the capacity of the industrial water pump on site?'

'I'll have to find out,' said Joydeep, scratching his head. 'What should I tell the bank?'

'Find out the capacity of the pump and I'll tell you when we can meet the bank,' replied Arvind.

A few minutes later, Joydeep had the information that Arvind wanted. 'The pump house uses a German machine. It has a capacity of five hundred litres per minute.'

Arvind did some calculations. 'A meeting should be fine as long as it is more than thirty-eight hours away. Go ahead and fix it.'

He paused. 'Also, tell the production manager to do what I have asked,' said Arvind. 'And open a new bank account for the company at United Federation Bank today. Transfer a few lakhs into it and pull it out the same day. Repeat the process tomorrow.'

'Sure. Care to explain what you're up to?' asked Joydeep.

'So this is what we're going to do…' began Arvind.

The officials from Central Commercial Bank were ushered into the managing director's cabin. Arvind sat inside the wood-panelled office looking relaxed.

After mutual introductions they got down to business.

'We are surprised that you bought this company, sir,' said an oily-haired executive. *Perfect for an edible oil relationship,* thought Arvind. He mentally named the executive Mr Oily.

'All the assets of the company are mortgaged to the bank and our board has decided to call in the loan,' said Mr Oily. 'If the company is unable to pay up, we shall auction the assets.'

'I am equally surprised that you have decided to auction the assets after waiting for three years,' replied Arvind smoothly. 'You are aware that what you will recover will only be a fraction of the loan. You are only calling in the loan because the new management has the financial resources to pay up. I call it deceitful.'

'No, no, sir. We want to maintain cordial relations with you,' said Mr Oily hastily.

'My factory is now running at full production as you would have observed,' said Arvind.

Mr Oily nodded. 'It is a pleasure to hear the sound of machinery once again, sir,' he said to Arvind.

'Joydeep, show them the bank statement,' said Arvind. Joydeep placed it in front of the bankers.

'From this statement you will see that I have brought in funds. These have been paid out to raw material suppliers. There have been inflows from our customers too. Again, these have been used to discharge raw material costs. The cash flow is back,' said Arvind.

The bankers listened carefully.

'Now if you will accompany me, I would like to show you something,' said Arvind. He got up and the bankers followed.

They headed over to the storage tanks and Arvind climbed the ladder of the first tank. The bank officials followed. He opened the hatch and asked the bankers to peek inside. The tank was full to the brim with oil.

'See what a tight production schedule can do?' asked Arvind. He asked them to follow him to the next tank. Again, it was full.

'I suggest that you allow your auditors to check all the tanks,' said Arvind. 'I am holding 11,36,000 litres of refined oil. As of date, my closing stock is more than adequate to meet your loans.'

Mr Oily had lost his voice.

'Of course, if you would rather auction the assets, be my guest. I shall be happy to get one of my companies to buy the assets at the fractional prices that they will fetch. I would imagine the auction should fetch you around thirty paisa to the rupee.'

'I don't know how you did it, Arvind, but the bank has agreed to renegotiate the tenure and terms of the loan,' said Joydeep excitedly.

'I knew that they would,' said Arvind.

'They have agreed to take a haircut on the interest outstanding,' said Joydeep. 'The total amount payable to them has come down by 25 per cent! How did you know that they would take the bait?'

'Simple. The factory had a storage capacity of a thousand tonnes. I noticed that each tank had a few inches of oil at the bottom. The specific gravity of oil is less than that of water. That's why oil floats on water. All I needed to do was to fill the tanks with water and it would give the impression that the tanks were full of oil!'

'But why the thirty-eight-hour wait?' asked Joydeep.

'Because the water pump in the factory could pump in water at 500 litres per minute. We needed a thousand tonnes or approximately 11,36,000 litres to be pumped in. Do the arithmetic. It would take around thirty-eight hours to fill the tanks.'

'You took a huge risk,' said Joydeep. 'They could have discovered that it was water if they had tested the samples from the outlets below.'

'That's why the bank account showing the flow of funds was necessary,' said Arvind. 'The fact that the machinery was humming even though no raw material was going through was also important. It gave the right impression.'

The two friends smiled at each other. 'Now what?' asked Joydeep.

'Tell Hilda to book a PP call to Mr Sampat Tejpal in Ahmedabad. She has the number.'

'Who is he?' asked Joydeep.

'The country's biggest exporter of edible oil,' answered Arvind. 'Last year our country exported 77,000 tons of groundnut oil, but this year there is a shortage. The price used to be around 1700 rupees per tonne but has already reached 2300 per tonne. This is a terrific time for the edible oil producers but a terrible time for the exporters. They have signed supply contracts and commitments that they cannot fulfil.

'You want to sell him oil?' asked Joydeep.

Arvind smiled. 'Joydeep, what happened yesterday at the Tokyo Olympics?'

'The Indian hockey team scored a gold,' said Joydeep proudly.

'I did the same yesterday. I scored a gold,' replied Arvind.

'How?' asked Joydeep.

'I have sold the factory to Mr Sampat Tejpal for three times the price that I bought it at.'

'You've earned 200 per cent? That's an incredible amount of money, Arvind!' exclaimed Joydeep.

Arvind thought for a moment before he spoke. 'You know, Joydeep, when we had just started out in business, I thought that money was the singlemost important thing in life. That was several years ago.'

'And now?' asked Joydeep.

'Now I know that it's true.'

The location was Hotel Horizon in Juhu. The ballroom of the hotel had been used numerous times. One simply had to see the last ten movies produced that year and one would find that almost every room used for fights, dances, songs and drama was the same one in Hotel Horizon. The actors and actresses changed, their costumes changed but the room didn't. It had an embellished ceiling with a cornice of plasterwork depicting flowers and leaves. The pale green walls bore stuccoed white peacocks while statues of dancing nymphs punctuated the carpeted floor.

Paromita looked as resplendent as Meena Kumari in her blue georgette saree and sleeveless blouse. Her long silky hair cascaded to her hips as she absent-mindedly played with the distinctive ruby pendant around her neck. She was a picture of perfection. When she smiled, the world around her rejoiced. When she was sad, the world desperately wanted to comfort her in order to make her smile again.

The director, Pinakin Deb, chain-smoked as the lighting crew snaked cables across the room. Pinakin Da had positioned himself behind the camera, having cast aside the cameraman to see if his efforts had paid off.

'I want more sunlight on her face,' he shouted and immediately two nervous boys positioned sunlight reflectors near the windows. Pinakin Da had a terrible temper and was capable of slapping crew members who got on his wrong side. Everyone attributed it to artistic perfectionism but insiders knew that it was alcohol. Lots of it. Arbaaz sat in the corner watching the proceedings with some amusement. Abdul Dada had sent him to check on the filming schedule.

Abdul Dada's latest mistress, Anjum Azad, was a beautiful ghazal singer from Kashmir. Her hair was a lustrous shade of mahogany that flowed in waves to frame her porcelain-complexion. Her emerald-green eyes twinkled mischievously each time that she smiled. She had everything going for her except her luck. She had tried transitioning into movies but had never made it big. She now wanted Abdul Dada to finance a film for her

'I know nothing about films,' Abdul had said.

'And I know everything there is to know. We've already signed Shashi Kapoor and Pran. Pinakin's niece is playing the female lead. You could make a lot of money,' she had said, unzipping his trousers and allowing her fingers to play with his tumescence. The discussion had lasted less than five minutes before Abdul Dada had agreed to finance the project.

'Everyone ready?' shouted Pinakin. 'Lights, camera a-a-n-d… action!' The sound of the camera whirring was the only sound as Paromita began her dialogue.

'Cut!' shouted Pinakin. The team readied themselves for expletives.

'*Chudir pola*!' he shouted at the lighting supervisor, exceeding all expectation. The hapless man remained quiet as he was called a son of a whore in Bengali. Arbaaz smiled. He now knew why this sector was called the entertainment industry. This was undoubtedly entertaining.

'I told you I want sunlight on her face, *chudir bhai*!' shrieked Pinakin Da. The lighting supervisor quickly rearranged the reflectors and wondered how he had gone from being the son of a whore to the brother of another.

'Everyone ready?' shouted Pinakin again. 'Lights, camera and… action!' The camera started whirring as Paromita began to speak.

Arbaaz looked at her for the hundredth time that day and felt guilty for feeling that Faiza paled in comparison to this ravishing woman. Her dusky complexion, deep languid eyes, hourglass figure and dimples that eddied every time she smiled were driving him mad.

Arbaaz forced himself to turn away and look at the others. *An actress like her will go out with movie stars, not scum like me,* he reasoned. He was right. The news was that she was having an affair with a rising star.

They met at the usual haunt. Plates of idlis accompanied by hot sambhar and chutney arrived in front of them. They tucked in.

The mood in India was festive. The Indo-Pakistan war had ended. It had started with Pakistan mounting Operation Gibraltar, a plan to infiltrate men and materials into Kashmir to foment an insurgency against India in 1965. Shastri had retaliated by launching a full-scale military attack on West Pakistan. The seventeen-day war had killed thousands on both sides and ended with a ceasefire.

'You were right,' said Murali, slurping his sambhar noisily.

'What do you know?' asked Arbaaz, taking a sip of his sweet milky coffee.

'Mustafa should take a 10-per-cent commission on all bets and share 65 per cent of that with Abdul Dada. What he notes down in the betting register is much less. Dada barely gets half of the actual,' explained Murali.

Arbaaz nodded. 'I knew it. What does he do with the money? Where does he park it?'

'He has an interesting little business on the side,' said Murali. 'He employs bookies for the horse races that happen at the Royal Western India Turf Club. They take off-the-turf bets on the phone even though it is not legally permitted.'

'Any idea how many bookies are involved?' asked Arbaaz.

'Lots,' said Murali. 'I wouldn't be surprised if he accepts bets worth three or four lakhs each day.'

Arbaaz whistled. 'That's a lot of money,' he said. 'Obviously his skimming has helped.'

'What will you do?' asked Murali. 'Inform Dada?'

'Let's keep this between ourselves for the moment, Murali. I think I can find a way to teach this rascal a lesson that he won't forget!'

'Dada, I have an idea,' said Arbaaz.

'What?' asked Abdul Dada.

They were seated in the Sardar Vallabhbhai Patel stadium at Worli at a wrestling match. Dara Singh was fighting his Hungarian rival, King Kong. The stadium was packed but the best seats had been cordoned off for Abdul Dada and his security ring.

'It's an idea about horses,' said Arbaaz.

'Horses?' asked Dada.

The crowds were going crazy. Dara Singh, weighing 130 kilos, had lifted King Kong who weighed over 200 kilos over his head and was twirling him around.

Abdul Dada laughed uproariously. 'I like that. Dara Singh is not just a wrestler, he's also a showman.'

King Kong was yelling at the referee. The twirling was not part of the accepted rules. The referee ran over to stop Dara Singh's exhibition of victory. But before he could intervene, Dara Singh threw King Kong out of the ring. He fell barely a few feet from the crowd.

'Um, about the horses, Dada,' asked Arbaaz.

'Talk,' said Dada to Arbaaz, tearing his eyes away with difficulty from the diverting spectacle before him.

'The Royal Western India Turf Club, which borders this wrestling stadium, has become very popular these days,' said Arbaaz. 'I think that you should own a horse.'

'What's cooking in that fucking fertile mind of yours?' asked Dada as Dara Singh was declared the winner.

'The inaugural Indian Invitation Cup was held at Mahalaxmi the previous year. This year, there's the Indian Fillies Triple Crown. This could be a profitable venture.'

'What do you need?' asked Abdul Dada, smiling.

'Just some seed capital and your complete secrecy and support,' replied Arbaaz.

'Fine,' said Dada. 'Just remember one thing though.'

'What?'

'I love making money but hate losing it even more.'

He was standing inside a stable that smelt of horseshit. At the present moment Arbaaz couldn't be bothered. To him the smell of that horseshit was nothing less valuable than that of expensive cologne.

'Is Riding Hood ready?' asked Arbaaz.

Santosh, a relatively unknown trainer in Bombay, nodded. The horse was a loser and he knew it. The jockey, Rustom, too, hadn't won a single race in more than two years. This particular horse and jockey were the laughing stock of the racing circuit.

'Good,' said Arbaaz. He had been working on the scheme for over three months. The next few days would reveal whether his efforts would pay off.

He had enlisted the services of two racehorse trainers: Santosh Tawade, based in Bombay, and Rajan Dhoble, from Poona.

Santosh had been provided with a chestnut racehorse of rather limited capability. The paperwork identified this horse as Riding Hood. But another horse, also called Riding Hood—and also chestnut in colour—was being trained to perfection by Rajan Dhoble in Poona.

'Enter Riding Hood into the Indian Derby,' said Arbaaz to Santosh as he got up to leave. 'Let's see how we do.'

Waiting outside the stable was Murali. 'Take me to the phone,' instructed Arbaaz. Murali led him to the sole public phone box near the betting booths.

'Usually, Mustafa's men occupy the booth throughout the race. When one man leaves, the other one in line is also Mustafa's man. They use the phone to communicate with their bookies.'

Arbaaz smiled. This was going to be fun.

Arbaaz was in Abdul Dada's Bandra house. He picked up the phone and dialled 180. The operator's disinterested voice came through, 'Trunk call booking.'

'I need to make a PP call to Poona,' said Arbaaz. An operator-assisted Person-to-Person—or PP—call was the only way to reach someone in another city.

'Phone number?' asked the operator.

'It's 60428,' answered Arbaaz. Memorizing Poona's five-digit phone numbers was relatively easy.

'Who is the PP?' asked the operator in her monotonous voice. Most operators seemed to forget that PP stood for person-to-person. By asking that question they were actually asking 'Who is the person-to-person?' which, obviously, made no sense. It was quite ridiculous. *It felt like I'll show you my pee-pee if you'll show me your pee-pee.*

'Rajan Dhoble,' answered Arbaaz, putting down the receiver.

An hour later the phone rang. The Bombay and Poona operators had put the call through. 'You have six minutes,' said the operator drily.

'Hello? Rajan?' asked Arbaaz. 'Ah! Good. You need to bring the horse from Poona to Bombay. I have arranged the truck. The watchman at Mahalaxmi Racecourse will allow the truck through without noting the details into the register. I have taken care of it. And yes, the driver knows that he has to take the Bombay horse back to Poona.'

'Now what?' asked Abdul Dada, his eyes twinkling. He gestured for both his new bodyguards to leave the room. Arbaaz had handpicked them for Dada.

'The horse from Poona will be swapped for the one that is currently inside the Mahalaxmi stables,' said Arbaaz.

'And then?' asked Dada. He loved a good scam.

'I have asked Murali to arrange for multiple bets to be placed but we need to be careful. If the bookies see too much interest in a given horse, they'll end up getting suspicious.'

'What are we doing about that?'

'I have had two lesser horses entered into the races—Bloody Mary and Snow White. Bloody Mary has been entered into the race that happens ten minutes before Riding Hood's. Snow White has been entered into the race that takes place ten minutes after Riding Hood's. I have asked Murali to place accumulator bets only. Both Bloody Mary and Snow White will be withdrawn moments before their respective races.'

Abdul Dada marvelled at Arbaaz's ingenuity. Accumulator bets were multi-race bets. Selections were made on horses in each of several races to win or place. In effect, Arbaaz was placing vast bets coupling Riding Hood's future with the two other horses. Of course, the two others had been entered as decoys—decoys that would be withdrawn at the last minute thus putting the bookies off the scent.

Murali's punters knew that the other two horses would be non-runners. Thus, all the money wagered on accumulator bets would end up being rolled over on Riding Hood.

Arbaaz picked up the phone again. This time he did not need to make a trunk call. It was a local one.

'Hello? Santosh? Yaar, make sure that you rub soapflakes on the horse that comes in from Poona.'

Santosh said something. Then Arbaaz resumed.

'I know. But Mustafa's men will be checking out all the horses. We want it to look like Riding Hood is sweating profusely. You understand? Good. Have it done.'

He paused for a think. 'One more thing, Santosh. Tell our jockey, Adil, to pretend that he has difficulty in mounting the horse. It will prompt the bookies to lengthen the odds.'

'You seem to have thought this through,' observed Abdul. 'You have already invested five lakhs of my money in horses, trainers, jockeys and bets. I hope this ends up being a worthwhile proposition. I also hope this Adil is a better jockey than the one you have currently?'

'The jockey listed in the *Cole* and in the newspapers is Rustom. He hasn't had a win in two years. But Rustom will declare himself sick and his place will be taken by Adil. He is a top Bangalore amateur but has ridden the real Riding Hood several times in Poona.'

'I could have simply finished off Mustafa,' said Abdul Dada. 'Why go through this routine?'

'Because we're hitting him where it hurts him most,' said Arbaaz.

Arbaaz sat patiently in the members' enclosure, his binoculars glued to his eyes as he watched the one and only race that he was there for. He ignored the perfumed ladies in their chiffon sarees and the dapper gentlemen in their straw hats.

A few minutes previously his man had cut the phone line to the telephone box. Now there was no way for Mustafa's team to communicate.

By the time the race started, more than three lakh rupees had been placed as bets on Riding Hood, Snow White and Bloody Mary. All the bets were long ones with massive pay-outs in the event that Riding Hood won.

The announcer's words were running faster than the horses.

They're all set. And, away they go… what a great start!

At number one we have Golden Biscuit. She's on a roll. She's a filly that likes to make her run on the outside. Kit Kat following close behind will probably go to the lead…

Mystic Magic is following at third place…

The jockey's got to figure out a way to get back behind Golden Biscuit and ease his way out somewhere down the rearside. Ah, what do we have here? Riding Hood is catching up…

She's being ridden by Adil Taraporewala because her usual jockey Rustom Shroff took ill. The jockey change seems to have made a difference…

The track is pretty even at this point. The same depth on the inside rail as it is towards the outside rail. And you know what? Riding Hood seems to be the pacesetter in this race…

Golden Biscuit is still ahead… Mystic Magic has dropped behind to the fourth position.

Riding Hood was a long shot at odds of forty-to-one while Golden Biscuit was the favourite…

And Riding Hood is like an express train today, closing the gap with each and every stride…

And Riding Hood is coming home to score…

And Riding Hood has won! In impressive style… routing the field by fifteen lengths at mouth-watering odds of forty-to-one!

Arbaaz quietly left the members' enclosure. Revenge was something to be savoured privately.

'Did you hear the news?' asked Arbaaz.

'What news?' asked Abdul Dada.

'Mustafa committed suicide last night,' said Arbaaz. 'Put the revolver in his mouth and splattered his brains on the wall when he was asked to pay out over a crore.'

Abdul Dada was quiet. 'I almost adopted him, Arbaaz. I treated him like a son. I never thought that it would come to this.'

Arbaaz had never seen the old man get emotional.

It had been a bad day across India. Prime Minister Lal Bahadur Shastri had gone to Tashkent to sign the ceasefire agreement with Pakistan's Ayub Khan and had died in mysterious circumstances the following day.

'Dada, let's go to the Taj. I'm told that Reita Faria is going to be there,' said Arbaaz, desperately trying to cheer up the old man.

'Who is she?' asked Abdul Dada.

'Reita has won the Miss Bombay crown and the Eve's Weekly Miss India. She's tipped to win the Miss World 1966. Meeting her may remedy your melancholy,' said Arbaaz.

'There is a remedy for everything in life, dear Arbaaz,' said the old man. 'It's called death.'

'If you say no to the Taj, we could go to Breach Candy and get you a slice of that cake you like at Bombelli's,' said Arbaaz.

'Come on, let's go,' said Abdul, assenting at last.

'What made you change your mind?' asked Arbaaz.

'I've had my cake. I may as well eat it too.'

Arvind and Joydeep were at Victoria Memorial's *puchka* joint.

'Why do we keep coming here?' asked Joydeep.

'Because the deal is bloody brilliant! Thirty-two puchkas for one rupee. Also, neither you nor I have girlfriends. We're stuck together,' replied Arvind as he popped another one in his mouth and was instantly gratified by the explosion of mint, lime and tamarind water mixed with the stuffing of semi-mashed potato, dates and raw mango pulp.

Arvind was convinced that puchka was really not the same as *golgappa* or *paani puri*. The fine, deep-fried spheres filled with a spicy mix of potatoes and channa, dunked in tamarind water were entirely different to their cousins.

To really appreciate the puchka one had to get one whole into one's mouth, without spilling the goods. If one could do that, ecstasy awaited.

'So what did you want to discuss?' asked Joydeep.

'Lal Bahadur Shastri's death in Tashkent means that the top job is up for grabs once again,' said Arvind.

'Death? You mean assassination!' Joydeep corrected him indignantly.

Apparently, Lal Bahadur Shastri's body had turned blue. The official explanation was that it had been embalmed but not many believed it. It was difficult for the nation to believe that the diminutive PM, who had given General Ayub Khan a bloody nose in battle, would die of a heart attack in a lonely dacha. In the capital, rumours were rife that the CIA had been behind Shastri's death in order to support their ally, Pakistan.

'I think I should speak to Dipankar Da,' said Arvind.

'Why?' asked Joydeep.

'If Shastri is dead, it means that the road is now clear for Indira Gandhi. Kamaraj would prefer to have her rather than Morarji Desai as PM. You watch, Morarji Desai will be side-lined.'

'So?' asked Joydeep.

'She will need to band together all the Left-leaning forces of the country. It's time for me to liquidate my portfolio in Indian banks. Knowing her she could nationalize them any time.'

'What should be our business strategy?' asked Joydeep.

'I think we need another big deal,' replied Arvind. 'I should go to Bombay.'

'To meet Paromita?' asked Joydeep, instantly regretting having mentioned her name. After their break-up Arvind had refused to acknowledge that he was affected by her departure. He had attacked his work with double his usual enthusiasm. It wasn't normal.

'No,' said Arvind. 'I need new hobbies. Golf and botany seem like good candidates for the description.'

'But why Bombay?' asked Joydeep.

'Because my trainers live there,' said Arvind, stuffing another puchka into his mouth without permitting a single drop to spill. 'Also, I believe that Bombay's Willingdon Sports Club has a reciprocal arrangement with Calcutta's Tollygunge Club. I will be able to use the Willingdon Club since my father is a member at the Tolly.'

Joydeep scratched his head wondering what bizarre new scheme was being cooked up. He gave up. Most of Arvind's plans were simply too complicated for Joydeep's circuitry.

'While I'm away in Bombay, do one thing, Joydeep,' said Arvind writing down a name on a slip of paper.

'Yes?' asked Joydeep.

'Incorporate a new company with the Registrar of Companies. It should be called Trac Technology Private Limited,' said Arvind handing over the slip.

'One more thing,' said Arvind.

'Yes?' asked Joydeep.

'I need you to apply for a patent under the Indian Patents and Designs Act of 1911.'

Abdul Dada blew a ring of smoke that floated up into the air, dissipating as it ascended. Arbaaz watched it dissolve.

'I think that this could be an excellent opportunity, Dada,' said Arbaaz.

'I agree,' said Abdul Dada. 'But how would it work?'

'There are hundreds of lenders in this city who have borrowers who refuse to pay back,' said Arbaaz. 'The same holds good of tenants who refuse to vacate landlords' properties. We will collaborate with lenders and landlords to help them.'

'Terms?' asked Abdul Dada.

'Nothing for signing up,' said Arbaaz. 'The service is free.'

'That's ridiculous,' said Abdul. 'We're not a charity!'

'Dada, for a moment I want you to imagine a huge concert hall,' said Arbaaz.

'Sure,' said Dada reluctantly. 'I still think this is a stupid idea.'

'Now imagine that the concert hall has two gates—one for entry and the other for exit.'

'Fine,' said Dada, closing his eyes to visualize the venue.

'Now imagine that the entry gate has no one checking tickets,' said Arbaaz. 'In effect, one could enter for free.'

'You'll have thousands of people coming but no revenue,' said Abdul. 'Foolish.'

'Hold on,' said Arbaaz. 'Now imagine that at the exit gate, the charge for leaving is a hundred rupees.'

Abdul laughed loudly.

Arvind looked at the 'Terms & Conditions' of the auction once again. It was a beautiful house on Alipore Road. Arvind had made up his mind to bid for it.

Participants must register in order to participate in the auction. The deposit amount required for participation is one lakh rupees.

The property is being sold on an as-is-where-is basis. Prior to submitting a bid, participants must review the purchase and sale agreement, any applicable addenda, seller's disclosure documentation, and all other transaction documents.

It is each participant's responsibility to conduct its own due diligence and investigate all matters relating to the property, including, without limitation, legal matters, physical condition and attributes, environmental matters, economic matters, encumbrances, and all other aspects.

This property has a minimum selling price established by seller, or Reserve Price. The Reserve Price is fifty lakh rupees. Bids below the Reserve Price shall not be accepted.

The winning bidder will be required to deposit 10 per cent of the bid price, in the form of cash or cheque, after deducting the initial participation deposit before 3 pm on the auction date.

If the highest bidder fails to tender the 10 per cent deposit before the deadline on the auction date, his participation deposit shall be forfeited and the second highest bidder shall be notified and be given opportunity to tender 10 per cent of the second-highest bid price.

'Get two participation deposit cheques made,' said Arvind to Joydeep.

'Why?' asked Joydeep. 'Who else is bidding?'

'You are,' said Arvind. 'In addition to me.'

'Why are both of us bidding?' asked Joydeep.

'I will be the first one to raise my hand and bid. Given that one cannot bid lower than the reserve price, I will bid fifty lakh,' said Arvind.

'And then?' asked Joydeep.

'You will bid immediately after me,' said Arvind. 'Do not allow anyone to raise their hand before you. This is absolutely critical.'

'Why?'

'Because you will bid three crore,' said Arvind.

'That's several times the market value!' sputtered Joydeep. 'Why buy a house at that price?'

'Because no one will want to bid beyond that ridiculous number,' answered Arvind. 'You will be easily declared the winning bidder.'

'But we will win it at many times the market price!' argued Joydeep.

'Once you have won, the auctioneers will ask you to deposit 10 per cent of the bid amount by 3 pm. You will not do so. Your deposit of one lakh rupees will be forfeited.'

'And then?'

'The auctioneers will have to offer the house to the second-highest bidder.'

Arvind looked at the outdoor hoarding advertising *Pyaar Karte Jaa*. It was directed by Pinakin Deb and starred two newcomers.

Arvind ignored the male lead. He only had eyes for the female one.

He always had.

Her name was Paromita.

The new Bagadia home was double the size of the original house although it continued to remain on Alipore Road. Arvind's affluence had also brought two new cars into the driveway. One was a Premier Padmini—in addition to the Ambassador that Brijmohanlal had bought earlier. This was used by his mother Shakuntala when she visited the club for her weekly game of bridge. The other was a GM Holden with an all-coil suspension and an extended wheelbase that Arvind used.

'Don't you think it's time you got married?' asked Shakuntala Bagadia one day. 'You've been spending so much time away from us these days.' Arvind had indeed been travelling a great deal. He had returned the previous day from Delhi on the newly introduced Rajdhani Express—a distance of 1,445 kilometres to Howrah Station in just seventeen hours. With every trip, he seemed to add a few more lakhs to the bank balance.

'Leave the boy alone,' said Brijmohanlal to his wife, fully aware that Arvind hadn't been himself after the affair with the Bengali girl had ended.

'Actually, I'm quite open to the idea,' said Arvind, pouring himself a cup from the teapot. He was comfortably seated on an oversized sofa and was wearing a tee shirt sporting a logo of the Beatles. The four musicians had visited Rishikesh a couple of years ago to attend an Transcendental Meditation camp at the ashram of Maharishi Mahesh Yogi. Arvind, a die-hard Beatles fan, had succeeded in worming his way in. The shirt had been a present from John Lennon.

'What did you say?' asked his mother. It was a severe shock to her. She had been pestering him about marriage for the past few years but he had been adamant about being unwilling to see any girls that were proposed through the arranged marriage network of pandits, aunts and family friends.

'I said I'm open to the idea,' said Arvind, sipping his tea. 'If you have a decent girl in mind, I'm willing to meet her.'

'What made you change your mind?' asked Brijmohanlal.

Arvind put away the *Amar Chitra Katha* comic that he was reading. He had ditched *Indrajal* for *ACK* these days.

'Madhubala died last year,' replied Arvind sarcastically. 'Any hopes I had of marrying her are now dead.'

'Seriously, son,' said Brijmohanlal.

'Marriages are simply working partnerships between businessmen and housekeepers. I could manage with such an arrangement.'

'You would marry without love?' asked his mother.

'All these days I was ready to try love without marriage. Why shouldn't I try marriage without love?' asked Arvind.

The next day, the Bagadias visited the home of the Goyals. They were jute traders like Brijmohanlal, and the horoscopes of Arvind and their daughter had matched on thirty-two *guna*s out of thirty-six. This was considered excellent. Under the *Ashta-Kuta* matchmaking system, over thirty-one was excellent, over twenty-one was good, over seventeen was average, and sixteen or less was inauspicious.

Her name was Abhilasha and she was appropriately three years younger and three inches shorter than Arvind. Her family were from the same community as the Bagadias and were slightly poorer. Marry your daughter into a family that's richer and take a daughter-in-law from a family that's poorer, had been the old maxim.

The rites were solemnized a month later during the auspicious day of *Akshay Tritiya*. One of the visitors at the reception was Sir Gyanchand Seksaria, seated on his throne-like wheelchair. The old man smiled as he blessed the couple, muttering, 'Your turn came before mine' into Arvind's ear.

Arvind had sent a handwritten note to invite the only politician he knew, Atal Bihari Vajpayee. The latter had written back congratulating Arvind and expressing his inability to come to Calcutta at that time. The death of the Jana Sangh's general secretary, Deendayal Upadhyaya, had placed the mantle of the leadership of the Jana Sangh on Vajpayee and he had just taken over as the national president of the party.

The next visitor was Munimji Tarachand Agarwal, who had taught Arvind all the tricks of accounting. Arvind and Abhilasha bent down to touch the old man's feet. He blessed them and then dispensed another one of his famous adages.

'There are two rules for a happy marriage,' he began.

'Really?' asked Arvind. 'What are they?'

'No one seems to recall what they are,' said Munimji smiling.

ॐ त्रियम्बकं यजामहे

सुगन्धिं पुष्टिवर्धनं ।

644 CE, Prayag

उर्वारुकमिव बन्धनात्

मृत्योर्मोक्षिय मामृतात् ।।

The Chinese monk watched the grand assembly on the riverbanks of Prayag. What had the emperor called it? A *Kumbh Mela*? Whatever it was, Xuanzang was moved deeply. It was an act of charity so vast in scope that it seemingly metamorphosed king into beggar.

By imperial decree, all the poor, destitute, orphaned and downtrodden from all five Indies had been invited to Prayag as guests of the king. Over half a million had come. The emperor fed thousands of people on each day of the assembly.

Over the next seventy-five days, Emperor Harsha gave away his treasury's accumulated surplus. Gold, precious stones, grain and other commodities were distributed to Brahmins, Buddhists and beggars alike. Harsha's charity was like that of a man possessed. He only retained horses, elephants and military equipment required for defence and public order.

'What is left to give?' thought Xuanzang as he saw the emperor part with the kingdom's wealth. It was almost as if he had no attachment to anything.

His detachment wasn't surprising.

Harsha hadn't been the official heir apparent to the throne. It was only a twist of fate that had placed him there. An enemy king had murdered Harsha's elder brother and had taken his sister captive. What had started out as Harsha's quest to liberate his sister and avenge his brother's death had magnified into a conquest of the whole of northern India. Harsha's empire now stretched from the Brahmaputra delta to Kathiawar, and from Punjab to the Narmada River.

But in his heart, Harsha was a spiritually inclined poet and artist, not conqueror. Harsha had transformed the kingdom of Kannuaj into a vibrant land renowned for its poets, artists, musicians and philosophers. The emperor had even written three Sanskrit plays himself.

Born a sun-worshipper, he had become one of the greatest patrons of Shaivism and Buddhism. The previous year he had banned the slaughter of animals in his kingdom. He was one of the most generous benefactors of Nalanda, a university that accommodated over 10,000 students and monks.

What is left to give? thought Harsha to himself. He quickly turned his attention to his personal jewellery and clothes. His necklaces, crown jewels, bracelets, amulets and rings went first. Next were his clothes. Having thus reduced himself to a naked pauper, he smiled and requested his sister for an ordinary used garment. Covering himself with it like a commoner, he then proceeded to pray, thanking the Almighty for having given him the opportunity to be of use to others.

The emperor then spoke to his people.

'The Kumbh Mela has an unfortunate legacy of deceit tagged to it,' he began. 'According to our holy scriptures, the Devas and Asuras fought each other for a pot of nectar even though they pretended to cooperate with one another while churning the ocean.'

There was pin-drop silence. The monarch was loved and respected by his people. They were eager to catch his every word.

'It is said that Vishnu, having transformed himself into the seductress Mohini, grabbed the pot from the Asuras and ran,' continued Harsha. 'A chase followed and Vishnu passed the pitcher to his flying mount, Garuda. In the struggle that followed, a few drops of nectar fell in four places. One of these places was Prayag. Tradition holds that ever since that eventful day, the Kumbh Mela has been held every three years, duly rotating between these four places, with the one in our beloved Prayag being the most important one.'

Harsha paused for breath.

'The importance of this sacred spot has been emphasized time and time again in our shared history,' said Harsha. 'Thousands of years ago, Prince Bharata had followed his brother Rama, Sita and Lakshmana to Prayag where they were staying at the ashram of Rishi Bhardwaj. Bharata pleaded with Rama to return to Ayodhya but he refused. Bharata had to reluctantly turn back and rule Ayodhya in Rama's name.'

The king directed his gaze towards the Chinese monk.

'Many centuries later, Gautama Buddha had visited Prayag in order to preach here. Three centuries after the Buddha, Emperor Ashoka had arrived in order to construct Buddhist stupas. Our wealth lies in this spiritual and historical heritage.'

A jubilant cheer of approval arose from the crowd.

Harsha waited for the cheers to die down before resuming. 'Ours is a land of immense wealth but we should be careful that our wealth never becomes a curse. Let us ensure that we do not fight over the pot of nectar. Whatever wealth my kingdom has, it is for the service of my people!'

Chants in praise of the monarch resounded.

Later that day at the palace, Harsha requested Xuanzang to join him in his private chambers.

Xuanzang was no ordinary monk. Having defied the Chinese Emperor Taizong's orders to not venture out beyond the borders, he had clandestinely left China and travelled to India. He had spent the next seventeen years travelling across the subcontinent, studying at Buddhist centres of learning and chronicling his experiences.

Upon his return to China, Xuanzang would carry Harsha's letters establishing diplomatic relations with China and would spend several years translating sacred Buddhist texts into Chinese. Xuanzang was thus a monk, scholar, diplomat, traveller and translator, all rolled into one.

'I wish to show you something,' said the emperor. 'It has been in the custody of my most trusted deputy, Mitravasu, the chancellor of Nalanda University.'

The emperor clapped his hands, and a wrinkle-faced monk entered. In his hands was a bundle wrapped in crimson cloth. He carefully placed it on the low table in front of the emperor and opened the knot.

Inside it lay a set of dried and smoothed giant talipot palm leaves that had been cut down to a uniform size. A cord passed through a hole in the centre of each leaf, holding the bundle together. A pair of wooden covers above and below held the delicate manuscript together. On each of the wooden covers was a carving of a jellyfish.

The chancellor opened the ancient book. On each leaf was a set of inscriptions. It was evident that each letter had been painstakingly etched on the leaves with a stylus and had then been rubbed over with lampblack.

Xuanzang squinted his eyes to read the script. It was not the script that he had learned in Nalanda. Harsha smiled. 'It's Brahmi, not Kutila,' he explained. 'You will be unable to read it.'

'Then why are you showing it to me, oh, Emperor?' asked Xuanzang.

'Because you should know what lies at the core of this golden age,' said Harsha. Turning to the monk, he said, 'Mitravasu, could you read out some of these pages to our learned friend?'

The old man nodded and began reading.

'Svedana… Mardana… Murchana… Uthapana… Patana… Rodhana… Niyamana… Sandipana…'

Book Three

1970-1980

Abdul Dada was wearing a Chinese dragon-print dressing gown and smoking a fat Cuban cigar in his office while the pink lady massaged his shoulders. On the desk in front of him were plates of sponge cake, cheese straws and puff pastries. 'What's all that about?' asked Arbaaz, pointing to the food.

'You remember that young boy you rescued? The one whose father had opened a mithai shop and ended up indebted to loan sharks? The boy's grandfather, a retired magistrate, had sought our help?'

'Yes,' replied Arbaaz.

'The father now works for the Monginis shop at Fort. He dropped in with some complimentary stuff for me to try.'

Arbaaz smiled. It was good to hear that the family had moved on.

'I gave him some money for his grandson,' said Abdul Dada. 'Which one should I take?'

'You mean between the cake and the puff pastries?' asked Arbaaz.

'No, chutiya. I mean these rings!'

In Abdul Dada's hand were two diamond rings. He was examining them both to see which one was better for Anjum Azad, his lady love.

'I'm hardly an expert in diamonds,' replied Arbaaz. 'I would choose the cheaper one.'

'Did you hear the news?' asked Abdul Dada as Arbaaz helped himself to a piece of cake.

'What?' asked Arbaaz with his mouth full.

'Indira Gandhi has abolished the Privy Purse,' said Dada. 'I told you that this government could never be trusted!'

The Privy Purse was a fee paid to the royal families of erstwhile princely states as a condition for their integration with India in 1947. Having secured their surrender, Indira Gandhi's government was now conveniently reneging on that promise.

'My immediate problems are far greater,' said Arbaaz.

Abdul Dada looked up from the diamond rings. 'Tell me,' he said, signalling to the masseuse to leave.

'As you know, there is a new Police Commissioner in town,' said Arbaaz. 'He's being rather difficult.'

'How?' asked Dada.

'He stopped a consignment of hooch that was coming into the city; he conducted raids at three of the matka dens; he picked up five of our drug pushers from Colaba Causeway; he told…'

'Big deal,' interrupted Abdul Dada. 'All commissioners need to be broken in. They need to be housetrained like puppies. You can use one of my Pandavas.'

Abdul Dada always nurtured five people at key places. 'They are the holy five,' he had explained to Arbaaz. Arbaaz had soon realized that it meant permanently looking after a key contact in the police, judiciary, Municipal Corporation and Income Tax. 'Who's the fifth?' Arbaaz had asked.

'God,' answered Abdul patly.

'It's proving not to be so easy with this man,' said Arbaaz. 'He's stark honest. He's been transferred to the city from Nagpur. The Bombay *hawa* has still not got to him. Your Pandava in the police is also fed up with this guy.'

'All honest men have hidden flaws,' said Dada. 'Find them.'

'We've looked into everything. He doesn't take bribes. He doesn't smoke, drink or gamble.'

'Women?' asked Dada.

'Faithfully married to the same woman for twenty-one years,' replied Arbaaz. 'Not the slightest whiff of an affair, mistress or call girl.'

'We could simply bump off the *ghanta*,' said Abdul Dada, blowing a perfect smoke ring. Arbaaz once more watched the ring expand and then dissolve into nothingness.

'Three of our chaps are serving time in prison,' said Arbaaz. 'They could be compromised if it were all-out war with the cops. You taught me that gentle persuasion is better than a revolver.'

Dada laughed. 'But sometimes gentle persuasion with a revolver in hand is more effective,' he said. 'You are right, though, no point in having an open war with the cops. Let's call Hameed.'

Hameed came in. Since the suicide of Mustafa, Hameed had acquired more importance. Rangarajan Pillai's murder had wiped out the Pillai gang almost entirely except for their hard-core support pockets in Matunga and Dharavi. The result was that Dada's writ ran large. Bombay was now entirely his fiefdom. It also meant that the vastly increased kingdom was now being ruled by two trusted men of

Abdul Dada—Arbaaz and Hameed. The matka business was now being operated by Murali who had succeeded in tripling profits for Dada.

'Does the man have any hobbies?' asked Arbaaz.

'Only two. Coin-collecting and watching Rajesh Khanna movies,' answered Hameed. 'He has done substantial research on ancient coins and is considered somewhat of an expert.'

'What about the Rajesh Khanna obsession?'

'He has watched all the smash hits of the superstar. He goes first day, first show. Apparently he saw *Aradhana, Do Raaste, Kati Patang* and *Anand* more than five times each.'

'Which is Rajesh Khanna's next big release?' asked Arbaaz.

'*Andaz*,' replied Arbaaz. 'Releasing next month. It's only a guest appearance by the superstar though.'

'What's the star cast?' asked Arbaaz.

'Hema Malini, Shammi Kapoor and Simi Garewal—besides the superstar,' replied Hameed.

'Producer?'

'Ramesh Sippy,' replied Hameed. 'They say that the movie has a song called '*Zindagi Ek Safar Hai Suhana*' in which Kishore Kumar yodels.'

'Does he know about the song?' asked Arbaaz.

'He listens to Ameen Sayani's *Binaca Geetmala* on the radio all the time. Our men assigned to watch him are fed up of listening to the same songs repeatedly,' said Hameed.

'Isn't there someone on that radio show who mimics Rajesh Khanna?' asked Arbaaz.

'Sure,' replied Hameed. 'His name is Niranjan something.'

'Hameed, get this Niranjan something to meet me,' instructed Arbaaz. Turning to Abdul Dada, Arbaaz asked, 'Dada, can you arrange four tickets to the premiere of *Andaz*?'

Abdul Dada nodded. 'There's nothing in Bollywood that I cannot arrange.'

Arbaaz smiled. Abdul Dada looked at him.

Dada knew that when Arbaaz smiled it could only mean one of two things. He had gotten even. Or he had found a way to get even.

The building opposite Crawford Market that had been built in 1896 was a fine example of Anglo-Gothic architecture. The thick cover of coconut trees made it almost invisible from the main road. Once inside, one had to walk through several Victorian-arched corridors and cross several forbidding portraits of former police commissioners before arriving at the Police Commissioner's office.

Commissioner Dube's cabin was massive, with an oversized teakwood desk topped with glass. On the wall behind him was an insignia of the Bombay Police. On his side credenza were three telephones. One had no rotary dial, it was an intercom to his secretary. The second was a hotline between him and the state Home Secretary. The third was his direct line.

The third line began ringing. It was an irritating—and rather terrifying—shrill ring produced by most rotary phones. Dube picked it up.

'Yes?' he said.

'Is that Commissioner Dube?' asked the voice of Rajesh Khanna. Dube leapt up from his seat. He didn't even do that for the Chief Minister or Governor.

The voice that had driven him mad all these years was calling up for him… for Dube!

'Is that really you, Kaka?' asked Dube, using Khanna's pet name, his voice trembling with excitement.

The voice at the other end laughed. '*Haan, mein hi hoon, yaar*. It's me. My PA tells me that you are a fan.'

'Of course, Kaka!' said the Commissioner emphatically. 'Who isn't a fan of yours? My wife and daughters are also crazy about you. We see every movie of yours many times. All of us are dying to meet you! I'm dying right now!'

'*Zindagi aur maut uparwale ke haath mein hai*,' said the voice taking a cue from the famous film *Anand*. 'Life and death are in the hands of God only, but I called to ask you for a small favour.'

'Your word is my command, sir,' said Dube.

'As you know a new film, *Andaz*, will be releasing soon,' said the voice. 'I have done a guest appearance in it.'

'We are all eagerly waiting for it,' said Dube.

'The movie will premiere at Apsara and you possibly know what happened there the last time?'

Dube who had never attended a movie premiere in his life, pleaded ignorance.

'The girls wanted to plant their lipsticked kisses on my car. Some even wrote love messages in their own blood on my windows. A sea of humanity lined up on either side of the road and it became impossible to get inside the movie theatre,' complained the famous voice.

'What would you like me to do, sir?' asked Dube.

'The Chief Minister has also been sent an invitation. It is for 6 pm.'

'So, is there a problem?' Dube asked, almost obsequiously.

'I am hoping that this movie will be my fifteenth successive super hit. I have consulted my astrologer and he insists that the premiere should be at 7 pm, not 6.'

'Why don't you ask the CM to come later?' suggested Dube.

'I would but he has a meeting with the Prime Minister at 9 pm. If we start at 7 o'clock, he will have to leave an hour earlier. He insists that the movie must be shown at 6 pm. I am in a terrible fix.'

'I understand, Kaka,' said Dube, commiseratingly.

'Could I request you to delay his convoy a little before it reaches Apsara theatre and hold it there for about thirty minutes? It would prevent the CM's ego being bruised and, given the traffic snarls in the area, it would ensure that he reaches closer to 7 pm.'

'He is the Chief Minister, how do I stop him?' asked Dube.

'I have someone who might be able to help you,' said the voice. 'Her name is Rani.'

'What will I need to do?' asked the Commissioner.

'I'm arranging invitations for you, your wife and your daughters. Please do come for the premiere. Be there at sharp 6 pm so that I may introduce you to the entire cast.'

'What about Rani?' asked the Commissioner.

'She'll meet you shortly. Please pay her 500 rupees. I shall reimburse you.'

The Chief Minister and his wife sat inside their white Ambassador car with the red beacon. The Chief Minister's wife was dressed in her Sunday best—a pale blue lace saree with a string of jasmine flowers in her hair. She had been putting together her ensemble for over a week in preparation.

The Chief Minister had left several pressing matters to attend the premiere. He justified it to his bureaucrats by telling them that he needed to 'motivate and encourage the cinematic industry'. His Principal Secretary gently pointed out that cinema had been flourishing since Dadasaheb Phalke gave India its first full-length feature film, *Raja Harishchandra,* in 1913. The CM gave him a stern look that immediately shut him up.

With a single pilot car in front of theirs, the couple headed towards Apsara Cinema. Their car made brisk progress through Kemp's Corner and Hughes Road before reaching Opera House. It was when their car took a left for Lamington Road that it happened.

A horde of eunuchs surrounded the Chief Minister's car. It wasn't a small horde. It seemed as though all the *hijra*s of the world had been assembled. In their usual quirky style they began tapping the windows of the car, clapping loudly and singing risqué songs.

The two policemen in the pilot car got out of their vehicle to clear the way for the Chief Minister but there was little that the two men could do when surrounded by a massive transgender group. The original group of ten eunuchs seemed to attract even more. Within a few minutes there were over fifty of them.

'Get us out of here!' shouted the CM to his driver. The chauffeur was a pious man. He attempted to explain to the CM that when Rama was leaving for the forest upon being banished from Ayodhya, he had asked all the men and women who were following him to return. The eunuchs had stayed on because they were neither men nor women. Rama, overwhelmed by their devotion, had sanctioned them the power to confer blessings.

'There is nothing to worry about, saheb,' said the driver. 'They have divine sanction to give blessings.'

One of the eunuchs had mounted the car's bonnet and was doing a vulgar dance, gyrating against the windscreen.

'Will you get us out of here or should I bless you?' shouted the CM furiously.

The Chief Minister and his wife arrived at Apsara Cinema a full hour later, at 7 pm. By the time they were escorted to their front row seats, almost sixty-six minutes of the 166-minute movie had elapsed.

The entire team, consisting of the director, producer and cast were already seated. They saw that the CM's hair was dishevelled while his wife's blue lace saree looked crushed. The jasmine flowers in her hair had fallen off and the string that had held the dainty flowers together was prominently visible in her hair.

Police Commissioner Dube got up from the second-row seats where his family had been seated and rushed to the CM. 'Is everything all right, sir? I was worried when you were late,' he whispered, his words loud enough to disturb most viewers. The CM mumbled something unintelligible and the Commissioner hurried back to his seat.

The Commissioner had arrived at Apsara at 6 pm sharp with family in tow. The invitations that he had received specified that invitees needed to be seated by 6 pm. He wondered what the point was if the movie was only going to start at 7 pm. But then, who was he to question Kaka? Kaka seemed to have entirely ignored him, without showing him the courtesy of thanking him for his efforts or reimbursing him the money spent. It was only when the

Commissioner went up to Kaka and introduced himself that the star smiled politely and shook his hand. The funny thing was that when the Commissioner winked at the star conspiratorially, Kaka seemed to have a puzzled look on his face.

Twenty minutes later the lights came on. It was intermission. The CM met all the stars and excused himself—on account of pressing matters of state. Actually, his wife had told him that she wanted to go home because she wasn't being able to follow the story, having missed an hour of the beginning. The Police Commissioner also got up to accompany the CM to his car.

Once they were outside the theatre, the CM's Ambassador pulled up to the kerb. The Commissioner held open the door for the couple. Suddenly, there was a commotion. It was Rani, the chief eunuch of the group that had obstructed the CM's journey.

'The deal was for double the amount that you gave me,' said Rani to the Police Commissioner, waving five notes of hundred at him. 'We did everything that you asked us to, so why aren't you keeping up your end of the deal?'

The poor Commissioner's face drained of colour as the CM looked on angrily, the rage clearly evident in his eyes.

The tenure of Police Commissioner Dube was one of the shortest ever recorded in the history of the Bombay Police.

'I need you to go to Hyderabad,' said Abdul Dada to Arbaaz.

'Sure, but why?' asked Arbaaz.

'We own a parcel of land in Banjara Hills—a very valuable piece of property,' explained Abdul. 'The state government is planning to acquire some of it for public use.'

'How do you want me to handle it?' asked Arbaaz.

'I have arranged for a meeting with H.V. Reddy,' said Dada.

'Who's he?' asked Arbaaz.

'He has access to the Chief Minister,' said Dada.

'We're going to bribe the CM?'

'Can't do that. He's stark honest. All we can do is appeal. Maybe he'll allow us to substitute some other land. Alternatively, he might help reduce the amount of land that is acquired.'

'Can you get him to come to Hyderabad?' asked Arbaaz. He was with Murali at the local Udupi restaurant in the morning.

'I'm not sure but if you could take him along, it would give you an edge like no other,' said Murali. 'Ah, he's here.'

A tall and thin European man with a goatee walked in. He was not out of place because he was dressed in a kurta and jeans.

'Let me introduce you to Pierre Lacroix, Arbaaz,' said Murali. Arbaaz and Pierre shook hands and they sat down. They then ordered breakfast.

'I'm what is known as a linguist,' explained Pierre.

'What does a linguist do?' asked Arbaaz.

'I study the practical and theoretical elements of languages—grammar, syntax, semantics and phonetics,' replied Pierre. 'I'm here because India has the maximum number of living languages.'

'Murali told me that you are having some difficulties,' said Arbaaz.

'I was to receive a grant from the Indo-French Council,' said Pierre. 'Unfortunately, the funding hasn't come through. I shall have to return to France.'

'What if I told you that I could get my boss to sponsor you?' asked Arbaaz.

'That would be incredible,' said Pierre. He then frowned. 'What's the catch?'

'You would need to make a trip with me to Hyderabad.'

Pierre Lacroix slept on the flight from Bombay to Hyderabad. Seated next to him was Arbaaz.

The co-pilot of the Caravelle aircraft, a young twenty-six-year-old, had chatted with Arbaaz briefly when Arbaaz had sought permission to go into the cockpit. 'Weather's a bit rough because of the pressure disturbances but we should be fine,' he said. When Arbaaz asked him his name, he said that it was Rajiv Gandhi.

Across the aisle from Arbaaz was another gentleman who was busy reading the newspaper that carried the headline 'Cyclone Kills 10,000 in Orissa'. According to the news, a cyclone had crossed the Orissa coast near Paradip early in the morning of 30 October 1971 with wind speeds of 170 kmph, leaving utter destruction in its wake.

'Terrible news,' said Arbaaz to the man across the aisle.

The man looked up from his newspaper, turning sideways to look at Arbaaz. 'Yes, really bad stuff,' agreed the man. 'Ten thousand have died and one million are homeless.'

'Do you go to Hyderabad often?' asked Arbaaz.

'Once in a while, when business takes me,' replied the man.

'Which is the best hotel to stay in?' asked Arbaaz. 'I'm dropping in to meet the Chief Minister but have no clue where to put up.'

'Hyderabad isn't like Bombay, Delhi or Calcutta,' replied the man. 'No decent hotels. If you like, my company guesthouse can accommodate you.'

'That's so kind of you,' said Arbaaz. 'But wouldn't you be staying there? I'd hate to be a bother.'

'I'm attending a wedding in the family of the Nizam,' said the man. 'My arrangements have been made by the bride's family so there's no bother.'

'I'm truly grateful. By the way, I'm Arbaaz Sheikh,' said Arbaaz, reaching out across the aisle of the Caravelle to shake hands.

'I'm Arvind Bagadia,' said the man, shaking Arbaaz's hand.

After getting to Hyderabad and settling into the Bagadia guesthouse, Arbaaz had called up H.V. Reddy who had been expecting his call. 'I'll arrange for the meeting with the CM but the rest is up to you,' he said to Arbaaz. 'What should I say that you are coming for?'

Arbaaz had explained.

Arbaaz had gone into the meeting along with Pierre. During the next three hours there was no discussion of land, property or business. The Chief Minister was an intellectual man, devoted to Indian literature. He was fluent in several languages including Telugu, Marathi, Hindi, English, Tamil, Urdu, Kannada, Oriya, Sanskrit, French and Spanish. He could speak seventeen languages in all. He was interested in translating the great Telugu work *Veyipadagalu* into Hindi as also the Marathi *Pan Lakshat Kon Gheto?* into Telugu.

The CM was fascinated by Pierre and, after cancelling many of the day's appointments, readily offered to sponsor him with a government grant.

'I do not need that, sir,' said Pierre. 'Arbaaz has very kindly taken care of all my financial needs. This was just a courtesy call.'

Then they got up to leave. The CM patted Arbaaz on the back and said, 'Thank you for bringing him here. It was an enlightening afternoon. Don't hesitate to get in touch if I can be of help.'

'Now that you mention it, sir…' began Arbaaz.

Arvind scanned the room as he adjusted his tie. He was at the Tollygunge Club, a venerable institution established in 1895. Spread over a hundred acres, the grounds had originally been an indigo plantation owned by the Johnson family. The main clubhouse had once been that family's home. What had started out as a meeting place for British bankers and merchants had morphed into a club for Indian traders and industrialists and was familiarly called the 'Tolly'. These days, rows of neatly laid-out tables with crisp white linen and gleaming silverware were usually occupied by the elite of Calcutta enjoying their *burra* peg or Darjeeling tea.

At a distant table Arvind saw the men he was looking for. Both men were drinking whisky as they observed the comings and goings in the ornate room. The first was Ghanshyam Das, the maverick textile magnate-turned-financier. The second was Ram Lal Khaitan, the merchant banker who was now the city's most famous dealmaker. Both men were in their fifties and were dressed in business suits. The two men spent most of their waking hours at that particular table, striking deals. The Tolly was almost their office and second home. Arvind waved to the men and headed over to their table.

'How are you, my boy?' said Ghanshyam Das. Arvind's goldmine and edible oil deals had been the talk of Calcutta, hence the sudden affection.

'By your blessings, all is well, sir,' replied Arvind, respectfully standing until asked to sit down.

'Join us for a drink,' said Ram Lal Khaitan, draining his own glass.

'I will sit down, sir, but I shall not have anything. I fast on Tuesdays,' said Arvind putting on the perfect façade of a well-brought-up Marwari boy.

'So, what is it that you wanted to talk about?' asked Ghanshyam Das.

'Well, I have been tinkering around with the idea of developing a transportation system,' said Arvind hesitantly. Ghanshyam Das raised his bushy eyebrows in surprise. The auto space was hardly an industry worth considering for investment. The Licence Raj allowed the Indian government to dictate what could be manufactured and at what price it could be sold.

The first motorcar in India had arrived in 1898 on the streets of Bombay. By 1903, an American firm had established a public taxicab service with around fifty cars in the city. By the time the First World War happened, around 4,000 vehicles had been imported into India. Two companies, Premier Automobiles and Hindustan Motors, had gone on to establish Indian factories in the '40s. These factories had started out with assembly, eventually leading to manufacture. In the meantime, Mahindra & Mahindra had started assembling Jeep CJ-3A utility vehicles. But the fact of the matter was that the automobile sector remained one of the most heavily regulated sectors ever.

'Why would you look at an industry that is so capital-intensive and so heavily government-controlled?' asked Khaitan.

'I have been working alongside a bunch of very bright individuals,' replied Arvind. 'We believe that we can develop a transport system that is unique. It will require virtually no fuel and hardly any maintenance. Most importantly, the government will love it because all the components will be built in India from day one. Import requirements will be zero.'

'Not a very interesting proposition,' murmured Ghanshyam Das. 'High capital outlay and long gestation. Not really my cup of tea.'

'The system is called TRAC—Transport Replacement Alternative for the Commonwealth. It will allow erstwhile British colonies like India to develop less expensive vehicles for the common man. It will be the people's vehicle,' said Arvind.

'No vehicle will ever be for the common man,' said Khaitan. 'A car is a luxury and luxuries are the prerogative of the rich!'

'I understand, sir,' said Arvind, getting up from the table. 'I truly appreciate the time that you spared for me. Thank you so much for listening to my idea.'

The next week Arvind sauntered into the club along with a friend. They sat down at a table which was a few tables away from the one regularly occupied by Ghanshyam Das and Ram Lal Khaitan. They ordered tea and sandwiches and then began an animated discussion that involved several sheets of paper and a pencil.

The atmosphere at the Tolly was normal but the situation on the streets of Calcutta was far from that. Thousands of refugees from East Pakistan had been pouring into Bengal since the onset of 1971. Pakistan's General Yahya Khan had resolved to crack down on all supporters of Mujibur Rahman. The American President, Richard Nixon, who called Indira Gandhi by the endearing term 'that bitch' was doing everything possible to support Yahya.

'Do you see who that Bagadia boy is with?' asked Khaitan. Ghanshyam Das took off his reading glasses and squinted his eyes into the distance.

'Isn't that Dr Venkatesh Subramaniam?' asked Ghanshyam Das.

'Absolutely,' replied Khaitan. 'The famous scientist from the Tata Institute of Fundamental Research. His work on reduction of friction is considered to be pathbreaking stuff in the commercial world.'

'What is he doing here in Calcutta? Doesn't he live in Bombay?' asked Ghanshyam Das.

'He's obviously here to meet our young friend,' said Khaitan. 'Maybe he's involved in that transport venture?'

Arvind and Dr Subramaniam were oblivious to the two old men who were chatting about them. Dr Subramaniam even laughed several times.

A month later, Arvind was back at the club. At his table was a stockbroker from Bombay. It was the same broker who had recently extended a massive loan to a Birla Group company in Calcutta. His name was Rakesh Dalal. Tall, loud and boisterous, Dalal seemed out of place in the cultivated and refined environment of the Tolly. Both Arvind and Rakesh were in golf attire, having just concluded a round on the club's eighteen-hole course. 'That was brutal,' said Arvind, having lost badly.

In fact, it was the Bangladesh situation that had become brutal. West Pakistani forces were perpetrating mass killings, rape and religious cleansing of Hindus. The Bangladeshi Declaration of Independence had been proclaimed from Chittagong in response to the crackdown. A group called the Mukti Bahini had begun waging a guerrilla war against Pakistani forces, quite evidently supported by India.

'Do you know who that is?' asked Ghanshyam Das. Both men were staring at Arvind's guest.

'Rakesh Dalal,' answered Khaitan. 'He just mounted a successful takeover bid on a Dalmia company and was bloody successful. He is known for investing in good ideas. He is the Walchand Hirachand of our times.'

'What do you think he has in common with Arvind Bagadia? Could he be investing in that transport venture of his?' asked Ghanshyam Das. The two men continued staring uncomfortably at Rakesh Dalal.

'Do you think we made a mistake by not listening to the Bagadia boy's proposal?' Khaitan whispered.

Arvind was enjoying his milkshake in the veranda of the club when the two old men of Tollygunge cornered him.

'How are you, my boy?' asked Ghanshyam Das. Arvind stood up respectfully to greet them.

'No, no, sit down, sit down,' said Ghanshyam Das. 'We don't want to disturb you. We simply want to let you know that we have had a chance to think about your idea and we're open to discussion.'

'Really, sir?' asked Arvind. 'That is so awfully kind of you but my problem is that I already have an investor.'

Both the men sat down without waiting for an invitation from Arvind. Ghanshyam Das leaned over conspiratorially. 'You mean that Rakesh Dalal? He is too concerned with quick profits! He will dominate your management meetings and eventually take you to the cleaners.'

'But sir,' began Arvind, delicately wiping the corner of his mouth with his napkin, 'Rakesh Dalal is not interested. He was with me only for a round of golf…'

'Don't lie to me, Bagadia,' said Khaitan. 'Dalal meets no one unless he is interested in investing… even if it's over a game of golf. Let us guide you. After all, we're your well-wishers!'

'I am blessed to have advisors like you, sir,' said Arvind. 'It's just that the technology that we're working on… '

'You mean the technology that you have designed along with Dr Venkatesh Subramaniam?' asked Ghanshyam Das.

'Sir, I promise you that he is just a fellow botany enthusiast in rare flora and fauna,' replied Arvind. 'I requested him to be my guest because this club has acres of rare flowers and plants.'

'Why are you being so secretive all of a sudden?' asked Khaitan, patting Arvind on his back. 'Let me make this easy for you.' He snapped his fingers to call one of the turbanned waiters.

'Get me paper and a pen,' he instructed. 'Also get me carbon paper from the secretary's office.' Khaitan was chairman of the club so no instruction could ever be ignored by the staff. When the stationery arrived, Khaitan sandwiched the carbon paper between two blank sheets and handed over the set to Arvind. 'Write down the terms on which you wish to do the deal. No negotiations. The money is yours.'

'Sir, I can't take your money. I only need your blessings,' said Arvind.

'Write,' said Ghanshyam Das firmly.

Arvind sighed, shrugged his shoulders, took the paper and pen and wrote:

By this agreement dated the nineteenth day of December, 1971, it is agreed between the parties that 51 per cent of the shares of the company known as Trac Technology Private Limited shall stand vested in equal parts to Mr Ghanshyam Das and Mr Ram Lal Khaitan in return for a sum of rupees 2,00,00,000 (rupees two crore) with an advance payment of rupees 1,00,00,000 (rupees one crore) on signing this agreement. The transportation system envisaged under TRAC has been thoroughly tested on Indian roads. It is economical, cost-effective and requires virtually no fuel. It also requires very little maintenance. All the parts and components for the vehicle have been manufactured in India thus allowing this system to be scaled up without any government licence restrictions. The buyers of the shares are fully aware that Mr Arvind Bagadia does not hold the patent on TRAC although the same has been applied for. Mr Arvind Bagadia makes no claims, promises, warranties or representations other than the above.

'Sign it,' said Khaitan. Arvind signed off at the bottom. 'Sir, this is not really proper. I had promised Dr Subramaniam and Rakesh… '

'Promises are like babies,' said Khaitan. 'Easy to make but hard to deliver. Let *us* deal with them, dear boy. You are now a silent partner with minority shares.'

Khaitan looked at the agreement and smiled. It had been easy. He took out his chequebook and signed a cheque for fifty lakh. Ghanshyam Das did the same. The two men handed over their cheques to Arvind.

'We will need the share certificates and signed transfer forms,' said Khaitan.

'They will reach you later today,' said Arvind.

'When do we get to see the vehicle?' asked Ghanshyam Das.

'I will get one of our test vehicles driven over to the club tomorrow,' said Arvind. 'Lunchtime—around twelve-thirty?'

Ghanshyam Das and Ram Lal Khaitan had ordered champagne. A third space had been kept ready for Arvind. It was time to celebrate the consummation of a terrific business deal.

The overall mood was upbeat that December of 1971. India had joined the Bangladesh war in that month after Pakistan launched air strikes on north India. The subsequent Indo-Pak War saw battle on two fronts—the Bay of Bengal and the Arabian Sea. On 16 December, Pakistan surrendered. The end of the war had resulted in the emergence of a new country, the newly liberated Bangladesh. Mrs Gandhi had emerged as the conquering hero.

One of the older waiters walked over to their table and discreetly informed them that a driver from Trac Technology was waiting on the main road with a vehicle that was to be shown to them.

'Main road?' asked Khaitan. 'Why hasn't he come into the club premises?'

'The guard at the main gate was not sure whether to allow him in,' the waiter explained.

'Nonsense,' said Khaitan. 'Tell the guard to let him in. We shall see the vehicle in the portico of the club.'

The waiter hurried off to convey the instructions.

'Shouldn't Bagadia have come by now?' asked Ghanshyam Das.

'He must be celebrating,' said Khaitan. 'He sent over the shares and signed transfer forms. He deposited the cheques and they were cleared.'

Fifteen minutes later, Khaitan called the waiter to their table. 'Has the vehicle come to the main portico of the clubhouse?'

'It's on its way sir,' said the waiter. Ram Lal Khaitan looked at his Rolex Tudor gold watch. Arvind should have been with them half an hour ago. How would the company be managed with such inefficiency?

Thirty minutes later, the vehicle had arrived but Arvind had not. 'Let's go have a look,' said Ghanshyam Das. 'Can't understand why it took so damn long to come inside from the main gate.'

The two men walked out of the dining room, through the lobby and out to the portico. There was no car in the portico, only a bullock-cart.

'Where is the vehicle?' asked Ghanshyam Das of the waiter who had obediently followed them.

'That is it,' said the waiter pointing to the bullock-cart.

The driver of the cart got off. He was wearing blue overalls that had the TRAC logo emblazoned on the pocket.

'Good afternoon, sir,' he began. 'Mr Bagadia has asked me to describe to you this vehicle that has been thoroughly tested on Indian roads. It is economical, cost-effective and requires virtually no fuel. It also requires very little maintenance. All the parts and components for the vehicle have been manufactured in India thus allowing this system to be scaled up without any government licence restrictions... '

The blood drained from both Ghanshyam Das's and Ram Lal Khaitan's faces.

'Our company has applied for a patent,' continued the driver. 'This is an experimental lightweight cart. This one has pneumatic tyres and an axle made of steel. It has low-friction bearings for free movement. The pull beam is made from steel pipes and the body is made of light steel sections.'

The driver turned around to point hospitably to the cart for the benefit of the two main investors in Trac Technology Private Limited, asking, 'Would you like to take a test drive, sirs?'

On the back of his blue overalls was the TRAC acronym in reverse.

It spelt CART.

Arvind and Joydeep were seated in oversized leather chairs surrounded by highly polished wooden bookshelves containing thousands of bound legal volumes. They were in the offices of Digby & Dastur, Calcutta's oldest law firm. The conference was with Mr Darius Dastur, the grandson of one of the founders, G.C. Dastur.

'As expected, we have been served a legal notice by Mr Ghanshyam Das and Mr Ram Lal Khaitan,' said Mr Dastur, a smile hovering on his lips. 'Frankly, the notice is a bluff. Their own solicitors would have advised them that nothing will come of it.'

'Can they do anything to us?' asked Joydeep.

'We had originally drafted the agreement that Mr Bagadia signed with Mr Das and Mr Khaitan,' said the lawyer. 'I am happy to see that Mr Bagadia had memorized it perfectly and reproduced it in his own hand word for word.'

'*You* drafted it?' asked Joydeep incredulously.

'Yes,' replied Mr Dastur. 'Mr Bagadia came to me after his goldmine deal with Mr Rao and honestly revealed to me that he had used my firm's name without referring the matter to me. However, he was in need of legal services given that he had just received substantial monies from Mr Rao for the sale of his mining rights. I told him that in future he must come to me *before* executing such deals, not *after*!'

Arvind smiled but kept quiet.

'So the agreement is foolproof?' asked Joydeep.

'Absolutely,' replied Mr Dastur. 'The cart *has* indeed been tested widely on Indian roads, it *is* economical and cost-effective. It requires virtually no fuel except if you count the bullock's fodder. There can be no dispute about the fact that it requires very little maintenance. All the parts and components of the vehicle *have* actually been made in India. There is no government licensing required for making bullock-carts.'

'But what about the patent?' asked Joydeep.

'It is very possible that the Controller-General of Patent Designs and Trademarks may reject the company's patent application on the grounds that it is not a new technology but the agreement clearly states that the buyers are fully aware that Mr Arvind Bagadia does not hold the patent on TRAC although the same has been applied for. The last line is the clincher—*Mr Arvind Bagadia makes no claims, promises, warranties or representations other than the above.* Let the two gentlemen take this case to court. I shall relish the idea of having it thrown out within the day!' thundered Mr Dastur.

Arvind entered his alma mater and the memories came flooding back. He walked into the round chapel circled by grand Corinthian pillars and stared at the honours boards that listed Founder's Day medallists. He had never made it to any of those boards. But the boys who had made it to the honours boards were usually not to be found on the boards of massive business enterprises.

Next to the chapel was the beautiful library. The main building was composed of rows of classrooms, with the dormitories on the top floor. Arvind turned and headed to the western wing of the building, walking up a flight of stairs until he reached the Principal's office.

The secretary in the outer office, Miss Matthew, was waiting for him. She quickly ushered him into the Principal's cabin. 'Arvind, my boy, delighted to see you,' said Father Anthony, walking around his desk to shake Arvind's hand.

'Good to see you too, Father,' said Arvind. 'Neither you nor the school has changed. Every step feels like a walk down memory lane.'

'How are your parents?' asked Father Anthony. 'And your wife, Abhilasha?'

'All well, by the grace of God,' replied Arvind. 'And that is precisely why I am here.'

'Old boys only come to meet me when they have children who need admission to the school,' said Father Anthony.

'Well then, I'm the exception. I'm here for CPC.'

'CPC?' asked the befuddled Principal.

'Catchick Paul Chater,' said Arvind.

'Ah!' said the Principal, nodding his head. Sir Catchick Paul Chater had been a student in La Martiniere from 1856 to 1863. He went on to become a very wealthy and respected banker in Hong Kong. When La Martiniere was in financial trouble and on the verge of closing down, he had provided funds that had saved the school. The grateful school had included Chater's name in the school prayer and had named an annual holiday after him.

'I wish to make a donation,' said Arvind.

'I will get Miss Matthew to bring the donation box,' said Father Anthony.

'It probably won't fit inside the box,' said Arvind as he handed over a generous cheque to the thunderstruck Principal.

Abhilasha sighed as she turned the pages of *Love Story*. She mentally thanked Erich Segal for having written it the previous year. Some lines had brought tears to her eyes.

Reading brought some activity in her otherwise boring life. Joydeep, Arvind's friend and manager, was also fond of reading and they would regularly exchange books. Arvind was so completely preoccupied with work that he never had any time for her. Even dinner was often eaten separately because he would invariably get delayed at work. He would be travelling out of Calcutta for at least two weeks of the month.

Abhilasha had initially tried to compensate for his absence by meeting her friends more often. After a while that had also become irksome. How much idle gossip could one digest? She had tried joining her mother-in-law, Shakuntala, when she did her prayerful rounds of temples, but she soon found that the religious scene bored her to death. Visiting places of worship and meeting greedy pandits who were quick to recommend new ceremonies at 'special' prices was not really her idea of spiritual fulfilment.

When they had initially met before getting engaged, Arvind had said, 'Marriage is a partnership. I will manage the business and you will manage the home.'

'What about love?' she had asked.

'Love is an optional extra,' he had replied unemotionally. 'If we're lucky, it will come as a bonus.' The bonus had not made an appearance to date. At the time she had not thought about the implications of his statement. And then it struck her. The solution was so very simple.

Children.

She had turned on the Voltas window air-conditioner an hour in advance to keep the room cool. She had turned down the lights and made the bed, using fresh cotton sheets. She had sprinkled *eau de cologne* on the bed and had placed on the coffee table a bottle of French wine that she had procured through their bootlegger earlier in the day, along with a tall vase of fresh gladioli. Two glinting flutes lay invitingly next to the bottle.

She had then showered and slipped into a simple blue saree with a sleeveless blouse that showed off her slim arms. Around her neck was her pearl string. She brushed her hair vigorously and applied a touch of lipstick, blush and eye shadow. Nothing overdone. Abhilasha looked gorgeous.

Arvind was on his way home. She had spoken to him before he left the office. She looked at the dainty watch on her wrist. It was 8 pm. She had spoken to him at 6 o'clock. How could it take two hours to get home? He knew that it was their wedding anniversary. She sat down on the bedroom couch and picked up *Love Story* to kill time even though she felt like killing him.

She poured herself a glass of wine and drained it when she reached page sixty-six. By page 150 she was three glasses down. She reached the last page with tears in her eyes.

'Oliver,' said my father urgently, 'I want to help.'

'Jenny's dead,' I told him.

'I'm sorry,' he said in a stunned whisper.

Not knowing why, I repeated what I had long ago learned from the beautiful girl now dead. 'Love means not ever having to say you're sorry.'

And then I did what I had never done in his presence, much less in his arms. I cried.

Abhilasha fell asleep crying, not only from Oliver's broken heart but also her own. When she awoke three hours later, Arvind had still not arrived.

Paromita walked into the hotel room that was booked for her at the Hotel Horizon. It served as her multifunction dressing room, restroom, make-up station and hairdressing parlour. She was tired. They had started the shoot at 7 am. She looked at her watch. It was 8.15 pm. They had been shooting for over twelve hours. But she was grateful nonetheless.

Earlier that year, the sultry Meena Kumari had passed away of cirrhosis. At the time of her death, her financial condition was no different from the poverty of her parents when she had been born. There had been no money to pay her hospital bills. It was a grim reminder of the momentary nature of fame and fortune. Paromita had not attained the fame of Meena Kumari but the three films that she had done with Pinakin Deb hadn't done too badly either.

She sat on the stool in front of her dressing table and painstakingly took off her make-up with cotton swabs. The air-conditioning felt good. Pinakin had switched off the AC units in the ballroom because they were making too much noise. Paromita discarded her clothes and climbed into the shower. Five minutes later she wrapped a towel around herself and walked back into the room.

It was a special room, one that had a television set installed in it. It had an indoor antenna and clunky buttons but it was state-of-the-art for 1972. A Doordarshan Kendra had been established at Worli and it had started transmitting a few hours' worth of black and white programming in the evenings to Bombay's residents. Paromita mulled over the idea of switching it on but recoiled in horror as she realized Pinakin was inside her room.

'What are you doing here, Mama?' she asked her maternal uncle.

'I have made you famous,' he said, staring at her breasts. 'I could make sure that you get roles with other directors too.'

'Thank you, Mama,' she said uncomfortably, tightening the towel around her. 'I am grateful.'

'How grateful?' he asked, stepping behind her and placing his hand on her wet shoulder. Paromita shivered involuntarily and took a few steps to get away from his touch and to reach for the dressing gown on the bed.

Before she could turn around and tell him to leave, he grabbed her from behind, tore away the towel and pulled her down on the bed. He tried to kiss her but she refused to let him. Frustrated, he placed a hand over her mouth so that she couldn't scream and quickly gagged her with her own towel. He then turned her over and bound her hands with the sash of her dressing gown.

Turning her over yet again he roughly cupped her breasts. Paromita shuddered. 'No, please…' she whimpered to her uncle but no words emerged, just muffled sounds under the gag. He unbuttoned his trousers and climbed on top of her before penetrating her violently.

She struggled but it was of no use. 'Yes, sweetheart, struggle a little more. I like that,' said Pinakin as he brutally used her. Paromita's eyes were wide open with terror but her vision faded. She realized that the tears in her eyes had clouded her visibility.

Twenty minutes later it was all over. 'If you breathe a word about this to anyone, your career will be finished. You will be unemployable, except as a whore. Got that?'

Arbaaz drove his car towards Hotel Horizon. Abdul Dada had suggested that he drop in and have a word with Pinakin. Too many unexplained expenses were mysteriously appearing in production budgets these days. The three movies that he had directed and produced hadn't done brilliantly either, one of them turning out to be a complete dud.

Suddenly, Arbaaz saw a figure that he recognized. Paromita! She was dressed in a pink cotton saree but her hair was dishevelled and she was wearing dark sunglasses. She was walking slowly, and with a stoop, as though she were attempting to keep her head down.

He pulled up near the kerb and said, 'Excuse me, Paromitaji, may I drop you somewhere?'

She looked at him briefly and said, 'Leave me alone. I'm fine. I'll be taking a taxi.'

Arbaaz whistled softly to himself. *The woman has some attitude,* he thought. *Move on.* He put his car back in gear and started driving away. When he looked in his rear-view mirror he saw that she had fallen on the pavement before she could reach the taxi-stand.

He quickly stopped the car, got out and ran over to her. He knelt down beside her. That was when he noticed the blood on her saree and the tears on her face. *Shit! I've been such a jerk,* he thought. *Someone's really messed her up bad.*

'Where do you live?' he asked. 'Let me drop you off. You are in no condition to walk.'

'No… no… I can't go back home in this condition,' she stammered. 'I'll be fine. Leave me alone and I'll manage.' The tears were cascading down her cheeks.

'I'm not leaving you alone,' said Arbaaz. 'And you will tell me which bastard did this to you. In the meantime, I'm taking you home to my mother. She'll fix you up.'

Paromita shuddered. She was in no position to trust a man yet again. *What if he, too, wanted to have his way with her?*

'I know what you're thinking,' said Arbaaz softly. 'Please trust me. I won't let anyone harm you.'

Before she could reply, he scooped her up into his arms and laid her down on the rear seat of his car as he drove towards his Colaba flat.

Shabana watched the poor girl sip the tea inside her bedroom as she sat up in bed. It had taken an hour to undress her and clean her up. Calling the police was of no use. The laws were stacked against women and there was simply no point in subjecting her to further humiliation at the hands of an uncaring cop.

Earlier that year, in 1972, a sixteen-year-old tribal girl from Chandrapur in Maharashtra had been dragged to the police station by her relatives because she had been attempting to elope with her lover. Instead of recording her statement, the two policemen on duty that day had raped her while her relatives sat complacently outside.

Shabana held Paromita's hands in her own and tried to comfort her. She had provided the girl with a fresh saree and had placed the bloodied one in a bucket of hot water. She did not have a daughter of her own but wondered how she would feel if her own daughter had been raped. She tried imagining the overwhelming feeling of hopelessness and despair.

In the case of the tribal girl, the Sessions Judge had held that attempting to elope with her boyfriend implied that she was habituated to sex. That being the case, she could not have been raped. Incredible logic! The High Court had reversed the judgment, delivering a six-year sentence to the policemen but the Supreme Court had overturned that order. The judges felt that because the girl had not raised an alarm, she must have given the men her consent.

There was a knock on the door. Shabana unlocked the door and saw that Arbaaz was standing outside. 'How is she?' he asked.

'Still coming to terms with the incident,' explained Shabana. 'Luckily, her bruises will heal quickly. I'm not as sure about her mental state.'

Arbaaz walked into the bedroom. 'I need to know who did this to you,' he asked.

Paromita burst into tears yet again.

'Stop it, Arbaaz,' said his mother. 'She isn't ready for this just yet.'

Arbaaz knelt by the bed. He whispered. 'I promise that I will handle this discreetly. Neither the police nor your parents will ever know. Now, tell me, who was it?'

Arbaaz had met Abdul Dada first. 'The bastard raped his own niece,' explained Arbaaz.

Abdul Dada had listened patiently. 'Take Hameed with you. Do what is needed,' he had said.

'But you have money invested in him,' said Arbaaz.

'Directors are paid employees. I can always find another clown on hire. This is about avenging a wrong. No money can ever come in the way of that. Now go!'

Arbaaz and Hameed got into his car and drove towards Juhu. The house was quiet when they arrived. The bastard had probably drunk himself to sleep.

The watchman outside was quickly neutralized by Hameed. He quickly bound and gagged him and left him near the gate. The two men then made their way to the front door. A minute later they rammed the door open, using the security guard's bench.

Pinakin, dressed in dhoti and vest, came running down the stairs when he heard the commotion. His wife, wearing a frilly nightgown, stood at the head of the stairs shouting for help.

A young servant emerged from the kitchen but a swift blow from Hameed knocked him down. Arbaaz charged towards Pinakin and slammed his fist into the director's mouth. Pinakin crashed to the floor, as his blood and teeth rained on the ground.

Pinakin's wife was frantic and kept shouting desperately for help. 'Shut her up,' said Arbaaz as he tied Pinakin's hands behind his back and stuffed a rag into his mouth.

Hameed took the stairs two at a time and reached Mrs Deb. He grabbed her by her shoulders, shook her violently and whispered into her ears, 'Your husband forcibly shoved his cock into another woman's pussy. He violently raped her. Do you really want to save him?'

Mrs Deb calmed down and stopped shouting. There were a few seconds when Hameed and Mrs Deb stared at each other with neither speaking. Then she spoke. 'The bastard is all yours. Untie the watchman on your way out since you've broken my door.'

Hameed and Arbaaz shoved Pinakin into the trunk of the car and drove off. It was an hour later that they opened the trunk. They had reached a deserted stretch along Vasai creek. Two men from Abdul Dada's team were already waiting for them. One of them was Chikna, the one who had helped recover the kidnapped boy along with Arbaaz.

'All set?' asked Arbaaz.

'Yes, Arbaaz Bhai,' replied Chikna. 'Have a look.'

An extra-large barbecue spit had been organized. All the ingredients for a barbecue had also been laid out: firewood, charcoal, ghee, diesel and tongs.

'Get him out of the trunk,' instructed Arbaaz. As the dazed Pinakin was dragged out, Arbaaz asked for him to be stripped naked.

The fear in Pinakin's eyes was all too apparent but the rag in his mouth prevented him from pleading or screaming.

'You took her like an animal, right? Now we're going to treat you like one,' said Arbaaz. 'Tie his hands to the spit and apply the ghee lightly to the soles of his feet and his palms.'

'Why?' asked Hameed curiously, a Charminar hanging from the corner of his mouth.

'You'll see,' said Arbaaz as he watched Pinakin being made to hang on the spit by his hands and legs. His bare buttocks faced the ground.

Arbaaz walked over to him and took out the rag from his mouth.

'No, please…' Pinakin whimpered.

'Did she also plead like that?' asked Arbaaz.

Pinakin struggled, attempting to sway his torso and topple the spit. 'Yes, sweetheart, struggle a little more. I like that,' said Arbaaz. 'Isn't that what you said to her?'

'We're ready,' said Chikna, who had been busy piling firewood and charcoal under Pinakin.

Arbaaz took the bottle of diesel and sprinkled it on the wood. He then lit a match and dropped it in. The firewood and charcoal burst into flames, the first licks singeing Pinakin's skin.

He screamed.

'Yes, I like it when you scream,' said Arbaaz. 'This is nothing. Just wait till the flames reach your feet and hands. They will soon ignite. Ah, the smell of barbecue. Oh, I forgot. You're a pig and I can't eat pork… nonetheless, Chikna here is a Hindu from Goa. You love roast pork, don't you, Chikna?'

The year 1974 turned out to be a difficult one. In the east, Jayaprakash Narayan, Indira Gandhi's most vocal critic, sounded the bugle for 'total revolution'. In the west, the *Nav Nirman* agitation in Gujarat caused 100 deaths, left 3,000 injured and led to 8,000 arrests. Clouds of political uncertainty were playing havoc with business sentiment.

'We need a great sales-oriented and dynamic chief executive,' said Arvind to Joydeep, realizing that the business environment needed someone who relished challenges. Someone a little less like Joydeep and a little more like Arvind.

'Why?' asked Joydeep. 'We don't even have anything to sell. Before we can even start running a business, you sell it.'

'Precisely. We sell it. You and I need someone who can ensure that there is a quick turnaround on deals. With me as chairman and you as vice-chairman…'

'Since when did I become vice-chairman?' asked Joydeep.

'Since this moment,' replied Arvind smiling. 'I have suggested that you should get married on several occasions but you have failed to do so. I figure that a grander title may get you a bride!'

The men laughed. 'So now we need a new chief executive,' said Arvind.

Interviews were scheduled the next week and were conducted by Arvind and Joydeep at the company's conference room in their Chowringhee Road office.

The first candidate came in.

Taking out a pen from his pocket, Arvind placed it on the desk and said to the candidate, 'Sell me this pen.'

The poor candidate initially looked worried. He then began hesitantly: 'This is a great pen. It writes beautifully and looks good too. It is easy to grip and easy to fill.'

'Thank you,' said Arvind.

'He's not our man,' he said to Joydeep as soon as the candidate left.

The second candidate walked in. Picking up the pen from the desk, Arvind placed it before the candidate and said, 'Sell me this pen.'

The candidate began confidently. 'Do you need to remember things? Do you need to jot down things that would otherwise be forgotten? Do you need a reliable tool that can help you? Here's the pen for you.'

Arvind thought about the pitch and then said, 'That was good but I need better. Thanks for coming.'

The third candidate entered. Arvind held the pen up and repeated his instructions. 'Sell me this pen.'

'Have you ever chanced upon a colleague dozing off at work? With this terrific pen you can jab him into alertness.'

Arvind laughed. The idea was witty but something was missing.

The last candidate entered Arvind's office. Arvind pushed the pen towards him and instructed. 'Sell me this pen.'

The candidate thought about it for a minute.

He took out a chequebook from the bag that he was carrying. He used the pen to sign the cheque and handed the blank cheque over to Arvind. He put the pen in his pocket and asked Arvind, 'Wouldn't it be great if you had a pen right now?'

Arvind smiled. He had his man.

Satyapal Mittal.

Satyapal Mittal had been born to a poor family in Patna. His father was a dealer in scrap—a *raddiwalla*. The family was so poor that Satyapal's father could not afford electricity.

Satyapal would study by the light of a temperamental kerosene lamp, the smoke making his eyes water.

Satyapal noticed the difference between his home and those of his classmates. His was the only one in which there were no light bulbs. He sheepishly approached his father and asked if they could get a light bulb. Instead of turning down the request, his father asked Satyapal to work hard so that one day he would be able to afford light bulbs for their house on his own.

The school that he attended, Shree Vishnu Mahadev Vidyalaya, offered a token scholarship of a hundred rupees to the student who stood first in school. Starting from the fifth grade onwards, Satyapal won the scholarship each year until he had put aside 300 rupees. He then went to the market and bought a bulb and a table fan. It was the proudest moment of his life. It was also an exceedingly proud moment for his father.

That day, his father took the young Satyapal to a meeting of Jeevan Prakash that was being conducted in Patna. 'Why are we going there, Father?' asked Satyapal.

'Because I can see that you will be very successful in life,' said his father.

'If I will be successful, why do I need Jeevan Prakash?' asked Satyapal.

'Because dealing with success is sometimes harder than dealing with failure,' answered his father wisely.

'What should be the next venture?' asked Arvind. 'I want us to do something that can leverage Satyapal's terrific skills of salesmanship and PR.'

Joydeep opened his mouth to speak but Satyapal beat him to it. 'Why don't we create a licence bank?' he asked.

'What the hell is that?' asked Joydeep.

'As you know, in India, we have what we like to call a planned economy,' said Satyapal. 'All aspects of the economy are controlled by our *sarkar*. The Planning Commission has ensured that we have created a complicated web of licences, permissions and regulations that one must get past before setting up a manufacturing facility.'

'So?' asked Joydeep.

'Sometimes the number of government agencies that one has to satisfy can be well over eighty. In each case liaison, influence-peddling and bribery are par for the course.'

'What do you have in mind?' asked Arvind.

'If you can use your contacts to stay informed of possible plans of various firms, we could do the groundwork in advance,' said Satyapal.

'But how would that help us?' asked Joydeep.

'Simple, really,' replied Arvind on Satyapal's behalf. 'Let's say that Kissan—the company that makes ketchup and jams—is looking to diversify into squashes or canned foods. I keep Satyapal informed. He then does the rounds of ministers and bureaucrats in advance and secures the licence in favour of a special-purpose company.'

'Why wouldn't Kissan do that on its own?' asked Joydeep.

'Two reasons,' replied Satyapal. 'One: We would have invested several months doing the legwork. It would be easier for them to buy our special-purpose company thus saving them time and hassle.'

'And?' asked Joydeep

'Two: When a licence is issued to manufacture 50,000 bottles of squash per year, the corollary is that it blocks another group from applying for it. The government wants national resources to be used without wastage.'

'In effect we build a bank of licences that can be bought in the secondary market by interested manufacturers at a premium,' translated Arvind.

'I'll have to park myself in Delhi,' observed Satyapal.

'We'll need to rent a place for you,' said Joydeep.

'Not really,' replied Satyapal. 'There's this little place called Hotel Vikas at Paharganj. I'll put up there. It's cheap.'

'Are you sure you'll be comfortable there?' asked Arvind.

'Absolutely,' replied Satyapal. 'There's an excellent *paranthawalla* around the corner, an even better *dahi bhalla* guy next to him and a *barfi* chap down the block. It's perfect. I stayed there a month ago.'

'What took you there?' asked Arvind.

'I am a follower of Jeevan Prakash. They conduct spiritual meetings at a huge ground in Paharganj.'

Satyapal fished out a photograph from his wallet and passed it on to Arvind. 'That's me at one of the camps of Jeevan Prakash.'

'Who's the American hippie standing next to you?' asked Arvind.

'Oh, some guy on a quest to find a guru called Neem Karoli Baba near Nainital. Told me his name. Steve Jobs, or something like that. He was also staying at the same hotel and he tagged along.'

'We need to consider operating a few legitimate businesses,' said Murali.

Abdul Dada, Arbaaz and Hameed stopped eating the chicken makhanwala the restaurant was famous for. They were at the Samarkand, the buzzing coffeeshop of the recently opened Oberoi Sheraton Hotel. When Abdul Dada walked in, several diners stopped to stare at him. The staff had rushed to get him a table and pull out his chair for him. Abdul Dada was not a man that one pissed off unless one had a lurking death wish.

'Why?' asked Arbaaz.

'It will give us more flexibility,' replied Murali. 'Indira Gandhi is now supreme dictator of India. The Emergency is here to stay. The government has passed COFEPOSA—the Conservation of Foreign Exchange and Prevention of Smuggling Activities Act. The law provides wide powers to the administration to detain individuals on the mere apprehension of their involvement in smuggling activities. It's time to have a respectable façade.'

'I quite like this Emergency,' said Arbaaz, dipping his naan into the makhanwala. 'The trains are running on time and people seem to be working harder. One often needs a healthy dose of fear to motivate people. And we've even increased our territory. Sikkim has been added as an Indian state, finally.'

Indira Gandhi had made President Fakhruddin Ali Ahmed issue the declaration of Emergency under Article 352 (1) of the Indian Constitution on account of 'internal disturbance'. The order bequeathed several powers on the PM—the authority to rule by decree, to suspend elections, to curb civil liberties, to imprison political opponents and to censor the press. The *Indian Express* and the *Statesman* had left the lead editorial space of their newspapers blank as a mark of protest.

'That's all very well but that son of hers—Sanjay—has a squad that is apparently rounding up men and having their sperm-tunnels forcibly snipped!' said Hameed. 'Although the government denies that.'

'Then it must be true,' joked Arbaaz. 'But it's probably a good idea. See the sort of scum we have in our country!' He was thinking of Pinakin, the movie director.

'What sort of business would we get into?' asked Abdul Dada, reverting to the original topic.

'Let's finance a few more films in a structured manner… given our strength in real estate we could consider a couple of hotels… given our gambling focus we could also look at legitimate share investments on the Bombay Stock Exchange,' replied Murali as he pushed aside his vegetarian option—vegetable makhanwala.

'And pay tax?' asked Hameed, his Charminar breath reaching everyone at the table. 'Why the fuck are we listening to this crap, Dada? Our dhanda is fine as it is. Why are we behaving like pussies?'

Abdul Dada ignored Hameed. 'How will getting into these businesses help me?' asked Abdul, using the final piece of his naan to wipe the rich gravy off his plate.

'In several ways,' replied Murali. 'Your travel abroad would be justified. You would have income streams that allow you to trade and invest officially. You could also convert black income into white or white income into black, as required, from time to time.'

'So how do you suggest I get started?' asked Abdul Dada, licking the remaining gravy off his fingers.

'Let's incorporate a company in which you are the sole shareholder,' suggested Murali. 'This company could then become the vehicle for investments in profitable opportunities. Any suggestions for a name?'

'Dhanda Holdings Private Limited,' said Arbaaz. 'White or black, taxed or untaxed, legal or illegal… it's all merely dhanda.'

Murali Iyer stretched his arms above his head in order to rid himself of the fatigue of being glued to a chair for five hours. During those five hours an analyst from the United Federation Bank had taken him through thirty balance sheets of various companies in Bombay, Delhi, Calcutta and Madras.

Murali had been very specific. 'Find me companies that are owner-driven, preferably by first-generation entrepreneurs. Show me balance sheets of companies that you would have no hesitation in lending to. Tell me about businesses that will be giants twenty years from today.'

The chairman of the United Federation Bank, Mr Kishore Deshmukh, was indebted to Abdul Dada. The strike by the UFB Bank Employees Union would have crippled the bank entirely had it not been for Abdul Dada's intervention. In his banking world, every credit needed a debit. Upon receiving a call from Abdul Dada, Deshmukh had immediately assigned his best financial analyst to Mr Murali Iyer.

'Parle Exports,' said Murali. 'They're working on an Indian cola.'

'Privately held by the Chauhan family. No outsiders hold shares,' replied the analyst.

'Vimal,' said Murali.

'You mean Reliance,' said the analyst. 'They'll go to the stock exchange soon. We'll pick up a huge chunk of shares for you during the IPO.'

'Godrej,' said Murali.

'Tightly owned by the Godrej family. Doesn't fit in with your criteria of first-generation. They were established in 1897.'

'Emami,' said Murali.

'Good option,' said the analyst. 'They're first-generation. Driven by two chaps who quit the Birla Group. They're in the process of acquiring another Ayurvedic company. They will need cash. I'll open discussions.'

'Kwality,' said Murali. 'The ice cream guys.'

'Started in 1940 by the Lamba family. Next generation has just entered the business. Will find out more.'

'Nirula's?' asked Murali.

'The fast-food company in Delhi? They don't need money. The single outlet at Connaught Place is raking it in. But I'll find out.'

'What else?' asked Murali.

'Ever heard of BRAID?' asked the analyst.

'Enlighten me,' said Murali.

'It's an acronym for B. Ravi And I. Daga. The company invests in ventures such as mining, edible oils, hotels, consumer goods and commodity speculation. Rarely talked about. Rather low-profile but very impressive returns.'

Arbaaz stood before the door to the apartment nervously. The nameplate on the door read K.C. Bannerjee. The apartment was located in Hyderabad Estate on Napean Sea Road. The ten-acre property had once belonged entirely to the Nizam of Hyderabad but had eventually become the site of dull and poorly maintained blocks of government quarters.

It had been several months since the incident. Paromita had withdrawn from the movies temporarily while Abdul Dada found himself another director. The gap suited her. She needed time to recover. The trauma of that terrible day had simply been too much to bear. She had wondered if she could ever tell her parents what had happened. How on earth was she to tell her mother, 'Your brother raped me and I told someone in the underworld who went after him and killed him for me?'

The flat in Bandra that she had bought with her Bollywood earnings was locked up. She simply couldn't bear living alone. She had shifted in with her parents at Hyderabad Estate.

Pinakin's body had never been found. The police file still listed the case as one of missing persons. Arbaaz took a deep breath and rang the bell, hoping that Paromita would open the door.

He was in luck. She opened the door but was taken aback to see him. 'Arbaaz, you? Here? My mother is at home!' she whispered.

'Relax, I'm leaving. I need to meet you. Whenever I call on the phone, someone sounding like your mother answers,' said Arbaaz.

'Who is it, Paromita?' came her mother's voice from within.

'Just someone doing a survey, Ma,' answered Paromita, a light smile playing on her lips.

'Will you meet me?' asked Arbaaz.

'Yes, I will,' replied Paromita. 'Now please... go.'

'When?' asked Arbaaz.

'Tomorrow... go.'

'I'll wait for you at Shamiana, the Taj coffeeshop tomorrow—Friday—at 5 pm,' said Arbaaz as he quickly turned around to briskly walk down the stairs the moment he saw Paromita's mother approaching.

Arbaaz and Paromita sat by the window table at the Shamiana. It had opened a few years back and had quickly become the go-to joint in Bombay. It was a new concept in which Gujarati wall hangings were used as canopies to create the effect of a tent—or *shamiana*—supported by dark maroon poles. Unlike other restaurants which attempted to project a Westernized image, the Shamiana menu unabashedly boasted of items like pav bhaji, Goa fish curry and masala dosa.

'I'm glad you came,' said Arbaaz, stirring several cubes of sugar into his cappuccino.

Paromita smiled. 'I couldn't thank you enough for what you did,' she said. 'I will never be able to settle the debt that I now owe you.'

'You owe me nothing,' said Arbaaz. 'I have a confession to make, though...'

'What?' asked Paromita.

'Ever since I saw you, I have felt strangely drawn towards you,' began Arbaaz hesitantly. 'I'm not really sure what it is and it's possible that given your circumstances you may say no to me... I'd really like to be your friend.'

'I'd like that too,' said Paromita, taking a sip of her Coke Float, Shamiana's famous concoction of Coca-Cola and vanilla ice cream.

There was a slight flutter in the restaurant as two khaki-clad policemen made their way towards the table at which Arbaaz sat. One of them was Deputy Commissioner of Police Sawant; the other was Sub-Inspector Waghamare.

'Arbaaz Sheikh?' asked DCP Sawant.

'Yes?' said Arbaaz, his heart beating wildly.

'I'm here to arrest you,' said Sawant.

'You have a warrant?' asked Arbaaz.

'It's a cognizable offence. We don't need a warrant,' said Sawant.

'What's the charge?' asked Arbaaz.

'Murder,' said Sawant.

Sitting a few tables away was a senior policeman in civvies. He smiled when he saw the man who had fucked up his career path being arrested. His name was Dube. *Revenge is sweet*, ex-Commissioner Dube thought as he sipped his own Coke Float.

Arbaaz was taken in a police jeep to Arthur Road Jail and booked under sections 302 for murder and 307 for attempt to murder as per the Indian Penal Code.

Paromita had been reluctant to leave. He had forced her to take a taxi back to her house and sit tight. He would get in touch with her after he was out.

'Take off your clothes,' said Sub-Inspector Waghamare to Arbaaz.

'Why?' asked Arbaaz. He received a resounding slap.

'I am not a fucking tour guide who explains everything,' said Waghamare, his breath reeking of paan and tobacco. 'We need to check for drugs, knives, guns and the like.'

Arbaaz stripped and was cavity-searched by a medical supervisor. The Sub-Inspector seemed to take sadistic pleasure from watching the supervisor probing Arbaaz's rectum. Once the checking was over, Arbaaz was given back his clothes to wear. His belongings—watch, wallet, cash, belt and pen—were taken from him and noted in a register that he was made to sign on.

'Take him to barrack eight,' said the Sub-Inspector to the warden. Arbaaz had heard of it. Drug addicts, ragpickers, beggars and rapists were usually lodged there. Arthur Road had an official capacity of around 800 prisoners but usually accommodated well over 3,000.

As expected, the barrack was overcrowded. As the gate slammed shut behind him, Arbaaz walked to a corner and sat down.

'That's *my* place. Get the fuck out of it,' said a hulk of a man. He was twice the size of Arbaaz and a terrible stink emanated from him—of stale urine.

'Go fuck yourself,' said Arbaaz. A low growl emanated from the hulk as he reached down to grab Arbaaz's shoulders and pull him up to give him the pummelling of his life. Before any of that could happen, Arbaaz swung his right hand viciously against the hulk's massive penis. The hulk doubled up in agony, giving Arbaaz just enough time to get up and kick his balls from behind. By now all the inmates had crowded around the hulk, who was lying on his side holding his balls. *Iqbal's training has finally paid off,* thought Arbaaz.

Arbaaz bent down and whispered into the hulk's ears, 'You look at me, I'll murder you. You touch me, I'll murder you. You mess with me, I'll murder you. Do you follow, *kutiya*? If not, I'll murder you.'

Standing up, Arbaaz announced to the inmates, 'I am Arbaaz Sheikh, right-hand man of Abdul Dada. No one, I repeat, *no one* here should fuck with me if they value their fucking lives.'

'Visitor for you,' shouted the voice of the warden. He was pointing at Arbaaz.

Arbaaz followed him to the Jail Superintendent's office. Sitting with the Superintendent was Abdul Dada and another man.

'Sit down,' said the Superintendent. Arbaaz occupied the third visitor chair. 'You are not supposed to be meeting me or anyone else right now. You are in police custody, not judicial. This is an unofficial meeting.'

'You were ratted out,' said Abdul. 'We can speak freely. The Superintendent is my old friend.'

'By whom?' asked Arbaaz wonderingly.

Abdul Dada looked Arbaaz in the eye and said, 'Hameed.'

'But why?' asked Arbaaz.

'He was never too happy with the new state of affairs after Mustafa died. He thought you had usurped his position. It's partly my fault. I should never have sent him with you when you went after that dog, Pinakin Deb.'

'So now what?' asked Arbaaz.

'With me is Mr Darius Dastur, one of the best lawyers in India. He has come from Calcutta on the request of Murali. He will do everything that is needed to set you free.'

'How long will I need to be here?' asked Arbaaz.

'Don't worry, son,' said the Superintendent. 'I will make sure that you get bedsheets, tea, decent food and playing cards—all of that *without* paying outrageous bribes to your barrack warden.'

'Superintendent,' said Abdul. 'Please shift him to the Boodha Barrack. You know—the one for senior citizens. That one is relatively clean and safe. Also, attach an inmate with him as his servant. I'll pay the fee. The fucking toilets in this hellhole are always overflowing. Get someone to clean them up before he has to use them. And get his cell fumigated for those bloodsucking *khatmal*s.'

'Yes, Dada, I'll see to it,' said the Superintendent.

'So when do I get out?' asked Arbaaz, ignoring the housekeeping instructions.

'You have been arrested under non-bailable sections of the IPC,' explained Mr Dastur. 'We need to first get you out of police custody and into judicial custody so that you can't be interrogated. We then need to apply for bail before the magistrate.'

'So when do I get out?' repeated Arbaaz.

'They have a detailed confession from Hameed. This case is not really difficult but you need to follow my instructions perfectly,' said Mr Dastur.

Abdul Dada quietly placed a bundle of notes wrapped in brown paper on Mr Dastur's lap. It was four times his usual fee.

'So when does he get out?' asked Abdul Dada.

'In a day if Arbaaz agrees to what I have in mind,' said Mr Dastur.

'I'll do whatever you ask,' said Arbaaz.

'First, narrate to me the exact conversation that happened with the police when you were arrested,' said Mr Dastur. Arbaaz spent the next ten minutes going over the events at the Shamiana.

Mr Dastur made careful notes.

He then asked Abdul Dada, 'Do you know the Magistrate? The one before whom Arbaaz will need to be produced tomorrow—Saturday?'

'He's straight as an arrow,' replied Abdul. 'If that's what you're asking.'

'In that case do you know who the Duty Magistrate for Sunday is?' he asked Abdul.

'Yes, but Arbaaz's matter won't be placed before him. In any case, the man's a twit. All that he likes doing is playing rummy,' answered Dada.

Turning to the Superintendent, Mr Dastur asked, 'Do you have a place where Arbaaz can hide?'

It was past midnight when he was woken up by his temporary servant. 'Superintendent has called for you.'

Arbaaz quietly made his way to the Superintendent's office. There were just the two of them waiting. Locking the door behind them, the Superintendent asked, 'Are you ready?'

'Sure,' replied Arbaaz, sitting down on the chair.

The Superintendent swung his fist into Arbaaz's face.

'Shit!' gasped Arbaaz. 'Did it have to be so hard?'

'We need to do this right,' said the Superintendent. 'Let me see your eye. Good. Now take off the shirt.'

Arbaaz pulled off his shirt, remaining seated.

The Superintendent picked up the plugged-in clothes iron and asked Arbaaz to bend over so that he could access Arbaaz's back. 'This will hurt but we'll keep it for less than three seconds. That should be sufficient,' said the Superintendent.

'It won't hurt as much as a prison sentence,' said Arbaaz, gritting his teeth. He wanted to scream as the hot iron was pressed into his back for a few seconds.

He felt slightly weak when he got up from the chair. The Superintendent helped him put his shirt back on. Arbaaz winced slightly as he felt the fabric graze his back.

'Now what?' asked Arbaaz.

'You will hide until 8 pm.'

'Where?'

'Right here in my office. It shall stay locked as I am supposed to be out of town for a conference. The canteen boy has left provisions in the cabinet. You can use the attached private toilet. The door will be locked from the outside.'

'Your honour, my client has been arrested on charges of murder and attempt to murder without the police having even found a body. Where is the murder?' said Mr Dastur.

The Magistrate looked at Mr Dastur and then the Public Prosecutor. 'What does the Public Prosecutor have to say?'

'Your honour, the body was roasted on a fire until it disintegrated into ashes. We have a detailed witness account from Mr Hameed Ibrahim. Given the fact that the body was charred to ashes, there can be no body,' said the Public Prosecutor confidently.

Mr Dastur was a tennis player and Wimbledon addict. *Love-Fifteen,* thought Mr Dastur to himself.

'Your honour, my client, Mr Arbaaz Sheikh, was arrested from a coffeeshop at the Taj Mahal Hotel. As you know there are five basic requirements for a proper arrest,' continued Mr Dastur. 'One: the right to see the warrant; two: the right to consult a lawyer of choice; three: the right to be informed about applicability of bail; four: the right to be informed of the reasons for his arrest…'

'Yes, yes, Mr Dastur, I am aware of the law,' interjected the Magistrate.

'Oh absolutely, I hope your honour will indulge me for a moment more,' continued Mr Dastur smoothly. 'And five: the right to be produced before a Magistrate within twenty-four hours of arrest…'

'What's your point?' asked the Magistrate.

'His offence was cognizable. Hence there was no warrant,' said Mr Dastur. 'So condition number one does not apply. He was allowed to see me, which means that the second condition was met. Given that the charge was for a non-bailable offence, the question of informing him about applicability of bail did not arise, hence condition number three was also met. Unfortunately, the same cannot be said for conditions four and five.'

'What do you mean?' asked the Magistrate.

'When he was arrested by DCP Sawant, my client specifically asked what the charge against him was. The DCP answered that it was murder.'

'Seems fine to me,' said the Magistrate.

'There were two charges against my client: Murder under section 302 of the Indian Penal Code and Attempt to Murder under section 307 of the Indian Penal Code. The DCP informed my client of the first but not of the second.'

'Is that true?' asked the Magistrate, looking at the Public Prosecutor who could be seen in a huddle with the DCP. They seemed to be having an animated discussion.

'I don't have all day,' said the Magistrate to the Public Prosecutor.

The Public Prosecutor cleared his throat and said, 'The arresting officer believes that he did inform the accused of both charges…'

'I have a witness—a lady who was having coffee along with my client—who will vouch for the fact that only one charge was communicated during arrest,' said Mr Dastur quickly.

'… but it's possible that the arresting officer may have slipped up,' completed the Public Prosecutor hastily.

The Magistrate took off his glasses and rubbed his eyes as he took a short break to consider the issue.

Fifteen-All, thought Mr Dastur.

The Magistrate put his spectacles back on. 'Carry on, Mr Dastur.'

'Thank you, your honour. As regards condition number five, my client was arrested at 5 o'clock in the evening on Friday. In accordance with the law he should have been produced before you by 5 o'clock on Saturday evening at the very latest.'

'Today is Monday,' noted the Magistrate. 'Why the delay?'

The Public Prosecutor coughed uncomfortably. 'Your honour, the accused was untraceable by the jail authorities until 8 o'clock on Saturday night. By that time it was too late to bring him before a Magistrate. This was followed by Sunday when you had your weekly off…'

'Why did you not place the matter before the Duty Magistrate on Sunday?' asked the Magistrate.

'He had called in sick,' replied the Public Prosecutor.

'Nonetheless, it is police carelessness that resulted in the accused remaining in police custody for far more time than the sanctioned limit,' said the Magistrate. 'What sort of prison are you running where prisoners are untraceable!'

Thirty-Fifteen, thought Mr Dastur.

'Anything else that you wish to say, Mr Dastur?' asked the Magistrate.

'Your honour, it pains me to bring this up,' began the crafty lawyer.

'Do go on,' urged the Magistrate helpfully.

'My client was viciously tortured while in police custody. If the court permits, I would like my client to stand before you,' said Mr Dastur.

'This is preposterous, your honour,' began the Public Prosecutor.

'Accused may approach the Bench,' said the Magistrate ignoring the Public Prosecutor. Arbaaz walked up to the Magistrate so that he could look at him from close quarters.

'What happened to your left eye?' asked the Magistrate when he saw the shiner.

'I'd rather not say, your honour,' said Arbaaz. *Do not say that the investigating officer beat you. That would be perjury.*

Arbaaz took off his shirt and turned around with his back towards the judge. Visible on his back was the burn mark of a clothes iron.

'Who did that to you?' asked the Magistrate.

'If I say anything, I might get beaten again,' said Arbaaz. *Remember that you don't need to respond to a question with a definite answer.*

Forty-Fifteen, thought Mr Dastur.

'Your honour,' interjected Mr Dastur. 'I would like to state that my client's life is at risk with the police. Arrest protocols have not been followed. The charges are trumped up on the basis of the confession of a known gangster, Mr Hameed Ibrahim, who has several criminal charges pending against him…'

'You want bail for your client?' asked the Magistrate.

'I don't want bail,' said Mr Dastur.

Arbaaz sucked in his breath. *What is this mad* Bawa *doing?*

'I want you to dismiss this sorry excuse of a case,' said Mr Dastur.

'I'm not sure I can do that,' said the Magistrate.

'Section 203 of the Criminal Procedure Code states, and I quote, *"If, after considering the statements on oath, if any, of the complainant and of the witnesses and the result of the inquiry or investigation, if any, under section 202, the Magistrate is of opinion that there is no sufficient ground for proceeding, he shall dismiss the complaint, and in every such case he shall briefly record his reasons for so doing."*'

The Magistrate considered Mr Dastur's submission.

'You *do* have the power, your honour,' urged Mr Dastur.

'It seems I do,' said the Magistrate.

Game, Set and Match.

Abdul Dada paid a visit to his house. The old man was overjoyed.

'How is the Monginis cake shop getting along?' asked Dada.

'Wonderful. My son has been promoted. He is now the manager.'

'And your grandson, Prasad? Which class is he now in?'

'He is no longer in school, Dada. He is now working as a shop floor supervisor at a printing press in Nashik.'

'How time flies,' said Abdul Dada, shaking his head. 'How old are you now?'

'Only eighty,' replied the old man with a grin. 'I'm still young at heart though.'

'When did you retire as a Judicial Magistrate?' asked Dada.

'Twenty years ago. The Sunday Duty Magistrate was my junior,' said the old man.

'What did you tell him?' asked Dada.

'Simply that he needed to call in sick for that particular day and spend the day playing rummy with me. He was delighted to do it.'

'Dube is the bastard who had me arrested,' said Arbaaz to Abdul Dada. 'He needs to be taught a lesson.'

'He simply got back at you for conning him into holding up the Chief Minister's car,' said Abdul. 'The matter is over. You screwed him. He screwed you.'

'He may become a pain in the future too. I need to set him right,' said Arbaaz.

'You've already done that. After his stint as Police Commissioner, he should have been promoted as Director of the Intelligence Bureau. That never happened.'

'True, but I'm informed that he will now be deputed to the Central Bureau of Investigation and will become a coordinator for all matters relating to Interpol. Not a good situation given our narcotics and smuggling trade. Better to be rid of him.'

'How many more people will you kill?' asked Abdul Dada, lighting up his cigar.

'I have no intention of killing him,' said Arbaaz. 'See this.'

Arbaaz placed a small box on Abdul Dada's desk. Abdul Dada looked at it and laughed. 'You think of everything. Go ahead and do it.'

Dube held his passport, ticket, boarding card and embarkation card while one of the constables carried his bag for him at Santa Cruz Airport. He was headed to London for an Interpol conference. That rascal Arbaaz Sheikh had screwed up Dube's career but he thanked his stars for resurrecting him from the ashes. It had been difficult but he had somehow muddled through. The Home Secretary had put in a word to the CBI Director who had recommended Dube's name as Interpol Coordinator.

Many of his erstwhile colleagues had come to the airport to see him off. It was a usual occurrence with Indians leaving on trips abroad. For every one individual who flew, another ten would come to see him off, many bearing kitschy garlands, flowers and useless gifts. *I'm about to board a flight and you expect me to lug on board the cheap bouquet that you bought near the airport taxi-stand?*

Among the individuals who came to the airport was Mr Sushil Tiwari, an Income Tax officer then with the Directorate of Inspection. Both men had known each other for many years because their families stayed in the same government quarters in Bombay. Mr Tiwari affectionately carried out a parting ritual for Mr Dube. It was a common tradition to offer the departing traveller a nibble of mithai while placing a vermillion tilak on his head and handing over a one-rupee coin. It was the customary way of wishing the traveller a safe voyage. 'Have a safe and successful trip,' said Mr Tiwari as he waved goodbye to Mr Dube.

Mr Dube cleared passport control in a jiffy. The immigration officer stamped his passport with the date of exit—5 April 1976. He was accompanied by the duty manager of the airport, so the security check was waived.

Just as they were about to proceed to the VIP lounge, a man tapped Mr Dube's shoulder from behind. 'Excuse me, sir, but I need to have a word.'

Mr Dube swung around to see a white-uniformed customs officer. His badge indicated that he was a Vigilance Officer. The Airport Duty Manager intervened. 'What seems to be the matter?'

'Please do not interfere,' said the Vigilance Officer to the Airport Duty Manager curtly. 'We have specific information that requires us to ask Mr Dube a few questions. Please accompany me, sir.'

'Do you know who I am?' asked Dube, visibly irritated.

'Of course, sir. Former Police Commissioner, presently on deputation with the CBI. Now, would you please accompany me, sir?'

Dube followed the Vigilance Officer to a small curtained booth. A stern look from the Vigilance Officer had ensured that the Airport Duty Manager had slunk away. 'Please empty your pockets and open your briefcase on the table,' said the Vigilance Officer.

'I am going to report this harassment to your seniors,' said Mr Dube angrily. 'I am being needlessly searched. A senior government functionary is being prevented from discharging his onerous duties by your callous attitude.'

'Sure, sir. You were about to have a cup of tea at the VIP lounge—an onerous duty indeed. You may submit your complaint to the Office of the Chief Commissioner of Customs, Zone III. Now, please empty your pockets and open your briefcase on the table,' said the Vigilance Officer with an unwavering expression.

Mr Dube realized that he had no alternative. He placed his briefcase on the table and opened it. He then took out the wallet from his back pocket, his keys, kerchief and pocket change from the front ones, and his pen and visiting cards from his shirt pocket, placing all of them on the table.

The Vigilance Officer scanned the material on the table. He quickly zeroed in on the coins and picked up a one-rupee coin. Holding it up, he examined both sides of the coin.

'This is a rare coin, sir,' said the Vigilance Officer. 'A one-rupee coin minted in 1875 with an image of Queen Victoria engraved on the head.'

Mr Dube looked at it. 'That's not mine. It belongs to my friend, Mr Tiwari. He gave it to me as a parting good luck gift. He knows that I like old coins.'

'It does not matter how the coin came into your possession, sir,' said the Vigilance Officer. 'It's an offence to be carrying this coin out of Indian territory under the Antiquities and Art Treasures Act.'

'Don't be ridiculous,' said Mr Dube. 'That Act only comes into force on... on...'

'Let me refresh your memory, sir,' said the Vigilance Officer. The Antiquities and Art Treasures Act was passed by the Indian Parliament four years ago, in 1972. It came into force on 5 April 1976. Today is the 5th.'

'But—but—this is hardly an antique. There are hundreds of East India Company coins in this country!' sputtered Mr Dube.

The Vigilance Officer handed over a small booklet to Mr Dube. It was a copy of the Antiquities and Art Treasures Act, 1972. 'Please read the underlined portions,' he said. Mr Dube looked at the underlined bits.

'... in this Act, unless the context otherwise requires "antiquity" includes any coin, sculpture, painting, epigraph or other work...

'... it shall come into force in the whole of India (except the State of Sikkim) with effect from 5 April 1976.

'... any article, object or thing declared by the Central Government to be an antiquity for the purposes of this Act, which has been in existence for not less than one hundred years...'

'What year is engraved on the coin?' asked the Vigilance Officer, taking back his booklet.

'1875,' said Mr Dube, scrutinizing the coin.

'Which year are we in?' asked the Vigilance Officer.

'1976,' replied Mr Dube.

'Your coin is 101 years old—in effect, more than a hundred years old,' said the Vigilance Officer. He flipped to another page of the booklet and handed it back to Mr Dube. 'Read the underlined bit,' he said.

'If any person, himself or by any other person on his behalf, exports or attempts to export any antiquity or art treasure in contravention of Section 3, he shall, without prejudice to any confiscation or penalty, be punishable with imprisonment for a term which shall not be less than six months but which may extend to three years.'

'Proceedings of the fifth Annual General Meeting of the shareholders of B. Ravi And I. Daga Private Limited held on 18 August 1976 at 10 am at the Oberoi Grand Hotel, Calcutta,' noted the secretary, Hilda Fonseca, as Arvind looked on.

'Attendance: 116 shareholders or their proxies holding 25,000 shares and representing 100 per cent of the Share Capital. The chairman of the Board, Mr Arvind Bagadia, opened the meeting and took the chair. He welcomed the shareholders and formally introduced the directors on the dais.'

'Mr Joydeep Chakraborty, vice-chairman.'
My trusted friend, thought Arvind.

'Mr Satyapal Mittal, managing director.'

My brilliant salesman, thought Arvind.

'Mr Brijmohanlal Bagadia, partner, Bagadia & Co.'
My patient father, thought Arvind.

'Mr Darius Dastur, partner, Digby & Dastur.'
My astute lawyer, thought Arvind.

'Mr Kishore Deshmukh, chairman, United Federation Bank.'
My resourceful banker, thought Arvind.

'Mr Tarachand Agarwal, chief accountant, Bagadia & Co.'
My clever Munimji, thought Arvind.

'Pursuant to Section 174 of the Companies Act 1956, the chairman announced that the necessary quorum was present and that timely notice of the meeting had been given as per Section 171. He accordingly declared the meeting in order.

'The chairman commenced his address to the shareholders by summarizing the events of the year gone by. In particular he drew the attention of shareholders to the fact that India had carried out its first nuclear test, Smiling Buddha, the previous year and had launched its first satellite, Aryabhatta, earlier in the year. These developments augured well for the country's progress. He then discussed the company's financial results for 1974—75 and the outlook for the next financial year. He underlined the fact that the company would not get into permanent businesses but only those in which a high exit valuation was possible.'

Our business is not to buy or sell things; our business is to buy and sell businesses, thought Arvind.

'The chairman was happy to bring to the attention of shareholders the fact that Rs 100 invested in the company in 1960 was now worth Rs 29,192, representing a compounded annual growth rate of 50 per cent annually, an achievement unparalleled in the Indian corporate sector.'

A good growth rate is achieved by knowing the rules; a great growth rate is achieved by knowing the exceptions, thought Arvind.

'The AGM then proceeded to the items of business listed in the published agenda:

One: Approval of the previous year's annual report and financial statements.

Two: Vote on appropriation of available earnings and dividend declaration.

Three: Appointment of statutory auditors for the current year.

Four: Re-election of directors whose tenures had ended.

'All necessary resolutions were passed by a vote of 25,000 in favour with nil abstentions. The chairman then left the floor open for shareholders.'

Mr Tarachand Agarwal rose to speak. 'While all of us are delighted with your progress, Arvind Babu, I would like to take this opportunity to congratulate you on the three new Income Tax assessments.'

'New assessments?' asked Arvind. 'We've not incorporated any new companies or firms.'

'I meant the arrival of your two sons—Vinay and Vinit,' said Munimji, smiling.

Arvind laughed while his shareholders clapped. 'Thank you, Munimji. Yes, it's true that my wife Abhilasha and I have been blessed with a pair of identical twins. But Munimji, even if we start their Income Tax files, that's still only two.'

'Under the Income Tax Act 1961, you are allowed to create an HUF—Hindu Undivided Family—as a third assessee, hence my congratulations for three assessments,' said Munimji as he sat down.

One of the proxies from Bombay, Mr Murali Iyer, representing Dhanda Holdings Private Limited, suggested that the company should be listed on the Bombay Stock Exchange without delay in order to release shareholder value. The chairman was in concurrence and indicated that plans for an Initial Public Offering were underway.

Before the close of the meeting, Mr Kishore Deshmukh praised the chairman's tremendous experience, entrepreneurial vision and impressive leadership capabilities and congratulated him on the dramatic results that he had produced.

There being no further requests to speak, the chairman thanked the shareholders for attending and closed the meeting at noon. He then announced that lunch had been organized in the adjoining room. He also announced that a special screening of *Sholay*—that was completing fifty-two weeks at the box office—had been arranged for the shareholders at 3 pm at Jyoti Cinema.

Arvind and Abhilasha got into the backseat of his car. Vinay and Vinit had been bundled up into matching blue jumper suits. Arvind held Vinay while Abhilasha held Vinit. Vinay was the older one, having arrived at 10.47 am, a full minute before Vinit, who emerged at 10.48.

Another car would follow theirs, the second car carrying the two maids who took care of the boys. They were headed to Tarakeshwar, around fifty-eight kilometres away from Calcutta. Located in the Hooghly district, Tarakeshwar owed its name to the Taraknath Temple built by Raja Bharamalla in 1729. It was Shivratri and Abhilasha had promised Lord Shiva that she would go there and perform a puja during Shivratri if he blessed her with a child. He had blessed her with two so the promised contractual obligation had to be fulfilled.

Just as the driver was about to pull out of the porch, their old servant came running up. ‘Arvind Babu, there’s an urgent call for you,’ he panted.

‘Give me a minute,’ said Arvind, handing over Vinay to Abhilasha. He got out of the car and went to the phone that sat on a highly-polished teakwood credenza near the stairs. He picked up the phone and listened.

He walked back to the car where Abhilasha awaited with the boys. ‘You carry on, Abhilasha,’ he said. ‘I need to go to the office for ten minutes. I need to sign some papers urgently.’

‘Will you follow?’ asked Abhilasha, a tad irritated.

‘I’ll be there an hour after you,’ said Arvind as he signalled the chauffeur to proceed with Abhilasha and the boys in the car.

Abhilasha knew that he would not come. It was the same pattern that invariably repeated itself.

The premiere of *Dharti Aur Aakash* starring Vinod Khanna, Paromita Bannerjee and Prem Chopra was held at Eros Cinema in October 1978. Because it was a premiere, the audience would be spared the usual ads by Vicco Vajradanti, Gold Spot, Nirma and Four Square.

A huge cut-out of Vinod Khanna had been perched atop the building while the name of the movie was proudly displayed in black cut-out letters placed carefully in white channels above the theatre’s entrance.

Paromita knew that it was probably the last movie she would act in. She was in her thirties and Bollywood was notorious for discarding heroines at the peak of their careers.

Everyone who was someone was present. This movie was director Avijit Basu's follow-up film to his massive 1976 hit *Meri Prem Kahani*. Paromita sat in the front row along with the director and her co-stars. Also seated in the front row were Arbaaz and Abdul Dada who had saved the film from financial ruin after Pinakin Deb's 'sudden disappearance'. Most people in Abdul Dada's team refused to call it murder because that would only implicate Arbaaz. In any case, these days the newspapers were entirely focused on Billa—Ranga, a brutal rapist-cum-murderer duo.

Seated behind Paromita on the second row should have been her parents. It would have been a proud moment for them but it was not to be. Having barely recovered from the trauma of the Pinakin incident and Arbaaz's arrest, Paromita had been delivered yet another body blow. Paromita's father, K.C. Bannerjee, had been promoted by the Indian government and had been invited to attend a conference in New York earlier that year. Unfortunately, the Air India flight 855 which Paromita's parents boarded had crashed off the coast of Bandra on New Year's Day of 1978, barely a few minutes after take-off. All 213 passengers and crew on board had perished.

Paromita had requested for the premiere of the movie to be delayed and Avijit had obliged her by pushing it a few months later into the year.

Paromita had always kept her friendship with Arbaaz secret from her parents. Her father was a Bengali Brahmin who proudly traced his descent from Rarheya Brahmins of the Shandilya clan of Kannauj. He would never have accepted the notion of his daughter having a Muslim boyfriend or marrying a Muslim man. But with her parents gone, Arbaaz had ended up becoming her only source of support and solace.

Six months after the death of her parents, Paromita moved out of the flat allotted to her father in Hyderabad Estate. She sold her own locked-up flat in Bandra and bought herself a small apartment in Colaba, just one floor above Arbaaz's house. She furnished it rather simply, using some of the furniture that had belonged to her parents. On the day she moved in, she organized a small puja ceremony followed by lunch. Arbaaz, his mother, the director Avijit Basu and a few of Paromita's colleagues from the sets had attended.

After everyone left, she cleared away the dishes and cleaned up the apartment. She was wealthy enough to hire domestic help but there was comfort in loneliness. She put on the headphones of her Walkman, a Japanese gadget that Arbaaz had gifted her on her birthday. She placed an audio cassette of ABBA in it and began listening to her favourite track, *'Take a Chance on Me'*, while contemplating which book would be her friend for the night.

As the track ended she heard the doorbell ringing. Looking through the peephole she saw Arbaaz standing at the door. Excitedly, she opened the door and fell into his arms. 'I was worried,' he said. 'I've been ringing the bell for several minutes.'

'Your fault for giving me that contraption,' she said smiling. There was an awkward pause. *What the fuck is wrong with you? You're behaving like a schoolboy,* thought Arbaaz to himself.

Paromita cut short his reverie by kissing him. That night was the very first time that they made love. She had been worried about whether she would ever be able to let another man touch her after the repugnant incident with Pinakin. But Arbaaz was caring and gentle and she forgot that terrible day as soon as Arbaaz kissed her. She even forgot all the other men that she had slept with during her film career.

The next morning she awoke to find that Arbaaz had made tea for her. 'I could get used to this,' she laughed, pushing her hair away from her face.

'So could I,' he said simply.

'The madarchod is likely to get out on bail,' said Arbaaz, as he drummed his fingers on the steering wheel of the Datsun Bluebird. He was talking about Hameed.

Abdul Dada was sitting in the passenger seat next to him. The car was parked at Bandra's Drive-In theatre. Though the capacity was 800 cars, the response to that night's show seemed lukewarm. Arbaaz had rolled down the window so that the speaker mounted on the pole at every parking slot could be heard. The movie playing was *Muqqadar ka Sikandar* starring Amitabh Bachchan, Vinod Khanna, Raakhee, Rekha and Amjad Khan.

Around them were assorted cars with assorted occupants. Some people had got out of their cars and were seated on folding chairs. Others had clambered up to their roofs. Cars parked in the distance contained couples who were looking for that little extra privacy.

Hameed had turned approver in order to supply evidence against Arbaaz but then the case against Arbaaz had been dismissed by the Magistrate. The angry cops had locked up Hameed for past crimes that were not covered by the pardon. After he had cooled his heels for a couple of years, the news was that he would be out in a couple of days.

'How do you want to play it?' asked Abdul Dada.

'I want to rip off his balls,' said Arbaaz, simply.

'Not a good idea to be angry,' said Abdul Dada. 'Retribution is like ice cream. It tastes terrible if it's melted.'

'What do you suggest, Dada?' asked Arbaaz.

'The two men I trusted—Mustafa and Hameed—are no longer with us. Murali is smart but can't really handle the heavy lifting. Your friend from the docks is still around?'

'Raju?' asked Arbaaz.

Abdul Dada nodded. 'You can be a capable general only if you have a strong army…'

'You are the general, Dada, not me!' said Arbaaz.

'Thank you, but I'm more like a field marshal.'

'What's that?' asked Arbaaz.

'It's like a lifetime achievement award,' explained Abdul Dada, savouring his cigar. Apparently, the ones he smoked were hand-rolled on a Cuban woman's thigh. That simple fact excited the don no end. 'It means that I don't have to really do anything. You do it for me. So you're the general. But where's your colonel?'

'Raju's almost fifty years old,' said Arbaaz.

'So what? One can only begin to pick up speed when one is over the hill,' said Dada. 'One more thing… '

'Yes, Dada?'

'You need to set up a meeting with the Shiv Sena bosses,' said Dada. 'I know that Keshav Gadgil, one of their top leaders, would be happy to meet you.'

'Why would we want to meet them?' asked Arbaaz. 'They've always had a pro-Hindu agenda.'

'Politics is like theatre,' said Abdul. 'Each politician plays his part according to the lines that are given to him. But backstage, the hero and the villain enjoy their drink together. And remember one thing that was said by some philosopher or the other: when it's a question of money, everybody is of the same religion.'

'But what do we need them for?' asked Arbaaz.

'We are in dhanda—in business,' said Abdul. 'We need to be friends with everyone from every political party.'

'But why the Shiv Sena?' persisted Arbaaz.

'You live in Bombay,' said Abdul. 'Your business operates from Bombay. Don't expect to achieve much in this city without political friendships. At the top of that list is the party of Balasaheb Thackeray.'

'How did he die?' asked Abdul Dada.

'Two men walked into this hotelier's office and shot him at point-blank range,' said Arbaaz.

'Had he contracted us to settle his property dispute?' asked Abdul.

Arbaaz nodded.

'His partner was not agreeing to go along with the expansion of the hotel even though all municipal permissions had come through. He asked us to persuade his partner.'

'Which means that his partner decided to use someone else,' observed Abdul. 'Who?'

'Dawood Ibrahim,' answered Arbaaz.

'How can we be sure?' asked Abdul.

'He's keen to control the narcotics, contract-killing and extortion businesses. With this single killing, he has achieved something in all three areas.'

'How?' asked Abdul.

'First: he took a *supari* and executed our man,' said Arbaaz. 'The word is out that it was a contract-killing. Second: he was keen on acquiring the hotel property. His extortion tactics worked. Third: the hotel is the single-biggest narcotics trading hub. He now has it.'

Dawood Ibrahim had become bigger than the mobster who had trained him—Haji Mastan. In recent years he had established control over *hawala* channels—the commonly used underground system for transferring money globally.

'Let him take the narcotics, extortion and contract-killing business,' said Abdul Dada. 'We don't need it. Focus on gambling and land banks.'

'Why cede space to him?' asked Arbaaz.

'Because he's bad news,' replied Abdul. 'You and I will never kill without a reason. This man can and does. The days when the mafia operated with a code of ethics are over.'

Arbaaz nodded.

'I need you, Raju,' said Arbaaz, placing a paan offered by Raju into his mouth. He didn't really care for the stuff but didn't want Raju to feel offended.

'I'm a simple dockhand, Arbaaz,' said Raju.

'And I'm Mother Teresa.'

Raju laughed. 'I'll come. I'll be your deputy but only on one condition.'

'What?' asked Arbaaz.

'Marry that woman. She's so pretty.'

Arbaaz laughed. Raju was talking about Paromita. Arbaaz owed his first sexual experience to Raju who had taken him to Bachchuseth ki Wadi and Bilqis Begum.

'I wish people placed more conditions like that one before me,' said Arbaaz.

He paused. 'This new man Dawood Ibrahim has suddenly become very active in Bombay.'

'How do you want to play it?' asked Raju.

'Let him take over the narcotics, contract-killing and extortion businesses,' said Arbaaz. 'I would much rather control gambling and land banks with you in charge of them. The money from these businesses will flow to Murali who will give it a legitimate face. In the next few years, I will be seen as a businessman rather than an underworld chief.'

Raju nodded. 'You're sure about ceding ground to Dawood? Abdul Dada is fine with it?'

'Yes,' replied Arbaaz. 'It's his idea. There is a time and place for everything and Dada has understood that better than me. Now listen, I need you coordinate this little matter.'

'Hameed?' asked Raju.

'How did you know?' asked Arbaaz.

'News is that he's getting out soon,' shrugged Raju. 'Any of your boys inside Arthur Road?'

'Some at Yerwada, others at Byculla and Nagpur,' replied Arbaaz. 'They shifted out our men when Hameed went in.'

'The canteen operator is loyal to the Shiv Sena,' said Raju. If you can use your relationship with the local Shiv Sena *Shakha Pramukh* to make an introduction, it could help.'

'I can do that. Ever since Abdul Dada told me, I have established relationships at various levels, especially with Keshav Gadgil. But even if I get you access to the canteen operator, the jail staff will look the other way but won't help stamp out the cockroach for us,' said Arbaaz.

'So let's not stamp out the cockroach,' said Raju. 'Fumigation should do the trick.'

'Fumigation?' asked Arbaaz.

'Herbal remedy. Ever heard of *tilpushpi*?'

Hameed counted his coupons. One could only use the damn coupons at the canteen inside the jail premises. One could buy milk, biscuits, bread, butter and cigarettes using them.

The fucking place is a shithole, thought Hameed. One had to almost stand to use the toilet because of the massive pile-up of excrement. He was lodged in barrack number eleven and it was packed like a tin of sardines. At night the men were required to sleep in three parallel rows, maintaining a four-inch gap between one inmate's foot and the other's head. The guards never turned off the lights for reasons of security. It was impossible to sleep. The food was terrible—usually watery dal, bland veggies, rice and leathery chapattis—and it was always served in filthy aluminium bowls. *What am I, a dog?*

Hameed handed over his remaining coupon to the canteen operator and eagerly took the Charminar cigarette from him. The canteen sold the cigarettes as singles only. He used the smouldering end of the coir rope that hung in the corner to light up longingly, his moustache quivering and his hands trembling in anticipation of the nicotine rush.

He took a deep breath, allowing the smoke to flood his lungs before falling dead to the ground.

The autopsy showed that he had inhaled the fumes of foxglove, a herbaceous short-lived perennial plant. It was called digitalis in the West but Indians had known it for ages as tilpushpi.

Much had happened during the two years when *Dharti Aur Aakash* had been in production.

The year 1977 had seen Indira Gandhi voted out and the Janata Party voted in. Morarji Desai had taken oath as Prime Minister. The 'illiterate' masses of India had shown that they could use their votes to punish errant governments intelligently.

In the corporate world, Coca-Cola and IBM had been asked to quit India by the new Minister for Industries, George Fernandes. In the meantime, a new company called Reliance Textiles Industries Ltd, promoted by someone called Dhirubhai Ambani, had made an Initial Public Offering in the capital market. Dhirubhai was already quite famous as the owner of the 'Vimal' brand and the issue was oversubscribed seven times. One of the significant subscribers to the issue was a company called Dhanda Holdings Private Limited.

Four months after the Reliance IPO, a lesser-known company called Braid Investments, BRAID being an acronym for 'B. Ravi And I. Daga', had also quietly listed on the Bombay Stock Exchange. The issue was oversubscribed only twice. The main subscriber to the issue was Dhanda Holdings Private Limited.

The next year, in 1978, American President Jimmy Carter had paid the country a visit. His otherwise boring speeches had been made more interesting by the microphone catching him unawares. He had forgotten to turn off the microphone while whispering to his aides that a 'cold and blunt message' ought to be delivered to India over its nuclear ambitions. It had probably made the Foreign Minister, a fifty-four-year-old man called Atal Bihari Vajpayee, laugh heartily over his evening tipple.

More importantly, *Dharti Aur Aakash* became a massive hit. Due to bad marketing and lacklustre reviews, it saw rather poor collections in its first two weeks. From the third week, however, audiences increased. This was primarily due to positive word of mouth. The movie was spurred on by a soundtrack release and the film was soon being called a blockbuster. It would end up running in theatres for over a hundred weeks. With the success of the movie, Paromita also became an overnight sensation. Thus her forthcoming court marriage to a Muslim man with a shady underworld connection became the juiciest news in India.

Both Arbaaz and Paromita had decided that they would retain their respective religious identities. Thus the easiest way to get married was a court wedding.

'You do realize that my world is dark and murky?' asked Arbaaz.

'Maybe I'll let in some light?' replied Paromita. She knew of Arbaaz's reputation. The moment his name was mentioned it caused an abrupt 'Oh!' among people. The tone was usually one of fear and awe.

On a cool, breezy day of December 1978, Arbaaz and Paromita stepped out of a Mercedes-Benz car loaned by Abdul Dada and walked into the Old Customs House, a stone's throw away from the docks where Arbaaz's story had commenced.

Three witnesses were needed to solemnize the marriage. Abdul Dada, Shabana and Avijit Basu had done the honours. The bride and groom had signed their marriage certificate and read out an oath before the Marriage Officer. 'You are now husband and wife under the Special

Marriage Act of 1954,' he had informed them. Arbaaz and Paromita had placed garlands of roses around each other's necks and the deed was done. Cold drinks—a new fizzier cola called Thums Up—and Cadbury chocolates were served to everyone present. Then they stepped out of the courthouse.

Hundreds of photographers descended upon them, hoping to get the perfect shot for the next day's papers. They quickly got into the car and headed to a suite at the newly opened Sea Rock Hotel in Bandra. A grand wedding reception had been organized for the evening at the Sea Rock because most of the Bollywood crowd stayed in the vicinity.

Just before the reception started, Abdul Dada had placed a sealed envelope in Arbaaz's hand. 'My wedding gift,' he said simply.

The second person to meet Arbaaz was Keshav Gadgil of the Shiv Sena. 'Balasaheb conveys his regards. He is unable to come due to a family commitment. He wishes both of you a long and happy married life.'

The reception venue had been lavishly done up with flowers. 'I love flowers,' said Paromita, looking around the ballroom.

'Then you must also love funerals,' joked Arbaaz. 'Lots of flowers there, too.'

Paromita pretended to slap him for his impertinence. 'There's a big difference between a wedding and a funeral,' she said.

'What?' asked Arbaaz.

'You can pick your own flowers for your wedding,' she joked.

The next day the newlyweds took a flight to Switzerland—usually pronounced as *shwee-jar-land* in most Bollywood flicks—for their honeymoon.

Seated in the upper deck lounge for first class passengers of the Jumbo 747, Arbaaz suddenly asked, 'May I tell you something?'

'Sure,' said Paromita.

'You have the prettiest smile I've ever seen,' he said earnestly.

Paromita froze and a wave of guilt washed over her as she remembered Arvind.

Arvind looked at the newspaper before him. 'Paromita Ties the Knot' was the headline. It was accompanied by a picture of Paromita and her husband emerging from the courthouse looking very happy as newlyweds.

She still looks so beautiful, thought Arvind.

Arvind felt sad. Then he felt angry. Actually, he didn't really know what he felt. He looked at the picture of her husband again. The face looked very familiar. He read the report beneath the photograph.

The marriage of the year happened yesterday in Bombay. Paromita Bannerjee, the leading lady of Dharti Aur Aakash, *tied the knot with Bombay businessman Arbaaz Sheikh. The romance had been the talk of the town for several months but the suddenness of the wedding announcement caught everyone off guard. Present to bless the couple was Abdul Rahim, Bombay's much-feared don. Inside sources reveal that Arbaaz Sheikh is tipped to be Abdul's successor although the recent rise to prominence of Dawood Ibrahim may interfere with such plans. It would be recalled that Arbaaz Sheikh was arrested a few years ago on murder charges that were eventually dropped.*

Arvind racked his brain. *Arbaaz Sheikh, where had he heard the name?* He had not just heard the name but had seen the man, his face looked so familiar.

Then he remembered his flight from Bombay to Hyderabad.

The windows of the Intensive Care Unit at the Breach Candy Hospital overlooked the Arabian Sea but none of the patients could really enjoy the view from their beds. Inside the ICU, on a metal bed, lay Abdul Dada. His ghazal-singer mistress sat outside in the ICU lobby. His wife had been informed of his condition and she had apparently said, 'I'm not coming to the hospital to see him. I'll wait for the funeral.'

Arbaaz and Paromita had arrived on the very first flight that they could get, cutting short their intended month-long honeymoon by a week the moment they received the news.

The month had been a hectic one for Abdul Dada in Arbaaz's absence because the old man was no longer attuned to operating without the younger man by his side. To add to his woes, the Reserve Bank of India had decided to demonetize currency notes of 1,000, 5,000 and 10,000. It was being done with a view to curbing the circulation of unaccounted money. People holding these notes were required to exchange them at banks after providing an explanation about the source of funds. This, quite obviously, was impossible for Abdul Dada's operations. Murali had swung into action and bought up vast quantities of gold and silver for Dada, thus temporarily solving his problem. Dada had simply sat in his office rolling cigarettes from the unused notes and smoking them.

Unfortunately, the pressure—and possibly the currency cigarette smoke—had triggered a heart attack in Abdul Dada. He had been rushed in an ambulance to the hospital where a new procedure known as coronary bypass surgery had been carried out on him. The surgeon working on him was one who had pioneered the treatment in India three years earlier.

'How is he?' asked Arbaaz anxiously.

The surgeon looked at the clipboard. He then measured his words carefully. 'Post-operative atrial fibrillation is the most common adverse event among patients. We will need to observe him carefully for the next five days.'

Arbaaz spent the night at the hospital, curled up on one of the uncomfortable chairs of the ICU lobby after sending Paromita home. The next morning he caught the surgeon on his rounds.

'How is he?' he asked again, with mounting anxiety.

'He's had acute renal failure and so we've hooked him up to the dialysis machine. We're keeping him under close observation.'

Arbaaz went home, showered and returned to the hospital, after being forced to eat lunch by his mother who had temporarily moved into Paromita's apartment. He spent another night on the uncomfortable chair but was instantly alert by the time the doctor came around the next morning.

'How is he?' asked Arbaaz.

'We're seeing a nosocomial infection which is quite common to one in five cardiac surgery patients. We can only observe for the moment.'

Arbaaz stayed on. Murali and Raju dropped by to report on various matters. They had tea together from the snack cart downstairs. Arbaaz saw the doctor walking towards him. Arbaaz put down his cup and strode up to him.

'How is he?' asked Arbaaz.

'Unfortunately, he's passed away,' said the doctor.

'Are you still planning to keep him under observation?' asked Arbaaz angrily, tears streaming down his cheeks as he mourned the man who had given him the love of a father.

Bombay had started out as seven islands separated by mosquito-infested swamps. The area was originally part of Ashoka's Mauryan Empire but in 1343, the islands were conquered by the Sultan of Gujarat. Two hundred years later, the Portuguese seized the islands and set up a trading centre there. They called the area *Bom Bahia*—meaning 'the good bay'.

Bom Bahia grew steadily along with the trade of silk, muslin, rice, cotton, chintz, onyx and tobacco. By 1661, Bom Bahia had a massive warehouse, a friary and a shipyard. Houses and mansions had also started appearing for the prosperous merchants who lived there. In that year, King Charles II of England married Catherine of Braganza. Catherine's family handed over Bom Bahia to the English king who had no desire to rule the mosquito-infested swamps. He quickly handed over the islands to the East India Company for a rent of ten pounds of gold each year. The English called the islands Bombay.

Bombay was a deep-water port and great ships could dock there. So the East India Company set about building a fort, a quay, warehouses and a customs house besides equipping it with a garrison of 1,500 soldiers for defence. This was followed by linking causeways, a church, a hospital, and a mint. By 1675, Bombay's population was 60,000 and the East India Company had made it their Indian headquarters. After an attack by Mughal forces, the Company created a fleet, called the Bombay Marine, to patrol the Malabar coast. Bombay was now entirely secure.

The result was that all types of people—goldsmiths, weavers, ironsmiths, merchants, shipbuilders and moneylenders—moved into the city. Massive engineering projects were undertaken and by 1854 the seven islands had become one large island with the swamps having been filled up. In 1853, the city got its first railway line, from Bombay to Thana, and a year later it got its first cotton mill.

The cotton mill needed workers, and labourers came from various parts of the country. One of them was Muhammad Rahim. He died in 1903, leaving behind several children. One of them was Aazam Rahim who flourished as a petty thief until he died of cholera in 1946, a year short of Independence. Aazam never married but had an illegitimate son from a prostitute. His name was Abdul Rahim, but everyone would eventually know him as Abdul Dada.

Abdul Dada married a woman called Zeenat. She bore him a son and a daughter. The son died in her womb while the daughter died during childbirth, when her breath was suffocated by the umbilical cord during delivery. Bitter and sad, Zeenat led a lonely existence which became even lonelier when Abdul Dada left her for his mistress.

His death in 1978 was the end of an era.

Arbaaz had not bothered to open the sealed envelope handed over to him by Abdul Dada but his passing away forced him to. Inside it was a simple two-page legal document, typed on a Godrej typewriter. It was Dada's will.

I, Abdul Rahim, aged eighty-one years, a Muslim adult and Indian inhabitant residing at Hill Road, Bandra, Bombay

400050, do hereby revoke all my previous Wills, Codicils and writings of testamentary nature and declare these presents to be my last Will and Testament.

1. *I appoint my trusted lieutenant, Arbaaz Sheikh, to be the Executor of this Will.*

2. *It is my desire that upon my demise all my rights, title, interest in the house that I own in Dongri and the rights and benefits incidental thereto including the right to use and occupy on ownership basis the said premises shall devolve upon and stand bequeathed to my wife, Begum Zeenat Rahim.*

3. *It is my desire that upon my demise all my rights, title, interest in the house that I own in Bandra and the rights and benefits incidental thereto including the right to use and occupy on ownership basis the said premises shall devolve upon and stand bequeathed to my loving companion, Anjum Azad.*

4. *I am the sole shareholder of Dhanda Holdings Private Limited owning all 1,000 shares of the said company. It is my desire that upon my demise all my shares in the company together with rights and benefits incidental thereto shall devolve upon and stand bequeathed to the son that I never had, my trusted lieutenant, Arbaaz Sheikh.*

5. *Any further assets remaining after disbursing my just debts and liabilities including taxes shall also devolve and stand bequeathed to Arbaaz Sheikh.*

In witness whereof, I, the said Abdul Rehman, has hereunto set my hand at Bombay this 21st day of December, 1978.

He had signed the will on the day that Arbaaz got married. Arbaaz cried softly as he realized that he had lost his second father.

More than half of the *Times of India* was filled with photographs of the glittering event that had been held the previous night at Shanmukhananda Hall. The lead story said:

The 26th Filmfare Awards were held at the Shanmukhananda Hall yesterday. Raj Khosla's Main Tulsi Tere Aangan Ki *was named the Best Film of the Year. Amitabh Bachchan won his second consecutive Best Actor Award for his double role in* Don. *Satyajit Ray won his sole Best Director Award for* Shatranj Ke Khiladi. *Paromita Bannerjee won her first Best Actress Award for her role in* Dharti Aur Aakash. *Both Paromita and her husband Arbaaz Sheikh were seen at the function…*

817 CE, Kannauj

ॐ त्रियम्बकं यजामहे

सुगन्धिं पुष्टिवर्धनं ।

उर्वारुकमिव बन्धनान्

मृत्योर्मोक्षिय मामृतात् ॥

'Paramabhattaraka, Maharajadhiraja, Paramesvara, Nagavaloka!'

The titles were announced by the court crier in his usual resounding voice as King Nagabhata II walked up to his throne without the slightest hint of a hunch or slouch. It was thus ironic that Nagabhata's capital was known by the unfortunate epithet of *The City of Hunchbacked Girls.*

According to legend, an infuriated rishi had cursed the hundred daughters of the town's ruler thus turning them all into hunchbacks. Since then, the town had been known as *Kanyakubja,* or the city of hunchbacked girls. It would eventually come to be known by a shortened version of the epithet: *Kannauj.*

The Rajasuya ceremony was in progress. A series of ritual offerings during the preceding year had concluded with divine power being taken on by the king. As the priests chanted mantras comparing the monarch with Indra and Prajapati, the king took three steps on a tiger's skin. By virtue of those three steps, the king was now an incarnate of Vishnu, whose three paces covered earth and heaven. The Brahmins chanted one final hymn:

Of mighty power is he who has been consecrated
Now he has become one of yours
And you must protect him

The king sat down and smiled at his courtiers. It was a confident smile, that of a victor. The previous year, he had captured Kannauj from Chakrayudha, who had crumbled before his army in spite of the protection that he enjoyed of the Pala rulers.

'Today, I wish to pay my thanks to Shiva, whose blessings have made the Pratihara kingdom prosperous,' began the king. 'Our beloved Somnath temple was destroyed by Junaid, the wicked Arab governor of Sind, about a century ago. That sacrilege still rankles me each day of my life. It shall be my highest priority to restore the abode of Shiva to its fullest glory!'

'Paramabhattaraka, Maharajadhiraja, Paramesvara, Nagavaloka!' chanted the court in unison.

'Precious offerings must be made available to the Lord,' continued Nagabhata. 'I am happy to announce that the revenue of 10,000 villages shall be provided for the construction and upkeep of this temple. A thousand Brahmins will be employed in the service of the Lord and 500 maidens shall sing and dance for his pleasure. In order to ensure that no human can easily destroy it, I have asked the royal engineers to build this divine monument in red sandstone.'

'Praise be to the king!' shouted the courtiers as the king retired to his private chambers, his umbrella and flywhisk-bearing female attendants following him.

In the privacy of his personal living room, the king continued discussing his pet project but only after he had dismissed all his attendants. Now there were only two other people in the room. The first was Nagabhata's trusted *kulguru*, Rishi Garga. Rishi Garga held in his lap a bundle that had been carefully wrapped in a cloth that bore a jellyfish motif.

The second was the crown prince, Ramabhadra.

'My son,' began Nagabhata. 'The architects tell me that they will be building fifty-six pillars of teak. All of these shall be covered in precious metal and gems. We shall need jewelled chandeliers. A chain of gold bells weighing 200 *maans* is required to wake the Brahmins for worship. Idols of gold and heavy vessels encrusted with jewels shall be needed for religious ceremonies.'

'Why are you telling me this, Father?' asked Prince Ramabhadra.

'Because it is possible that this project may not get completed during my lifetime,' replied the father. 'If I should die, it shall be your responsibility to bring it to fruition.'

Turning to Rishi Garga, the king said, 'We live in troubled times, wise guru. These days the kings of Andhra, Sindhu, Vidarbha and Kalinga strive to strike alliances with me. Why? Because they see me as a valuable ally. But in politics there are no permanent friends or enemies. You are among those who know how much I have struggled to reach here.'

'Why do you worry, oh King? Your victories over Anartta, Malava, the Matsyas, Kiratas, Turushkas and Vatsas have given you a stature that no other king has,' opined the sage.

'True, but I needed the help of allies to defeat Dharmapala,' replied the king. 'In our world, alliances are marriages of convenience. Allies can become foes when circumstances change. It is only divine intervention that can ensure our continued success.'

Rishi Garga nodded. The king was right. He knew what was coming.

'Promise me that you will use your divine powers to make my dream of Somnath come true,' said the king, as expected.

'It shall be done, oh King,' said Garga, as he cautiously clutched the crimson bundle on his lap and mentally recited:

Svedana… Mardana… Murchana… Uthapana… Patana… Rodhana… Niyamana… Sandipana…

Garga closed his eyes, meditating on the words in his head.

Gaganagrass… Carana… Garbhadruti… Bahyadruti… Jarana… Ranjana… Sarana… Kramana… Vedhana… Bhaksana.

Book Four
1980-1990

A week after Abdul Dada died, Arbaaz moved the office from the Bandra house—which had been willed by Dada to his mistress—to new premises at Ballard Estate. Murali had recommended it. It would give Arbaaz a veneer of respectability. 'All the old and respectable multinationals still have their offices there,' Murali had said.

The old building that had once been used by Raju and Arbaaz for storing and despatching their stolen goods, Crescent House, had been up for sale. Arbaaz had quickly bought it and converted one floor into a spacious office. *Life comes full circle,* he had thought to himself the first day that he had stepped into the renovated building.

The only thing that Arbaaz had requested from Anjum Azad, Dada's mistress, had been Dada's chair. Sitting on it made him feel a sense of closeness to the old man's spirit. He couldn't explain it. Anjum had been happy to part with it. Arbaaz had used the chair along with new furniture and interiors to give his place of work a look of solidity and seriousness.

Even though the office location and interiors had changed, the work that carried on inside it had not. Like his mentor, Arbaaz was always willing to welcome people who were in difficulty into his chambers. He would give them a patient hearing, judge for himself whether the individual's case warranted his assistance or not and then take quick corrective action.

The person who sat before him today was Yash Dhar.

Yash's story was an interesting one. Born in Kashmir to a Pandit family, he had attended Tyndale Biscoe School in Srinagar and then studied economics at St Stephen's, Delhi, while learning to fly at the Delhi Flying Club. Upon graduating, he had worked as a pilot for Indian Airlines for several years. Then one day he had experienced chest pains. The doctor who conducted his medical examination told him that he was suffering from angina pectoris. Unfortunately, angina pectoris was one of the medical conditions that disqualified him from being a pilot. His flying career crashlanded that day.

The only other passion that Yash had was reading newspapers. He was a news junkie, devouring everything that he could lay his hands on. A friend from St Stephen's had got him a job at the *Hindustan Times* and within two years he was writing articles that were being appreciated by his bosses at the paper. A year later he had been offered a terrific opportunity in Bombay by a newly launched tabloid, *Mid-Day*. He had switched jobs and relocated to Bombay along with his wife and young son.

Yash had proved himself to be an outstanding investigative reporter. The problem was that no investigative reporter could ever do his job without stepping on other people's toes. While investigating the deaths of twenty-three undertrials at the state's prisons, he had ended up antagonizing the Chief Minister as well as the Police Commissioner.

Pressure tactics had started in a subtle way. His landlord had suddenly decided that he could no longer offer the flat to him on rent. The school in which his son had almost been admitted decided that they had too many applicants and could not release the remaining seat. Yash had ploughed on.

Then the pressure had become less subtle. When he commuted to his place of work, he was always followed. The person following made no effort to be discreet. The state machinery had long arms when it wanted to go after someone.

Then one day he and his wife, Shaila, started receiving phone calls in which the caller refused to speak. Instead, the caller would play audio cassettes of Mohammad Rafi songs. It was a sinister threat that Yash would soon be dead, like Rafi, who had passed away just a few months back.

'I need your help, sir,' said Yash as he sat in the visitor's chair in front of Arbaaz's desk

'The problem is that we have no way of finding out who is behind this without pissing them off,' said Arbaaz. 'It's like the light in your refrigerator.'

'Huh?'

'Is the light on when the refrigerator door is shut? The only way to find out is by opening the door, in which case the door is no longer shut,' said Arbaaz.

'So what should I do?' asked Yash.

'Let me first ask you a question: why have you come to me? You are an investigative reporter. You obviously know who I am and what I do.'

'Your name was mentioned to me by Anjum,' replied Yash.

'Anjum Azad? Abdul Dada's mistress?' asked Arbaaz.

'Yes, she's from Kashmir and our families know each other,' replied Yash. 'When I met her last week, she said that there was only one person in Bombay who could help me and that was you.'

'I know the current Police Commissioner,' said Arbaaz. 'His son runs an art studio that I financed. I can ask him to get his men to lay off. But…'

'But what?' asked Yash.

'Asking him to lay off is like asking a whore to adopt celibacy,' said Arbaaz.

'Then what is the solution?' asked Yash worriedly. 'My wife is insisting that we get the hell out of this city. I don't blame her.'

'If the Police Commissioner is doing anything to pressure you, it means that he has received instructions from the Chief Minister. It is the Chief Minister who needs to understand that you should not be harassed.'

'Isn't the CM supposed to be committed to the safety and security of his people?' asked Yash in righteous anger.

'The only thing that this CM is committed to is the CM,' replied Arbaaz. 'But I think I have a way. It will mean spending some money on your behalf.'

'Thank you so much,' said Yash. 'I'll not forget the favour.'

'I know you won't,' said Arbaaz. 'I'm treating the money as an investment.'

The massive shamiana in the open grounds at Paharganj was a sea of white. The canvas of the gargantuan marquee was white, the mattresses upon which the disciples sat were white, the clothes of everyone at the assembly were white.

'Pure white light,' said Adhyapika Jyoti into the microphone. 'The universe is simply light. You are light, I am light… and yet we continue to live in darkness.'

Jeevan Prakash had come into existence in Varanasi at the turn of the twentieth century when the founder,

Mahashiva Baba, had experienced a series of visions. His visions had revealed some rather simple ideas about the nature of the universe, the human soul and God. He had shared his visions with an intimate band of followers and Jeevan Prakash had been born. For several years, Jeevan Prakash had remained a close-knit community, devoting time to spiritual studies, reflection, meditation and self-transformation but as the number of followers grew, it also began to undertake projects that could help humanity. Within a decade it had established several universities, schools, hospitals, orphanages and shelters.

In the years following the partition of India and Pakistan, Jeevan Prakash had run several camps, like the massive one at Kurukshetra, to accommodate the flood of humanity from Pakistan into India. Mahashiva Baba had personally supervised the camp and had ensured that thousands of refugees were clothed and fed.

At the Kurukshetra camp, one among the thousands of refugees had caught his attention. She was a young woman called Parmeet. He had noticed that her attention was always directed towards helping others although she was a refugee herself. Mahashiva Baba used to hold a *satsang* each evening at the camp to offer solace and comfort to the refugees and Parmeet would always be there, listening intently to him.

All of Mahashiva Baba's senior disciples took on the title of *Adhyapak*—or teacher. Female equivalents were called *Adhyapikas*. It was their responsibility to teach humanity how to come out of darkness and into light. Mahashiva Baba soon conferred the name 'Adhyapika Jyoti' upon Parmeet.

Adhyapika Jyoti would go on to take Jeevan Prakash to unimaginable heights. By 1980, there were over a thousand Jeevan Prakash ashrams in 103 countries. Estimates of follower count varied from six million up to nearly fifty million. Mahashiva Baba, who was said to be immortal, had decided to proceed for penance in the Himalayas and had left the entire organization in the capable hands of Adhyapika Jyoti.

The Paharganj satsang was the largest one and was attended by people from all over the country. Seated towards the front were Arvind, his wife Abhilasha and the two baby boys, Vinay and Vinit. Satyapal had urged Arvind to attend the satsang of Jeevan Prakash, having derived comfort from it himself.

'You think that God is this person who sits in judgement over us,' continued Adhyapika Jyoti. 'That is a fallacy. God is simply energy—pure white light. This energy manifests itself in myriad ways. We come from light and we return to light.'

Please spare me the mumbo-jumbo, thought Arvind to himself.

Arvind looked around the shamiana. There were probably at least a quarter of a million souls in the gigantic tent that day but there was pin-drop silence as Adhyapika Jyoti spoke. Whatever baggage of scepticism Arvind brought with him when he arrived began to magically fall off his shoulders. There was something intensely spiritual about Adhyapika Jyoti. She wasn't like the usual godmen or godwomen one encountered. Her simplicity of conduct and speech drew one to her.

An hour later, Adhyapika Jyoti withdrew to her simple temporary room backstage. A disciple brought her a glass of nimboo-paani. Arvind poked his head in. 'Ah, come in, Arvind,' she said. Arvind had made a sizeable donation to Jeevan Prakash and hence the first-name familiarity.

Arvind entered and was followed by Abhilasha, each parent carrying one of the twins. Adhyapika Jyoti smiled at the parents and stretched out her arms signalling that the infants be brought to her. She took each one of the children into her arms and whispered into their ears:

'Om tryambakam yajaamahe
sugandhim pushti-vardhanam,
Urvaarukam-iva bandhanaan
mrityormuksheeya maamrataat!'

Arbaaz had spent the previous evening at Sardar Vallabhbhai Stadium watching the heavyweight boxer Muhammad Ali take on former heavyweight champion Jimmy Ellis.

After the event, an impertinent reporter had questioned the weakness of Ali's left hook. Ali had challenged the reporter to get into the ring with him. He went on to say, 'In my forty-nine fights I have knocked out thirty-two of my opponents and I haven't suffered much punishment. You see my face? Do you see any scars or disfigurements? It looks nice and clean isn't it? That's it! That's why I'm the greatest!'

Arbaaz had loved it.

'Deposit another 5,000 rupees into the account,' said Murali on the phone. He had been getting various people to deposit similar amounts in cash into the same account number.

'How much has been deposited in total?' asked Arbaaz as Murali put down the phone.

'Including that last instruction, we've put 2,50,000 into the account. Fifty deposits of 5,000 each,' replied Murali. 'I'll be receiving a confirmation on the telex machine in the next hour or so.'

Arbaaz looked across the table at Yash Dhar. 'Have you typed up the draft article that I asked you to?' he asked.

Yash nodded as he passed a sheet of paper to Arbaaz who quickly read it.

Informed sources in the Education Ministry indicate that around fifty students have been made to pay bribes to the spouse of a senior minister in the state Cabinet with a view to securing their admissions to engineering and medical colleges in the state. It is still unclear who accepted the bribes but sources tell us that the racket has links to the very top echelons of government.

'Good,' said Arbaaz.

'Should I have it published?' asked Yash.

'The value of a bullet is much more when it is still inside the revolver,' replied Arbaaz. 'No need to publish it.'

Turning to Murali, he asked, 'Are you sure it's her account?'

'I rechecked with my man at the United Federation Bank. It's definitely the savings account of the Chief Minister's wife.'

'Murali, get a copy of the bank statement from the manager,' said Arbaaz. 'Next we shall send Yash's draft article as well as the bank statement to the CM.'

'Then?' asked Yash Dhar.

'You will drop in to see him.'

'Then?' asked Yash Dhar.

'You will ask him if he has any comments to make regarding your article. That's known as Ali's knockout punch.'

'I've been getting calls for several months about your dates,' said T.K., her secretary. After the resounding success of *Dharti Aur Aakash*, Paromita had been inundated with love letters from star-struck fans. She had been left with no alternative but to hire a full-time secretary to handle her correspondence and calls.

Paromita scanned the important letters and postcards that he had distilled for her. 'Hrishikesh Mukherjee loved your look in the movie. He sent word that he would like to consider you for a character role in his next one,' said T.K.

'Oh God, that's a dream come true!' said Paromita excitedly. 'I've waited for this day all my life.'

'Ramesh Sippy has also been in touch. He thinks that you will be ideally suited for a new movie that stars Shashi Kapoor,' said T.K. 'It's not the leading role but nothing to scoff at either.'

'Anyone else?' asked Paromita.

'Ravi Chopra is preparing for a venture which has Dharmendra and Hema Malini already signed up. He needs another woman in the story. You are his first option.'

'You will have to say no to all of them, T.K.,' said Paromita.

'Why?' asked T.K., mystified.

'I have to discuss it with Arbaaz first,' she said.

Later that night, Arbaaz took her out to dinner at the Supper Club. They then headed to Studio 29 on Marine Drive. It was a members-only nightclub and Arbaaz was one of its earliest members.

Studio 29 had replaced a barber's saloon called Wanderers at the Bombay International Hotel. Expensive sound equipment, lighting, turntables, a big shiny disco ball, and even the DJs had been imported from England by the owner, Sabira Merchant. The décor consisted of scarlet walls, shimmering curtains, velvet-upholstered chairs and Marilyn Monroe memorabilia. The Billboard hit being belted out was '*When You're in Love with a Beautiful Woman*' by Dr Hook.

Arbaaz held Paromita close to him on the dance floor. Some of the most beautiful women of Bombay were there that night. Dancing next to Arbaaz and Paromita were Anna Bredemeyer, the winner of the Miss Asia Pacific 1976, and Sangeeta Bijlani, Miss India 1980, but Arbaaz couldn't care less. *This is the only woman that I shall ever need,* thought Arbaaz as they gyrated to the music. *This is the only woman that I shall ever love.*

'I need some air,' said Paromita. Arbaaz quickly led her out of the nightclub. They crossed the road and strolled along the sea-hugging pavement on Marine Drive. Arbaaz's bodyguards followed at a discreet distance.

'What's the matter, baby?' he asked. 'Is it a new movie offer? Are you worried about taking up a project now that we're married? I don't really care if you…'

'I'm pregnant,' she said.

Arbaaz looked at the priest carefully. He wore a white cassock which matched his white hair perfectly. His black leather shoes were mirror-polished. This was a man who groomed himself to perfection. His name was Thomas V. Koshy.

'What can I do for you, Father?' asked Arbaaz, leaning forward as he sat in Abdul Dada's chair.

'As you may know, St Thomas Cathedral was completed in 1781,' said the priest. 'In fact, Churchgate owes its very name to the church which was located at the gate of the fort of Bombay.'

'I didn't know that,' said Arbaaz, wondering how long this was going to take.

'The police have been unable to help and everyone says that you are the man who gets things done,' said Koshy.

'That's why I've come to you even though the diocese was against it.'

'Do explain, Father,' urged Arbaaz.

'One of the most prominent features is an antique eagle lectern,' said the priest. 'It's a distinctive brass support for holding the Holy Bible during church services.'

'What about it?' asked Arbaaz.

'It was discovered missing from the church the day before yesterday. We informed the police but nothing came of it. We're worried that if more time elapses the thieves will have a better chance of getting away.'

'How heavy is it?' asked Arbaaz.

'Around thirty kilos,' said Thomas Koshy.

'Give me thirty hours,' said Arbaaz.

Arbaaz bade goodbye to Thomas Koshy and called for Raju. He quickly explained the situation.

'It's thirty kilos in weight. Something like that can't be moved easily. Seems like an inside job,' said Raju.

'I agree,' said Arbaaz. 'It's a busy area in the commercial district. It could not have been moved out during the day. If it was moved at night, it couldn't have been moved without the security guards noticing.'

'What do you want me to do?' asked Raju.

'Find out everything that there is to know about the night shift security guards. If any of them has a drug, drinking, gambling or womanizing habit, I'm sure our boys will know.'

An hour later, Raju was back. 'You were right, boss,' said Raju. 'One of the security guards is a chap called Lobo. Heavily in debt to our matka den.'

'Speak to him nicely,' said Arbaaz. 'Tell him we'll waive the debts if he puts the lectern back in place. His name will not be revealed to the police or diocese.'

'What if he says "no"?' asked Raju.

'He can opt to be buried in one of the marble tombs within the church,' said Arbaaz.

'Why are you so keen on helping this man, Thomas Koshy?' asked Raju.

'It's my duty,' said Arbaaz. 'It's also an investment that will pay off in five years.'

'Have you heard of Siri Fort?' asked Satyapal. They were in the luxurious conference room of the Calcutta office of Braid Investments.

'You mean that swamp in Delhi?' asked Arvind.

'Precisely,' replied Satyapal. 'That swamp could be the next goldmine.'

'What do you mean?' asked Joydeep.

'India will be hosting the 1982 Asian Games there,' said Satyapal.

'Don't they announce these things several years in advance?' asked Arvind.

'Actually, the decision to host the games in India was taken in 1976, but then the Emergency was called off. The Janata Party came to power. Political uncertainties prevented any work from happening. Mrs Gandhi returned to power this year and I'm told that work has already started in full swing.'

The Janata experiment had proved to be a disaster from the start. The only thing that had united the disparate Janata elements was their hatred of Indira Gandhi. Parliament had imprisoned her for a week at Tihar Jail because it was the one issue that they could actually agree upon. It was a foolish move. It showed them as petty. And it won her pity. Lots. From the Indian public.

Prime Minister Morarji Desai had been toppled within twenty-eight months of his term only to be succeeded by Prime Minister Charan Singh who had an even shorter tenure of less than six months. Fed up with the political bickering and squabbling, Indians had brought back Mrs Gandhi with a landslide majority. The Jana Sangh, which had been a constituent of the Janata Party, had eventually reconvened as the Bharatiya Janata Party—or BJP.

In the previous year, Pakistan had chosen to hang their former Prime Minister, Zulfikar Ali Bhutto. Some observers had commented that at least Mrs Gandhi's ordeal could be remedied through elections. Bhutto's could not.

'So who's in charge of putting the Asian Games together?' asked Arvind.

'Sanjay Gandhi was supposed to handle it but with his death in that plane crash, Rajiv Gandhi is handling it along with Delhi's Lieutenant-Governor, Jagmohan.'

'What will happen at Siri Fort?' asked Arvind.

'As you know, the area is a forgotten wilderness and becomes a swampy wasteland during the monsoons. A new Siri Fort Sports Complex is coming up. Next to it will be an Asian Games Village. A massive 60,000-seater stadium called the Jawaharlal Nehru Stadium is also being built there.'

'Interesting,' murmured Arvind.

'Delhi will be transformed,' continued Satyapal. 'Flyovers and roads are being built and the government is sanctioning prime land for those who wish to put up hotels.'

'Ah,' said Arvind, finally beginning to understand where Satyapal was going.

'I know that the Taj Group is likely to build a second hotel in Delhi,' said Satyapal. 'Hyatt and Holiday Inn are also surveying plots.'

'What's on your mind?' asked Arvind.

'See this,' said Satyapal, passing on a copy of a three-day-old *Hindustan Times*. It contained a government advertisement. Arvind read it aloud.

Invitation of Expression of Interest (EOI) for the development, completion and management of Five-Star Hotels in New Delhi. The Government of India is entrusted with the construction of five Five-Star hotels at prominent sites of New Delhi to meet the increased tourist demand that will arise from the Asian Games to be hosted in New Delhi commencing November 1982 and thereafter. The government proposes to initiate the process of identifying and appointing hotel developers who will undertake planning, detailed engineering and designing, financing, construction, marketing, and operation and maintenance (O&M) of the proposed projects. Information about each site and project proposed is available from the secretariat upon payment of a standard fee of Rs 100. All EOI submissions would first be evaluated in terms of financial and technical capability of the applicants. Successful applicants will be intimated by Registered Post and will be required to submit their sealed commercial bids thereafter. No change in applicant or in the ownership structure of an applicant company will be permitted once EOI is submitted, listed entities excepted.

Arvind remained lost in thought.

'Arvind?' asked Joydeep. 'What do you think?'

'I'm looking at the last line,' said Arvind. '*No change in applicant or in the ownership structure of an applicant company will be permitted once EOI is submitted, listed entities excepted.* It means that we will not be in a position to apply for a licence and resell it to someone else. We will also be unable to sell the company once it has been allotted the licence and the land.'

'I think we should seriously consider building a hotel rather than trading in hotel permits,' said Joydeep.

'No,' said Arvind. 'Remember that our business is not to buy or sell things but to buy and sell businesses.'

'If trading hotel permits will not work then how does one get in and get out while still making a killing and not getting stuck running a hotel?' asked Joydeep.

'I think I have an idea,' said Arvind.

'Find me a company that's for sale and is listed on the Bombay Stock Exchange,' said Arvind to his *paan masala*-chewing chartered accountant from Bombay as he himself concentrated on buttering his toast. Joydeep, Arvind and the chartered accountant were in the sprawling garden of Bagadia House on Alipore Road. Abhilasha had arranged for breakfast to be served to them on the lawns.

'What sort of company are you looking to acquire?' asked the chartered accountant as he sucked the juices from the crushed paan masala in his mouth. He had chosen to give breakfast a miss for the masala. 'Any specific sector or business?'

'No preference,' said Arvind. 'Just a defunct company in which the shares are available for a song… and with no hidden liabilities.'

'Acquiring a listed company is a complicated process,' began Mr Paan Masala. 'It requires approvals from shareholders, management and compliance of the rules set by the Controller of Capital Issues… '

'My data shows me that at least nineteen companies, which traded actively on the Bombay Stock Exchange, are available at valuations of less than ten lakh rupees,' said Arvind. 'I don't care about whether they have income streams or not. In fact, I would prefer companies which do not have any running business. Ideally, with no accumulated Income Tax dues or hidden labour liabilities.'

'I'll get on it immediately,' said Paan Masala, getting up.

'What are you up to, Arvind?' asked Joydeep when they were alone. 'Our company Braid Investments is already listed on the BSE. Why are we acquiring another company?'

'It takes months to list on the stock exchange,' replied Arvind. 'Our capital markets are governed by two archaic laws—the Capital Issues Control Act of 1947 and the Securities Contracts Regulation Act of 1956. I have neither the desire nor inclination to jump through hoops for a mere listing.'

'But why do we need another listed company at all?' asked Joydeep.

'For submitting the hotel EOI—the Expression of Interest,' said Arvind.

'Ah, that's good news,' said Arvind on the call from Bombay. 'How many shares can we buy immediately?'

He listened to the voice at the other end of the phone connection. The disturbance was not due to a poor connection. It was the sound of paan masala being chewed vigorously at the other end.

'That would give us around 70 per cent of the shares? Right, you go ahead and buy the shares for eleven rupees each…'

Arvind listened yet again.

'You need a Power of Attorney to buy and sell shares on my behalf? I will send it to you. One of my employees will fly to Bombay with it.'

There was some more masticating and talking at the other end.

Arvind resumed. 'Yes, I will leave the POA as general as possible so that you can act on my behalf in all matters. The money needed for the share purchase has already been sent to you as a loan. Please have the loan agreement signed and delivered to me.'

Arvind put down the receiver and looked at Satyapal and Joydeep. 'How is the work on the Expression of Interest?' he asked.

'Paperwork's all done,' said Satyapal. 'I'm just waiting for you to give me the name of the company in which we should submit it. Once the eggs are scrambled, I can't unscramble them.'

The intercom rang. Arvind picked it up. 'There is a call for you from your wife, sir,' said Hilda.

'Tell her I'm in a meeting and that I'll call her back,' said Arvind into the intercom. Hilda followed his instructions but felt terrible. How many times could she find creative excuses that would lessen Abhilasha's pain?

'Arvind, it's past 6. Abhilasha must be waiting because the twins are celebrating their fifth birthday,' said Joydeep. 'I'm supposed to ensure that you reach home on time.'

'It completely slipped my mind,' muttered Arvind. 'Do me a favour, Joydeep. Pick up the birthday presents that Hilda has gift-wrapped and head home. Give them to the boys. I'll finish the phone calls with Satyapal and follow shortly.'

'What about those school admission forms?' asked Joydeep. The twins would need to start school soon.

'Drop them off for me to Father Anthony's office,' said Arvind.

'I'm told that there's a long waiting list at La Martiniere,' said Joydeep.

'The waiting list disappeared for me the day I assumed the role of Sir Catchick Paul Chater,' said Arvind.

The real estate broker from Bombay was quick to respond to the phone call from Mr Arvind Bagadia. His reputation preceded him.

'How may I help you, Bagadiaji?' asked the broker.

'I need a small office space,' said Arvind. 'On rent.'

'Any idea in which locality?' asked the broker.

'Prime commercial area,' answered Arvind. 'Nariman Point.'

'Rentals in that area are very high these days, around ten rupees per square foot,' said the broker. 'I have an office of around 3,000 square feet that's available. It has a sea view.'

'Something smaller, please,' said Arvind.

'There's another one but it overlooks shanties. It's a thousand square feet,' said the broker.

'Something smaller, please,' said Arvind.

'Five hundred square feet. The office doesn't have any windows. I'm not too sure if there is any air-conditioning system installed,' said the broker.

'Something smaller, please,' said Arvind, unrelentingly.

'How many shares do we now own?' asked Arvind.

'Around 97 per cent of the company,' said the paan masala-addict chartered accountant. 'We are unable to trace the balance of 3 per cent shareholders.'

'It doesn't matter,' said Arvind. 'That's too small a chunk to worry about. I hope that you have not yet submitted the share transfer forms?'

'No. We'll do it as a single lot. We were worried that the share price would begin rising if there was suddenly too much interest in the scrip.'

'Good,' said Arvind. 'I now need you to apply for a change of the registered office and name.'

'What will be the new registered office?' asked the chartered accountant.

'I have rented a small 100-square-foot space in Nariman Point,' said Arvind.

'One hundred square feet?' asked the chartered accountant. 'A wee bit small, isn't it?'

'We're paying double the usual rent but even then it gives us a very respectable address for a marginal amount,' said Arvind.

'And what will be the new name?' asked the chartered accountant.

'Qurbani Hotels Limited,' answered Arvind. He had watched the Feroz Khan film *Qurbani* the previous week and the song '*Aap Jaisa Koi Meri Zindagi Mein Aaye*' sung by a young Pakistani singer called Nazia Hassan was still playing on an infinite loop inside his head.

'Why Qurbani?' asked Joydeep.

'"Qurbani" means "sacrifice",' said Arvind cryptically. Changing the topic, he said, 'Joydeep, I need you to find out which senior management executives retired from their jobs last year.'

'In which city?' asked Joydeep.

'Bombay, Delhi, Calcutta and Madras,' replied Arvind. 'Only look at people who were in top positions with very large companies but are now too old to be gainfully employed. Age—mid-sixties to early seventies.'

'Anything else?'

'They should be individuals who worked with public sector companies, the really big and bureaucratic ones.'

'And?'

'They should be socially connected… people who attend lunches, cocktails, dinners and weddings.'

'Sure,' said Joydeep. 'Any other criteria?'

'Yes,' said Arvind. 'They should all have slightly tarnished reputations. You know, the sort that may have indulged in a few not-so-straightforward deals on the side.'

'On that topic, Arvind...' began Joydeep hesitantly.

'Yes?' asked Arvind.

'I'm not sure if I'm too happy with what we're attempting to do here,' finished Joydeep. 'It seems unfair.'

'Nothing is fair in business,' said Arvind.

'But I want to have a clear conscience,' said Joydeep.

'Joydeep,' said Arvind. 'A businessman with a clear conscience is an oxymoron.'

Arvind looked at the final list in front of him. There were four names on the list.

1. *Mr Jagdeep Arora, 71, retired from the Steel Authority of India, Delhi*
2. *Mr Anurag Sen, 65, retired from the State Bank of India, Calcutta*
3. *Mr Venkat Ramaswamy, 69, retired from Coal India Limited, Madras*
4. *Mr Santosh Parulekar, 66, retired from the Life Insurance Corporation, Bombay*

'Have you approached all four of them?' asked Arvind.

'Yes,' replied Joydeep. 'It was done via an agency so that I would not need to personally interact with them.'

'Good. Have all four given their consent to serve as directors?'

'Yes. Most of them are delighted that they get to earn a remuneration in spite of their advanced years,' said Joydeep. 'Two of them were rather surprised that *anyone* had approached them to serve as directors.'

'Excellent,' said Arvind. 'Satyapal, you may now submit our Expression of Interest in the name of Qurbani Hotels Limited. When will bidding happen?'

'In two weeks,' said Satyapal. 'How much do you plan to bid?'

'Absolutely nothing,' said Arvind.

Joydeep scanned the room until he spotted Mr Anurag Sen. He seemed older than his stated age of sixty-five. He was dressed in a conservative business suit and was getting the waiter to pour a mixture of soda and water into his whisky. It was one of those usual cocktail parties at a five-star hotel where complete strangers learnt more about you in an hour than your spouse ever could in a lifetime.

Joydeep walked up to him and said, 'I see that you're like me, sir. You, too, like a mixture of soda *and* water in your whisky!'

The old man looked at Joydeep and screwed up his eyes as though attempting to recognize him. 'We've never met, I'm Joydeep Chakraborty,' said Joydeep, extending his hand.

Anurag Sen shook hands with the young man. 'Anurag Sen,' he introduced himself.

'You're not *the* Anurag Sen?' asked Joydeep excitedly. 'The one who was with State Bank of India?'

There was a smile on Mr Sen's face. It was obvious that no one had ever referred to him as '*the* Anurag Sen'.

'Yours truly,' said Mr Sen, almost taking a bow with his first sip of whisky.

'Let me convey my congratulations to you, sir,' said Joydeep.

'Congratulations?' asked Mr Sen.

'You know what I mean,' said Joydeep winking at the old man.

'Er, refresh my memory, son,' said Mr Sen.

'Ah, I see. I guess the directors are not supposed to talk about it. Keeping it under wraps, eh? My apologies for bringing it up,' said Joydeep, continuing to be a royal pain in the ass. Arvind's training had rubbed off.

Mr Sen looked even more bewildered.

'You have my assurance, sir, that the news of Qurbani having swung—in advance—the bid in your favour shall remain secret. I shall not breathe a word to anyone,' said Joydeep.

'I don't believe you,' said Mr Sen under his breath.

'Everyone should believe in something,' said Joydeep, calling for one of the waiters bearing a drinks tray. 'I believe I'll have another drink.'

Joydeep picked up the phone on the third ring. It was Arvind calling from Bombay.

'Did you meet him?' asked Arvind.

'Absolutely,' said Joydeep proudly. 'Played it exactly the way you asked me to.'

'Good. In that case I shall ask Paan Masala to place 10,000 shares on the market for sale,' said Arvind. 'We bought at eleven rupees. I think fifteen rupees should be fine. Enough to send a signal to the market that something's up.'

'Any further instructions?' asked Joydeep.

'Yes, ask Satyapal to meet Jagdeep Arora. You go to Madras and find a way to meet that doddering fool, Venkat Ramaswamy.'

Arvind watched as the group of golfers tackled the seventeenth hole of the eighteen-hole golf course of the Willingdon Club. He could hear Santosh Parulekar giving advice to his friend. 'This is an easy hole to par if played conservatively. Did you notice, at the dogleg, the fairway turns significantly to the left and then straightens?'

His friend nodded and looked into the distance.

'See, old boy, this hole is best played as a hop, step and jump hole. An easy 220-yard drive, a 150-yard mid iron and another short wedge into the green.'

His friend seemed to be hoping that Santosh Parulekar would shut up and let him play the shot but Parulekar continued, 'The challenge of the tee is to avoid the left and be in the fairway. A draw of the tee is ideal. The rough of the fairway is thick and sturdy and very tough to get out of.'

His friend took the shot, probably to get Parulekar to shut up.

Arvind quickly made his way to the tearoom. He knew that the group would eventually make its way there. He ordered a fresh lime soda for himself and waited. The men walked in about twenty minutes later.

Arvind pretended to be reading a letter while casually sipping his drink. The men ordered tea and sandwiches.

'Crap!' muttered Arvind, loud enough for the men to hear. He was ignored.

'Fuck!' said Arvind as he slammed down the letter on the table in front of him and spilt his drink. Through the corner of his eye he noticed Parulekar looking at him. He got up and apologized to the men.

'My sincerest apologies, I should learn to keep my own thoughts in check, sir,' said Arvind, humbly.

'What's the matter, son?' asked Parulekar. 'You seem disturbed.'

'I shouldn't be bothering you with my problems, sir,' said Arvind. 'Utterly unprofessional.'

'No, no, no…' said Parulekar. 'Come join us. Sit down.' Arvind pulled up a chair to their table and sat down.

'What seems to be the matter?' asked Parulekar. 'Romantic troubles?'

'Oh no, sir. Business.'

'Care to share?' asked Parulekar.

'My name is Arvind Bagadia,' said Arvind. 'I run a company called Braid Investments.'

'Ah yes, I've heard of it,' said Parulekar. 'Nice to meet you, young man. I'm Santosh Parulekar.'

'Not *the* Santosh Parulekar? The one who was at the Life Insurance Corporation?'

Parulekar instantly puffed up. 'Well, I *was* with LIC…'

'Amazing to meet you, sir,' said Arvind excitedly. 'It's just that a business deal that I've been working on has fallen through.'

'What sort of deal?' asked Parulekar.

Arvind pulled closer to Parulekar conspiratorially and whispered, 'My company was about to bid for a hotel project up for grabs in Delhi's Asian Games…'

'And?' asked Parulekar.

'We've been beaten even before bidding. An unknown company called Qurbani has fixed it in their favour.'

Arvind noticed the instant recognition on Parulekar's face as the name was mentioned.

'Please don't mention it to anyone,' said Arvind. 'My share price will be hammered while Qurbani will make a killing.'

Joydeep telephoned Arvind in the evening. 'How did it go?' asked Arvind.

'Perfect,' said Joydeep. 'Venkat Ramaswamy loves playing bridge. I managed to meet him at his weekly game.'

'Hmm. I met Parulekar today. I believe that the time has come to unload another chunk of shares.'

'How much have you already sold?' asked Joydeep.

'Only 10 per cent. But that was to get the ball rolling. I think we can put 20 per cent of the shares on the market now. Does twenty bucks sound like a good price?'

'Did you meet Jagdeep Arora?' asked Arvind.

'Yes, he was on a train from Delhi to Chandigarh. I hopped on,' replied Satyapal.

'What happened?' asked Arvind.

'He dropped his walking stick when I mentioned Qurbani and the fact that it seemed to have emerged as the only company to go through the first round of evaluations,' said Satyapal.

Arvind laughed.

'I have takers at fifty,' said Paan Masala to Arvind.

'Sell another third of the shares but hang onto the rest,' said Arvind.

'Why?' queried Paan Masala. 'I doubt you'll get more for what is an otherwise worthless company.'

'I'll take my chances,' said Arvind.

Arvind stepped into the offices of the Old Lady of Bori Bunder. The *Times of India* was Bombay's most widely read newspaper. God, Tea and the *Times of India* were the Holy Trinity of the Bombay morning—morning prayers, followed by tea and a dose of the news.

Arvind carried a leather satchel as well as two brown manila envelopes under his arm as he walked through the maze of offices filled with people and clickety-clacking typewriters. He finally reached the corner office of T.R. Ganesan.

Known for his investigative skills, Ganesan had been responsible for many of the insightful reports that occasionally accompanied the newspaper's otherwise bland diet of ads, pictures and verbatim newswire articles. Ganesan was never interested in information that could be accessed in the normal course. His interest lay in information that no one else knew about.

'Good to see you, Mr Ganesan,' said Arvind. 'Thanks for meeting me at such short notice.'

'I've heard a lot about you,' said Ganesan, offering Arvind a chair.

'Some of it was good, I hope,' Arvind laughed as he sat down, placing the two envelopes on Ganesan's desk and the leather satchel on top.

Ganesan smiled. 'How can I be of help to the chairman of Braid Investments?'

'Actually, I'm here to meet you in my personal capacity,' said Arvind. 'I'm told that you are one of the most knowledgeable people in Carnatic music.'

'Absolutely. I have one of the largest collections of D.K. Pattammal, M.L. Vasanthakumari and M.S. Subbulakshmi recordings.'

'How exciting,' said Arvind. 'My wife is very interested in Carnatic music because her family lived in Madras for some years. She asked me to find out if she could correspond with you from time to time.'

'I shall be delighted to hear from her,' said Ganesan. 'I had no idea that any north Indian would ever be interested in Carnatic music.'

'Oh, she's an enthusiast. She prefers male vocalists such as Muthiah Bhagavathar, Mysore Vasudevachar and Chintalapalli Venkata Rao,' said Arvind, hoping that he had got the pronunciations right. Joydeep's research had helped.

'Excellent, hopefully we shall have lots to discuss,' said Ganesan. 'What's her name?'

'Abhilasha,' replied Arvind. 'I shall give her your address and ask her to write to you. How do I say thanks for your help?'

'Just give me the inside business scoop from time to time,' said Ganesan, winking.

Arvind laughed as he arose to leave. 'I certainly shall. It's just that I'm so forgetful these days, you may have to remind me!'

He picked up his leather satchel and envelope, tucked them under his arm, and made a quick exit.

After he had left, Ganesan noticed that one of Mr Bagadia's envelopes had been left behind by him on the desk.

Arvind laughed to himself as he exited the newspaper office. Forgetfulness could often be used as a strategic advantage. In any case, it was always better to tell journalists openly and honestly anything that they could discover some other way.

Sitting inside his stuffy office of the *Times of India,* Ganesan looked at the memo yet again.

From: *Satyapal Mittal*
To: *Arvind Bagadia*
Subject: *Delhi Asiad Hotel Project*
Date: *3 December 1980*

As per my discussions with you I have been doing the rounds of the Delhi Development Authority, the Tourism Department and the Urban Development Ministry. It seems that Expressions of Interest have been received from various parties. The problem is that most of them have been disqualified during the stage of financial and technical evaluation owing to political considerations. Apparently only one company 'meets' the stringent criteria, a relatively unknown company called Qurbani Hotels Limited. If we could start acquiring shares of this company, it might be another way to access this lucrative opportunity.

Ganesan smiled. He pulled up his typewriter and began writing a story.

'The market's gone crazy,' said Paan Masala. 'I'm getting calls from the stockbrokers asking to pick up shares at 250.'

'Any idea who's buying?' asked Arvind.

'Mostly the four directors' friends and families,' said Paan Masala. 'As you know, the insider trading regulations are never enforced in India. We don't even have a market regulator! The newspaper article has also prompted a rush of unrelated investors. One of the big ones is a company called Dhanda Holdings Private Limited.'

'Shit,' muttered Arvind.

'What happened?' asked Paan Masala.

'I would have preferred that they had not invested in Qurbani Hotels,' said Arvind. 'They're investors in my company, Braid Investments. Can you find a way to cancel the share transactions with them?'

'Impossible,' said Paan Masala. 'They've paid upfront. Their banker seems rather excited about the *short-term punt* as he described it.'

Arvind sighed. 'In any case, we can't do anything now… go ahead and sell the remaining shares at 250,' said Arvind.

'Are you sure?' asked Paan Masala. 'The *Times of India* article says that Qurbani is a frontrunner for winning several hotel projects for the Delhi Asian Games.'

'I've already played the games that interest me,' said Arvind.

'What about the profits? How do you want them paid to you?' asked Paan Masala.

'Cash,' said Arvind. 'There should be no trail linking me to the share price movements of Qurbani.'

The four directors of Qurbani Hotels Limited made their way to the company's first board meeting after the board's reconstitution.

'Are you sure that this is the address?' asked Parulekar.

'Of course I'm sure,' said Ramaswamy. 'Read the notice.'

A meeting of the Board of Directors of Qurbani Hotels Limited shall be held on 10 December 1980 at the company's registered office, 1st floor, Suite 11-A, Maker Towers VI at 10 am.

They knocked on the door that bore the number 11-A again but there was no response. Finally, Jagdeep Arora tried the handle and found that the door swung open.

It was a ten-by-ten janitor's closet. All along the length of three walls were shelves on which brooms, buckets, mops and other assorted cleaning equipment and supplies sat.

They stood in silence, absorbing the shock of their surroundings.

'I think that we've been royally screwed,' said Anurag Sen to the others. 'How many shares did each of you get your friends and family to buy?'

There was a reason why Arvind Bagadia had called the company Qurbani. Someone had to be sacrificed.

'How much did you say they are at?' asked Murali. He waited for his banker from United Federation Bank to convey the news.

'How did the price crash from two-fifty to nine rupees in five days?' asked Murali. 'This was meant to be a short-term punt, in and out with a tidy profit. And how am I supposed to explain the staggering loss to Arbaaz?'

The banker mumbled something about the fact that he had helped Murali make twenty brilliant investments. One bad investment wasn't the end of the world.

'Find out who owned the shares that we bought,' said Murali firmly. 'Find out who the directors are. Access the tax returns and hotel bids. I want to know everything. And I mean *everything*! Got it?'

Sitting 1200 miles away in Calcutta, Arvind looked at the statement yet again.

Shares of Qurbani purchase value	Rs 9,47,300
Rent, brokerage, travel and director fees	Rs 2,61,557
Total investment including expenses	Rs 12,08,857
Sale proceeds of Qurbani shares	Rs 1,02,62,416
Profit	Rs 90,53,559

A clean profit of ninety lakh with a whopping nine-fold return in two weeks.

'I know we've made our profit without even bidding but Qurbani has been shortlisted at the EOI stage. Do you still want us to bid for the hotel?' asked Satyapal.

'Ever noticed the toilet paper roll in the bathroom?' asked Arvind.

'Sure,' said Satyapal, wondering where the conversation was headed.

'Have you noticed how it rolls much faster as you get to the end? We're reaching that point. Leave it.'

Arbaaz sat with Murali and Raju for their weekly lunch at Gaylord.

Murali and Raju were now his right and left hands. Raju had effortlessly taken over all the shady parts of Abdul Dada's business while Murali was rapidly building a respectable corporate front for Arbaaz.

Gaylord had always been Arbaaz's favourite haunt. Started in 1956 by two partners—Ghai and Lamba—they had decided on the name 'Gay Lord' because the name used the 'G' of Ghai and the 'L' of Lamba. Those were simpler times when being 'gay' meant being happy!

Paromita, in particular, loved the Waldorf salad, baked Alaska and chicken stroganoff. But today's menu was channa bhatura for Murali and butter chicken for Arbaaz and Raju.

'How are we doing with our key areas?' asked Arbaaz looking at Raju. 'How's the betting revenue doing?'

'Very well,' replied Raju. 'Since the beginning of this year we've opened fifty more matka dens. The result is that we've increased the daily take by more than 50 per cent.'

'You should consider how we can start taking bets on other activities like cricket,' said Arbaaz. 'How's the hooch?'

'Again, under control,' replied Raju. 'The only problem is intermittent police raids. Sometimes we get an advance tip-off from one of the cops on our payroll. Sometimes that doesn't happen.'

'Consider moving our distillation units into slum areas. This will make them less accessible to the cops,' said Arbaaz. 'Smuggling scene?'

'Good,' said Raju. 'We've really expanded the range of items—electronics, perfumes, watches, gold, garments, foodstuffs, cosmetics… maximum demand these days is for VHS players and colour television sets.'

'Why?' asked Arbaaz

'Because the government has announced that it will launch colour transmission on Doordarshan soon. The launch will coincide with the Asiad.'

'Drugs?' asked Arbaaz. 'Any good news?'

'Very good news, in fact. The government is likely to pass the Narcotic Drugs and something-something Act as well as the Prevention of Illicit Trafficking in Narcotic Drugs and something-something Act. If these are passed, the entire trade will shift underground.'

'Start building up additional supply channels for heroin,' said Arbaaz. 'How's the land bank?' asked Arbaaz.

'Brilliant,' answered Raju. 'This chap Datta Samant has struck fear into the hearts of mill-owners. There is every possibility that the entire textile industry may go into a strike. We're doing side deals with the owners for a third of the land value. In the meantime, we're occupying vacant land near the airport with our own slumlords.'

'Good,' said Arbaaz. 'And you, Murali? Anything to report?'

'You want the good news or the bad news?' asked Murali.

'What's the good stuff?' asked Arbaaz.

'We've struck gold with almost twenty of our investments. Your company is a large shareholder in several very large corporations. In some of them, I already occupy a board seat on your behalf. Many new start-ups are also on our horizon. A small company called Infosys has come up in Pune. We're keeping our eyes on that as a potential opportunity.'

'In money terms?' asked Arbaaz.

'Our capital appreciation has been over three crore for the year,' said Murali. 'Keep in mind that the BSE index is only 227. My own prediction is that in ten years the index should multiply ten times. We are all set to make a killing. The second piece of good news is that the government is in the process of announcing a special bearer bond that will allow you to launder your unaccounted cash.'

'So what's the bad news?' asked Arbaaz.

'We got conned by the owner of Braid Investments Ltd. His name is Arvind Bagadia. We lost around thirty lakh.'

'The name sounds familiar,' said Arbaaz. Then he remembered the flight to Hyderabad and the stay at Bagadia's guest-house.

'How did you end up losing so much?' asked Arbaaz.

'We invested in a company called Qurbani Hotels Limited. The rumours were that it was in line to get a lucrative hotel project in Delhi. We got in thinking that it would be a short-term investment, not realizing that it was an elaborate con by Mr Bagadia.'

'How well do you know him?' asked Arbaaz.

'We invested in his company, Braid Investments. He's a smart guy—exceptionally bright. Damn, I even praised him during his company's Annual General Meeting.'

'Business is business, Murali,' said Arbaaz. 'Calm down.'

'We lost a lot of money, Arbaaz. Your money! And it happened because I allowed that blasted banker to convince me that Qurbani was a good short-term punt.'

'Don't get mad,' said Arbaaz. 'Get even.'

'How?' asked Murali.

'Your way or my way?' asked Arbaaz.

'What do you mean?' asked Murali.

'Your way means we find a way to get back our money with profit. My way means I get his legs broken or receive his corpse in a body bag.'

'Er, my way is better in this instance. We also need to preserve and protect our corporate reputation,' said Murali quickly.

'Fine,' said Arbaaz. 'So do you have a plan?'

'If I simply dump his company's shares in the market, I'll cause his share price to crash,' said Murali.

'But how will you gain?' asked Arbaaz. 'No, I suggest that you meet Mr Tiwari.'

'Who is he?' asked Murali.

'The Chief Commissioner of Income Tax, the one who helped us fix ex-Police Commissioner Dube at the airport,' replied Arbaaz. 'We need leverage on Mr Arvind Bagadia.'

'Will Mr Tiwari work?' asked Murali.

'Most government servants are like faulty guns,' replied Arbaaz.

'Huh?'

'They don't work and you can't fire them. In any case, let's try,' said Arbaaz.

Murali laughed. 'You have a smile on your face. What idea is brewing behind it?'

'The scheme is called PLPLPL,' said Arbaaz.

'PLPLPL?' asked Murali.

'You remember that Parsi lawyer whom you brought from Calcutta to get me released from Arthur Road Jail?' asked Arbaaz.

'Darius Dastur?' asked Murali.

'That's the one. I've been in touch with him. He put me in touch with someone who manages the records of the Bombay Parsi Panchayat.'

'Whatever for?'

'They maintain a *Paidast* list,' said Arbaaz.

'A what?'

'A Paidast list is a funeral list. A daily updated list of deaths among the Parsi community,' replied Arbaaz. 'My contact keeps me informed.'

'Should I ask why?'

'Did you know that nine landowners together own a fifth of Bombay's land?' asked Arbaaz.

'Really?'

'The six biggest ones are Godrej & Boyce, the Byramjee Jeejeebhoy Group, the A.H. Wadia Trust, the F.E. Dinshaw Trust, Hirjibhai Dinshaw Billimoria and Jeejeebhoy Ardeshir. What's common between them? They're all Parsi!'

'How did that happen?'

'The East India Company gifted land as a reward to attract people to Bombay. Prosperous Parsi traders and merchants not only received huge tracts of land as gifts but also reinvested their profits into acquiring additional land. This land has been passed down through the generations,' explained Arbaaz.

'How does this concern us?' asked Murali.

'The Parsi population in India is dwindling,' said Arbaaz. 'It's less than 72,000 people. Twenty years ago it was over a lakh. The result is that many Parsi widows lead a very lonely existence. I simply meet them occasionally, chat with them over a cup of tea, and take a few gifts for them from time to time. They call me their *dikra*—or son—and confide in me.'

'All this out of the goodness of your heart?' asked Murali, cynically.

'Yes,' replied Arbaaz. 'Also, the fact that massive tracts of land across Kurla, Bhandup, Vikhroli, Deonar, Malad and Goregaon—not to mention some fabulous heritage properties—are owned by them. By the time that they are ready to pass on, I am the only one that they ever want to include in their last will and testament. The kids rarely bother about these lonely ladies. That's why my programme is called PLPLPL.'

'What does that stand for?' asked Murali.

'Properties of Lonely Parsi Ladies Private Limited,' said Arbaaz, winking.

'I've had three contractions,' said Paromita to Arbaaz who was glued to the TV set. He wasn't watching anything. He had a little contraption called a Sinclair ZX81 hooked up to the television and was playing a game called 3D Monster Maze. His smugglers had started bringing in a bunch of these gadgets that people called personal computers and they were selling like hot cakes in the new Heera Panna Shopping Centre at Haji Ali.

Arbaaz remained glued to the computer. He was caught in a maze with one exit and a hostile *Tyrannosaurus rex*. He was concentrating on traversing the maze and escaping through the exit without being eaten, something that he did almost each day in his line of work.

'I've had three contractions,' said Paromita again. This time Arbaaz looked up.

'What? Why didn't you tell me earlier?' he said. Shoving the ZX81 away, Arbaaz drove Paromita from their Colaba flat to Bombay Hospital like a man possessed. They reached their destination in less than ten minutes.

'Are you okay?' he asked as he helped her out of the car.

Paromita smiled. 'Relax, Arbaaz, the contractions are far apart and not very hard as yet. We're here in good time.'

Paromita was admitted into the maternity wing and a few hours later she was wheeled into the delivery room. Her gynaecologist was Bombay's best, a young Maharashtrian doctor whose overall look was that of a Bollywood star.

'I suggest that you wait outside, Mr Sheikh,' he said to Arbaaz. The last thing that the doctor needed was a paranoid husband inside the delivery room.

He quickly had the nurse prop up her up on the delivery table and asked her to breathe deeply and then push. She could feel an intense contraction building up in her uterus and she screamed as she felt a sensation that bordered on tearing muscles.

The doctor asked the nurse to dab her face with a cold towel. 'Pause for a moment, take a very deep breath, wait for the spasm and then push again.'

Paromita did as he asked, taking a deep breath. Then she began to push with a determined expression. 'I can see the head,' said the doctor.

The baby emerged, face down. 'We've got the baby out till the shoulders,' said the doctor. 'I need another long and decisive push from you.'

As Paromita grunted, her baby emerged, rotating gently from back to front as the rest of the body from the shoulders down came out. 'Let's get the placenta out and the umbilical cord severed and we're done.'

Emerging from the delivery room ten minutes later, the doctor handed over a little bundle to Arbaaz. 'You have a beautiful little baby girl. Congratulations!'

His daughter's eyes blinked open and one corner of her mouth crinkled as though she were smiling at Arbaaz. He fell in love for the second time in his life that day.

Abhilasha asked her driver to drop her off at the Fairlawn Hotel. It was not a hotel that was frequented by Arvind even though the hotel had stood on the junction of Madge Lane and Sudder Street since 1783. One of the reasons for her choosing this particular hotel was because they did not ask too many questions.

She ignored the reception and quickly made her way to the second floor. She knocked on the door and it was opened almost instantly. She walked in and fell into his arms.

'I've missed you,' she said.

'So have I,' he said as he bent down to kiss her.

They remained locked in a passionate embrace as his hands wandered down towards the swell of her hips. 'I can't wait,' he said, pulling away to help her undrape her saree.

Abhilasha savoured his passion and warmth. She savoured his mere presence. She felt excited, adventurous, young and sexy. She also felt guilty about how she was betraying Arvind.

Then she remembered the long nights when she had cried herself to sleep waiting for him. She remembered the postpartum days when Arvind had ignored her even though she desperately needed him. She remembered all the family vacations that had been cancelled owing to last-minute business commitments and the movies that she had watched alone.

'Hey, what's on your mind?' he asked, unbuttoning his shirt.

'Nothing,' she said, smiling as she helped him take off his clothes.

Paromita was feeding little Alisha. She looked tired and bleary-eyed. Alisha had kept her up all night.

Arbaaz was dressed in khaki trousers and a loose linen shirt. In his hands were a bunch of flowers and a box of chocolates.

Paromita looked at him. Seeing Arbaaz freshly bathed and immaculately groomed, accessorized as though he were heading out on a date, made Paromita want to scream at him.

'Where are you going?' she asked.

'Property deal,' he replied.

'With flowers and chocolates in hand?' she asked, adjusting Alisha in her arms.

Arbaaz laughed. 'Jealous?' he asked. He could see the rage building up in Paromita.

He quickly put down the flowers and chocolates and walked over to the easy chair on which she was sitting and feeding Alisha.

'I already have the two most beautiful girls in my life,' he whispered, kneeling down next to Paromita. 'I don't need another.'

'Who are the chocolates and flowers for?' asked Paromita suspiciously.

'Her name is Mrs Gulnaz Batlivala,' replied Arbaaz. 'She's part of a social initiative that we've undertaken. It's called PLPLPL.'

Arbaaz held Alisha in his arms as he and Paromita got out of the car at Aarey Milk Colony. It was a long drive to Goregaon East but entirely worth it. Gardens, lakes, restaurants, an observation pavilion, picnic facilities and 16,000 head of cattle on 1,287 hectares of land made it almost possible to forget that one was in Bombay.

The picnic had been Paromita's idea and she had packed a basket of food along with another bag containing Alisha's baby supplies. Arbaaz had been enthusiastic about the idea and had spoken with his contact at the Maharashtra Public Works Department to give them access to areas that were usually off-limits to regular visitors.

Arbaaz's bodyguards had been given strict instructions by him to remain at a distance. Raju had quietly overruled Arbaaz. 'Remember what happened with Rangarajan Pillai when he asked his bodyguards to remain at a distance? Stay out of sight but be on very high alert. If anyone is able to touch a hair on Arbaaz's body, I will shoot all of you. Got that?'

Arbaaz and Paromita sat down on the soft grass and placed little Alisha in her crib. No sooner had they settled down, there was a squeal from a young girl in the distance.

'Look, Papa, Paromita!' The young girl ran up to Paromita along with a pad and pen, requesting her for an autograph. Before long, they were surrounded by several fans.

Arbaaz's bodyguards appeared on the scene but Arbaaz gave them a stern look to shoo them away. Paromita looked incredibly happy as she autographed pieces of paper, shirts and even arms. Arbaaz looked at her and smiled. When the crowd had dissipated he said to her, 'Thanks, *jaan*.'

'Thanks? For what?' asked Paromita, opening the basket.

'For giving up all this on account of me,' said Arbaaz. 'I'm probably the luckiest man alive.'

'I think you ought to remove the word *probably* from that sentence,' joked Paromita as she passed him a sandwich.

He looked at her with a serious expression on his face. 'I have had only two teachers in my life,' he said.

'Who?' asked Paromita.

'Abdul Dada and you,' he replied.

'How can you compare me with him?' asked Paromita, almost outraged by the statement.

'He taught me how to be feared. You have taught me how to love and be loved.'

Mr Sushil Tiwari listened to Murali patiently in his spacious office at the Income Tax headquarters. He was the Chief Commissioner of Income Tax in Bombay, having served the Indian Revenue Service for thirty years before occupying the high post of Chief Commissioner.

Tiwari massaged his temples in the hope of driving away the splitting headache caused by his hangover. The night before, there had been a concert by Jagjit and Chitra Singh at the President Hotel. Mr Tiwari had sat on a spotless white mattress downing peg after peg of whisky while the duo rendered his favourite ghazal, '*Ahistaa Ahistaa*'. Mr Tiwari had ignored the advice to go slow. Jagjit Singh and whisky were a potent combination for Mr Tiwari. So were Pankaj Udhas and whisky. Or Ghulam Ali and whisky. Anything and whisky.

Tiwari's rise had not been without its fair share of controversies. He had been part of the special cell within the Directorate of Inspection that had been created in 1972 to oversee the Income Tax cases of big industrial houses. There had been rumours of department information being leaked to corporate groups but none of it could ever be traced back to him. He had also been assigned a new directorate known as the Directorate of Vigilance in 1978 but much of the actual work had been held up owing to directives from him. Again, no action was ever taken against him.

The secret of Mr Tiwari's unhindered ascent within the Indian Revenue Service was the fact that he had friends in all the right places. Several people who had occupied the critical posts of Revenue Secretary and chairman of the Central Board of Direct Taxes had been assiduously nurtured by Mr Tiwari. He was seen as a man who could 'get things done'. If a school admission was needed for a child, Mr Tiwari was the man to approach. If a telephone line needed to be allotted out of turn, Mr Tiwari could handle that too. If an appointment with a senior doctor at a hospital was not possible, Mr Tiwari could pick up a phone and organize that in a jiffy. Mr Tiwari was a miracle man of sorts.

Mr Tiwari's secret formula had been Abdul Dada. Abdul had fostered his relationship with Tiwari to ensure that his premises and homes were never raided. Most of the officers were too terrified to raid him anyway but it always helped to have one's own man inside the department. In fact, any effort to make Abdul Dada fall in line was aggressively stymied by Mr Tiwari almost instantly. Mr Tiwari was one of Dada's Pandavas, the five people that Abdul Dada always wanted on his side—the police, Income Tax, Municipal Corporation, the judiciary and God.

'Why these five in particular?' Arbaaz had once asked. Dada had replied, 'The police are our partners. Without them we cannot carry on our business. The Income Tax people are our partners-in-waiting. They want a piece of the action but we don't want them in so we keep them happy with a few morsels thrown their way now and then. The municipal authorities are the partners that we want. They can bring us untold riches through land-grabs but we have to woo them to join. The judiciary is the angry partner, the one who is not getting any piece of the action. We need to keep this partner cool so that he doesn't harm us.'

'And God?' Arbaaz had asked.

'He's the senior partner. Without his blessings and agreement, nothing can move.'

Murali watched Mr Tiwari examine the documents carefully. 'If he did all this, he would not be stupid enough to take his profit on the books. This would be an entirely *benami* transaction,' said Mr Tiwari.

'Precisely,' said Murali. 'And that's why I'm here.'

'Leave this with me,' said Mr Tiwari. 'I'll come up with something. Tell Arbaaz Bhai not to worry. I always find a way.'

The office of Chander Lakhotia a.k.a. Paan Masala, was located on Kalbadevi Road, a congested area named after the Hindu goddess of that name. Hundreds of goldsmiths, cotton yarn traders and steel utensil merchants had their operations here.

Kalbadevi Road began near Metro Cinema and stretched up to Bhuleshwar Road and Khetwadi Road. Bombay's two main cloth wholesale markets, Mulji Jetha Market and Mangaldas Market, were located here and could be accessed from Hanuman Galli. Towards Bhuleshwar was Zaveri Bazaar, a patchwork of exceedingly narrow lanes, occupied by hundreds of jewellers from whom emerged two-thirds of all gold trades in India. Towards the end of Kalbadevi, near Bhuleshwar Road, was the Cotton Exchange.

Chander Lakhotia had been born and brought up in in this area. His father was a cotton trader in Mulji Jetha Market and his elder brother worked alongside his father. Chander had always been academically bright and had managed to clear both groups of his intermediate as well as final exams with flying colours. It was joked that CA actually stood for 'Come Again' instead of 'chartered accountant' but Chander had been able to clear all his papers in the very first attempt.

The truth was that Chander Lakhotia was a chartered accountant whom one employed when one wanted something that bordered on illegal to be executed in as legal a manner as possible. His oiled hair, safari suit and paan masala-stained teeth were testament to that.

Chander had married his college sweetheart in what was called an 'intercommunity' marriage—Marwari boy marrying a Gujarati girl. The romance had blossomed at a famous eatery of the area known as Shree Thaker Bhojanalay. Established in 1945, the restaurant served the finest Gujarati *thaali* in all of Bombay, including *farsan*, veggies, *rotis*, *pulao*, *dal*, *kadhi*, buttermilk and creamy *shrikhand*. A visit to Shree Thaker Bhojanalay was part of Chander's daily lunchtime ritual and he always used the time to meet with clients over food. Once the meal was over, he would take out a small silver box from his pocket containing paan masala and savour the wrap-up of the meal.

There was no jeweller, cloth merchant or stock market operator in Kalbadevi who did not avail of his talents. Besides the usual accounting and taxation advice, Chander was famous for his niche services branded among those in the know as 1-2-2-1. He could take your official money and make it unofficial and vice-versa, hence the moniker *One ka Two aur Two ka One*. Chander's introduction to Arvind Bagadia had been through Tarachand Agarwal, Brijmohanlal's old munim who had also joined Arvind's board. The Marwari network was amazingly resourceful when it came to matters of money.

That Tuesday, Chander was settled at his usual two-seater table awaiting a jeweller who wanted assistance in avoiding a huge tax liability. The decade of the '70s had produced an Indian tax structure that was unrealistic. At its peak, the maximum marginal rate of tax for an individual was a staggering 97.5 per cent. It was but obvious that the demand for Chander's services would be substantial.

Chander looked at his watch. His client was late. A minute later the second chair at his table was occupied. Not by his jeweller client but by a stranger.

'What's good in the thali today? I hope they're serving *basundhi* instead of shrikhand,' remarked Mr Sushil Tiwari, Chief Commissioner Income Tax. 'I haven't been here in ages. Is the food still as wonderful?'

'I have no clue about that transaction,' said Chander Lakhotia defiantly to Sushil Tiwari.

'You just threw a stone at me,' said Mr Tiwari. 'People who live in glass houses should not throw stones at Income Tax officers.'

'I don't know what you mean,' said Chander defensively, still chewing his afters.

'Why don't we start with the April transaction that you did with Bhimji Maniklal? You paid him a commission of several lakhs. Pray, what services did he render that required such significant payment? It's obvious that you were helping him convert his ill-gotten *kuchcha* gains to *pukka*.'

Chander Lakhotia kept quiet.

'And then there's the June transaction that's even more interesting. You bought and sold huge quantities of raw steel. As far as I can recall, you are neither in the steel trading business nor are you in the construction industry.'

Chander Lakhotia stayed quiet.

'There's the August transaction that's truly remarkable. You bought uncut diamonds worth lakhs and then allowed the diamonds to be resold at a fraction of the value. Quite obviously you were assisting someone to launder their money. Given that the diamonds were imported, I could quite easily ask the boys at the Enforcement Directorate to see if any provisions of the Foreign Exchange Regulation Act have been violated. As you well know, non-compliance involves criminal prosecution and a prison term. Do you want me to go on?'

Chander Lakhotia was no longer quiet.

'Why don't you simply tell me what it is that you want? Money?' he asked.

Sushil Tiwari laughed. 'Nothing as cheap as money, Mr Lakhotia. All I need is Mr Arvind Bagadia. Help me and I'll be on my way and you can get on with all your dodgy transactions.'

'We now have enough material to warrant an Income Tax raid on Mr Arvind Bagadia and all his business establishments,' said Sushil Tiwari.

'But how will an Income Tax raid help me recover my money?' asked Murali. 'All it will do is to give you an opportunity to line your own pockets.'

'There are twenty-two locations besides his home and corporate office that would need to be raided,' said Mr Tiwari. 'If you like we can raid just a few of the locations.'

'How will that help?' asked Murali.

'You could coordinate the rest,' winked Tiwari.

'Tiwari has lost it, Arbaaz,' said Murali, sipping his coffee. 'He says that he will just conduct a couple of the raids and the rest could be done by us. What sort of an offer is that?'

'A good one,' replied Arbaaz.

'How?' asked Murali, even more confused by Arbaaz's reply.

'You recall what happened a couple of years ago at a jewellery shop in Bombay? A group of men posing as Income Tax officers executed a fake raid on the shop.'

'How did they manage that?' asked Murali.

'The kingpin placed a classified advertisement in the *Times of India*, calling for applications from candidates who wanted to be security officers,' replied Arbaaz. 'The ad asked the applicants to report for an interview to an office address the next day. The kingpin interviewed the candidates, selected two dozen from the candidate pool and asked them to report the next day for a mock raid.'

'Then what happened?' asked Murali, leaning forward, his interest piqued.

'The next day he loaded them into a bus and took them to the target jewellery shop. Once there, he introduced himself to the owner as an Income Tax officer and produced a forged search warrant. He then seized much of the inventory and cash and provided the owners with a receipt. He left to "supervise another raid" while leaving his team "in charge". An hour later the owner called the police when he realized that the team members who had remained behind were not Income Tax officers.'

Murali and Arbaaz laughed heartily.

'It was the heist of a lifetime. He was never caught. That is what Tiwari is referring to. While he mounts genuine Income Tax raids on a few select locations, our men can conduct fake raids on the remaining locations. The Income Tax team will torment Arvind Bagadia mercilessly while we recoup all our losses and, possibly, garner a handsome profit on top of it.'

'I can't fucking believe what you are telling me,' screamed Arvind. 'How could this happen?'

There was a hushed silence as his team attempted to come to grips with the situation.

'Yesterday we spent all day answering the questions of the Income Tax department,' shouted Arvind. 'And today you tell me that only the raid at the Bombay office was real...

that the other raids at our Calcutta corporate office and our branch offices in other cities were a scam. Didn't any of you bother to check IDs and warrants?'

'All the raid parties were carrying search warrants and Income Tax ID cards,' replied Joydeep. 'The raid at the Bombay office happened at 10 am. When the other raids followed at 11 am, we assumed it was the same thing.'

'Assumed? Assumed? I don't fucking pay you all to assume anything!' screamed Arvind. 'How much have we lost?'

'The cash that was available at all the locations was a little in excess of two crore,' said Satyapal. 'They took it away and gave us receipts.'

'In the meantime, the real authorities that had raided the Bombay office have seized records and books of account,' said Joydeep. 'The Chief Commissioner of Income Tax is someone called Mr Sushil Tiwari. He is personally calculating the proposed liability for the transaction that we did with Chander Lakhotia.'

'It's evident that Chander Lakhotia leaked,' said Satyapal.

'If Lakhotia leaked then someone made him leak,' said Arvind. 'The question is who.'

'Come to Calcutta Medical College,' said Abhilasha on the phone. She sounded tired and stressed out.

'What's the matter?' asked Arvind.

'It's Babuji,' she said. 'He's had a heart attack.'

Arvind left everything and got into his car without giving any of his usual instructions to Hilda. *When it rains, it bloody pours,* he thought.

He instructed the driver to get him to College Street double-quick. As soon as he reached Calcutta Medical College he ran towards the cardiology wing. He found his mother and wife outside in the hallway. Both looked terribly distraught.

'How is he?' he asked, ignoring the usual hospital commotion around him. His mother reached out and hugged Arvind tightly as her tears began flowing.

Abhilasha looked on, feeling even more guilty.

Two important business people died in 1983. They were two individuals who were rather different in their approach. First, there was the doyen of Indian industry, Ghanshyam Das Birla, who passed away in London on 11 June. Then there was Brijmohanlal Bagadia who followed a day later in Calcutta.

The cremation of Birla was held at Golders Green Crematorium in London. The cremation of Brijmohanlal Bagadia was held at the Keoratola burning ghat. Arvind held the bundle of burning grass as he circled his father's body. The priest then instructed Arvind to light the pyre. Brijmohanlal's body was soon engulfed in flames on a bed of wood, bamboo and grass. Tending to the pyre was a Brahmin who was reciting verses in praise of Shiva.

The funeral was attended by bankers, industrialists, traders, landlords and bureaucrats. There was no one in Calcutta who hadn't had business dealings with Arvind, and all his friends were present. Arvind's enemies, too, were present. Births, marriages and deaths were never reserved for one group or the other. *Who will cry when you die? Quite a few if your son is rich and powerful.*

Several members of the extended Bagadia clan were also present. This was a family that had banished Brijmohanlal and declared him persona non grata. They had only chosen to remember Brijmohanlal after his son Arvind had become a millionaire.

Brijmohanlal's life had been complicated. His father, a senior manager at a tea plantation in Darjeeling, had been keen for him to take up a factory manager's position at the plantation. Brijmohanlal had been adamant about shifting to Calcutta and getting into the jute trade. He had done so against the wishes of his father.

There was a reason for Brijmohanlal's father's views. The reason went back to 1652. Brijmohanlal's distant ancestor, Hiranand Sahu, had emigrated from Marwar's Nagaur—a dusty town midway between Jaipur and Bikaner—to Patna in 1652. In Patna he had emerged as the main lender to local rulers as well as foreign merchants. His eldest son, Manik Chand, had moved to Dhaka, which used to be the key commercial centre of Bengal in the seventeenth century. In Dhaka, Manik Chand had added commodity trading to his portfolio of activities.

When the first Nawab of Bengal, a Hindu Brahmin-raised Muslim, Murshid Quli Khan, had transferred the capital of Bengal to a new town, Murshidabad, which he named after himself, Manik Chand had also moved. By the time he died in 1714, his business had grown by leaps and bounds. The business now had branches in Delhi, Hooghly, Calcutta, Dhaka and Varanasi besides Murshidabad.

The family reached its zenith under Manik Chand's son, Fateh Chand, who was conferred the title *Jagat Seth* by the Mughal emperor in 1722. The title meant 'banker to the world' and indeed he was. He managed the Murshidabad mint, financed local rulers and foreign merchants and was the designated state treasurer. He alone lent almost four lakh each year to the East India Company!

Ironically, it was the British who were the reason for the downfall of the Jagat Seths. The Jagat Seths supported the British during the Battle of Plassey in 1757 thus helping them gain control of Bengal. As British domination and administration strengthened, the position of the Jagat Seths weakened. The British eventually subsumed many of the functions that the Jagat Seths usually performed.

By the nineteenth century, the family was compelled to seek a pension from the British and by the twentieth century, their descendants were forced to look at employment opportunities. Brijmohanlal's great-grandmother had been a Jagat Seth and had married Nathulal Bagadia of Fatehpur. Successive generations, including Brijmohanlal's father, had always taken up employment and shunned business.

Brijmohanlal's obstinacy to engage in a business of his own and his subsequent decision to marry Shakuntala, who was from a lower caste than the Bagadias, had severed almost all family connections. The struggle to make ends meet without any family support had taken its toll on the couple. Luckily for Brijmohanlal, one of his schoolfriends had been the manager at Kamarhatty, one of the oldest jute mills in Bengal. He had offered Brijmohanlal his first deal. It had set the ball rolling. Brijmohanlal hadn't become a millionaire but had succeeded in securing a life that would be called affluent by most standards.

Arvind watched the flames consume his father's body. He remembered Paromita. He remembered her reciting the verses of Omar Khayyam to him.

Ah make the most of what yet we may spend, before we too into dust descend!

The twenty-fifth of June 1983 was a sunny day in London, but it was in front of a television set in Bombay at five minutes before midnight that four Indian men were sweating profusely as they shouted their lungs hoarse.

The 25,000 spectators who crowded the stands at Lord's had their eyes glued to the ball as it swirled in the air, heading towards the outfield. Back in India, millions of Indians also had their eyes glued to their television sets, keeping their fingers crossed that the transmission link would not go down at that critical moment only to be replaced by footage of Mohammad Rafi singing Shammi Kapoor hits.

It had been a series of unexpected twists that had propelled India to the final. Kapil Dev had played the best ODI knock against Zimbabwe; Yashpal Sharma and Sandeep Patil had simply hung in there during the semi-final; Balwinder Sandhu had bowled an awesome in-swinger to stun Gordon Greenidge… the list was endless.

During the final match that day, India had been restricted to 183, and Richards had led West Indies to 50 for 1 in a strong reply. Caribbean celebrations had begun in advance. And then Kapil had miraculously run back from his position, extended his long arms, his eyes never leaving the ball, only to take out Richards at 33. Indians had erupted in joyful madness. Then Madan Lal and Mohinder Amarnath had wobbled the ball around and incredibly taken three wickets each, thus dismissing a stunned West Indies for 140. For every Indian around the world, God had delivered victory to them. And Kapil Dev was God.

The four Indian men who were going crazy in front of the television set were Arbaaz, Murali, Raju and a fourth invitee—Yash Dhar.

On the urging of Arbaaz, Raju had started accepting cricket bets for the Prudential World Cup. No one had ever given Kapil Dev's team the remotest chance of defeating West Indies and it had ended up doing precisely that. Even on the day of the final, the odds being offered in London for bets on India to win were 66—1. Kapil Dev was in his very first season as team captain, having assumed the mantle from Gavaskar just a few months previously. Murali had done his calculations wisely and advised Raju to offer odds of 11—1 on an India win. Less than 3 per cent of Indian punters had placed their money on India. The net result was that Arbaaz had made a killing.

'This event has changed cricket for ever,' said Arbaaz as he downed his drink.

'How?' asked Raju as he took out a paan from a small box and placed it in his mouth.

'First, live television with colour transmission is here to stay,' explained Arbaaz. 'Second, the shorter format of the game will replace Test matches. Third, huge money will flow into advertising and sponsorships. Four, we will make a killing on betting.'

'Yes, big changes are in the offing,' echoed Yash.

Ever since the day Arbaaz had helped get the CM off his back, Yash had become indebted to Arbaaz. Giving up his job in journalism, he had hooked up with his old friends from the world of flying. One of them was an airline pilot called Rajiv Gandhi. Three months later, Yash had joined the Congress party. Yash had built and nurtured his relationship with Arbaaz thereafter. After the excitement of the win had died down, Yash proceeded to convince Arbaaz that he needed to join the Congress party too.

'What will that achieve?' asked Arbaaz.

'The country needs people who can get things done, it doesn't matter how they get done,' replied Yash. 'The country is spiralling out of control. The news is that Jarnail Singh Bhindranwale will occupy the Golden Temple very soon. Punjab is in a mess. The situation down south is also politically precarious. N.T. Rama Rao defeated the

Congress in Andhra Pradesh and we now have a non-Congress state government there.'

'You misunderstood my question,' said Arbaaz. 'I meant what will joining the Congress achieve for *me*?'

Yash laughed. 'Come with me to Delhi. Meet the party bosses. You will find out.'

'Did you hear the news?' asked Yash on the phone.

'What news?' asked Arbaaz.

'Mrs Gandhi has been assassinated,' replied Yash.

'What?! By whom? And why?' asked Arbaaz, his head spinning.

'She was at her residence at Safdarjung Road. Two of her Sikh bodyguards shot her using their service weapons,' said Yash. 'Apparently, it was retribution for Operation Bluestar.'

Five months earlier, the Indian Army had stormed the Harmandir Sahib complex in the Golden Temple, holiest of the holy to the Sikhs, to eject Jarnail Singh Bhindranwale and his armed followers from inside it. The action had led to massive Sikh agitations and anger. Sikh soldiers in the Indian Army mutinied, some Sikhs resigned from government positions and many returned awards, honours and medals they had earned from the government.

'What will happen now?' asked Arbaaz.

'The body's at the All-India Institute of Medical Sciences,' said Yash. 'It's most likely that Rajiv will be sworn in as Prime Minister and fresh elections will be called. You need to come to Delhi… on second thoughts, wait until I call you.'

'Why?'

'There have been instances of looting and violence,' said Yash. 'Let things settle down and then I'll call you.'

'No, Yash, I should come,' said Arbaaz. 'I should be visible at the funeral. I'll bring my bodyguards.'

Delhi was bathed in Sikh blood during those seventy-two hours.

Arbaaz was staying at Yash's house in Maharani Bagh when the trouble started. Although the violence was maximum in colonies such as Trilokpuri, Kalyanpur and Mangalpuri, looting and killing soon spread to Connaught Place, Vasant Vihar, Maharani Bagh, New Friends Colony, Lodhi Colony and Hauz Khas.

The first targets in Sikh-dominated areas were the gurudwaras. Rioters would desecrate the Guru Granth Sahib by urinating on it and this would be followed by the gurudwara being burnt down. The next targets were chosen through visible symbols—turbans, uncut hair and beards. Attackers invaded Sikh homes and pulled out the men, tore away their beards, beat them with rods and finally killed them by placing flaming tyres around their necks. The Delhi Police was conspicuous by its absence.

'Stay inside and let this play out,' said Yash to Arbaaz.

'Why are you behaving like a pussy?' argued Arbaaz. 'People are being killed in broad daylight and you fucking hide yourself in your house!' *How do I tell you that many politicians are actively assisting the troublemakers?* thought Yash.

That afternoon a mob reached Yash's house but it was not touched. Two blocks down, a house belonging to Sardar

Harpal Singh was targeted. He and his family were abroad but there was a house guest staying there.

Hearing shouts and screams, Arbaaz ran outside to see a woman being dragged by her hair to the street by intoxicated hoodlums. 'Blood for blood, spare no *sardar*,' the crowd was shouting.

Arbaaz's blood boiled. Grabbing the watchman's lathi, he jumped in. His two bodyguards also rushed behind him. Arbaaz remembered the training that had been imparted to him by Iqbal at the taleemkhana. He had been made to stand on a cot, below which Iqbal had placed a hen. It all came flooding back to him as he wielded the lathi around him like the propeller of an aircraft, making it impossible for any of the attackers to touch the woman without getting their heads split wide open.

A few minutes later, a reluctant Yash came running out and commanded the hoodlums. 'She is not to be touched. Go home!'

The anti-Sikh pogrom eventually killed 2,733, leaving 1,300 widows and 4,000 orphans in its aftermath. Some days later, Rajiv Gandhi philosophically suggested that when a big tree fell, it was only natural that the ground around it would shake. It had taken Atal Bihari Vajpayee's wit to refute the words of Rajiv. Vajpayee had responded that Rajiv was too young to understand that it was the other way round—trees usually fell when the earth shook.

'Who are you?' asked Arbaaz, as he escorted the Sardarni to Yash's house.

'My name is Adhyapika Jyoti,' she said.

'The house that I was staying in belongs to Sardar Harpal Singh and his wife Kamaljot. Harpal is a wealthy businessman who divides his time between India and Bhutan,' said Adhyapika Jyoti. 'He and his family are my disciples. Whenever I am in Delhi, I stay at their house. I had come home for a quick shower when the commotion began.'

She said it in an entirely calm manner. It was as though she had just come out of meditation. There wasn't the slightest hint that she had been affected by the goons or their attack on her.

She sipped the tea offered by Yash's servant and said to Arbaaz, 'I have always believed that the Almighty finds a way to protect us if our time has not yet come. He protected me through you, my son.'

Arbaaz smiled, slightly embarrassed by the praise. Here was a mafia don who controlled most of Bombay, feeling like a schoolboy in the presence of this intensely spiritual woman.

'What is your name, son?' she asked.

'Arbaaz,' he replied.

'And is this your house?' she asked.

'No, I live in Bombay,' he replied. 'This is my friend Yash's home.' He pointed to Yash who was seated next to him on the sofa.

'Well, Arbaaz, I should be going,' she said. 'You shall have my abundant blessings, always.'

'Are you sure you want to go back to that house?' asked Arbaaz. 'Should I send one of my men to protect you?'

'I am not going back to the house, Arbaaz,' she replied. 'I plan to go door-to-door to provide a shoulder to cry on. Hundreds have been killed, raped or orphaned. I am needed by many.'

'It's not safe for you to be wandering about,' protested Arbaaz.

'What will they do? Kill me? They can only kill my body, not my soul. My soul is immortal,' she said as she stood up to leave.

'I'm not sure whether I want to contest on a Congress ticket,' Arbaaz told Yash.

'Why?' asked Yash. 'Because of the killings in the anti-Sikh riots? Isn't that a bit rich, coming from Bombay's most powerful don?'

'I kill for business, not for pleasure,' said Arbaaz.

'There has never been a time that India has been free from communal clashes,' countered Yash. 'Everyone is naked under their clothes, Arbaaz, every community—be it Hindu, Muslim, Christian or Sikh—has been guilty. Even the greatest emperor of ancient India, Ashoka, put 18,000 followers of the Ajivika sect to the sword.'

Arbaaz was quiet.

'The most liberal Akbar also ordered the death of 8,000 Hindus at Chittor,' said Yash.

Arbaaz remained quiet.

'The great Maharaja Ranjit Singh asked his governor to demolish the Jama Masjid of Srinagar and to kill thousands of Muslim Pashtun tribals,' continued Yash.

Arbaaz stayed deep in thought.

'The illustrious Tipu Sultan destroyed twenty-seven churches and captured 60,000 Syrian Christians at Seringapatam. Some 20,000 of them died during a forced march,' said Yash.

Arbaaz remained in thought.

'The Portuguese Catholics established the Inquisition that tortured and killed hundreds of Hindus in Goa,' said Yash.

Arbaaz made up his mind.

The next day, he dropped in to meet a man he had met twelve years earlier in Hyderabad. He had been the Chief Minister of Andhra Pradesh at that time and Arbaaz had taken a linguist, Pierre Lacroix, to meet him.

The former CM was now the Minister of External Affairs. His name was P.V. Narasimha Rao. The day after their second meeting, Arbaaz formally joined the Congress party.

Back in Bombay, Arbaaz received a bouquet of flowers. It was from Keshav Gadgil of the Shiv Sena. The note that accompanied it said, 'Welcome to the political arena. I look forward to our duel.'

General elections were announced on 14 November 1984.

Arbaaz charged headlong into campaigning. There were 644,716 voters on the rolls for his constituency. It was his job to reach out to each one of them. Murali and Raju had been sceptical initially but seeing Arbaaz's enthusiasm they quickly set up an election office staffed with Arbaaz's loyal supporters.

Arbaaz would address at least five public meetings each day. Murali had bought a new Maruti 800—launched the previous year in India—so that Arbaaz could zip in and out of congested areas in a fraction of the time it would normally take. Arbaaz never spoke from a prepared text, always gauging the mood of the crowd first and then choosing his words. On one occasion, Murali accompanied Arbaaz to that day's meetings and came away astounded.

At the first meeting of the day, he said to a crowd of Muslim youth, 'I am your father. I am your mother. Haven't I always looked after you like a parent?'

At the mid-morning meeting he said to an assembly of construction workers, 'There are those who say that I am a bad person? Yes, I am a bad person. I am bad to those who torment the poor and the downtrodden. Is it too much to demand two square meals, clothes on one's back and a roof over one's head? Shame on the pathetic politicians that you voted in. I am not *a* choice. I am your *only* choice!'

In the afternoon meeting, he told a group of slum-dwellers, 'God Almighty once asked me what more he could give me. I answered, help me help others. I want to serve you by serving them. There are hundreds of people here whose tears I have personally wiped away. All I want is the chance to wipe away some more. Hopefully, I'll also bring a smile to those tearful faces.'

In the evening he addressed a labour union. He said, 'You need someone tough. Someone who can stand up for you. Someone who can demand justice and dignity on your behalf. I am the only one who can do that for you.'

At night he addressed a youth conference. 'My opponents are weak. Yesterday, I sent each of them a box of bangles. None of them have the guts to face me in the street, how will they face me at the ballot-box?'

Murali was convinced that Arbaaz would win. Muslims had already decided to vote for him. His winning would depend on swinging the Hindu vote. He spoke to Arbaaz about that and Arbaaz quickly incorporated temple darshans into his schedule.

Campaigning ended on 23 December 1984 at 5 pm. The fate of 5,301 candidates and forty-six political parties would be decided after the votes were tallied. All of 389 million people were eligible to vote and each of them knew the power of the ballot. It was the same ballot that had thrown Mrs Gandhi out. It was the same one that had brought her back.

As it turned out, Rajiv Gandhi romped home with a landslide victory in the elections. It was a victory like no other. The Indian National Congress won 404 seats in a 533-seat Lok Sabha, managing to muster more than 50 per cent of the popular vote. The tragedy of Mrs Gandhi's assassination had played a vital role in consolidating the vote for the grand old party.

Atal Bihari Vajpayee, who had rebuked Rajiv Gandhi for his 'falling-tree' statement was left with a party that had been decimated. The BJP had been expected to gain from the backlash following Mrs Gandhi's assassination but this did not happen and the party was able to win a mere two seats after contesting 224. N.T. Rama Rao's Telugu Desam Party emerged as the second-largest party by winning thirty seats. For the first time in India, a regional party was now the main Opposition party.

Arbaaz Sheikh, MP, Bombay South, stormed into the Lok Sabha along with 403 colleagues from the Indian National Congress. They included a famous Bollywood star, Amitabh Bachchan, who won his Allahabad seat by polling 68 per cent of the votes. Arbaaz had 2,05,192 votes in his favour. The next highest candidate—Keshav Gadgil from the Shiv Sena—pulled in 1,96,313 votes. One of Arbaaz's 403 colleagues who won was Yash Dhar who had contested the Chandni Chowk seat in Delhi.

In the heat and dust of election campaigning and the exhilaration of victory, scant attention was paid to the fact that three weeks previously, the pesticide plant of Union Carbide India Limited at Bhopal had sprung a leak. Over half a million people were exposed to deadly methyl-isocyanate gas. The official death toll was 2,259. It would subsequently stand revised to 3,787 but the unofficial estimates were 8,000.

Joseph Stalin, the Soviet dictator, had once famously observed, 'A single death is a tragedy; a million deaths is a statistic.'

The BJP had contested 224 seats and won only two. The two seats that it won were Mehsana in Gujarat, where the BJP candidate, Dr A.K. Patel, romped home, and Hanamkonda in Andhra Pradesh where the BJP candidate, P.J. Reddy, won. The losing candidate was the Congress party's P.V. Narasimha Rao.

Arvind dictated a letter to Hilda before leaving for his meeting at the Bengal Club.

31 December 1984

Shri Atal Bihari Vajpayee
Bharatiya Janata Party

Dear Atalji,

This letter is to remind you that the darkest hour is just before the dawn. I am certain that you shall see the glorious sunrise soon enough.

My very best wishes,

Arvind Bagadia

Arvind arrived for his meeting with Mr Deshmukh, the former chairman of United Federation Bank, at 12.30 sharp. It was to be lunch at the Bengal Club.

Arvind's father, Brijmohanlal, had initially attempted to apply for membership to the club. Founded almost seventy years before the Tolly, the Bengal Club boasted an ancestry no less than that of the Athenaeum, the Carlton or the Reform Club. And unlike the Tolly, the Bengal Club refused to be addressed by a nickname. Unfortunately, one of the seventeen members of the membership subcommittee of the Bengal Club had decided to blackball Brijmohanlal. 'We're not sitting on this subcommittee to admit riffraff,' the blackballing member had haughtily confided to one of the others. That single veto had been sufficient to bar Brijmohanlal from the white club of the brown sahibs. But the Tolly had been nicer to Brijmohanlal.

The bastards who had blackballed his father had now been forced to accept Arvind at the Bengal Club. *Money makes everything right*, thought Arvind as he entered the dining room that was famous for its offerings of smoked hilsa, honey-glazed ham, lobster thermidor and gazpacho. Arvind was vegetarian. The white-gloved waiters knew that his meal would consist of boiled rice, vegetable curry and yoghurt. He settled down at his usual table and ordered tonic water, lemon and ice.

After a long stint as managing director, then chairman, Mr Deshmukh had retired and then taken over as secretary-general of the Chambers of Indian Commerce and Industry, more commonly known in business circles as the CICI.

When conveyed the news of his new position by Mr Deshmukh a few weeks earlier, Arvind had asked Mr Deshmukh, 'Why the demeaning title of secretary? It makes one sound like a typist!'

Mr Deshmukh had laughed. 'The word "secretary" comes from the medieval Latin word *secretarius* which means a person entrusted with secrets. That's why America has a secretary of state, it's why the Communist Party has a general secretary, and it's why the United Nations has a secretary-general.'

Arvind sipped his tonic water and looked at his watch. 12.35 pm. He saw Mr Deshmukh arrive along with another guest, a rather good-looking man impeccably dressed in a linen suit. Arvind waved to Mr Deshmukh from his table as a waiter accompanied the two men to Arvind.

'Let me introduce you to the new Minister of State for Food and Civil Supplies, Mr Yash Dhar,' said Mr Deshmukh as the men shook hands.

'Minister of State?' asked Arvind.

'Junior minister,' explained Yash. 'But wait for the next Cabinet. I'll have Cabinet rank then.'

'So what secret can I get out of you today?' asked Arvind jokingly of Mr Deshmukh as he and Mr Yash Dhar sat down.

'He who keeps a secret,' said Mr Deshmukh, 'must also keep it secret that he has a secret to keep!' The men laughed.

After they had ordered, Arvind spoke. 'I am grateful to Mr Deshmukh for getting us to meet each other,' he said to Yash. 'I am certain that there could be areas of mutual interest.'

'Areas of mutual interest?' asked Yash. 'A nice euphemism for making money. The problem is that our Prime Minister has been dubbed "Mr Clean" by the general public. He now needs to live up to the name.'

'The truth,' said Arvind, 'is that there are three ways that serious money is currently made in India. One: a resource-grab; two: a licence-grab; three: a land-grab. Very few have bothered with the fourth.'

'What is the fourth?' asked a curious Yash.

'An information-grab. The ability to get information well in advance. That's where you can help me.'

Emerging from his lunch at the Bengal Club, Arvind got into the rear seat of his Mercedes-Benz 300TD Wagon and asked the driver to take him back to his office which was located a few minutes away along the Chowringhee Road stretch.

His car stopped momentarily at the traffic junction at the corner of Chowringhee Road and Sudder Street. Arvind noticed another car that looked familiar. 'Take a right on Sudder Street,' he told his driver. The chauffeur efficiently did what his master requested.

He was right. It was Joydeep's blue Toyota Corona. The one that Joydeep had picked up at an auction from the State Trading Corporation. Arvind saw Joydeep's car heading into the driveway of the Fairlawn Hotel.

He was about to follow, thump him on the back and suggest that they have a cup of tea together when he saw another familiar car and another familiar face.

Kalyan Sarkar was dressed in civvies when he was off duty. In any case, his position in the West Bengal police force was not due to his remarkable efficiency, intelligence or discipline.

Since 1980, West Bengal had been ruled by the CPM. It had brought about successful land reforms in the state and the party had used the political capital earned by it to quickly create a system that could preserve power. The system of patronage it created was so all-encompassing that the politburo's writ ran from Writers' Building to even the remote rural panchayats. Kalyan Sarkar was simply a product of that system. He knew which buttons had to be pressed and which gears to be lubricated.

The result was that even though Kalyan Sarkar drew a government salary, his primary income came from hiring out cops for private services. It was a flourishing business. Arvind had used his services several times and paid him a monthly retainership. 'Ask not what your police officer can do for you, ask what you can do for your police officer,' was the accepted motto for Kalyan Sarkar and his men.

Arvind took out a bundle of cash from his briefcase and placed it inside a manila envelope. He handed it over to Sarkar.

'Put your best chap on the job,' Arvind said to him.

'Don't worry, boss,' said Kalyan, grinning obsequiously. 'I have never put anyone less than the best on assignments that come from you.'

Joydeep walked into Arvind's office excitedly. 'I've found out what happened,' he said, sitting down on one of the visitor's chairs.

'Where were you?' asked Arvind.

'Doing some research. Chander Lakhotia, our chartered accountant, was pressured by the Chief Commissioner of Income Tax, Mr Sushil Tiwari, to squeal on us.'

'I already know that,' said Arvind, absentmindedly playing with a solid silver paperweight on his desk. His mother had given the paperweight to him as a present on his last birthday. It was a silver disc with a diameter of around five centimetres and thickness of a centimetre. Wrapped snugly around the disc was the copper kada that Arvind had wanted from his mother all his life. Shakuntala had had the paperweight handcrafted by her silversmith, and it looked stunning.

'Yes,' said Joydeep. 'But what you do not know is that our bank, United Federation Bank, has another client in Bombay. This client lost a huge amount of money when we rigged the share price of Qurbani Hotels Limited.'

'You mean Dhanda Holdings Private Limited?' asked Arvind.

'Precisely, Dhanda Holdings Private Limited. Its managing director, Mr Murali Iyer, had attended our AGM and had praised you eloquently.'

'I remember that,' said Arvind. 'What about him?'

'He's merely a front. The company is a massive money-laundering operation for the Bombay underworld,' said Joydeep.

'Who?' asked Arvind.

'Arbaaz Sheikh,' said Joydeep, putting a newspaper cutting of Arbaaz's Lok Sabha victory on Arvind's table. Arvind remembered the man on the flight whom he had extended his hospitality to in Hyderabad.

'And we goddamn allowed him to invest in Braid too,' said Arvind, suddenly irritated that Paromita was Arbaaz's wife.

'It's not your fault, Arvind,' said Joydeep. 'One can't be expected to judge people accurately all the time.'

'That's so true,' said Arvind, staring at Joydeep.

In 1985, a bomb placed by Sikh militants on an Air India flight from Montreal to London had blown up 31,000 feet above the Irish coast. All 329 people aboard—mostly of Indian origin—had been killed. The dastardly act was purportedly carried out to avenge Indira Gandhi's Operation Bluestar.

One of the passengers who died in that bomb explosion was Shaila Dhar. She was the wife of Yash Dhar, the Minister of Coal and Mines. She had been on a personal visit to Canada to spend a few weeks with uncles, aunts and cousins who were settled in Toronto. By an ironic twist of fate, her husband and son had been unable to accompany her owing to political commitments and school schedules.

Shaila was a lawyer who had valiantly fought for women's rights. One of the cases that she had advised on concerned the matter of a Muslim woman called Shah Bano Begum. Shah Bano, a sixty-two-year-old Muslim mother of five from Indore, had been divorced by her husband in 1978. She filed a criminal suit in the Supreme Court, in which she won the right to alimony from her husband. This was a landmark secular judgment in which the court decided that maintenance was payable even if it were in conflict with Muslim personal law—Sharia. India seemed to be moving towards a uniform civil code—one that did not distinguish between Hindu, Muslim, Christian or Sikh.

Several people in positions of power attended the prayer meeting held at Yash's house in Delhi that morning. There had been no funeral because her body was never found. 'Lost at sea' was the only observation that appeared against her name. Among the attendees were Arbaaz Sheikh and Arvind Bagadia. Mr Deshmukh was also there. Several politicians cutting across party lines were present. Being a friend and minister of Rajiv Gandhi, Yash had many friends from the secular Left. Being a Kashmiri Pandit, Yash also had many political friends from the Hindu Right. Yash's friends had often asked him where exactly he stood politically—Leftist, Rightist, centrist, conservative, liberal, democrat or socialist? Yash would reply wittily, 'I'm something between a socialist and a socialite.'

Today the wit was entirely absent as mourners, mostly dressed in white, sat under a canopy quietly as a group of sombre men and women chanted *Om Namah Shivay*. Seated in the front row was Yash's colleague, Arbaaz Sheikh. Two rows behind was Arvind Bagadia along with the banker, Mr Deshmukh. At night many of the mourners would be seen at the Ghungroo, the discotheque at Delhi's ITC Maurya Sheraton. There was no point in mourning beyond the morning.

As the prayer meeting wound up and the attendees spilled outside into the garden, Arvind was greeted by a familiar face. It was Chander Lakhotia, the paan-masala-loving chartered accountant. Arvind had seen him from a distance but had chosen to ignore him. Arvind was pretty certain that Chander Lakhotia had revealed critical information that prompted the Income Tax raid on him. But Chander was effusive in his warmth.

'It is so good to see you, Arvind Babu,' said Chander. 'I felt terrible about the way that the Income Tax authorities treated you. I wanted to call you but I knew that you would have your hands full with the passing away of your dear father.'

'What brings you here?' asked Arvind, not bothering to reciprocate the warmth.

'See those men there?' asked Chander, indicating the direction with a nod of his head.

Arvind looked at the mourners. Among them were Atal Bihari Vajpayee and L.K. Advani. 'You mean Vajpayeeji and Advaniji?' asked Arvind.

'Yes,' replied Chander. 'I'm a member of the BJP. My main task is to raise money from businessmen so that the party can mount a credible bid for power in the next general elections.'

'But elections took place only last year,' said Arvind. 'There's still lots of time till 1989.'

'This government won't last that long,' whispered Chander. 'Rajiv Gandhi plans to introduce legislation to overturn the secular Shah Bano verdict. It will be called the Muslim Women's Bill and will pander to his Muslim constituency. He doesn't yet realize that it will completely destroy his Hindu support base.'

'I see,' said Arvind, attempting to digest the information.

'Arvind Babu, let me introduce you to the party bigwigs. Who knows? Maybe one day you will join politics too?'

'Why not,' said Arvind, as they headed towards the BJP bigwigs.

How nice to see you, Arvind,' said Vajpayee as they approached. Arvind bent down to touch Vajpayee's feet. 'I was sad to hear about your dear father's demise.'

Chander Lakhotia slunk away when he realized that Arvind already knew the party bigwigs.

'Let me introduce you to Sardar Harpal Singh, a dear friend who spends more time in Bhutan than in India these days,' said Vajpayee.

Yash Dhar, the Minister for Food and Civil Supplies, had provided him with a list of everything that his ministry did. Arvind looked at the list again.

1. *Purchase of foodstuff for civil and military requirements*
2. *Coordination with the International Wheat Council, International Sugar Council, World Food Council and IFPRI*
3. *Treaties and agreements with foreign countries relating to trade and commerce in foodgrains and foodstuff*

4. *Acquisition of warehouses for storage*
5. *Interstate trade in respect of foodgrains and foodstuffs including sugar*
6. *Industries related to fruit- and vegetable-processing, sugar and milling*
7. *Management of Central Warehousing Corporation and State Warehousing Corporations*
8. *Price control and forecasting of foodgrains, foodstuffs and sugar*
9. *Matters related to the Directorate of Sugar, National Sugar Institute, Development Council for Sugar Industry and other subordinate offices*

He read the list twice and then looked at Satyapal. 'Do you see the opportunity?' he asked.

Satyapal read the list again. 'I can't seem to see anything other than government jargon,' he said.

'See item eight,' said Arvind. 'Price control and forecasting of food grains, foodstuffs and sugar.'

'How does that constitute a money-making opportunity?' asked Satyapal.

'The minister will always know the likely output of a given commodity and the likely price,' replied Arvind.

'So?' asked Satyapal.

'If he shares this information with us in advance, we could make a killing,' said Arvind.

'Our country does not have a commodity exchange,' said Satyapal. 'The Forward Contracts Regulation Act prohibits futures trading in almost all commodities.'

'That's true, but one doesn't need to trade in commodities to make money,' said Arvind.

'Then how?' asked Satyapal.

'The price of a commodity is often a proxy for something else,' said Arvind.

'You will need to explain that to me,' said Satyapal.

'A couple of years ago, they did an interesting study at the University of California,' said Arvind. 'Over 90 per cent of all American oranges used in frozen concentrated orange juice are grown in Florida. Thus, Florida's weather is a key factor influencing the price at which Orange Juice Futures—or OJF—are traded.'

'So?' asked Satyapal.

'The University of California study found that the reverse was also true. Price changes in OJF were an equally good predictor of Florida weather… if OJF prices went up it meant that temperatures were likely to dip.'

'Interesting,' laughed Satyapal.

'The point I am making is that the advance information that we receive from Yash Dhar could help us predict other variables,' said Arvind.

'Like?'

'If wheat is likely to be a bumper crop, it means that there will be a downward push on price. It means that a company like Britannia that depends heavily on wheat—for its biscuits and breads—would benefit,' said Arvind.

'Go on,' said Satyapal, making notes.

'If groundnut production is likely to be poor, then an upward movement of price would be detrimental to an oil producer like Postman. Conversely, if sunflower seed production is good, then a softening of prices would help Saffola.'

'Excellent, said Satyapal.

'If the sugarcane harvest will be higher this year, it means that the crushing by-product, molasses, will also be greater in quantity. That should be a happy situation for liquor companies such as Shaw Wallace or McDowells.'

'I'll put it into action immediately,' said Satyapal, getting up from the chair.

Arvind picked up the *Forbes* magazine that was lying on his table. The magazine had started tracking the world's billionaires. The only Indian on that list for 1987 was Aditya Birla. *One day I shall be on that list,* thought Arvind.

Next to the issue of *Forbes* lay the *Statesman*. The headline announced that the playback singer, Kishore Kumar, had died. Arvind didn't bother to think that one day he would also be on a list of dead people.

Arvind's phone rang. Picking it up, he listened. Satyapal waited at the door.

He then said, 'A Bengal Transport bus should be fine... I'll pay cash.'

Satyapal left.

Abhilasha sat in the living room watching Sunday morning primetime. *Ramayan,* a serial created by Ramanand Sagar that had become a weekly ritual in the Bagadia home—as it had in millions of homes around the country. Seated next to her was her mother-in-law Shakuntala. Vinay and Vinit also lay sprawled on the carpet, their breakfast untouched.

The Sunday edition of the *Telegraph,* a recent addition to Calcutta's newspaper options, lay on the coffee table. She ignored it. Nowadays the news was always about guns and war. Why couldn't the world watch the *Ramayan* and learn to be more peaceful? Who was to remind Abhilasha that the *Ramayan* had ended with a massive war in Lanka?

Next to the newspaper lay a dog-eared copy of *The Complete Adventures of Feluda* written by the great film director, Satyajit Ray. She ignored that too. She was simply not in the mood to read about death.

Ironically, the latest war was also in Lanka. Rajiv Gandhi had despatched tens of thousands of men to Sri Lanka to keep the peace. The force was known as the Indian Peace Keeping Force—or IPKF. At its peak, over 100,000 IPKF troops would be stationed in Sri Lanka. Closer home, the story of guns seemed to be the only story worth telling. Swedish Radio had alleged that massive kickbacks had been paid by the Swedish arms manufacturer Bofors to Indian politicians and defence officials. Rajiv Gandhi's government was looking increasingly shaky.

The day's episode came to an end and the television was switched off. Abhilasha asked the boys to get their homework done. She knew that it would not get done till the very last minute of the weekend. They were good kids but twelve-year-old boys had minds that were interested in everything but schoolwork.

Shakuntala was counting her beads and silently mouthing her prayers. Abhilasha picked up the newspaper reluctantly. The headline talked about the passing away of Hindi film legend, Raj Kapoor. She then absentmindedly skipped through the usual stuff about the IPKF and Bofors until a photograph in one of the inside pages caught her eye. The staff photographer had taken a picture of a car that had met with a terrible accident the previous day.

The report said that it had been travelling along Chowringhee Road when a bus belonging to Bengal Transport had lost control and crashed headlong into it. The driver of the car had died on the spot.

Abhilasha was stunned. It was a blue Toyota Corona.

'What's the matter, *beti*?' asked Shakuntala, observing that her daughter-in-law's hands were shaking.

'Nothing, Amma,' said Abhilasha, getting up. 'I had better check up on the boys.'

That year, in a ghastly incident, a young Rajput woman called Roop Kanwar had committed sati by sitting on the burning funeral pyre of her husband. As tears began welling up in her eyes, Abhilasha also felt like killing herself for the only man who had brought joy to her miserable life.

Joydeep Chakraborty was bathed and clothed in white. Before the final journey to the cremation ground, an impression of his foot was taken with red dye on a piece of paper. Joydeep was then carried to the cremation ground for the funeral. Arvind was one of the pallbearers.

Joydeep was placed on a pyre. His father, the retired college headmaster, looked utterly broken. He stood in a daze, giving his one and only son a final farewell.

The old man circled the pyre seven times and then performed the *pindo daan*. He then carried out the *daho sanskar*—lighting the pyre to the chant of mantras. Arvind waited on with the old man until the remains could be collected. They would be purified with milk and curd for the *asthi bisorjan*.

When they were alone, Arvind said to Joydeep's father, 'I lost my closest friend and you lost your only son. From today, all your expenses shall be borne by me. You may call me any time of the day or night. I am there for you—always.'

The old man looked at Arvind with tears in his eyes. He lifted his hand and placed it on Arvind's head in a silent gesture of blessing.

Chander Lakhotia shook hands with Arvind as he sat down.

'Good to see you, Arvind Babu,' he said jovially.

'Where does the BJP stand?' asked Arvind, dispensing with the small talk.

'They're going to support Raja Bahadur until such time as he self-destructs,' said Chander, sitting down.

The forty-first Raja Bahadur of Manda had been sworn in as the eighth Prime Minister of India on 2 December 1989. His name was Vishwanath Pratap Singh. His arrival as Prime Minister coincided with the arrival of a young man called Salman Khan whose movie, *Maine Pyar Kiya*, turned out to be the biggest grosser of the year. As it turned out, Salman Khan was to have a lot more staying power than Vishwanath Pratap Singh.

V.P. Singh had been the biggest thorn in Rajiv Gandhi's side. First, Rajiv had made him his Finance Minister. V.P. Singh had proceeded to conduct tax raids on the very businessmen who had supported the Congress party. Rajiv had been left with no alternative but to shunt him sideways into the Ministry of Defence. As Minister of Defence, Singh had launched investigations into the Bofors deal, eventually prompting Rajiv to shunt him out entirely. It was the opportunity that he had been waiting for. He had launched his own political outfit and ended up whittling down the Congress tally.

'How long will this government last?' asked Arvind.

'It's like that new girl, Madhuri Dixit, dancing to '*Ek Do Teen*'. Most likely—one year, possible but unlikely—two years, most improbable—three years,' said Chander, allowing a waiter to place a bowl of soup in front of him.

'Why not five years?' asked Arvind.

'V.P. Singh is entirely dependent on the support of the BJP and the Left parties. Internally, within his own party, there are people like Chandra Shekhar who are feeling sidelined.'

'What should be my strategy?' asked Arvind, tonelessly.

'Unlike the Congress, the BJP doesn't have too many benefactors. If you steadily contribute to their coffers, I think it will guarantee you a position by the time the party comes to power. In any case, you *do* have an old equation with Vajpayeeji,' replied Chander, leaving the bland soup untouched while continuing to chew on the strongly flavoured condiments habitually in his mouth. Secretly, he wished he were in Delhi's Chandni Chowk, enjoying a meal at Paranthe Wali Gali instead.

'I know that you were forced to rat on me by that rascal, Sushil Tiwari,' said Arvind suddenly, snapping his breadstick into two. It was a subtle gesture hinting that he could snap Chander in two just as easily.

Chander's face fell. 'I... I didn't...' he began. He scraped frantically with his teeth at the scented mishmash now liberally coating his tongue.

'I don't blame you,' said Arvind, scooping some butter onto his breadstick. 'I just want you to know that the breadstick did not know that I was going to snap it in two. That breadstick could very well be you one day.'

'Alisha's school admission will need to be made,' said Paromita to Arbaaz, switching off the television.

'What did you do that for?' asked Arbaaz, hastily turning the television set back on.

An India—Pakistan Test match was in progress in Sialkot. A sixteen-year-old boy called Sachin Tendulkar had joined Sidhu at 38 for four in the second innings. A Waqar Younis bouncer had hit Sachin directly on his nose. It was a deep cut and the boy had started bleeding. Instead of withdrawing, he had splashed water on his face and hit the next ball for four.

'*Wah, mere sher,*' said Arbaaz, as he looked at the young man. He quickly muted the television as he saw Paromita's irritated expression. Paromita hated cricket. Her only TV-watching happened on Sunday mornings although Ramanand Sagar's *Ramayan* had been replaced by B.R. Chopra's *Mahabharat*.

'Which is the best school in Bombay?' asked Arbaaz, knowing what the answer would be.

'Cathedral and John Connon,' said Paromita.

She said it hesitantly, knowing how difficult it was to get beyond those hallowed portals. Parents bided their time for years on a waiting list only to find that their child had been left out. Thousands would apply for a mere dozen vacant seats. The school that had begun in 1860 as a grammar school within the walled city of Bombay was heavily in demand 129 years later.

'I have got the forms that need to be submitted,' said Paromita. 'They've asked for lots of information.'

'Don't bother,' said Arbaaz. 'Alisha's admission will happen.'

'How?' asked Paromita.

'The school has a board of governors. There are twelve members,' said Arbaaz. 'They are appointed by the Anglo-Scottish Education Society.'

'And?' asked Paromita.

'One of them, Thomas Koshy, is someone I assisted in recovering a brass lectern from a church five years ago.'

'How fortunate,' said Paromita.

'It's not about fortune,' said Arbaaz. 'It's about foresight.'

'So he finally got his way,' said Arvind to Satyapal, speaking of the wily salt-and-pepper-bearded politician. Both men were in the backseat of Arvind's Merc.

'Can you blame him?' asked Satyapal. 'Chandra Shekhar was gypped out of the top job in 1989.'

V.P. Singh and Chandra Shekhar were rivals, both in contention for the PM's post. They had eventually decided to settle for a consensus candidate—Devi Lal. Accordingly, V.P. Singh had stood up in the Central Hall of Parliament and proposed the name of Devi Lal. Devi Lal had graciously refused the nomination saying that he would prefer V.P. Singh to be PM. The surprise of betrayal on Chandra Shekhar's face had been captured by television cameras.

Now it was payback time.

'V.P. Singh's fate was sealed with the Mandal Commission protests,' said Satyapal.

'No, his fate was sealed at Samastipur,' said Arvind. 'The writing was on the wall.'

The BJP had thrown its weight behind the Ram Janmabhoomi agitation. The party president, L.K. Advani, had toured India's northern states on a *rath*—a bus customized to resemble an ancient chariot. Arvind had donated generously to the BJP even though he did not agree with the idea of a *rath yatra*.

Chander Lakhotia, who was passionately in favour of a Ram temple being built at the site had once asked Arvind, 'Don't you think that we owe it to God?'

Arvind had replied, 'I'm not sure whether God created man or man created God. I do know that someone is watching over us. Usually, it's the Income Tax department.'

'So you're an atheist? You don't believe in God?' asked Chander.

'I believe in God but I don't trust his managers,' said Arvind. 'They're greedy, inefficient and overpaid. I'm not even sure whether they ever convey my messages to him.'

Before L.K. Advani could complete his yatra at Ayodhya, he had been arrested at Samastipur on charges of disturbing the peace and fomenting communal tension. The BJP had responded by withdrawing support to V.P. Singh's government. Singh had lost the vote of no-confidence 142 to 346.

'But how did Chandra Shekhar muster the numbers in his favour?' asked Arvind.

'Rajiv Gandhi's Congress is supporting him,' said Satyapal. 'And guess who engineered that support?'

'No!' said Arvind disbelievingly.

'Absolutely,' replied Satyapal, nodding his head emphatically. 'It was Yash Dhar.'

'What game is the Congress playing?' murmured Arvind.

'They feel it's too early for another election,' said Satyapal. 'They'll wait for a while before pulling the rug from under Chandra Shekhar and then go to an election saying that they are the only ones who can guarantee stability. The question is, what should we do till then.'

'Bet against the rupee and on the dollar,' said Arvind.

'Why?' asked Satyapal.

'The inside news is that we're heading towards a Balance of Payments crisis. India may have to go running to the International Monetary Fund for help. Possibly, we may even have to pledge our gold.'

'So what?' asked Satyapal.

'If that happens, the rupee will plunge against the dollar. We should start acquiring businesses that have dollar revenues.'

'For example?'

'Export-oriented businesses. Most of them do business against Letters of Credit that guarantee dollar revenues. Do your deals quickly.'

'Why?' asked Satyapal.

'Tell me, Satyapal. If you were offered a feast and were told that you could eat as much as you liked for an hour and then be locked away without anything to eat for a week, what would you do?'

Arbaaz drove to Nashik from Bombay in an SUV. In addition to his own two bodyguards was a police escort. Arbaaz Sheikh was now a Member of Parliament and thus entitled to the trappings of power and protection that came with the position.

It was nightfall by the time they arrived. He went directly to Prasad's house. The family was in mourning, Prasad having cremated his wife just that afternoon.

Arbaaz met Prasad and held his hands in a gesture of emotional support. 'Abdul Dada took care of your grandfather and father earlier. It is now my job to take care of you. Anything you need, you tell me,' said Arbaaz to the grateful Prasad.

'Her illness has put me in financial distress,' explained Prasad. 'In India you are not supposed to fall sick if you are poor. Only the rich have the right to fall ill.'

'Stop worrying about money,' said Arbaaz. 'When you were little, you were kidnapped by a loan shark. I saved you from him. Later, when I was in prison, it was your grandfather who helped secure my release.'

Arbaaz handed over a bundle wrapped in newspaper to Prasad. 'Keep it,' he said softly.

'How will I repay you?' asked Prasad.

'It does not need to be repaid, but I'll think of a way that it can,' replied Arbaaz.

'I want you to complete the purchase of that Nashik company.'

'The defunct printing press?' asked Murali.

'I want us to buy it,' said Arbaaz, nodding.

'Why?' asked Murali. 'It's obsolete. Most of the machinery is unusable. Why are we wasting money on this?'

'I have always wanted to bring joy into people's lives,' said Arbaaz. 'What brings greater joy than a wedding invitation card or a birth announcement?'

Murali sighed. It was impossible to get Arbaaz to change his mind once he had decided on something.

'The seller wants full payment upfront,' said Murali.

'Make it,' said Arbaaz, unfazed. "How many employees are there?'

'Twenty,' replied Murali.

'Tell them that their jobs are safe,' said Arbaaz. 'Tell Raju to give you another twenty men.'

'Why?' asked Murali. 'It's a loss-making business. Why overstaff it?'

'I need two shifts,' said Arbaaz. 'A day shift and a night shift.'

The house in Nashik was rarely used. Except for a few trucks that came in at night, it saw very little activity. It had belonged to a television actor whose cash had run out. He had been forced to sell and Arbaaz had been happy to buy it. It was the perfect location. It was just a few yards away from the printing press that he had bought in Nashik.

Arbaaz switched on the lights and sat down on a crate in the bare room. Prasad remained standing.

'Did you check at your printing press?' asked Arbaaz.

Prasad nodded. 'The procedure at ISP is that every three years we discard machinery and dye plates that are worn out. The rule book states that the plates that are to be discarded must be destroyed in the presence of a magistrate.'

'Your grandfather was a magistrate,' said Arbaaz.

'Precisely,' said Prasad. 'Using family connections, I have identified a magistrate who will be happy to sign off papers indicating that the plates were destroyed in his presence.'

'See? I told you that I would find a way for you to pay me back,' joked Arbaaz. 'So here's what will happen now. You will declare three specific plates as worn out. Then you will have the magistrate certify that they have been destroyed in his presence. You will bring the plates to my printing press. During the day, the regular shift shall print wedding cards and stationery. At night, Raju's men will print stuff using your plates. The material printed at night will be brought to this house and stored here so that no one in the regular shift sees it.'

Prasad nodded. He wasn't entirely comfortable with what was being done but his loyalty to Arbaaz was paramount. This was a man who had crushed a loan shark's knuckles with a hammer in order to save him.

India Security Press—or ISP—where Prasad worked, was responsible for minting coins, printing currency and bank notes, non-judicial stamp papers, postage stamps, visa stickers and passports. It reported to the Department of Economic Affairs in the Ministry of Finance.

'I don't understand,' said Raju. 'Here is someone who can give us access to designing, engraving, offset and Intaglio printing machines. Why not simply produce currency?

'You're right, Raju,' said Arbaaz. 'Prasad has access to the security systems, treatment facilities as well as numbering equipment. There is one thing that he does not have access to.'

'What is that?' asked Raju.

'Currency paper,' replied Arbaaz. 'It is imported directly by the government from Japan and Australia. That's precisely why stamp paper is a better bet.'

'Why?' asked Raju, carefully extracting another paan from the small box in his hand and placing it in his mouth.

'The paper used for stamp papers is made right here in India,' said Arbaaz. 'India Security Press has no control over production of security papers by the paper mills, most of which are in the private sector. In fact, even the dandy roll—the device used to create the watermark—is freely available.'

'What do you want me to do?' asked Raju.

'Last year the government ordered 5,281 lakh sheets of stamp paper from ISP,' said Arbaaz. 'ISP supplied 1,424 lakh sheets. There was a shortfall of 3,857 lakh sheets.'

Raju chewed his paan quietly.

'Even if we assume that the average value of each stamp paper was one hundred rupees, the shortfall is worth 3,857 crore per year. I need you to go meet stamp paper distributors all over the country. We can help plug the gap.'

Raju laughed. 'Abdul Dada would be proud of you.'

'Who knows,' joked Arbaaz. 'They may even put my face on a stamp one day!'

1521, Vijayanagara

ॐ त्रियम्बकं यजामहे
सुगन्धिं पुष्टिवर्धनं ।
उर्वारुकमिव बन्धनान्
मृत्योर्मोक्षिय मामृतात् ॥

As was his custom, Krishnadevaraya had risen before daybreak. He had consumed and then anointed himself with a third of a litre of sesame oil. Covered only by a small loincloth, he had worked out with earthen weights and then performed an exercise routine with his sword until his sweat had entirely expelled the oil from his pores.

With his body still wet, the king had stepped into the wrestling ring with one of the royal bodyguards who had strict instructions from the monarch to never go easy on him. After the bout, Krishnadevaraya had mounted his stallion and galloped into the countryside until the first rays of the sun emerged. That was his signal to return.

Now, freshly bathed and impeccably dressed, Krishnadevaraya, Lord of the Vijayanagar Empire, Victor of Andhra, King of Three Kings, examined the *Ratna Kireetam* that had been placed before him for his approval by Prime Minister Thimmarasu.

It was splendid. The jewelled crown weighed 8.27 kilograms and was studded with 2,822 garnets, 160 emeralds, 423 rubies, three sapphires, ten cat's eyes and 1,339 pearls.

'It's outstanding,' remarked the king. 'Where is the sword that goes with it?'

There was a flurry of activity as a nervous jeweller stepped forward and presented a velvet cushion bearing a sword with a diamond-encrusted handle to the king. 'They will suit your majesty,' said the foolish jeweller who had been given the task of creating the two pieces.

'Fool!' snapped the impatient king. 'These are not meant for a mere mortal like myself.' Prime Minister Thimmarasu smiled. He knew where the items were headed. To Lord Venkateswara.

'Have the three statues been erected at the entrance to the temple?' the king asked Thimmarasu.

'Yes, your majesty,' replied his trusted Prime Minister. 'All three statues—of you, Queen Tirumaladevi and Queen Chinnadevi—have been installed in the *Pratima Mandapam* facing the main shrine.'

'Have you seen the figures?' asked the king.

'Absolutely. All three have their hands joined in supplication. Very realistic and artistic. You will be delighted to see them, sire,' said Thimmarasu.

The king's donation to the Tirumala Venkateswara Temple may have been lavish but he did not think of it as such. Some years ago, the renowned saint Vallabhacharya had visited him. Krishnadevaraya had honoured the saint by performing *Kanakabhishekam*. The saint had been seated on a throne while vessels filled with 30,000 gold coins had been poured over the sage's person as an offering.

Krishnadevaraya was never found wanting in his generosity to temples, charities and holy men. He had visited the Venkateswara Temple seven times and each visit had been commemorated by a precious offering to the Lord—a *vidudhara* of solid gold, several pairs of *bhujakeerthi*s, three swords with sheaths, two pairs of *addigalapeta* with a solid gold chain, nine kinds of precious stones, a pair of *kadiyam*s, thousands of gold coins, and a *peetambaram* studded with nine kinds of precious stones.

'Where is Nilakantha Somayaji?' asked the king.

'He is on his way back from Tirumala, your majesty,' replied Thimmarasu.

'Remind me to thank him,' said the king. 'Without him, none of these benefactions to Lord Venkateswara of Tirumala would have been possible.'

Somayaji was Vijayanagara's most renowned mathematician and astronomer. He had written several scholarly works including the *Tantrasamgraha* and *Aryabhatiya Bhasya*.

But there was also a secret side to Somayaji. No one other than the king knew about the mystical chants that Somayaji had in his written possession. Somayaji had spent several years mastering them under the tutelage of a reclusive hermit.

The king knew that he would never have won his countless battles had it not been for the divine blessings of Lord Venkateswara. It was those blessings that had made him victorious against Bijapur, Golconda, the Bahmani Sultanate and Odisha.

But would those blessings have fructified without Somayaji and his crimson-covered notebooks bearing those jelly-fish symbols?

Book Five

1990–2000

'Arbaaz, wake up,' said Paromita.

'What happened?' asked Arbaaz. 'Is Alisha fine?'

'She's sleeping,' said Paromita. 'I was up and the radio was on. BBC Radio just announced that Rajiv Gandhi has been killed.'

'What?' said Arbaaz, getting out of bed. 'Are you sure you aren't mistaken?'

'I am pretty certain,' said Paromita.

Arbaaz quickly put on his clothes. 'Where are you going?' asked Paromita.

'The airport,' said Arbaaz. 'I had better get to Delhi.'

The details would only emerge later.

Rajiv had been on the campaign trail, hoping for a political comeback in the elections of 1991. After successful meetings in Visakhapatnam, his next stop had been Sriperumbudur in Tamil Nadu. When he reached the rally ground in Sriperumbudur, he got out of his car and started walking towards the dais. Several supporters, party workers and schoolchildren stopped him in order to put garlands around his neck.

At exactly 10.21, a young woman called Dhanu approached and greeted him. She bent down to touch his feet and detonated an RDX explosive-laden belt that lay tucked below her dress. Rajiv, Dhanu and fourteen others were killed in the explosion that followed. Dhanu was a member of the 'Liberation Tigers of Tamil Eelam'. India had just recalled the Indian Peace Keeping Force from the Sri Lankan civil war but the violence had not ended.

'Where is he?' asked Arbaaz once he was with Yash in Delhi.

'His body is badly mutilated by the severity of the explosion,' said Yash. 'They've airlifted the remains to New Delhi. From Palam airport, his body will go to AIIMS for reconstruction. That's what the fax message sent from the party says.'

Three days of voting had already taken place. It was another three days before the state funeral could be held.

Lakhs of grief-stricken people thronged the cortege's six-mile journey to the western bank of the Yamuna. Arbaaz stood along with many of his colleagues in a truck that followed the gun carriage that bore Rajiv Gandhi's body. It took three hours, starting at 2 pm, for the short distance to be covered. Rajiv had lain in state for two days at Teen Murti Bhavan.

Security concerns were uppermost in everyone's minds. The assassination of Rajiv's mother had resulted in an orgy of violence. Black Cat commandos rode in jeeps all around the casket that was escorted by platoons of thirty-three soldiers each, while an overhead helicopter monitored the procession, also intermittently dropping clusters of red rose petals on the gun carriage.

The crowds were continuously pressing against the windows of the car in which Rajiv's wife, Sonia, was travelling, urging her vociferously to take up the reins of the Congress party. Hundreds attempted to touch Rajiv's flower-strewn casket as cries of *'Rajiv Gandhi amar rahe'* pierced the air. Whenever the crowd crossed security lines they had to be beaten back with lathis.

An honour guard in dark green turbans and red plumage led Sonia and Rajiv's children—Rahul and Priyanka—to the brick platform at Shakti Sthal. Rajiv's body, wrapped in khadi, was placed in the sandalwood pyre, his head pointing south, as hymns from Hindu and Parsi scriptures were recited.

Rahul sprinkled water from the Ganges on the pyre before lighting it on the banks of the Yamuna. Foreign dignitaries from sixty countries watched as billowing black smoke arose in conjunction with the sounding of bugles. First his brother, then his mother, now Rajiv... seemingly there was a curse on the entire Gandhi family. Arbaaz watched the cremation from a respectful distance.

Standing next to him, Yash said, 'This election is no longer about BJP's Ram Mandir versus the National Front's Mandal card.'

Arbaaz turned to look at Yash.

'You are a lucky man, Arbaaz Sheikh,' muttered Yash.

'How?' asked Arbaaz.

'Because Maharashtra has not yet gone to polls,' said Yash. 'There will be a massive sympathy wave generated by Rajiv Gandhi's assassination. You watch. In your own constituency, all you will need is a small swing to sail through.'

'I'd rather lose miserably than win on the ashes of Rajiv Gandhi,' said Arbaaz to Yash.

Pamulaparti Venkata Narasimha Rao had almost retired from politics after his embarrassing defeat in the 1984 election that almost every other Congress candidate had won. But suddenly, the assassination of Rajiv Gandhi pulled him out of retirement in 1991. The very first person outside the Nehru—Gandhi clan to serve a full five-year term, Rao was also the very first PM from south India. Given that he had not contested the general elections, he participated in a by-election in Nandyal to reach Parliament. He won with a record victory margin of half a million votes and entered the *Guinness Book of World Records*.

This was despite the fact that it was a period of political uncertainties. The previous year, two newcomers had come to monopolize the politics of the Hindi heartland: Mulayam Singh Yadav in Uttar Pradesh and Lalu Prasad Yadav in Bihar. The best that anyone could predict was that Indian politics was unpredictable.

But P.V. Narasimha Rao was turning out to be one of the most sensible administrators that India ever had. He seemed to be keeping politics out of governance. Or possibly, he played the political game so well that no one realized he was playing politics.

He had broken convention by appointing a non-political economist, Dr Manmohan Singh, as his Finance Minister who was now busy dismantling the Licence Raj by announcing a new industrial policy. The PM had then appointed Subramanian Swamy, a member of the Opposition, to the Commission on Labour Standards and International Trade, a position that was the equivalent of Cabinet rank. His equation with Atal Bihari Vajpayee was legendary. He would regularly depute Vajpayee to UN meetings on behalf of India. He even went ahead and appointed one of the chief contenders for the PM's post, Sharad Pawar, to the position of Minister of Defence.

Among the various Cabinet appointments, two others were significant. Yash Dhar as Minister for Civil Aviation and Arbaaz Sheikh as Minister of State for Textiles. Arbaaz's winning streak from his constituency had prompted his rival, Keshav Gadgil of the Shiv Sena, to change his own. It had led to a win for both Arbaaz and Gadgil. Both men had met for a drink thereafter and toasted each other.

The appointment of Arbaaz had caused several flutters because his underworld background was well known, but P.V. Narasimha Rao was nothing if not a pragmatist. He knew that he needed a thug to handle the entrenched unions of the textile industry.

Yash Dhar's appointment as Civil Aviation Minister came as happy news. The happiest person was Arvind Bagadia. He immediately put in a personal request to the Hon'ble Minister to increase the routes offered to American Airlines, TWA and United. In addition he wanted further routes for Air France. Yash would be suitably compensated.

'I am an honest politician, Arvindji,' joked Yash. 'Are you trying to bribe me?'

'The term *honest politician* is a contradiction in terms,' replied Arvind. 'You can either be honest or you can be a politician.'

Having delivered that statement, Arvind embarked on a journey to Chicago and Toulouse.

Adhyapika Jyoti sat in her simple room, meditating. When she opened her eyes an hour later, she found her assistant waiting patiently.

'The Prime Minister was trying to reach you,' he said. 'I told his secretary that you will call back.'

'I know why he has called,' said Adhyapika Jyoti.

The government of P.V. Narasimha Rao had inherited an economy with a gaping black hole. Faced with a Balance of Payments crisis, the government was now contemplating pledging gold from its reserves in order to muster up loans.

'What should I tell the secretary?' asked the assistant.

'That the Prime Minister should meet me,' said Adhyapika.

The sixty-nine-year-old man was clearly enjoying himself. He had visited the Grand Canyon and from there had dropped in at Disneyland. At Disneyland he had tried out almost all the rides, after standing in long queues.

He had met up with his friends in New York and they had taken him out to his favourite Mexican restaurant. He had taken in several Broadway shows and had bought ice cream for himself and his travelling companions. He had then dropped in at Schwartz, the city's largest toy store in order to buy a bagful of toys for his adopted granddaughter.

At Schwartz he saw a familiar person walk up to him with folded hands saying, 'Namaste, Atalji.'

Atal Bihari Vajpayee recognized him instantly. '*Aap kaise ho, Arvind?*' asked the leader of the Opposition in the tenth Lok Sabha.

'I saw you from the street but was hesitant to disturb you. You seemed to be enjoying looking at the toys… so I followed you!'

Atalji laughed. 'Men are always boys… we always like our toys. This detour though is on account of my granddaughter.'

Unknown to the rest of the world, the wily politician's private persona was rather different to his public one. Besides reading and writing Hindi poetry, he loved taking his dogs for long walks and reading John Grisham books. He enjoyed travelling and on such trips the usual *dhoti-kurta* would give way to trousers and checked bush shirts.

'What brings you to New York?' asked Arvind.

'The Prime Minister has sent me to the United Nations yet again,' said Vajpayee. 'And you?'

'I'm here to sign an agreement with the Boeing Company. I've just come from Chicago and am heading back to India tomorrow via Paris.'

'Why Paris?' asked Vajpayee.

'I have a meeting at Airbus's headquarters in Toulouse.'

Yash Dhar looked at the documents on his desk. Then he looked up at Arvind. 'Seems like a good deal,' he said.

'It's the deal of a lifetime,' said Arvind. 'One that will make you and me rich beyond our wildest imaginations.'

'The best part of this deal is that both the companies will be unable to cry foul,' said Yash.

'Airlines around the world are ordering about 400 aircraft worth around thirty to forty billion dollars a year,' said

Arvind. 'The competition for this business is cutthroat between Airbus and Boeing. The company that does not get the order will complain that there has been bribery. The solution that I have put together takes care of all that.'

'What about discounts and performance guarantees?' asked Yash.

'Negotiated and closed.'

'And technical performance?' asked Yash.

'I have deputed Satyapal to go to Madras and meet with Dr Aravinda Muthu, your chief technical advisor at the ministry. Satyapal will ensure that Dr Muthu approves the machines of both Airbus and Boeing.'

'Then whom will the national carriers sign the contract with?'

'We have incorporated a company called Civil Aviation Lease & Finance in Bermuda. You and I are 50 per cent shareholders through our nominees. This single company shall trade with both Boeing and Airbus, representing neither,' said Arvind. 'It shall buy the aircraft and then lease them to the national carriers.'

'The aircraft manufacturers don't have a problem with that?' asked Yash.

'In fact, they're happy with it,' said Arvind. 'The US Congress passed the Foreign Corrupt Practices Act—the FCPA—several years ago. It forbids American companies, their officers or their representatives from bribing foreign officials. It helps that our Bermuda company is neither an officer nor a representative. Boeing is protected.'

'What about Airbus?' asked Yash.

'They are not subject to such constraints. OECD has been attempting to get France to ratify a convention outlawing bribery of foreign public officials but France has not done it,' said Arvind. 'Hell, the government even permits French companies to take tax deductions for giving bribes!'

'Then why not simply do the deal with Airbus?' asked Yash.

'Because Boeing will complain. We'll have a CBI enquiry on our hands,' explained Arvind.

'People are bound to ask why we are mixing up the fleet by splitting the order across two companies,' said Yash.

'That's the beauty of the situation,' said Arvind. 'We have two national carriers, Indian Airlines and Air India. Indian Airlines will get only Airbus aircraft and Air India will get only Boeing aircraft. No mixing of fleet.'

'Where will the money to buy aircraft come from?' asked Yash. 'I'm assuming that the Bermuda company has none.'

'The national carriers shall pay lease rent in advance plus a hefty deposit,' replied Arvind. 'The Bermuda company will use that money to buy the aircraft. The operational expenses of the Bermuda company are being borne by Airbus and Boeing.'

'Can the lease arrangement be questioned?' asked Yash.

'Unlikely,' answered Arvind. 'Undoubtedly, some aircraft are bought and sold in conventional ways but most are not. Around the world, many airlines are government-owned. Commission payments only end up increasing the capital cost. The increased capital cost means higher depreciation and higher depreciation means yet more red ink added to the airline's losses. A lease glosses over such commissions beautifully.'

'So how will we play this?' asked Yash, realizing that Arvind's way was the way to go.

'First, we will ask both companies to tender for outright purchases by the two national carriers. Both companies will quote prices that are very high. The quotes will be rejected.'

'Then?'

'Civil Aviation Lease & Finance in Bermuda will offer to lease the aircraft to the national carriers,' said Arvind. 'The very same aircraft that they would have otherwise have bought. Given the earlier inflated quotes, the offer from Bermuda will seem very economical.'

'The American and French governments tend to get resentful when the other nation's company gets an order,' observed Yash.

'That's why you are granting additional routes for their respective national carriers as quid pro quo,' said Arvind. 'This is the perfect deal—where everyone is happy.'

'Why are you helping that bastard?' asked Arbaaz.

'Arbaaz, we're politicians,' said Yash. 'We're not supposed to have any permanent friends or permanent enemies.'

'He's my enemy,' said Arbaaz. 'He screwed me out of a ton of money with that Qurbani deal.'

'And you repaid him with an Income Tax raid and theft. As I recall, you made a tidy profit over what you lost. You're even. You're more than even.'

'It doesn't work that way,' said Arbaaz. 'Once a foe, always a foe. I want you to call off the aircraft deal involving him.'

'I can't do that,' replied Yash. 'It will look damn suspicious. Then I'll have the CBI on my head.'

'You can't do that?' asked Arbaaz, his voice rising in anger. 'When you were in trouble, I was the one who helped you out. You told me that you would always be indebted to me. So I'm calling in the debt.'

'Be reasonable, Arbaaz,' said Yash. 'In any case, this deal does not harm you in any way. I promise I won't do any more deals with Bagadia. How does that sound?'

'As phoney as the time that you told me that you would always be in my debt.'

Mr Vijay Rao of Rao Enterprises sat in the first row of the Madras University Centenary Auditorium as the new Chief Minister of Tamil Nadu took the oath of office on 24 June 1991. She had wisely entered into an alliance with the Indian National Congress and the sympathy wave had ensured that her alliance won 225 of the 234 seats contested. Jayalalithaa Jayaram at forty-three was the youngest-ever Chief Minister of the state. She was an accomplished actress, having appeared in over 120 Tamil, Telugu and Kannada films. But this was the greatest role that she would ever perform.

Rao had wisely supported 'Amma's' party and was looking to leverage his political proximity to the AIADMK government. When he had just started out in business at age twenty-seven, the empire that he had inherited included textile mills, hotels, tea and tobacco. By thirty-seven he had exited textiles and strengthened his presence in hotels. By forty-seven, he had exited tea and built up his real estate business. And now, at fifty-seven, he had exited tobacco and entered financial services. The only fact that continued to niggle him was how he had been scammed into buying worthless goldmines by Arvind Bagadia.

A couple of rows behind him sat Dr Aravinda Muthu, the chief technical advisor to the Ministry of Civil Aviation. Next to him sat a visitor from Calcutta. His name was Satyapal Mittal. Dr Muthu waved out to Rao and Vijay waved back. Once the oath-taking was done, the audience filed out for refreshments.

'How are you, Dr Muthu?' asked Vijay Rao.

'Excellent, Mr Rao,' replied the scientist. 'By the way, allow me to introduce to you Mr Satyapal Mittal from Calcutta.'

'Calcutta, eh? Whom do you work for?' asked Vijay Rao.

'Arvind Bagadia,' replied Satyapal.

Arvind exited the Hotel des Bergues and crossed the Pont du Mont Blanc that ran across Lake Geneva. It was winter and Arvind was wearing a thick woollen overcoat and muffler over his merino wool suit. He walked along the Quai du Generale-Guisan before reaching his destination on Rue de la Scie.

The building was an unassuming one with a simple brass plaque outside that said 56 Rue de la Scie. He pushed open a solid oak door that led him to a foyer. Another door, this time of glass, lay beyond, locked. He pressed the brass button on the side and a man dressed in a dark blue suit opened it. Only once Arvind was inside did he see the name, Allenbach & Cie, neatly embossed in gold on a highly polished wooden wall.

'Mr Fehrmann, please,' said Arvind to the blue suit. Mr Blue Suit picked up a phone and spoke to someone. Within a minute, a middle-aged secretary, neatly coiffured, in a grey dress embellished with a brooch, emerged from an elevator and walked up to Arvind.

'He is waiting for you, Mr Bagadia,' said the secretary. 'Follow me, please.'

Arvind walked into the elevator and the secretary pressed a button that took them to the third floor. They walked through a series of carpeted passages, each containing doors to private conference rooms. The secretary eventually opened one of them and ushered Arvind into a small room containing a conference table and four chairs.

'May I get you something?' she asked as Arvind took off his coat and gave it to her. 'Tea, coffee, water?'

'Just water, please,' said Arvind, sitting down.

'Still or sparkling?' she asked.

'Still,' said Arvind as the door opened and Mr Fehrmann walked in.

The secretary left them alone and Mr Fehrmann opened the file that he carried. He took out a pair of thin wire-framed spectacles and put them on. He then pulled out a statement and showed it to Arvind. The closing balance was 66,105,213.06 Swiss francs.

'We have been regularly receiving commissions from Civil Aviation Lease & Finance in Bermuda,' said Mr Fehrmann. 'The last transfer happened a month ago.'

'What is the Indian rupee equivalent of the Swiss franc balance?' asked Arvind, sipping the Evian water that the secretary had brought for him.

Mr Fehrmann pulled out a small calculator from a drawer in the conference table. 'Yesterday, the rate was 30.2548 Indian rupees to the Swiss franc. It means that the value of funds in your account with us is approximately two billion rupees. What do you want us to do with it?'

'I need you to open some more accounts in your bank,' said Arvind.

'Another numbered account?' asked Mr Fehrmann.

'No,' said Arvind. 'These are current accounts for companies that I own in Mauritius.'

'Names?' asked Mr Fehrmann.

Arvind reached inside his suit pocket and took out a small Hindu prayer book called the *Ashtottara Shatanamavali.* He handed it over to Mr Fehrmann.

'This book contains 108 names of Shiva, the god of destruction. I have incorporated these 108 companies in Mauritius.'

'So you will need 108 accounts?' asked Mr Fehrmann without flinching. In his long career he had received many client requests that were extraordinary. 'What is the postal address of each of the companies?'

'All addresses are the same,' replied Arvind. 'C/O Blackhole Management Services Ltd, Suite 2045, Lancaster Court, Lavoquer Street, Port Louis. The Memorandum and Articles of Association of each of these companies, along with the list of directors and appropriate board resolutions for opening accounts at Allenbach & Cie, will be sent to you by my lawyers in Mauritius.'

'It shall be done,' said Mr Fehrmann, closing his file.

'Once the accounts have been set up, please transfer half a million Swiss francs into each of the 108 accounts from mine,' said Arvind, getting up from his chair and retrieving his overcoat from the corner rack.

'If I am not prying, Mr Bagadia, why are you doing this?' asked Mr Fehrmann, taking off his glasses and tucking them back into his pocket.

'In the old days, kings created forts and moats around their cities to protect themselves. This is merely my fort.'

Vijay Rao watched the two men as they fidgeted uncomfortably in their seats. It was evident that they were uncomfortable discussing the way they had been scammed by Bagadia. He could understand. He knew what a fool he had felt like after it had been discovered that the entire goldmine project was one big scam.

'This is an opportunity to get back at Arvind Bagadia but you need to come clean,' said Vijay Rao. 'If he scammed you—like he scammed me—then it is our duty to teach him a lesson.'

Ghanshyam Das and Ram Lal Khaitan looked at each other. They could still recall the precise moment when they had waited at the Tollygunge Club for a car to drive in and had been greeted in its place by a bullock-cart. It had been so embarrassing. And negative news had a habit of running around the world at blazing speed. It had meant many months of patient work to regain some of their lost prestige.

'He is scum,' said Ghanshyam Das. 'It's about time that someone put him in his place. Do you have a plan?'

'Well,' said Vijay Rao. 'I met with one of his employees the other day in Madras. We hit it off quite well. His name is Satyapal Mittal.'

On the fourth floor of the Oberoi Grand hotel, inside a darkened room that overlooked the pool, was a bed occupied by two people. Low moans emanated from it as the couple moved to their own urgent rhythm.

Scattered around the bed were clothes. Her saree, his trousers and shoes, his tie. Arvind was on top and rode her like an animal, pounding at her tirelessly. They switched positions and Arvind arched upwards as he tried to penetrate her even deeper. Both were covered in a thin film of sweat and she ground herself into him as she felt his climax approaching. A few seconds later he reached up to cup her breasts as he experienced the climax of his life.

They remained intertwined under the bedsheets for a few minutes before Arvind extricated himself. *Why did women want to hug and spoon incessantly after the act?* He was done.

When he had entered the room, she had been waiting for him on the bed, resplendent in her nakedness. He had instantly felt the tumescence between his legs as he had ripped off his own clothes and mounted her. But now he was done and wanted to be back at work.

He tried counting how many he had had. There had been the model from Bombay, the writer from Calcutta, the shady lady from Ahmedabad, the singer from Lucknow, the painter from Pakistan and the dancer from Kerala… he had lost count somewhere along the way.

He quickly put on his clothes while thinking of an appropriate exit line. Somewhere deep inside of him he was paying back Abhilasha for having an affair with his best friend. Another part of him told him that he was the culprit for having ignored his own wife all these years.

Somewhere inside Arvind, his conscience told him that he was wasting his time searching for the perfect lover, instead of rejoicing in perfect love.

Arbaaz sat in his Ballard Estate office dressed in a casual open-collar shirt. In front of him was an untouched cup of coffee. The man seated on the visitor's chair was having masala tea.

'Thank you for dropping in, Mr Lakhotia,' said Arbaaz to Chander Lakhotia.

'My pleasure Arbaaz Bhai,' said Chander. 'I have heard so many things about you.'

'Some of them good, I hope?' said Arbaaz, smiling.

'All good,' lied Chander. 'Now tell me how I may be of assistance to you.'

'You are an acquaintance of Mr Arvind Bagadia. Friend of his?' asked Arbaaz.

'I had thought that he was a friend, Arbaaz Bhai,' began Chander. 'Unfortunately, he no longer considers me a friend, even though I went out of my way to assist him.'

Arbaaz stared at Chander, attempting to pick up any facial tics that would indicate he was bluffing. There were none.

'How would you like to make some money?' asked Arbaaz.

'How much?' asked Chander. Arbaaz laughed.

'As you know, I am currently the Minister of State for Textiles,' said Arbaaz.

'Yes, sir, I am aware of what an important portfolio the PM has entrusted you with,' flattered Chander.

'There are around 1,900 textile mills in India,' said Arbaaz. 'They have almost nine lakh workers on their rolls. Of the mills, 546 are lying closed.'

'Datta Samant killed the industry,' said Chander, sipping his tea noisily.

'True. Already, 167 of the closed 546 mills have been transferred to the Board for Industrial and Financial Reconstruction—the BIFR—but it is unable to do much. The scale of the problem is staggering.'

'The commonly accepted joke is that BIFR means "Board for Industrial Funeral Rites",' said Chander.

'Precisely,' laughed Arbaaz, lighting up a Dunhill cigarette. 'I have come across one textile unit in Bombay that has not yet gone to the BIFR,' he went on, 'even though it is loss-making. It owns twenty acres of prime real estate'.

'Are you talking about Albert Mills?' asked Chander.

'Yes, that's the one. It is a prime candidate for the BIFR and, in the ordinary course, would have been referred to them…'

'But?' asked Chander.

'But I have held back the file,' said Arbaaz.

'Why?' asked Chander.

'Because I saw that the primary shareholder is Braid Investments Limited.'

'Arvind Bagadia's company,' whistled Chander.

'Exactly,' said Arbaaz. 'More than eighty per cent of the shares of Albert Mills are held by Braid Investments. Apparently, they were given by Mr Vijay Rao to Arvind Bagadia.'

'Why are you interested in the mill?' asked Chander.

'Because it is sitting on the very best real estate in Bombay,' replied Arbaaz. 'Most of the other defunct mills have legacy debts that cannot be repaid even if one redevelops the land. Albert Mills is different. If one redevelops it, one could make a fortune.'

'You want me to negotiate with Arvind Bagadia for the sale of his shares in Albert Mills?' asked Chander.

'No,' said Arbaaz. 'I am open to the idea of extortion.'

'There could be another way,' murmured Chander.

'What?' asked Arbaaz.

'Let me come back to you,' said Chander. 'I need to check my files.'

'There are three obstacles that we will need to overcome if we want to redevelop Albert Mills,' said Arbaaz.

Murali listened.

'One: we need to find a way to acquire a majority stake in the mill. Two: we need to get the municipal authorities to approve the redevelopment plans. Three: we need to settle the labour so that development can proceed.'

'How should we approach this?' asked Murali.

'Step by step,' answered Arbaaz.

Chander Lakhotia looked at the Companies' Act 1956 that lay open before him. The requirements for transfers of shares were:

1. *Original share certificates*
2. *Duplicate share certificates if (1) above are lost or misplaced*
3. *Share transfer form signed by transferor or duly authorized attorney duly stamped with adequate value as per section 12 of the Indian Stamp Act.*
4. *Attested Power of Attorney in the event that (3) above is signed by authorized attorney instead of transferor*

He laughed to himself. *Arvind Babu, your* qurbani *was not in vain. You shall now make a supreme sacrifice.*

'The company secretary of Albert Mills is Devendra Dixit,' said Chander.

'Where does he stay?' asked Arbaaz.

'Andheri,' said Chander, handing over a slip of paper containing the address to Arbaaz.

'Are you sure that your idea will work?' asked Arbaaz.

'I checked my files,' replied Chander. 'The document that I was looking for was there. I only need a letter from Mr Bagadia stating that his shares are lost. I'm getting that fabricated through someone I know. The only remaining issue is that of Dixit. You need to help me with that.'

'It shall be done,' said Arbaaz, calling for Raju.

'I have had Dixit tailed for the past few days,' said Raju to Arbaaz. 'He has a nasty little secret. I've had photos taken.'

'What is the secret?' asked Arbaaz.

'He's married and has two kids but he has a roaring affair going on,' said Raju.

'Big deal,' said Arbaaz.

'It *is* a big deal,' said Raju.

'Why?'

'Because the person that he's having an affair with is another man.'

Chander watched the man in Kalbadevi place a piece of tracing paper over Arvind's original signature. He saw the man use a pencil to very slowly trace over the signature with a steady but light hand. It was evident that he had done this many times before because his hand did not shake at all.

'People outside this business do not understand that it's not simply getting the loops, dots and lines right. The pressure applied on different parts of a signature are different,' said the master forger as he took off the tracing paper. 'This signature is relatively simple because it follows a natural slant towards the right but sometimes attention to detail is often the difference between a decent forgery and one that's easy to call out as fake.'

He reversed the tracing paper and used a thick sketching pencil to apply a layer of writing lead on it. He then placed the tracing paper above Arvind's name on the letter that Chander had typed. He adjusted the tracing paper at a slight slant. 'It's important to make it look like it was signed in a very natural way. This person doesn't sign in a straight line so we need to ensure that there is an angle.'

The forger used a sharp pencil to press over the traced signature and in less than sixty seconds a faint pencil impression of Arvind's signature was on the letter. He was careful to not press too hard because a deep impression would be a give-away.

He then walked over to a cabinet that contained hundreds of fountain pens, markers, ballpoint pens, holders, nibs and inks. He looked at the original signature to gauge what type of pen had been used. He tried out a couple of pens on blank paper before deciding. Then, after selecting one, he simply ran the pen without lifting his hand over the pencil impression.

He didn't bother to look at it again. He was a master at what he did. He handed over the letter to Chander.

Succeeding with fraud is so much better than failing with honour, thought Chander to himself as he looked at the perfect signature.

Chander looked at the papers in the Qurbani file once again. When Arvind had asked him to buy the shares of Qurbani and subsequently sell them, Chander had asked him for a written authorization to transact on his behalf—Power of Attorney. He looked at the first page of the notarized document:

To all to whom these presents shall come, we Messrs Braid Investments Ltd, a company registered under the Companies Act 1956 with our registered office at Chowringhee Road, Calcutta 700016, send greetings.

Now know all ye and these presents witness that we do hereby appoint, constitute and nominate Mr Chander Lakhotia, residing at Kalbadevi Road, Bombay 400002 (hereinafter referred to as the 'said attorney') to be our true and lawful attorney to act on behalf of us and in our name and on our behalf, to execute and perform all or any of the following acts, deeds, matters and things, that is to say:

1. *To buy, sell, transfer or otherwise deal in shares for and on our behalf.*
2. *To sign, execute and register in our name and on our behalf such deeds or instruments of transfer in respect of the said shares.*
3. *To sign all applications, transfer deeds, and other writings for the purpose of buying, selling, or mortgaging shares.*

And generally to do and execute all such deeds, instruments, acts and things in relation to the said shares in all aspects as we ourselves could have done if personally present as the said attorney shall deem fit and proper.

Chander laughed to himself. This was more than enough to do the job. At the time they had been executing the Qurbani transaction, Chander had asked for a General Power of attorney rather than a Specific Power of Attorney. This was to enable him to carry out all of Arvind's instructions effectively.

Tsk, tsk, Arvind Babu. Didn't anyone teach you that Power of Attorney should be as specific and as limited as possible? he thought to himself as he placed the Power of Attorney along with the forged letter in a plastic folder.

Devendra Dixit, the company secretary of Albert Mills, was a mild-mannered man with a small frame and wavy hair. He had stuck on with Albert Mills because other jobs were difficult to find. It had meant constant fights with his wife, a dominating and always-angry woman. Albert Mills had not paid salaries for years.

Devendra exited his office and reached the parking lot. It took him a couple of minutes to find his scooter. Pulling it out from the line of parked two-wheelers, he kick-started and mounted it. Before he could manoeuvre the scooter out of the parking lot, his world went dark.

A black bag had been pulled over his face. His hands were tied behind his back and a voice accompanied by garlic breath whispered, 'You will not be hurt if you behave yourself.' He was bundled into a car which drove through several twists and turns for the next hour.

When the bag was pulled off his face, he squinted his eyes against the harsh warehouse lighting. The shed looked abandoned, the massive beams overhead seemingly containing more rust than iron. He was seated on a wooden chair and there were several men surrounding him. One of the men looked out of place. He didn't seem like a thug, more like a lawyer or an accountant.

The out-of-place man stepped up. 'I am providing you with share certificate numbers,' said Chander. 'You will be required to issue duplicate share certificates to us.'

'You kidnapped me for just *that*?' asked Dixit. He received a stinging slap across his face from one of the thugs. 'Do you want to experience hell?' the thug asked him. 'We can arrange that for you, *gandu*. Or would you prefer that we tell your wife about that horny architect that you're fucking on the side?'

Chander placed a large photograph on Dixit's lap without saying a word. Dixit looked at it and went absolutely quiet. A minute later, tears rolled down his cheeks and splashed all over the photograph.

Chander picked up the photograph. 'No one holds your bisexuality against you but your wife may not be as understanding.'

'What do you want?' asked the broken Dixit.

'The shares of Albert Mills that belong to Mr Arvind Bagadia,' said Chander. 'You will issue duplicate certificates upon receiving a written application signed by him. You will then send the duplicate certificates to the address that I provide.'

'Mr Bagadia will fire me,' pleaded Dixit. 'I'll be out of a job.'

'Better to be fired than dead,' said Chander. 'Once we have received the duplicate certificates from you, we will apply for the transfer.'

'You would need a Power of Attorney for that,' said Dixit.

'I have it,' said Chander. 'You and your family will be taken care of. You will have enough money to last a lifetime. Just do what I tell you and everything will be fine.'

Arbaaz watched the man as he worked on the architectural drawings.

He first applied a yellow solution of potassium ferricyanide and ferric ammonium onto a thick linen canvas and allowed it to dry. He then placed the coated linen under a translucent drawing, weighted it with a sheet of glass, and exposed it to ultraviolet light. Satisfied that the exposure was adequate he removed the glass and the translucent drawing and washed the linen. What remained was an image of white lines on a Prussian blue background.

'Why are we doing this the old way?' asked Arbaaz.

'Because the original structures of Albert Mills were constructed before 1940,' answered the man. 'By the 1940s, cyanotype blueprints began to be supplanted by diazo prints which have blue lines on a white background. If you want this to look like it was approved in 1870—the year in which this mill was established—then it must be printed in the way that it would have been printed then.'

'What next?' asked Arbaaz, as the man took examined the blueprint with a magnifying glass.

'We need to create a rubber stamp for the officer who would have approved the plan,' said the man.

'How will you do that?' asked Arbaaz.

'I have checked files of the year 1870 in the Bombay Municipal Corporation's records,' said the man. 'Most of the plans of that time are signed by Arthur Crawford, the first Municipal Commissioner who joined the corporation in 1865. See this?'

Arbaaz peered over the man's shoulder. He saw a rubber stamp on one of the plans. It was slightly smudged.

Approved subject to the conditions mentioned
vide letter number .... dated ....
Signed Arthur Crawford, Commissioner
Bombay Municipality
as per provisions of
Bombay Municipal Act 1865

'See the font,' said the man. 'Bodoni, but of an older era. We will need to replicate that on our rubber stamp. After that you should be done.'

'But anyone examining it forensically would know that this is not an old blueprint?' asked Arbaaz.

'Yes,' replied the man. 'This would not stand up to scrutiny in terms of age even though we would give it an old look. Depends on what your objective is.'

'I need to show that there were several structures that were constructed on the twenty acres of land in 1870,' said Arbaaz. 'I could then apply for permission to repair those structures rather than apply for new permissions. It will shorten the bureaucratic process tremendously.'

'Ah,' said the man. 'But wouldn't there be a pre-existing plan in the files of the Municipal Corporation?'

'I have spoken to the filing clerk,' replied Arbaaz. 'He will remove the old plan and replace it with ours.'

'So once you have permission from the repair board, your concern is that someone looking at the plan later might be able to spot the fact that the plan is a later creation. Is that it?' asked the man.

'Yes,' replied Arbaaz. 'But I think I've already thought of a solution.'

The 1893-built headquarters of the Bombay Municipal Corporation stood at the junction of Dadabhai Naoroji Road and Mahapalika Marg, opposite the Victoria Terminus Station. Just above the signboard that announced its name hung a coat of arms that bore an inscription in Sanskrit—*Yato Dharmastato Jaya*. Translated into English, it meant *where there is righteousness, there shall be victory.*

Unfortunately, righteousness was in short supply at the BMC and victory usually meant personal gain—which suited Arbaaz just fine.

Some months earlier, the Chief Minister had been in a dilemma about whom to appoint as the Municipal Commissioner. 'It's like deciding which alcoholic will serve the drinks from the bar,' joked Arbaaz to Murali.

'More like deciding which lunatic will run the mental asylum,' observed Murali.

Arbaaz and Murali walked in and were instantly ushered into the large and spacious office of the Municipal Commissioner. He was in his fifties and had managed to hold on to his post in spite of several other political changes. It was a clear indication of the Commissioner's flexibility and tenacity.

'How nice to see you, Arbaaz Bhai,' said the Commissioner, getting up from his chair to greet Arbaaz and Murali. He quickly told the orderly to get tea and biscuits. 'How can I be of help to you?'

'I'm not here to help myself. I'm here to help you,' said Arbaaz.

'Really?' asked the Commissioner. 'How?'

Arbaaz handed over a slip of paper on which was written a file number. 'The plans in that particular file clearly show that there were several structures on the land that we call Albert Mills. I need you to issue repair permits quickly.'

'What if the plans are forged?' asked the Commissioner, a smile hovering on his face.

'After issuing the repair orders, you shall ask for the file to be sent to the Records Department,' said Arbaaz, placing a briefcase on the Commissioner's table.

'And then?' asked the Commissioner.

'You shall call the Fire Brigade when the Records Department catches fire owing to a short circuit,' said Arbaaz, as the Commissioner opened the briefcase, looked at the contents, closed it, and placed it reverently under his desk.

'Funny thing, really,' mused Arbaaz.

'What?' asked the Commissioner.

'All of you chaps in positions of importance are called Commissioners. Municipal Commissioner, Police Commissioner, Income Tax Commissioner.'

'What's funny about that?' asked the Municipal Commissioner.

'What's funny is that the government wants you to commission. We simply want your omission. For which we pay you commission.'

'Now what?' asked Murali.

'We need to get consent from the workers for the redevelopment,' said Arbaaz. 'Who is the union leader?'

'Vidyadhar,' replied Murali.

'The Maharashtra Mazdoor Union chap?'

'Yes.'

'Shit,' said Arbaaz. 'He's never amenable to negotiation. In another case, he asked the mill-owners to share the land proceeds with the workers.'

'There are 500 existing workers of Albert Mills,' said Murali. 'You will need to find a way to lay them off. Without doing that you will be unable to redevelop the land.'

'On the contrary, I plan to recruit more workers,' said Arbaaz.

'To be precise, I plan to recruit 1,167 new workers.'

'What?' asked Murali. 'We'll end up tripling our wage bill!'

'Appoint 1,167 new people, Murali,' said Arbaaz. 'They will receive a salary for doing nothing at all for a full six months.'

'What's the catch?' asked Murali.

'They need to sign up as members of another union,' said Arbaaz.

'And then?' asked Murali.

'Take their resignation letters in advance. The letters should be post-dated six months,' said Arbaaz.

'Why 1,167 additional employees in particular?' asked Murali.

'You are supposed to be the educated one, Murali,' said Arbaaz mock-reprovingly. 'Read section 13 (1) (ii) of the Maharashtra Recognition of Trade Unions & Prevention of Unfair Labour Practice Act, 1971.'

Arbaaz met the leader of the Maharashtra Mazdoor Union, Mr Vidyadhar, in his office. The man was entirely bald and certainly not more than five feet in height. But he packed a punch when he exhorted workers to strike.

'Sheikh,' he said impertinently to Arbaaz. 'The workers of Albert Mills are your responsibility. There are over 500 families whose livelihoods are dependent on the mill. You must not only compensate each one of them but must also share the profit from land redevelopment with them.'

'I plan to do no such thing,' said Arbaaz.

'In that case, we shall seek an injunction in court to prevent you from selling or redeveloping the mill land,' said Vidyadhar.

'You shall do no such thing,' said Arbaaz.

The trade union leader looked confused.

'Have you watched those television game shows in which a contestant can choose one of several doors?' asked Arbaaz. 'Depending upon which door he chooses he can win a prize. Well, I'm also offering you two doors to choose from.'

Vidyadhar opened his mouth to speak but was silenced by a look from Arbaaz.

'Now I'm sure you're wondering where the doors are,' said Arbaaz. 'They're imaginary! Behind one of the two imaginary doors is a bag containing twenty lakh in cash.'

'I am not one to be taken in by your bribes, Sheikh,' spat Vidyadhar. 'Marxism is my religion. My only love is for the working class.'

'I'm touched,' said Arbaaz. 'But you should know what's behind the second imaginary door.'

'You don't scare me,' said Vidyadhar defiantly.

'Behind the second imaginary door is a Union Derecognition notice,' said Arbaaz.

'You can't derecognize the union,' said Vidyadhar. 'All the workers of Albert Mills are with me.'

'Not quite,' said Arbaaz. 'You see we appointed 1,167 additional workers. We are now in a position to make an application to the Industrial Court under Section 13 (1) (ii) of the Maharashtra Recognition of Trade Unions & Prevention of Unfair Labour Practice Act, 1971.'

'For what?'

'For cancellation of the recognition of the Maharashtra Mazdoor Union on the ground that your union's membership in Albert Mills has fallen below 30 per cent of the total strength of workmen. Your representation is 29.99 per cent, to be precise.'

Vidyadhar chose the first imaginary door ten minutes later.

He walked out through the real door a minute later.

'I want the bastard arrested,' screamed Arvind at Satyapal. 'No one fucks with Arvind Bagadia.'

Except for the model from Bombay, the writer from Calcutta, the shady lady from Ahmedabad, the singer from Lucknow, the painter from Pakistan and the dancer from Kerala.

'I have asked Darius Dastur to file an urgent application before the Calcutta High Court to place an injunction on Arbaaz,' said Satyapal.

'It will be of little use,' said Arvind. 'By now, he will have transferred the shares of Albert Mills several times over. Those shares will have changed hands more times than a whore in Sonagachi. Any interim relief or stay will be irrelevant. Can't turn the clock back.'

'Scrambled eggs,' observed Satyapal. 'One can't unscramble them after they've been scrambled. What do you want me to do?'

'The problem is that we can't go after Chander Lakhotia because he used a valid Power of Attorney signed by me. So who do we go after?'

'I'm worried, Ma,' said Alisha to her mother. 'Last year at Stanford there were 38,828 applicants and only 2,210 were accepted. That's one in every seventeen!' She chewed on her pencil as she looked at the bulky application form. She looked devastatingly pretty as her hair fell over her face.

Alisha was simply gorgeous, having inherited most of Paromita's features. She had already caused many hearts to break at Cathedral School. Her focus, though, had been on scoring well in academics and hitting the right notes in extracurricular activities. The result was that she had been made head girl of the school that year.

'Your father is totally against the idea of sending you to America,' said Paromita. 'We've ended up quarrelling over this but I'm determined that you shall go. Stop worrying about the admissions process. It will work out. You have a brilliant school record.'

'It's not as easy as you think, Ma,' said Alisha. 'A reviewer has only fifteen minutes for a standard application review. Applicants whose parents were in Stanford get thirty minutes. Neither of you went there. I'm stuck with a fifteen-minute review!'

'I'm so sorry that we do not meet your requirements, dear,' said Paromita caustically.

'That's not what I meant!' said Alisha, getting up to hug her mother. 'You both have been great parents. I'm just trying to explain to you the fact that it's tough to get in.'

'You have an SAT score of 2100,' said Paromita. 'That must count for something.'

'Last year, candidates with perfect 2400 scores were turned away because of other reasons. I wish I knew the formula for getting the fat envelope,' said Alisha.

'Fat envelope?' asked Paromita.

'You either receive a fat envelope or a thin one in response to your application,' explained Alisha. 'The fat one means that you got in. The thin one is a rejection.'

'Poor dear,' said Paromita. 'I wish I could find a way to ensure that you got a fat envelope. Tomorrow I'll go to the Durga temple and pray for you.'

Devendra Dixit looked haggard and exhausted. He had been picked up by the police the previous evening and made to sit inside a hot and stuffy cubicle for several hours before being photographed, fingerprinted and then hauled into an overcrowded cell that stank of piss.

He had to be pulled out within half an hour because one of the inmates attempted to shove his penis into Dixit's mouth. Dixit was terrified. Why didn't I just tell my wife everything? Why did I allow myself to get blackmailed? Why was I such a fucking idiot?

After being arrested, he had tried reaching Chander Lakhotia. The cops had told him that he was entitled to one phone call to a lawyer or friend. When Chander eventually came on the line, Dixit said, 'I need your help, Lakhotiaji. I have been arrested.'

'Who is this?' asked Chander.

'Devendra Dixit,' replied the terrified man.

'I can't seem to recall the name,' said Chander.

'What the fuck do you mean that you can't recall the name?' shouted Dixit, spittle leaping from his lips and into the mouthpiece of the telephone. 'I fucking did everything that you…'

Click. Chander had disconnected.

'Someone to see you,' said the Sub-Inspector to Dixit as Arvind walked in along with Darius Dastur.

The contrast between Dixit and Arvind could not have been more striking. Dixit was wearing dirty clothes that he had been arrested in and a cloud of body odour hung over him. His hair was dishevelled and a discernible tremor had affected his speech. Arvind was dressed in a fresh white cotton shirt with double cuffs and the only smell that emanated from him was that of talcum powder and eau de cologne.

'You strayed, Dixit,' said Arvind as he and Darius Dastur occupied the chairs opposite him. 'I was hurt by your deceit.'

'Arvind Babu, I was blackmailed. Please believe me, I didn't want to do anything to hurt you…' babbled Dixit.

'Ssh,' said Arvind. 'I'm not here to find fault with you. I know that you had your reasons for doing what you did. The men that did this are rascals. They're the ones that I need to set right.'

'Get me out of here, Arvind Babu,' pleaded Dixit. 'I will do anything that you ask but I do not want to go back into that cell. The men have already started calling me their *randi*.'

'I have brought my lawyer, Mr Darius Dastur, with me. He will help get you out,' said Arvind. 'But first you will have to help me.'

'Anything,' said Dixit emphatically. 'I'll do whatever you want.'

Darius Dastur placed several sheets of green legal paper before Dixit. 'You will need to write down everything that happened from beginning to end. You must not leave out even the smallest detail.'

'Why?' asked Dixit.

'It's the only way that we can go after Arbaaz Sheikh and Chander Lakhotia,' said Dastur.

'And then you'll get me out?' asked Dixit.

'The magistrate is known to us,' said Arvind. 'You will plead guilty to the charges. The magistrate will give you a six-month prison sentence.'

'But I can't go back,' said Dixit. 'I'll be raped!'

'The magistrate will suspend the sentence for community service,' said Arvind. 'You will not need to spend another night in prison.'

The learned Additional Chief Metropolitan Magistrate of the eighth Court at Esplanade leaned to one side to quietly release the gas that had been created by his oily lunch. Satisfied that no one in court had noticed and relieved that the emission was odourless, he straightened up and asked for the next case. The bailiff yelled, 'Case number 984/1993.'

Darius Dastur stood up along with Devendra Dixit. 'May it please your honour, my client has already provided a detailed confession of the circumstances under which he acted. He throws himself at the mercy of the court and hopes that your generous spirit of forgiveness will prevail.'

The magistrate looked at the papers in front of him and then addressed Dixit. 'Do you understand this Hon'ble Court will issue process against you, the accused, under section 420 of the Indian Penal Code?'

'Yes, your excellency,' said Dixit, unaware that the magistrate was not an ambassador.

'You understand that this Hon'ble Court will be required to punish you, the accused, according to the provisions of the law?'

'Yes, your honour,' said Mr Dastur before Dixit could commit another blunder.

'Section 420 provides that whoever dishonestly or fraudulently removes, conceals or delivers to any person, or transfer or causes to be transferred to any person, without adequate consideration, any property… shall be punished with imprisonment of either description for a term which may extend to two years, or with a fine, or with both. Accordingly, I sentence the accused to two years imprisonment and a fine of 25,000 rupees.'

Dixit looked at the magistrate and then at Darius Dastur.

'I was supposed to receive a six-month sentence that would eventually be suspended,' he whispered to Dastur.

Dastur remained quiet as he placed his papers into his briefcase with his manicured hands.

'Bastard! You set me up!' cried Dixit as two policemen grabbed his arms.

'Quiet!' said the magistrate. 'If you continue to remain unruly I shall sentence you to additional time.'

Dixit managed to free his arms from the cops and lunged towards Dastur but the senior lawyer was already far away from his reach.

'Good news,' said Murali. 'The Banking Regulation Act has been amended by Parliament.'

'Why should that be good news?' asked Arbaaz.

'The Indian Economic Policy has come full circle,' said Murali. 'They nationalized banks in 1969. Now—in 1993—they're inviting new private sector banks to set up shop. Incredible!'

'Anyone interested?' asked Arbaaz.

'UTI is planning to set up a bank,' said Murali. 'So is HDFC. I'm told that the Hindujas and the 20th Century Finance Group are also evaluating possibilities. Bennett, Coleman & Co., too.'

'What's your idea?' asked Arbaaz.

'Our friend, Mr Kishore Deshmukh, is killing time as secretary-general of the Chambers of Indian Commerce and Industry. Why not use him as a front to set up a bank?'

'How much will it cost?' asked Arbaaz.

'The Reserve Bank of India requires that the bank should have a net worth of 200 crore and that the promoters should hold minimum 25 per cent of the capital.'

'What do you think?' asked Arbaaz. 'Is it something we should do?'

'Absolutely,' said Murali. 'Dhanda Holdings is sitting on excess cash. Raju keeps funnelling his ill-gotten collections into the company.'

Arbaaz thought about it for a day. The next day he called Murali to his office. 'What would we call the bank?'

'Dhanda Bank,' replied Murali, smiling.

The manager of the United Federation Bank passed on the two slips to Arvind for his perusal.

'What are they?' asked Arvind.

'Bank Receipts—or BRs,' replied the manager.

'Enlighten me,' said Arvind.

'These are used in Ready Forward transactions between banks,' said the manager.

'What are those?' asked Arvind.

'One bank sells shares to another bank through a broker. The selling bank buys them back at a higher price two weeks later. The difference between the buying and selling price is interest cost.'

'So?' asked Arvind.

'The shares do not change hands. What changes hands is this BR. It certifies that the selling bank is holding the shares and will deliver them when called upon to do so.'

'What's seems to be the problem?' asked Arvind.

'Hundreds of BRs are flooding the market,' said the manager. 'All of them emanate from three small banks—Bank of Karad, Metropolitan Cooperative Bank and…'

'And?'

'Dhanda Bank. There's something dodgy going on.'

'Why are you telling me this?' asked Arvind.

'Because your erstwhile chartered accountant, Mr Chander Lakhotia, seems to be arranging most of the deals as the middleman. He's sitting on a huge pile of cash borrowed against BRs.'

'Why would he need the money?' wondered Arvind.

'He's working on behalf of a big market operator called Harshad Mehta. Harshad Mehta is using the cash to drive up the price of ACC shares. That's what the market rumours are saying.'

'Anything else?' asked Arvind.

'Apparently the deal is that Harshad Mehta will concentrate on driving up the price of ACC while Chander will concentrate on driving down the price of your company—Braid Investments.'

'He's obviously working on behalf of Arbaaz Sheikh,' said Arvind. 'He doesn't yet realize that this is a game that I can play far better than he does.'

'Buy Braid shares on behalf of Maheshwara Traders Mauritius Ltd,' said Arvind, putting down the phone.

It rang again. He picked it up, listened to the price being quoted and said, 'Buy Braid shares on behalf of Shrikantha Traders Mauritius Ltd.'

The share price of Braid was being hammered down by the bears. It was a cartel of operators from Bombay who seemed to be working in tandem with people who had very deep pockets.

The phone rang yet again. 'Buy on behalf of Shambhu Traders Mauritius Ltd,' said Arvind. *I will make all 108 names of Shiva buy Braid shares until Shiva destroys Chander Lakhotia and Arbaaz Sheikh,* thought Arvind.

He put down the phone and looked at Satyapal.

'Arbaaz Sheikh's outfit—Dhanda Holdings—owns 30 per cent of Braid. That amounts to three lakh shares. How many have we transacted to buy in the last two days?' asked Arvind.

'At last count, 2,95,133,' said Satyapal, his eyes bloodshot from lack of sleep.

'Keep buying in the various names that I gave you,' said Arvind.

'Until when?' asked Satyapal.

'Until Friday,' said Arvind.

'How many shares have we bought?' asked Arvind.

'Three lakh shares,' replied a weary Satyapal who had been up all night. 'I'm assuming that Arbaaz Sheikh has now sold off his entire shareholding in Braid.'

'Keep buying till Friday,' said Arvind. 'They will want to drive down the price further. The only way to do that is by short-selling.'

Short-selling was a process of selling shares that one didn't yet own. It was done in the hope that prices would fall, thus enabling the seller to pick up the shares at a lower price in the future and make delivery at a later date.

'The brokers operating on our behalf are worried that we will go bust,' said Satyapal.

'Tell them that they stand to make the greatest killing ever made in the history of the Bombay Stock Exchange,' said Arvind.

'How many shares have we bought?' asked Arvind.

'Six lakh shares,' replied Satyapal.

'Good,' said Arvind. 'What day is it?'

'Friday.'

'Second Friday of the month?'

'Yes.'

'Now ask our brokers to demand delivery of all the shares that have been sold to our 108 companies,' said Arvind.

Settlement of shares at the BSE happened every second Friday. The brokers who had sold Braid shares would either have to deliver those shares or pay *undha badla,* a carryover charge demanded by the buyer to delay delivery for another fortnight.'

'If we demand delivery then we need to cough up cash,' said Satyapal.

'All the buying companies have cash,' said Arvind. 'Demand delivery.'

'What if they want to roll over delivery until the next settlement period?' asked Satyapal.

'Demand undha badla of 200 rupees per share to postpone delivery until the next fortnight,' said Arvind.

The first three lakh shares were delivered to Arvind's NRI investors without a hitch. *That was the easy part for you chaps,* thought Arvind. *You've simply delivered the shares that Dhanda was already sitting on. Let me now see you cough up the remaining shares!*

'There is panic on the Bombay Stock Exchange,' said Satyapal, his voice weary from stress. 'The bear operators never expected us to demand delivery. There is a mad scramble by them to buy Braid shares.'

'Do not sell at any price,' instructed Arvind. 'Let those bastards sweat some more.'

'They are saying that the market may have to be temporarily shut down due to the confusion,' said Satyapal.

'What's the price of Braid shares right now?' asked Arvind.

'Around 400 per share,' said Satyapal. He looked ready to drop.

'What was the highest price at which we bought our own shares?' asked Arvind.

'Three hundred,' replied Satyapal.

'Start offering small parcels of shares for sale at 500,' said Arvind.

'Why?' asked Satyapal.

'Six lakh shares were bought by us. Of these, three lakh shares belonged to Arbaaz Sheikh. The balance three lakh shares were never available with the sellers,' said Arvind.

'True,' said Satyapal. 'They were short sales.'

'In effect, the brokers who offered these shares for sale never expected that the buyers would demand delivery. Now they find themselves in a situation where they have sold shares at 300 but will now have to buy them at 500.'

'What if they roll over the delivery to the next fortnight?' asked Satyapal.

'It won't help,' said Arvind. 'They've bought at 300 and will have to pay another 200 undha badla to roll over. Better to buy at 500 and be done with it.'

'It will destroy all the brokers who indulged in short-selling our shares,' said Satyapal.

'Shiva always destroys,' said Arvind, unfeelingly.

Satyapal waited for Arvind to say thanks but it never happened.

Satyapal was not expecting long paeans of gratitude. Just a few words of appreciation would have sufficed.

Satyapal, I appreciate how you have stood by me...

I just want to tell you that I know how much you have done...

Thanks for supporting me through thick and thin...

You have my gratitude for perfectly executing my instructions...

But no words had emerged from Arvind.

It was just not Arvind's style to show gratitude. It was always the same story. The horse did the work and the horseman got tipped.

Bastard.

Murali looked at the financial statement yet again. He was a worried man. Arbaaz's decision to drive down the share price of Braid had been ill-conceived. They had lost a ton of money in buying shares at far higher prices than what they had sold at. To add to his woes, he had pumped in 200 crore into Dhanda Bank under the stewardship of Kishore Deshmukh.

Chander Lakhotia had misguided Arbaaz into thinking that he could bring about the downfall of Arvind. Much as Murali hated admitting it, the fact was that Arvind Bagadia was a financial genius who had left them with a bloodied nose.

He passed the statement over to Arbaaz. 'We've lost around a hundred crore from this single project,' said Murali.

'Don't worry, Murali, the Lord giveth and taketh away from time to time,' said Arbaaz. 'And remember, we have a stamp paper-printing machine working overtime in Nashik.'

'I guess you're right,' said Murali. 'It's only money.'

'No, no, it isn't *only* money. *Paisa khuda toh nahin par, khuda ki kasam, khuda se kam bhi nahin,'* amended Arbaaz.

Money isn't God but, by God, it's no less than God either.

Arbaaz peeped into her room. She was staying at the Jeevan Prakash guesthouse located at Navi Mumbai. She was dressed in her trademark white and was seated, cross-legged, on a simple sofa. 'Come in, beta,' she said to Arbaaz when he knocked lightly on the open door.

'Give me ten minutes,' said Adhyapika Jyoti to her other disciples who immediately got up, leaving her alone with Arbaaz.

He walked up to the sofa and paused for a moment before bending down to touch her feet, a gesture not really encouraged among Muslims. She smiled and blessed him. In front of the sofa was a thick carpet for her disciples. On either side of the sofa were chairs. Arbaaz ignored the chairs and sat down on the carpet in front of her.

'I don't know what has pulled me here,' he said to her. 'Ever since those terrible anti-Sikh riots in Delhi, when I met you, I have been counting the days.'

'Why count? You could have dropped in any time,' said Adhyapika Jyoti. 'Perhaps the counting of money got in the way?'

The gentle admonishment was not lost on Arbaaz.

'You're absolutely right,' he said. 'And I am paying the price. I lost a ton of money because of my own foolishness recently. And now my wife and daughter have ganged up on me, insisting that Alisha go to a university in America.'

'Birds sing after a storm,' said Adhyapika Jyoti. 'They do it because they're free. Liberate your daughter. Let her go. She loves you and will always remain your daughter.'

Arbaaz felt a lump in his throat. He fought back the tears. No one had ever spoken to him in this gentle and understanding manner before.

'You are joy. You are devotion. You are tenderness. You are freedom,' said Adhyapika Jyoti to him.

Arbaaz nodded, unable to speak.

'Share a little of yourself with your daughter. Humankind should remember that it's less important to be human and more important to be kind,' said Adhyapika.

'A disciple of mine needs your help,' said Adhyapika Jyoti to Arbaaz. 'Can you go meet him in Delhi?'

'Anything for you,' said Arbaaz.

The meeting happened at Sardar Harpal Singh's house in Maharani Bagh, the same one that Adhyapika Jyoti had been staying in during the anti-Sikh riots. They sat in the huge garden under a beige umbrella while the servant brought a tray of tea and snacks to them.

Sardar Harpal Singh was a handsome sardar with blue eyes. He was impeccably dressed in a crisp white kurta, churidar and black shoes. On his head was a white turban, tied to perfection. His grey beard and moustache looked like they had been groomed meticulously. There wasn't an inch of flab on his body and his skin radiated a glow of peace and wellness.

'Thank you for coming here to meet me,' said Harpal Singh, pouring a cup of tea and placing two samosas with chutney on a plate for Arbaaz.

'Once Adhyapika Jyoti instructs, I simply cannot say no,' said Arbaaz, gratefully accepting the cup but declining the samosas.

'I know the feeling,' laughed Harpal Singh. 'I was her very first disciple.'

'She said you needed my assistance,' said Arbaaz.

'Not for myself,' said Harpal. 'I run a charitable foundation in Bombay. It owns a huge piece of land in Malad. Unfortunately, illegal squatters are occupying the land.'

'Say no more,' said Arbaaz. 'I'll have them removed.'

'Oh no, son,' said Harpal Singh. 'I simply want them to be given alternate accommodation so that we may start building a charitable hospital on the land thus vacated.'

'But they're illegal squatters!' argued Arbaaz. 'I can simply have them removed for you. Why do you want to offer them alternative accommodation?'

'I wouldn't want anyone to be deprived of a roof over their head,' said Harpal Singh. 'How can one build a charitable hospital on a foundation that involves the misery of others?'

'Why do you need me, then?' asked Arbaaz.

'One of the squatters is a troublemaker,' said Harpal. 'He's preventing the others from taking our alternative accommodation offer. I'm told that you have powers of persuasion.'

'Don't worry,' said Arbaaz.

'You'll do it?' asked Harpal.

'Your word is my persuasion,' said Arbaaz.

'The job is done,' said Arbaaz on the phone.

'How did you convince him?' asked Sardar Harpal Singh.

'Did you ever watch the movie *Godfather*?' asked Arbaaz.

'The Marlon Brando one from the '70s? Yes, I did,' replied Harpal.

'Then you would be familiar with the statement: *I made him an offer he couldn't refuse.*'

Arbaaz looked at the man as he walked into his office. He had kept his bodyguards on full alert. One could never be certain.

'*As-Salaam-Alaikum*, Arbaaz Bhai,' said the man. He was dressed in a white pathan suit and an embroidered skullcap. Tied tightly around his neck was a taweez.

'*Wa Alaikumu Al-Salam,*' replied Arbaaz warily.

'Dawood Bhai sends you his greetings,' said the man.

'Please convey my best wishes to him too,' said Arbaaz.

'Arbaaz Bhai,' began the man. 'Dawood Bhai feels that Islam is under attack in India. Look at the way the Babri mosque was demolished by Hindus. See the riots that followed all over India. Enough is enough. This is the time to forget petty differences. All true Muslims should stand together.'

'What do you propose?' asked Arbaaz, controlling his breathing.

'Dawood Bhai has created a team. Tiger Memon, Yakub Memon, Hajji Ahmed, Hajji Umar, Taufiq Jaliawala and Dawood Jatt. The objective is, by the grace of Allah, to avenge the insult to the Muslims of India.'

'How do you propose to do that?' asked Arbaaz.

'By teaching the enemy a lesson he will never forget.'

'What do you want from me?' asked Arbaaz.

Arvind, Abhilasha, Shakuntala, Vinay and Vinit arrived in Bombay on a cool, sunny day. They had taken a flight operated by a new private airline called Jet Airways. In comparison to Indian Airlines, Jet had been a breath of fresh air with spotless interiors, well-trained staff and impeccable service. Arvind had wondered whether he should consider investing in the company.

They drove to the Bagadia guesthouse on Altamount Road and settled in.

Vinay and Vinit were headed back to Palo Alto after spending their winter break in Calcutta. Both of them had entered the undergraduate programme the previous year. Given that their flight to Los Angeles via Singapore was scheduled to leave three days later, Arvind had decided that they would all spend a few a days together in Bombay.

Even though they were twins, Vinay and Vinit were remarkably different. Vinay was interested in numbers but Vinit was interested in words. Vinay was outgoing but Vinit was reserved. Vinay took mostly business and quantitative subjects at college but Vinit had signed up for courses in humanities and the arts.

Arvind had never been one to show his emotions but the absence of his sons when they left for America affected him deeply. During their vacation in Calcutta, he had spent hours talking with them as young adults even though he had never had time for them when they were little kids. Vinit, who was turning out to be quite the poet, even read a line from Szymborska's *Nothing Twice* to his father.

Why do we treat the fleeting day
with so much needless fear and sorrow?
It's in its nature not to stay
Today is always gone tomorrow.

Arvind had organized a meeting with the brokers who helped defeat the bear cartel that was trying to hammer down the share price of his company. Arvind had ended up having the last laugh. By buying at an average price of 300 and selling back those shares at 500 he had netted a little over a hundred crore. Most of that money had been made by his Shiva web of Mauritius investment companies. Arvind and the twins headed over to the Bombay Stock Exchange for the meeting.

At the Stock Exchange meeting, Arvind sat with Vinay and Vinit on either side, facing twenty stockbrokers. 'We are indebted to you, Mr Bagadia,' said one of the stockbrokers who had made a killing by following Arvind's instructions. 'Going forward, there is nothing that our group would not do for you.' Vinay and Vinit smiled with pride at the compliments being showered on their father.

'The journey of life is dotted with obstacles,' said Arvind to the stockbrokers. 'If one has friends, the obstacles seem to disappear. Each one of you has been a loyal friend and Arvind Bagadia shall never forget it.'

There was applause from the brokers. One of them stood up to ask a question. As Arvind was answering it, Vinit stood up. 'I'm going downstairs,' he whispered in Vinay's ear. 'Come to the car when you and Dad are done.'

'Where are you going?' asked Vinay.

'One of the brokers has agreed to show me the trading floor. I want to read the *shloka* that adorns it,' replied Vinit, as he quietly slipped out of the meeting.

The broker quickly got Vinit inside the trading floor which was buzzing with traders. Nearly a thousand people were crammed inside. Shouting wildly at one another. The din was horrendous as middle-aged men screamed buy and sell orders accompanied by a series of hand gestures.

'What are the trading hours of the exchange?' shouted Vinit, over the din of the trading floor.

'Noon to 2.30 in the afternoon,' shouted back the broker.

'Why only two-and-a-half hours?' yelled Vinit.

'Could you keep up this shouting for longer than that?' asked the broker, smiling.

Before Vinit could ask his next question, all hell broke loose.

Shakuntala and Abhilasha were keen to give the boys protective Shrinathji pendants that they would be able to wear around their necks once they re-entered the 'big bad world' in America. Their first stop was Tribhovandas Bhimji Zaveri, the largest and most famous jewellery store of Zaveri Bazaar. The shop's oldest salesman, Bhagubhai, saw Shakuntala enter and immediately ensured that she and Abhilasha were danced attendance on. Old was gold.

He seated them on the plush sofa, organized water, tea and dry fruits, and then began showing them a wide variety of pendants that would be appropriate for young men.

Shakuntala and Abhilasha saw several pendants but couldn't find a design that was simple and elegant enough. The ones that they had seen thus far were rather garish. The boys would never wear anything that was so loud.

'Instead of gold, let's look at silver,' said Abhilasha to Bhagubhai. 'Smaller Shrinathji pendants in silver may also meet our needs.'

The salesman nodded respectfully and walked over to the glass cabinet behind him. Putting back the tray that he had just picked up from the counter top, he pulled out another tray with a series of pendants in silver.

The sound was deafening as the windows of the Stock Exchange Building shattered. Vinay leapt from his chair to protect his father. Shards of glass lay on the floor and Arvind and Vinay lay on the shards along with the brokers that they had been meeting.

Arvind got up, slightly dazed. 'Where is Vinit?' he asked Vinay, brushing himself down worriedly.

'Went downstairs to the trading floor,' said Vinay, his expression grim. 'What just happened?'

'There's been a bomb blast,' said one of the brokers.

Arvind ran like a man possessed with Vinay following. There was chaos inside the Stock Exchange building as swarms of people attempted to get out. The elevators had stopped working and thousands of people were falling over each other to use the stairs. Arvind and Vinay were prisoners of the crowd.

Someone in the crowd said that the bomb had exploded in the basement. It had been installed in one of the cars parked there. The maximum loss of life had happened on the lower floors.

Tears flowed down Arvind's face as he contemplated the grim possibilities.

Having bought two acceptable pendants with appropriate chains for the boys, Abhilasha handed over a bundle of cash to Bhagubhai. It was taken for granted that the transaction would remain off the books.

'There have been bomb blasts,' said a salesman, running inside. 'The phone lines are down. Many have died!'

'Where?' asked Bhagubhai.

'The Stock Exchange building and the Air India building,' said the distraught man.

Shakuntala felt faint. *Where was her son? Where were her grandchildren? Were they safe?*

She briskly walked out of Tribhovandas Bhimji Zaveri, asking Abhilasha to follow. 'I'm going there. We need to find out if everyone is fine,' she instructed Abhilasha who was taking delivery of the two small boxes.

Just then there was a massive explosion and the earth shook.

The trading floor of the Bombay Stock Exchange was littered with bodies by the time Arvind and Vinay reached downstairs. Blood was splattered everywhere—on the floor and the walls. Scattered along with shattered glass lay severed limbs that had been torn off bodies. It was a ghastly mess of exploded debris and human flesh with the overhanging smell of acrid smoke.

'Vinit!' shouted Arvind as he and Vinay started searching frantically but it was like looking for a needle in a haystack. More than 3,000 people had been inside the Stock Exchange at that time.

Arvind prayed fervently to God that his son had been spared.

When Arvind had arrived in Bombay he had noticed it. Bombay seemed more subdued than usual. On 6 December 1992, a massive gathering of Hindu *kar sevaks*—or volunteers—had destroyed the Babri Masjid in Ayodhya. It had led to communal riots in Bombay in which over 900 people had died. The tension between Hindus and Muslims had not dissipated even three months later.

On 12 March, 1993, Bombay was rocked by thirteen explosions scattered across various parts of the city. Records would later show that 257 people had died and over 700 people had been injured. It was the first ever coordinated terror attack in India in which RDX had been used as the explosive.

At 1.30 pm, the first car bomb exploded in the basement of the Bombay Stock Exchange. The twenty-eight floors were damaged but the maximum casualties were sustained on the lower floors. Around fifty were killed. Over the next two hours, car and scooter bombs exploded at Fisherman's Colony in Mahim Causeway, Zaveri Bazaar, Plaza Cinema, Century Bazaar, Katha Bazaar, the Air India building and the Passport Office. Grenades were lobbed at Sahar Airport while suitcase bombs exploded inside rooms at Hotel Sea Rock and the Juhu Centaur Hotel.

Among the hundreds who died that day was a sixty-nine-year-old lady in Zaveri Bazaar who had been getting into her car. Her name was Shakuntala Bagadia, the mother of the business scion, Arvind Bagadia.

Another person who was killed that day was an eighteen-year-old boy who had been visiting the Bombay Stock Exchange along with his father and brother. His name was Vinit Bagadia.

'I had fucking warned you that Dawood and his men were planning something terrible,' said Arbaaz. 'I even tipped you off about Gullu.'

'We nabbed Gullu's brothers,' said the Additional Commissioner of Police. 'That forced him to come to us and surrender.'

'But what did you do with the information?' asked Arbaaz. 'Nothing!'

Arbaaz had accepted the proposal that had come to him from Dawood's man. The man had wanted him to provide a safe house for Gul Noor Mohammad a.k.a. Gullu. Instead of merely providing a safe house, Arbaaz had tipped off the Additional Commissioner of Police.

Gullu was one of the nineteen men handpicked by Tiger Memon and sent to Pakistan via Dubai for training in the use of arms and bomb-making. He was also an accused in the Bombay riots case. After completing his training, Gullu had returned to Bombay via Dubai only to find that the police had arrested his brothers. Gullu had surrendered to the police in a futile attempt to secure the release of his siblings. He confessed to his role in the riots, his training in Pakistan, and a conspiracy underway to bomb major locations around the city, including the Stock Exchange, Sahar International Airport and the Shiv Sena Bhavan.

'Instead of listening to Gullu, your super-intelligent interrogators decided to dismiss his claims as mere bluff!' roared Arbaaz. 'All of you—each one of you—has blood on his hands!'

Ballard Estate had mercifully remained untouched by the bomb blasts. Arbaaz, Raju and Murali met to take stock.

'As it turns out, I was right about Dawood,' said Arbaaz. 'I always knew he was bad news. I just wish I hadn't been proved right.'

'Your other enemy, Arvind Bagadia, is also in town,' said Murali. 'He lost his mother and one of his sons in the explosions.'

'What?' asked Arbaaz. 'Hell! The poor man must be finished!'

'His wife is in hospital,' said Murali. 'She was saved because she was inside the Zaveri Bazaar shop. The mother-in-law was outside near the car and died in the blast.'

'Anyone else that we know has been affected?' asked Arbaaz softly.

'Chander Lakhotia is dead,' said Murali. 'His office was located at Zaveri Bazaar. He was walking back from lunch to his office when the blast happened.'

He was dressed in a simple white kurta and pyjama with a light shawl thrown around his shoulders. He hadn't shaved for many days. Arvind looked thirteen years older in thirteen days. Abhilasha stood next to him, her face still scarred by the glass shards from the shop windows of Zaveri Bazaar. She looked frail and almost ready to fall down.

It was the usual custom to bathe and dress the corpse before the last rites. She had burst out crying when she had seen what remained of her son. Arvind had gently held her and led her away from Vinit. Every father hoped that his son would light his funeral pyre, but God had made it incumbent for this particular father to light his son's funeral pyre instead. Both cremations had been carried out in Bombay.

Shakuntala had been in the process of getting into the car when a bomb placed in another car close by had exploded. Her head had been split open by a projectile from the car. She had died instantly but finding her body had not been difficult.

The situation with Vinit's body had been different. They never did find his entire body. The doctors had pieced together whatever they had been able to find. His head and torso had been separated entirely from his limbs. Arvind and Vinay had searched for hours in the Stock Exchange trading floor before finding anything.

Before leaving for the cremation ground in Bombay, both Shakuntala and Vinit's bodies had been positioned with their heads pointing north. Sandalwood paste had been applied to their foreheads and both had been garlanded with flowers and tulsi beads. Their bodies had been sprinkled with Ganga water using dried elephant grass. Then a leaf of tulsi had been placed in each mouth before Shakuntala and her grandson made the final journey. Three days after the cremation, Arvind, Abhilasha and Vinay had carried out the *asthi-sanchayana*. They had collected the ashes and bones in earthen pots and then made the journey to Haridwar to immerse them.

On the thirteenth day, a prayer meeting was held in Calcutta. It was attended by anyone and everyone in the city. Two large portraits of Shakuntala and Vinit had been placed on a platform along with flowers and burning incense. Arvind, Abhilasha and Vinay stood in a line, sombrely accepting condolences from those who passed by in single file.

Suddenly, Arvind froze.

'I tried meeting you in Bombay, Arvindji, but you had already left for Haridwar,' said Arbaaz, clasping Arvind's hands. 'I have come to Calcutta only as a father. As a father

I can understand what it is to lose a child. Whatever may be our business differences, I stand beside you in your hour of grief.'

Tears rolled down Arvind's cheeks as he nodded his head in silent acknowledgment. He remembered his dead son reciting:

Why do we treat the fleeting day
With so much needless fear and sorrow?
It's in its nature not to stay
Today is always gone tomorrow.

Arvind and Abhilasha lay on the bed in their usual fashion—both on their sides but looking at opposite ends of the room. It had always been like that. Two individuals sharing the same bed but little else.

Abhilasha's pillow was wet with her tears. She missed Vinit. She missed holding, hugging, kissing and nursing him. She even missed Vinay even though he was alive. The death of his twin brother had deeply affected him and he wasn't anything of his former self. She missed Joydeep, the only man who had truly loved and cared for her. She missed Shakuntala who had given her support and affection when there had been none forthcoming from Arvind.

She felt a hand on her shoulder. She turned her head slightly and saw Arvind's face. He was leaning on an elbow, his free hand on her shoulder. Abhilasha turned over to face him. No words were exchanged as they hugged. He enveloped her in his arms and allowed his own tears to flow.

'I am sorry for the way I treated you, Abhilasha,' he whispered to her as he continued to hold her. 'I miss my son. I miss my mother. Why is God punishing me in this way?'

Abhilasha felt safe in Arvind's arms. She continued sobbing softly but it was cathartic. Abhilasha and Arvind continued holding each other through the night. *I will never let you down again,* thought Arvind to himself. *I will never let you be unhappy again.*

A couple of hours later, Vinay walked in. His father had insisted that he proceed to America and join his class. How was he to explain to his father that he felt as if one half of him had been amputated? Vinay knew it would not be the same without Vinit. They had done everything together, including writing their college essays for one another and helping each other with girlfriend troubles.

Arvind got up from the bed and picked up the paperweight that he had brought from the office. Handing it over to Vinay, he said, 'Keep this with you. Your grandmother gave it to me and now I'm passing it on to you.'

Vinay took the disc-shaped paperweight from his father and bent down and touched his feet. Arvind hugged his one and only remaining son and then burst into tears.

Vinay lay down next to his parents and held them tightly, praying that the empty sensation that he felt after Vinit's death would go away.

Arvind sat at his desk in his study. A small television was switched to CNN but left on mute. The previous year, satellite television had arrived in the country. Five new channels—Star TV, Zee, ESPN, CNN and MTV—were now available to Indians through their cable operators who had created a criss-cross mesh of cables running between houses. Arvind ignored the television. His attention was on his desk. He looked at the envelope yet again. It was nondescript, bearing no return address.

He then looked at the photographs that it contained. They were black and white photographs that had been shot by a professional. They showed Arvind handing over a bundle of cash to another man who was standing in front of a bus bearing the words Bengal Transport painted on its side.

The phone on his desk rang.

'Mr Arvind Bagadia?' enquired the voice on the phone. It was muffled, as though the person at the other end had placed a kerchief over the mouthpiece.

'Yes?' replied Arvind.

'I hope you saw the photographs?' asked the voice. 'I have even more evidence if you want.'

'Who are you?' asked Arvind. 'And evidence about what?'

'Who I am is irrelevant,' answered the voice. 'The evidence is about the fact that you hatched a conspiracy to have your friend, Mr Joydeep Chakraborty, murdered.'

'What? You've got to be joking!' shouted Arvind into the phone.

Click. The person calling had disconnected.

Arvind picked up the phone the moment it rang.

'Hello?' he said.

'Sanjay Dutt has been arrested for simply receiving a weapon from Abu Salem,' said the voice. 'I wonder how many years you would get for conspiracy to murder?

'Bastard!' shouted Arvind. 'Why are you such a fucking coward. Why don't you come and meet me? I will set you right once and for all!'

'Tsk. Tsk. So much anger,' said the voice. 'Not good for your health, Mr Bagadia. Be reasonable. You scrambled your eggs. Expecting to unscramble them is unreasonable.'

'I do not do business with scum like you,' said Arvind.

Click. The person calling had disconnected.

The phone rang again. Arvind knew that it would be the same voice. He picked it up.

'Hello?' he asked.

'If you want me to send those photographs to your wife, I can do so,' said the voice. 'She will be devastated to know that you had her lover killed.'

'I did not have Joydeep killed,' said Arvind. 'I had foreign guests in Calcutta and the cash that I was handing over was hire charges for the bus. How was I to know that another Bengal Transport bus would kill my friend?'

'Touched,' said the voice. 'But that's not how it will seem to anyone looking at the photograph. Plus there is your connection with Kalyan Sarkar, the most corrupt cop in the state of West Bengal.'

'I only used him to follow Joydeep,' spluttered Arvind. 'Not to kill him!'

Arvind's voice softened. 'I have been through so much,' said Arvind. 'I've just lost a son and mother. Please…'

'My condolences. But business is business.'

'What do you want?' asked Arvind softly.

Vijay Rao looked at Satyapal Mittal as he put down the phone.

'It's sad to do this to a man who has just experienced such a tragic loss,' said Mr Rao. 'Unfortunately, the goldmine that Mr Bagadia sold me was a dud. He scammed me.'

The two other men nodded. Ghanshyam Das and Ram Lal Khaitan were also itching for revenge, having been made fools over an investment that had turned out to be nothing more than a bullock-cart.

'Are you sure this will work?' asked Rao.

'All the money that was pumped in to prop up the shares of Braid Investments was provided by a network of secret companies in Mauritius,' said Satyapal. 'The last thing that Arvind Bagadia wants is for the Income Tax authorities to get wind of those.'

'How many companies are there?' asked Rao.

'There are 108,' replied Satyapal. 'Each one is called by a different name of Shiva—like Maheshwara, Shrikantha, Shambhu, Parameshwara, Mahadeva, and so on.'

'Why not simply report him to the authorities?' asked Ghanshyam Das.

'How will that help us?' asked Satyapal. 'Blackmailing him into parting with the shares of those Mauritius companies will not only torment him but also make us richer.'

Vijay Rao, Ghanshyam Das and Ram Lal Khaitan smiled. Getting Satyapal Mittal on their side had been a masterstroke. He was the find of the century. A bit like a young Bollywood actor called Shah Rukh Khan who had suddenly become famous on account of two films called *Baazigar* and *Darr*.

'So it's decided,' said Rao. 'Whatever we get from Bagadia will be split in the following proportions: a third to me, a third to Satyapal and the remaining to be shared between Mr Das and Mr Khaitan.' The others nodded.

'Mr Satyapal Mittal, I am told that you are a pure vegetarian but your actions are those of someone who has tasted blood,' said Ghanshyam Das jokingly.

Satyapal grinned. 'I'm told that McDonald's, the American burger giant, has announced that they're entering India. Do you know who their partner is?'

'Who?' asked Ghanshyam Das.

'A chap called Amit Jatia,' said Satyapal. 'He was fourteen when he walked into a McDonald's for the first time—in Japan. All he could have was a milkshake because he was vegetarian. See what I mean?'

Arvind could feel the ground beneath his feet slip as he contemplated the alternatives. Some 1,627 kilometres away, the ground had actually slipped. In the Marathwada region of Maharashtra, a devastating earthquake had killed 10,000 in the districts of Latur and Osmanabad a few weeks previously.

Arvind thought about the alternatives. If he didn't cooperate, the photos of him paying the bus driver would reach Abhilasha. He had never brought up her affair with Joydeep. Neither had he discussed his own affairs. He wanted to erase all that from his memory. He just wanted to love his wife and his one remaining son. He wanted nothing to come between them now.

If he played hardball, there was also the possibility that the details of his Mauritian web of Shiva companies would be revealed. That would lead to problems with the Enforcement Directorate.

He scratched his head as he thought about the telephone conversation he had with the stranger. There was something that he couldn't quite place his finger on. Was it something the man had said? He desperately tried to recall what.

Tsk. Tsk. So much anger… Not good for your health, Mr Bagadia. Be reasonable. You scrambled your eggs. Expecting to unscramble them is unreasonable.

There was one man he knew who loved talking in metaphors about scrambled eggs.

Satyapal Mittal.

Satyapal Mittal saw the box lying on the floor to the right of the entrance door as he entered his home.

He had gone with his wife to see a special screening of a soon-to-be-released movie called *Dilwale Dulhaniya Le Jaayenge.* His wife had gone over to her mum's for dinner and Satyapal had headed home.

Satyapal looked at the box. It was of plywood, a little over two feet long and slightly over a foot wide. It was clearly labelled with his name and residential address in thick black felt marker.

'Who brought this?' he asked the servant.

'A delivery man came, *Sahib,*' said the servant. 'He said that you were expecting it and that I should ensure that you receive it.'

'Bring it into the living room,' said Satyapal to the servant. The servant did as he was instructed and placed the box on the coffee-table that lay in front of the sofa.

Satyapal used a kitchen knife to pry open the wooden lid of the box. On top was a thick layer of white thermocol.

He pulled away the thermocol and barely had a chance to register the contents before the doorbell rang.

'Are you Mr Satyapal Mittal?' asked the Superintendent of Police, Kalyan Sarkar.

'Yes, I am,' answered Satyapal, the sweat on his forehead glistening. When the servant had informed him that cops were at the door, he had hurriedly put away the carton under the sofa, hidden away from plain sight.

Kalyan Sarkar looked at Satyapal Mittal suspiciously. It had been an amazing career of promotions from Police Constable to Head Constable and Assistant Police Sub-Inspector. There had been short intervals before he made it to Police Sub-Inspector, Inspector, Assistant Superintendent of Police and, finally, Superintendent of Police.

'We have a warrant to search your house,' said Sarkar, relishing the idea of making a pig's breakfast of the house. He handed over the search warrant to Satyapal and snapped his fingers. Ten policemen trooped in, heading to various corners of the house.

'You seem nervous, Mr Mittal,' said Kalyan Sarkar. 'There's sweat on your forehead. Are you sure you're feeling all right? Hope you've not caught a bug. You do know that 693 people died of bubonic plague last year, don't you?'

'I don't have the fucking plague,' said Satyapal. 'I just need to sit down.' He quickly sat himself on the sofa, crossing his fingers that the box beneath the sofa would not be discovered.

'Yes,' said Sarkar. 'Stupid of me to think that you would catch the plague.'

'Why?' asked Satyapal.

'Because rats only spread the disease,' said Sarkar.

'Who gave this to you?' asked Sarkar, as he looked at the AK-47 machine gun inside the box.

'I have no clue,' said Satyapal. 'I arrived home and the servant told me that a delivery man had dropped it off for me in my absence.'

'Call the servant,' instructed Sarkar to one of his men.

'Did you see who brought the box?' asked Sarkar when the servant was presented before them.

'No, saheb,' said the servant. 'I assumed that Satyapal *Sahib* brought it here himself.'

'Why are you lying?' screamed Satyapal. 'You specifically told me that it was delivered by someone else!'

'A thousand apologies, *Sahib*,' said the servant. 'I cannot lie. I do not know what story you want me to tell the police. The fact is that there was no delivery boy. I saw the box in your bedroom last night and assumed that you had brought it with you.'

'I have no alternative but to arrest you, Mr Mittal,' said Sarkar, a smile on his lips as he delivered that statement.

'I'm being set up,' said Satyapal. 'And given your reputation I wouldn't be surprised if this was done by you.'

'You give me far more credit than I deserve, Mr Mittal,' said Sarkar. 'All I know is that yesterday some unauthorized arms were dropped from an Antonov An-26 aircraft in the Purulia district. The chief accused—Kim Davy—is now in our custody. We're simply acting on a tip-off that said that the arms were meant for you. Sanjay Dutt was arrested for a similar charge in Bombay, so what makes *you* immune?'

'Why in heaven's name would I need arms?' asked Satyapal. 'I'm a simple business professional.'

'Everyone needs arms,' quipped Sarkar. 'Just ask the *thakur* in *Sholay*. Now, even though I'm enjoying this conversation, I must ask you to come with me.'

'But I'm innocent,' argued Satyapal.

'In that case, drink some milk,' said Sarkar.

'What?' asked Satyapal, confused.

'A few months ago, the entire country went into a frenzy over statues of Ganesha that were seen drinking milk. It was a miracle! And that's precisely what you will need in order to get your sorry ass out of prison!'

Arvind took an early-morning flight to Hyderabad. Adhyapika Jyoti was touring the ashrams of the southern states and it was the only way to meet her. He flipped through the latest *Forbes* magazine he had received some days earlier. The annual list of the world's billionaires was out. He was happy to note that now there were two Indians on the list—Aditya Birla and Dhirubhai Ambani. *When will I be on that list?* he asked himself, momentarily forgetting everything else.

He ignored the *Times of India* in the seat pocket that discussed the implications of the passing away of JRD Tata during the previous month. JRD had never made it to the

Forbes list because the shares of the Tata companies were held by Tata Sons, which was mostly owned by charitable trusts. JRD would probably have found the endeavour of getting himself into the *Forbes* list rather pointless.

Adhyapika Jyoti sat at the head of the sea of white inside the white shamiana. Jeevan Prakash was now a regular in every nook and corner of India. Its global presence had also grown with the organization's footprint having spread from 103 to 114 countries.

Arvind and Vinay were ushered into her tent. She was seated cross-legged on a cot. Arvind immediately touched her feet. She gently placed her hand on his head and blessed him. Then she did the same for Vinay. They sat down on the ground next to her cot. She smiled.

'How are you, child?' she asked Arvind.

'I lost my mother and my son to bombs. Now I've lost my trusted companion, Satyapal,' said Arvind, tears welling up in his eyes.

'But you have a wife who still loves you very much,' said Adhyapika Jyoti softly. *A wife who was willing to have an affair with my best friend who is now also dead,* thought Arvind.

'And you have a son who yearns for your affection,' said Adhyapika as she turned her gaze on Vinay.

'But why do I feel so hollow?' asked Arvind. 'It was Satyapal who first told me about Jeevan Prakash. Now he's in prison because of me.'

'A moment of time cannot be bought by an inch of gold, child,' said Adhyapika Jyoti. 'At some point of time in your life you will stop chasing gold. That day, all your questions will stand answered.'

Alisha's palms were sweating and her heart was thumping. It was move-in day at Stanford. She had spent the previous three months imagining the day but nothing had prepared her for the actual thing.

In Bombay, Arbaaz had behaved like a heartbroken puppy, breaking into tears each time he thought of his little princess living away from him. 'I will call you every day,' he said. 'Eat properly. Keep the boys at a distance. No late nights. Stay safe…'

The list was endless. Alisha had found it easier to simply hug her father because that seemed to stem the flow of worries. At the airport, on the day of her departure, Arbaaz gave her a little box. 'What's that?' she asked.'

'It's a little copper *kada,*' said Arbaaz. 'My mother gave it to me so that it would protect me. I'm giving it to you for the very same reason.' Alisha opened the box and looked inside. It had been polished recently. It seemed to have some stuff engraved on it in a language she didn't understand.

She put her arms around her father, hugged him and whispered in his ear, 'I may be going to Stanford but I am and will always remain your little girl.'

Alisha had remained uncommunicative with Paromita throughout the journey from Bombay to Singapore and thereon to Los Angeles. She had remained equally quiet during the long five-hour drive from LA to Stanford. Paromita had attempted to get her daughter to talk but she had remained frozen.

She thawed only when they reached Roble Hall. All over, there were students holding up signs and blowing crazy horns. Alisha's nervousness began to dissolve. Everyone seemed so helpful. A couple of students offered to help with her luggage. Another asked for her name so that the DJ could announce it alongside the blasting Inner Circle hit '*Sweat-A-La-La-La-La-Long*'.

Alisha and Paromita walked through the maze of Roble Hall. Suddenly, a friendly Indian boy with a video camera slung around his neck, approached them. 'Are you Alisha?' he asked.

Alisha nodded. 'That's me.'

'Hi Alisha, I'm your RA,' he said.

'RA?' asked Alisha.

'Resident Assistant,' he explained. 'I'm here to help you with everything. Your room, luggage, settling in, dorm rules… anything! Follow me.'

One floor up via the elevator and a second floor up via the stairs, they were led into a room. It had stuff. Lots of it. Four girls' worth of stuff. After introductions, the girls started chatting as though they had known each other for decades.

Paromita knew it was time to say goodbye. She tried hiding her tears but it was impossible. She headed down to the Roble lawn where countless parents were dealing with the same emotions. She hugged Alisha tightly and whispered, 'I love you, sweetheart. I'll phone you every week.'

She turned to leave but Alisha wanted to hug her mother some more.

As Paromita's car drove off, Alisha walked back to her dorm. 'The first day is always a bag of mixed emotions,' said her RA at the entrance.

She smiled. 'Thanks for your help. What do I call you? RA?'

He laughed. 'I'm a sophomore. My name is Vinay Bagadia,' he said.

Alisha had initially found it difficult to adjust to the new style of learning. She had even been confused about the number of classes to take. Vinay had helped. 'It depends on the classes, the workload, and your other commitments. You should wait until classes start and attend as many of them as possible. By the end of the first week you'll be able to tell which set of classes is the best combination for you. You need to sign up for at least twelve units by the end of the first day of classes but the official add-drop deadline is only at the end of week three.'

She had eventually settled on four main academic classes—maths, Spanish, chemistry, and history. She would have liked to take more but Stanford did not allow first-quarter freshmen to take more than twenty units. 'Adjusting to Stanford and college life is at least the equivalent of a three-unit course,' her Academic Advising Director had said to her.

Alisha had listened to him.

Stanford was spread over a beautiful 8,180-acre campus in the northwest part of Silicon Valley. Alisha was like a child in a candy shop, struggling to take it all in. She visited the Main Quad and the Memorial Church; then the Cantor Centre for Visual Arts, the Stanford Mausoleum and the Angel of Grief; on another occasion it was the Hoover Tower, the Rodin sculpture garden and the Papua New Guinea Sculpture Garden... one could spend years and still not have seen everything.

In her third week she was at the Arizona Cactus Garden, a 30,000-square-foot botanical garden in the Stanford campus, when she saw a familiar face.

'Hey, there,' said Vinay. He was wearing a maroon Stanford tee shirt and plaid shorts. On his face were a pair of black

Oakley sunglasses. His feet were encased in comfortable hand-sewn Timberlands.

'Hey,' replied Alisha. 'What brings you here?'

'Oh, my roommate from Bhutan,' said Vinay. 'He's interested in plants—especially cactus and succulents. I'm along for the ride.'

Alisha looked at the young Bhutanese who was making notes in a diary. 'He seems rather serious,' she said. 'What's his name?'

'Karma Tshering,' replied Vinay. 'And yes, he's very serious.'

'What does he do?'

'Botany, chemistry, mathematics, history, languages… the list is rather long. And he's bloody good at all of them. But enough about him. Want to get some ice cream?'

Vinay ran madly from one end of the racquetball court to the other, breathing heavily, his heart pumping at full capacity. He thwacked the ball with all his might, sending it whizzing like a projectile towards the concrete wall.

'Dude, why are you trying to kill the ball?' joked Karma as he saw the ball coming at him and missed taking the shot. It was the equivalent of a cannon-ball.

'You're right,' said Vinay as the ball arched back towards him. He took yet another mad swing and slammed the ball again into the wall. 'I do need to calm down.'

Karma was puzzled. He had never seen his friend so worked up. He swung his own racquet with full force and sent the ball screaming past Vinay and into the front wall. He grinned at Vinay triumphantly but Vinay wasn't about to give up so easily. He tightened his grip on his racquet and smashed the ball again, sending it into a crazy zigzag around the court. Karma ignored it and shouted, 'Game!'

Vinay doubled over to catch his breath. 'So soon?' he asked.

'I'm worried that you'll break the concrete wall if you carry on,' said Karma. 'What's going on?'

'I think I'm in love,' said Vinay. 'And I'm not sure if she likes me. It's frustrating the hell out of me!'

Alisha's freshman year at Stanford passed by in a blaze. She had the opportunity to listen to brilliant speakers, performers and scholars from around the globe; she sang in an a cappella concert; she cheered for Stanford basketball; and attended the opening of a new exhibit at the Cantor Arts Centre. What remained constant across all of these activities was a young man. His name was Vinay Bagadia.

One day they had gone for lunch to Ann's Coffee Shop, a fixture on Santa Cruz Avenue in Menlo Park since 1946. The restaurant had changed little since then. It still used the original pancake recipe and its milkshakes were the real thing. The couple had then gone to watch *Four Weddings and a Funeral*.

'I love Hugh Grant,' said Alisha as they emerged from the dark interiors of the cinema.

'I wish I could say the same about Andie MacDowell,' said Vinay. 'She has massive teeth.'

'I didn't know that men were interested in teeth,' joked Alisha. 'I thought that the obsession was with teats.'

'What if I tell you that I'm obsessed with you?' asked Vinay seriously.

'I thought it was those women on television,' said Alisha playfully. 'Miss Universe Sushmita Sen and Miss World Aishwarya Rai. You watched both those shows end-to-end.'

'They pale in comparison to you,' said Vinay as he held her hand and led her to his car.

Arvind dictated the letter to Hilda. 'Bring me a draft,' he instructed. 'You may print it on my letterhead after I have had a chance to correct it.'

On the side credenza of his desk sat an unused Pentium PC. The supplier had installed two programmes called Netscape Navigator and cc:Mail that allowed Arvind to use the new technology known as the Internet and email. The machine was attached to a modem and phone line that took several minutes of screeching and squealing to establish a connection.

No, thank you. Arvind still preferred the feel of paper and pen. He looked at the letter as soon as Hilda placed it before him.

16 May 1996

Shri Atal Bihari Vajpayee
Hon'ble Prime Minister of India
New Delhi

Dear Prime Minister,

Please accept my heartiest congratulations on having assumed the country's greatest office. My heart is filled with joy that the people of India have chosen you to help fulfil their tryst with destiny.

Having met you when I was just a little boy in Kashmir and having seen your struggles during the Emergency days and your achievements during later years, I am in no doubt that the nation has chosen wisely.

Please do not hesitate to call upon me if I can ever be of service to you or the nation.

With respect and regards,
Sincerely,

Arvind Bagadia

He signed the letter with his thick-nibbed fountain pen, returned the letter to Hilda and then picked up the latest issue of *Forbes*. The Indian billionaires included by *Forbes* on the list were four in number: Kumar Mangalam Birla, Mukesh Ambani, Anil Ambani and steel magnate Lakshmi Mittal. *Don't worry, your time is near,* said an inner voice to Arvind.

'His government has fallen,' said Yash. 'Thirteen days is all that it took.'

Yash Dhar was inside Arvind's office. The peon had placed two cups of tea along with a small silver platter of biscuits in front of the men.

'Pity,' said Arvind. 'He would have been a good Prime Minister. What happens now?

'H.D. Deve Gowda is likely to make it,' said Yash. 'You see, while we Congress chaps have been undeniably defeated, no other party has undeniably won. And everyone around us has their own problems to grapple with. Lalu Prasad Yadav, the strongman of Bihar, is suddenly faced with a fodder scam. Can you believe it? Fodder!'

'More fodder for the fire,' observed Arvind. 'But the ragtag coalition of the United Front can't last too long. They need Congress support. Deve Gowda should learn from Charan Singh and Chandra Shekhar. In both cases the Congress pulled the rug from under their feet prematurely.'

Yash laughed. 'That's true. Our party loves doing that. Truth be told, names of Prime Ministers change. Politics doesn't.'

'If the Shiv Sena can rename Bombay as Mumbai and the DMK can rename Madras as Chennai, can Prime Ministers' names be far behind?' asked Arvind, sipping his tea.

The phone on his desk rang. 'Yes, Hilda?' he said. 'Yes, put her on.'

'Yes, darling, I'll be there,' he said to Abhilasha. 'What time? 5.30? Fine.'

Yash smiled. 'I see that you've become domesticated these days,' he observed.

'You should know,' said Arvind. 'I'm told that you have a stellar attendance record in the Lok Sabha.'

'What does that have to do with marriage?' asked Yash, contemplating picking up another biscuit.

'They say that no man is regular in his attendance in Parliament unless he is married!'

'How is your Congress colleague doing?' asked Arvind.

'You mean Arbaaz?' asked Yash. 'You gave him a bloodied nose in that share market brawl.'

'He started it,' said Arvind. 'He wanted to short-sell my shares.'

'But you made a fool out of him with that Qurbani thing,' argued Yash.

'For which he had me raided by the Income Tax authorities,' countered Arvind. 'He then topped it off with stealing Albert Mills by using forged documents supplied by that rascal, Chander Lakhotia.'

'When will this tit-for-tat end?' asked Yash. 'I know Arbaaz since the time he helped me out when I pissed off the CM. He became my friend. I also know you as a friend…'

'… and business partner in our aviation deal,' Arvind reminded him.

'Absolutely,' said Yash. 'Isn't it time that both of you let bygones be bygones and come together? Imagine what you could do if you worked together? It would be magic!'

'It's like asking Atal Bihari Vajpayee and Sonia Gandhi to fight an election on the same side,' said Arvind. A few days earlier, Sonia had delivered her first political speech at a rally in Sriperumbudur, the place where her husband had been killed. 'In any case, Arbaaz Sheikh stole my girl.'

'He never stole her,' said Yash. 'Paromita shifted to Bombay—sorry Mumbai—and he ended up with her. He didn't know that she wore a tag that read "Arvind Bagadia!"'

'I don't like him,' said Arvind, running out of issues.

'He came to the funeral,' said Yash. 'He was trying to reach out to you. Think about it.'

'I have an idea,' said Arvind. 'It's called the Mother Teresa formula.'

'What's that?' asked Yash.

'When contestants at beauty pageants are asked whom they admire the most, I'm told it's fashionable to answer, "Mother Teresa",' said Arvind. *God rest her soul,* thought

Arvind. The woman had passed away the previous year in 1997.

'So?' asked Yash.

'Let's invest in something that's fashionable these days.'

'Have you heard of the Internet?' asked Arvind.

'Sure,' said Yash. 'The papers have been full of it. A bunch of kids are making fortunes off it, it seems.'

'It's a bubble,' said Arvind. 'Don't mistake it for anything else. 'Whether it was the Tulip Mania of 1637, the South Sea Bubble of 1720, the Railway Frenzy of 1840 or the Great Depression of 1929… this is just one more in the series.'

'I don't really understand the business model of many of these companies,' said Yash. 'Technology was never my strong point.'

'You don't need to understand the technology,' said Arvind. 'You simply need to understand what happens during a bubble.'

'Enlighten me,' said Yash.

'A bubble is simply a phenomenon where trading in a particular type of asset happens in a price range that strongly deviates from its intrinsic value,' explained Arvind.

'But why does that happen?' asked Yash.

'Because it's almost impossible to observe intrinsic values,' replied Arvind. 'Bubbles usually get identified in retrospect. There is a sudden drop in prices—a crash—which follows the boom phase. The trick lies in being able to identify, in advance, the mismatch in valuation and value.'

'You want to invest in Internet start-ups?' asked Yash.

'Well, yes,' replied Arvind carefully. 'But I need a partner to play this game. Why don't you talk to Arbaaz?'

The meeting between Arvind and Arbaaz was awkward. Yash had arranged for them to meet in Delhi, which was neutral territory. Mumbai would have made Arvind feel slighted and Kolkata would have irritated Arbaaz. The location chosen was a private meeting room at the Belvedere, the exclusive business club of the Oberoi.

'This is a moment of change,' announced Yash, as though he were delivering a speech at a conference. 'Deve Gowda is gone and we now have Inder Kumar Gujral as our Hon'ble Prime Minister. All indications are that he will last for a year, unlike his predecessor who lasted just nine months.'

'And if he survives longer than that, it will be because the rug-puller in the Congress party is asleep,' joked Arvind.

Arbaaz and Yash laughed at the observation because it was true. The white-gloved waiter placed drinks and snacks on the table and discreetly left.

'Both of you have had your differences,' said Yash. 'But I am convinced that you would do brilliantly if you set aside your disputes and came together as a team.'

'Brothers in a family business can barely work together and you want two strangers who hate each other's guts to work as a team? You've lost it!' said Arbaaz.

'Each of you has had wins and losses,' said Yash. 'As I understand it, Arbaaz is busy printing money in Mumbai. And you, Arvind, are the largest institutional investor in the Indian stock market. What incredible power!'

'Thanks for the commercial,' said Arvind, interrupting the gushing Yash.

Yash continued smoothly, ignoring the barb. 'The Qurbani deal went in favour of Arvind... 1-0. In retaliation, an Income Tax raid happened... 1-1. Then Arbaaz managed to get Albert Mills redeveloped... 1-2. But Arvind was able to clean up in the stock market... 2-2. Hasn't enough blood been shed?'

Arvind interrupted. Turning to Arbaaz, he said, 'I lost one of my sons during the bomb blasts. I have seen the triviality of what I do. Irrespective of whether we do business together or not, and irrespective of whether we can be friends, let's not be enemies anymore.'

'I'll drink to that,' said Arbaaz, raising his glass.

'Now let's discuss the business proposition,' said Yash.

'It's simple,' said Arvind. 'Utterly foolish ideas are getting lapped up by investors across the world. 'A company called Boo.com is spending 188 million dollars to create an online fashion store. Do they really need 188 million dollars for that? Another company called Books-a-Million saw its stock price inflate by a thousand per cent in one week! Why? Because they simply announced an updated website.'

'Utter madness,' said Arbaaz.

'An unknown company called Pets.com aims to sell pet supplies to retail customers,' continued Arvind. 'It is spending millions on the forthcoming Macy's Thanksgiving Day Parade and an advertisement in the Super Bowl. It's as though they can't find enough ways to burn cash.'

'So what exactly do you have in mind?' asked Arbaaz.

'You and I will both invest in dotcoms here in India,' said Arvind.

'That's your plan?' said Arbaaz incredulously. 'Invest in dotcoms?'

'That's part one,' said Arvind. 'Part two gets more interesting.'

'What happens in part two?' asked Arbaaz.

'You've heard the phrase, I'll show you mine if you'll show me yours? This one goes like, *I'll invest in yours if you'll invest in mine!*'

The *Economic Times* carried the article on its front page on Monday.

Braid Investments Picks Up Equity Stake in BabaBolo

Kolkata-headquartered Braid Investments has invested an undisclosed amount in BabaBolo. The funds will be used by BabaBolo to experiment with new innovations in the B2B space. Braid will not be taking a board seat in BabaBolo. Unofficial sources confirmed that the investment in BabaBolo has been carried out at an enterprise valuation of 1025 crore. 'BabaBolo has proved itself as a terrific innovator and, coupled with its strong use of technology, it is creating an aggregation opportunity in the business-to-business space,' said Arvind Bagadia, chairman and managing director of Braid Investments. 'We hope that this latest round of cash infusion will allow BabaBolo to consolidate its leadership position in the space.'

'Now what happens?' asked Arbaaz on the phone.

'My company, Braid, is in the process of transferring 200 crore to BabaBolo,' said Arvind. 'Given that BabaBolo is controlled by you, you will place the money in a fixed deposit with United Federation Bank. Using the deposit as collateral, the bank will make the money available to your company, Dhanda Holdings. Dhanda will use the money to make an investment in DeshVidesh.'

The *Financial Express* carried an article about another company on its front page on Tuesday.

DeshVidesh Raises 200 Crore in Funding

Mumbai investment giant Dhanda Holdings has picked up an equity stake of 25 per cent in DeshVidesh. Financial Express *has learned that Bangalore-based DeshVidesh has raised 200 crore in new funding at a pre-money valuation of 800 crore. According to sources, DeshVidesh is likely to reach cash break-even in two years. Its page views have been growing at a rate of 67 per cent per month, one of the highest in the industry. A DeshVidesh representative says the company is on track to hit its goals of migrating more international business to its proprietary trading platform. Speaking about the investment, Mr Murali Iyer, chief investment officer of Dhanda, said, 'We are excited about the phenomenal growth opportunities offered by DeshVidesh. We hope that our investment will accelerate the path to positive EBIDTA for DeshVidesh.'*

'Now what?' asked Arbaaz.

'The money that I gave you has effectively come back to me because I own a controlling stake in DeshVidesh. We now need both companies to show revenue.'

'How?' asked Arbaaz. 'Neither of them does anything!'

'You will get BabaBolo to raise invoices on DeshVidesh for various services rendered,' said Arvind. 'We will pay you a hundred crore towards those services.'

'Then?' asked Arbaaz.

'DeshVidesh will raise invoices for an equal amount on BabaBolo,' said Arvind. 'BabaBolo will pay the money back.'

'But that would mean no-profit-no-loss. Each company would have a hundred-crore revenue and a hundred-crore expense,' said Arbaaz.

'True, but the market is not looking for the bottom-line, only the top-line,' said Arvind. 'It's called window-dressing!'

'These are companies with no track record, no revenue, no skilled management and certainly no prospect of ever being profitable,' said Arvind. 'Yet the market loves them.'

'You made the market love them,' said Yash as they reconvened a month later in Bangalore, neutral territory yet again.

'I didn't do that,' admitted Arvind. 'We simply hired a high-priced PR agency to ensure that the right spin was put on everything that went out. The other part was the robot.'

'The robot?' asked Arbaaz.

'I hired a techie from IIT,' said Arvind. 'He created a programme that visits websites and clicks on important links repeatedly.'

'What does that achieve?' asked Yash.

'One of the important metrics in evaluating the performance of dotcoms is visitor sessions and page views,' said Arvind.

'What's that?' asked Arbaaz.

'Simply put, the number of people who visit the website each day and the number of website pages that they view,' explained Arvind. 'The market loves the fact that our traffic is exploding.'

'Now what?' asked Arbaaz, smiling.

'Part three,' answered Arvind. 'Braid buys out Dhanda's stake in DeshVidesh at an appreciation of 100 per cent.

Dhanda buys out Braid's stake in BabaBolo, again at an appreciation of 100 per cent.'

'But that's ridiculous,' said Arbaaz. 'Nothing has changed to warrant a 100-per-cent increase in the value of those holdings.'

'Welcome to the world of dotcom valuations,' said Arvind.

The *Business Standard* carried an article on the front page of the newspaper on a Thursday.

DeshVidesh Valuation Pegged at 1600 crore

Mumbai investment giant Dhanda Holdings has divested part of its equity stake in DeshVidesh. Dhanda had invested 200 crore in Bangalore-based DeshVidesh at a pre-money valuation of 800 crore. Parties in the know of the latest developments have revealed that negotiations are at the final stages for Dhanda to exit at a massive premium on its entry price. 'We continue to remain excited about the incredible business model of DeshVidesh but we also recognize that it is time to let additional funds flow into the company prior to an Initial Public Offering. It is our intention to remain invested, financially and strategically, in DeshVidesh because we have utmost confidence in the abilities of the superlative management team.'

'What now?' asked Arbaaz

'The money for the sale of shares will come to Dhanda from Braid,' said Arvind. 'That money will be used by Dhanda to buy out our shares in BabaBolo. I have sent you a fax message as we speak. It shows the article that the *Hindu Business Line* will carry a day later.

Braid Exits BabaBolo with a Massive Valuation

Kolkata-headquartered Braid Investments had invested an undisclosed amount in BabaBolo. We are now told that this was a

19.5 per cent stake acquired for 200 crore. Insiders on the condition of anonymity have revealed that Braid has decided to sell out a substantial part of its stake for 400 crore. The holding period of the investment was less than two months. It is not yet known who the acquirer is but it is evident that BabaBolo's valuation has just doubled from 1,025 crore to 2,050 crore. 'BabaBolo has an excellent track record and some of the technologies it has invested in will drive it towards leadership in the business-to-business space,' said Arvind Bagadia, chairman and managing director of Braid Investments. 'We believe the time has come for BabaBolo to raise a fresh round of funding before it heads to an IPO. We will continue to hold a small stake until IPO.'

The next meeting happened in Chennai. Mumbai and Kolkata, as usual, had been ignored.

'So we've got two companies that do nothing, earn nothing, and yet attract eyeballs,' said Yash.

'Haven't you heard of the greater fool theory?' asked Arvind.

'What's that?' asked Yash.

'The greater fool theory states that the price of an object is determined not by its intrinsic value, but rather by irrational beliefs and expectations of market participants. As long as there is a greater fool around the corner willing to pay a higher price, the value will continue to rise,' explained Arvind.

'So now what happens?' asked Yash.

'Part four,' said Arvind. 'We find the greater fool. As of today, our investment bankers have identified five potential investors for the two companies.'

'And?' asked Arbaaz.

'We carefully select two of these,' said Arvind. 'BabaBolo will negotiate with one but ditch it at the last minute for the other.'

'And then?' asked Arbaaz.

'This will drive the ditched party to close out the DeshVidesh deal at any price,' offered Yash.

'Precisely,' said Arvind. 'We will have found the greatest fool.'

Turning to Arbaaz he said, 'The last transaction in which we paid you 400 crore needs to be routed back to us.'

Arbaaz nodded. 'The bankers tell us that it's on the way.'

'The bastard has gypped me again!' shouted Arvind. He and Yash were in his office.

'It could be a simple bank delay,' said Yash. 'Aren't you jumping the gun?'

'Balls!' said Arvind. 'I have been reminding him for the past two weeks. He finds all types of reasons why the money is held up.'

'Maybe he hasn't fully understood the cycle,' suggested Yash.

'What's there to understand? I invest 200 crore in his company, he invests it back in my company. I pay him 100 crore as revenue earnings for his company, he pays 100 crore as revenue for my company. I buy his stake for 400 crore, he buys my stake for 400 crore. Even a child of five would understand that!'

'Let me speak to him,' said Yash, hurriedly getting up before Arvind could throw something at him. He hated violence.

He had watched a new TV show called *CID* which had recently been launched on Sony Entertainment Television and had vowed never to watch it again.

Arbaaz and Yash met at the tony Belvedere club of the Oberoi. They had booked a private meeting room, the Corbett, so that they would be undisturbed.

'Why were you held up in Delhi?' asked Arbaaz.

'I happened to be at a party at the Tamarind Court when Manu Sharma shot Jessica Lal,' said Yash. 'The world has gone fucking crazy. People get shot for refusing to serve a drink! The cops wanted statements and shit.'

There was a pause in the conversation. 'I told you that if we simply remained patient we could get back at him,' said Yash, eventually. 'But he must never know that I teamed up with you to screw him. I'll be royally fucked if he spills the beans on that aviation deal.'

'My lips are sealed,' said Arbaaz.

'Here's to Arvind Bagadia,' said Arbaaz, raising his glass.

'The greatest fool ever,' said Yash, taking a sip.

'I had begun to think that you were on Bagadia's side,' said Arbaaz. 'I was convinced of it when you decided to do the aircraft deal with him. Then when you suggested that I pay him a condolence visit, I thought that you had lost it.'

'That was a masterstroke,' said Yash.

'The fact of the matter is that I genuinely felt for him at that time,' said Arbaaz. 'Whenever I begin to have feelings of goodness well up inside me, I just sit down and wait.'

'What happens then?' asked Yash.

'The feeling eventually passes,' said Arbaaz.

Arvind put down his issue of *Forbes*. No luck as yet. The Indians on the world's richest list were the usual suspects. The only new entrants were Azim Premji of Wipro and Shiv Nadar of HCL. *Patience,* thought Arvind, *your time will come.*

Arvind put away the magazine and called for Hilda. He dictated another letter to her. He made a few small changes when she brought the draft and then signed the final one with his thick-nibbed Mont Blanc fountain pen.

13 October 1999
Shri Atal Bihari Vajpayee
Hon'ble Prime Minister of India
New Delhi

Dear Prime Minister,

I am so very delighted to see that you have assumed the office of Prime Minister. Your first term lasted thirteen days. Your next one lasted thirteen months. I am certain that this term will last thirteen years. I am praying for it.

Your personal courage in pushing through the nuclear test at Pokhran against all odds has instilled hope in millions of Indians that they can finally be led by a fearless yet compassionate leader. Your bus trip to Lahore has been seen by the world as a genuine gesture of peace and friendship extended by India to Pakistan. Your subsequent courage and determination in fighting the Kargil incursion by Pakistan will go down in history as your defining moment.

Please do not hesitate to call upon me if I can ever be of service to you or the nation.

With respect and regards,

Sincerely,

Arvind Bagadia

Arvind looked at the letter again. Satisfied that it said exactly what he wanted it to, he closed the leather folder that held it and rang the bell for the peon who would pass it on to Hilda.

It was time to give up on conventional warfare. The nuclear option was far more effective, thought Arvind. *Arbaaz Sheikh, you haven't heard the last of me.*

1750, Thiruvananthapuram

ॐ त्रियम्बकं यजामहे
सुगन्धिं पुष्टिवर्धनं ।
उर्वारुकमिव बन्धनात्
मृत्योर्मोक्षिय मामृतात् ।।

The streets of Thiruvananthapuram lay quiet. Narrow, congested, and usually teeming with people and goods, the alleys were difficult to manoeuvre during the day. But they had a different feel at night.

All the streets eventually wound their way to the town's main attraction, the Padmanabhaswamy Temple. They were like the coils of a serpent. Rather apt, given that the city derived its name from *Anantha,* the serpent of Vishnu.

To the west of the Padmanabhaswamy Temple were the homes of the Nambudiri Brahmins. One of these was a stately homestead containing several rooms connected by verandas of elegant wooden banisters and sporting highly polished carved wooden ceilings. One among these many rooms was off limits to everyone except the master of the house. Massive brass bolts, chains and a solid doorknob indicated the importance of the room. Inside it, a man called Jayanthan pored over manuscripts by the light of two large oil lamps. Each of the manuscripts had a little jellyfish embossed in the centre of the covers.

'Svedana... Mardana... Murchana... Uthapana... Patana... Rodhana... Niyamana... Sandipana...'

He was preparing himself for his pre-dawn meeting. He rose, pinched out the oil lamps, stepped out and locked the door behind him. Jayanthan sniffed. What was that smell? He then smiled. Sandalwood and pepper. Sometimes the breeze carried the fragrance from the docks. Trading vessels of King Solomon had landed here five centuries ago and the city had carried on a flourishing trade in spices and ivory ever since.

Stepping into the waiting palanquin, Jayanthan settled into the seat and gave a quick command to the four burly men who would carry him to a modest house on the outskirts of Padmanabhapuram, a few hours away. The bearers always wondered why their master visited this particular house each month. They knew better than to ask.

The house was occupied by a very beautiful lady. She draped herself in the finest fabrics and used the most exquisite fragrances. Her voluptuous curves, flashing eyes and pouted lips could set any man on fire. She was waiting for Jayanthan and smiled as he approached. She led him away from the prying eyes of his bearers into a well-appointed parlour. Not a word was exchanged between Jayanthan and the woman once they were inside. She lit a torch from the oil lamp and silently handed it to him. In the centre of the parlour lay an inviting mattress, draped in silk and scented with rosewater. Generous cushions lay scattered on it.

Jayanthan looked at her and she smiled. She kneeled near the mattress and efficiently pulled it away to reveal a trap door. Jayanthan reached down, grasped the rope handle and pulled it open. 'I'll knock twice when I'm back,' he said to her as he walked down a flight of steps with the flaming torch in his hand. The tunnel was a perfect straight line and Jayanthan's walk lasted for less than an hour.

He emerged at the other end through an ornate door that led to a steep staircase. Walking up the stairs, Jayanthan arrived in a stately room with a glossy mirror-polished floor. The workers had used a mixture of burnt coconut shell, laterite, lime and sand to achieve the effect. The floor reflected images of the ornate carved ceiling that depicted ninety varieties of flowers.

Jayanthan had arrived in the *Upparika Malika,* the king's quarters. It was a four-storey building at the centre of the complex and contained the king's treasury, his sleeping quarters, study and worship chamber. Even though the wooden slats that allowed a cool breeze to regulate the temperature were shut, it was evident that it was still dark outside and that the residents of Padmanabhapuram Palace were asleep—except for the most important one.

Inside the study of his quarters, King Marthanda Varma was still at work. Pillar-mounted oil lamps illuminated the ornate room. The king looked battle-weary. though. Was there any value in being the only Indian ruler to have ever defeated the Dutch?

The king looked at Jayanthan as he bowed before him. 'Good to see you, Jayanthan,' said the king. 'I have called you here because of an important idea that I need to discuss with you.' Jayanthan sat down on a chair that was offered to him by the king.

'As you know, our kingdom of Travancore is bound by the tradition of matrilineal succession,' began the king. 'Upon my death, it shall be my eldest sister's son who shall succeed me rather than my own eldest son.' Jayanthan nodded.

'The problem with this system is that it creates two warring factions—sons and nephews. It worries me that in future years this struggle for the throne could place the entire kingdom in jeopardy.'

'Your majesty,' began Jayanthan, 'your excellent administration has resulted in new roads and inns, fresh military outposts, an internal water transport system, new canals for irrigation and new dams for water storage. The kingdom is at its strongest ever. Why do you worry so much?'

The king smiled. 'When I die, my nephew, Karthika Thirunal Rama Varma, shall succeed me. I do not want him or any future kings to inherit this kingdom,' he said.

'I am confused,' admitted Jayanthan.

'I have decided to dedicate the kingdom of Travancore to Sri Padmanabhaswamy, the royal family's deity. Everything in this kingdom shall belong to the deity.'

'But someone has to administer the kingdom,' said the perplexed Jayanthan.

'I—and my successors after me—shall continue to administer the kingdom, but as servants. We shall not be called kings. We shall all be *Padmanabhadasa*s—servants of the Lord.'

'What do you want from me?' asked Jayanthan.

'We need to ensure that the treasury of Sri Padmanabhaswamy is vast and bountiful so that future generations of this kingdom never have to worry. They can then wholeheartedly throw themselves into the service of the Lord and the people. The only one who has the power to ensure this is you.'

Jayanthan digested this information as the king continued speaking.

'Gold is tested by fire and people are tested by God,' said the monarch. 'I will tend to God if you will tend the fire.'

Book Six

2000-2010

The man arrived in Arbaaz's office draped in an orange *angavastram,* a vermillion tilak mark on his forehead, chunky beads around his neck and carrying a staff in his right hand. Arbaaz got up from his seat as Raju ushered him in.

Rudraguru sat down on the sofa, took off his slippers and pulled up his legs to sit cross-legged after adjusting his bright yellow lungi. Arbaaz folded his hands in a namaste and Rudraguru conveyed his blessings.

The tantric guru's reputation preceded him. He had first gained fame through his incredible astrological predictions. He had become even more famous when he met and offered his predictions to prime ministers, presidents, kings and queens.

'I was curious about why you wanted to see me,' said Arbaaz, still standing.

'Wonder no more,' said Rudraguru grandly. 'All will be revealed by Rudraguru.'

Arbaaz sat down on the chair opposite the sofa. 'May I get you something? Tea, coffee, water?'

The swami asked for a glass of water into which he poured a little sachet of colourless powder. It instantly turned blood red. He drank it and then used the cotton angavastram draped on his shoulders to wipe his mouth.

'Rudraguru is not only a spiritual practitioner, he is also a friend to his well-wishers,' he said, talking about himself only in the third person.

Arbaaz waited patiently.

'One of Rudraguru's well-wishers is a Polish businessman, Leszek Kulczyk. He is a billionaire with interests in oil, shipping, construction, transport and armaments. He would be interested in appointing you as his agent in India for defence orders.'

'Why me?' asked Arbaaz.

'Because Rudraguru suggested your name,' said the tantric. 'Rudraguru met your colleague Yash Dhar in America recently and Rudraguru was very impressed by all that you have achieved.'

'What's the catch?' asked Arbaaz.

'There's no catch,' said Rudraguru. 'Rudraguru helps his friends. His friends help him. Rudraguru only asks for your friendship.'

'How much will that friendship cost?' asked Arbaaz, smiling.

'Ten per cent,' said Rudraguru.

A soap by Ekta Kapoor called *Kyunki Saas Bhi Kabhi Bahu Thi*—literally translated to 'Because every mother-in-law was once also a daughter-in-law'—had hooked millions of housewives to the idiot box. Abhilasha had been watching the latest episode when Arvind walked in. 'How can you tolerate that crap?' he asked her playfully.

'Do I ask you about your watching *Kaun Banega Crorepati*?' asked Abhilasha, smiling. *Kaun Banega Crorepati* was the Indian version of *Who Wants to Be a Millionaire*. The Bollywood star, Amitabh Bachchan, had been roped in as the anchor and it had worked wonders. Arvind, who rarely watched any television, had gotten hooked.

'At least that's about general knowledge,' argued Arvind.

'Einstein said that imagination is more important than knowledge,' said Abhilasha. 'You watch your show about knowledge. I'll watch mine about imagination.'

Arvind retreated to the bar cabinet to pour himself a whisky when his mobile phone rang. He answered the call.

'Yes, Sardar Harpal,' he said softly. There was another pause.

'Yes, I do understand the need for confidentiality,' said Arvind. 'Certainly, I'll take the flight to Delhi on Thursday.'

He turned to Abhilasha with a smile on his face.

'What happened?' she asked.

'That was Sardar Harpal Singh, the business tycoon who is now an economic adviser to the government,' he said.

'What did he want?' asked Abhilasha.

'The BJP—NDA government is creating an economic think-tank that will advise the government on how to liberalize the Indian economy,' said Arvind. 'He wants me to be the chairman.'

Keshav Gadgil of the Shiv Sena was a thin man with a wiry moustache. His wireframe glasses accentuated his fragile frame. He had ordered a glass of lassi to combat his acidity. He was inside a room of the Marine Plaza Hotel along with

Arbaaz. Both men had entered the hotel separately and had reached the room five minutes apart. Arbaaz had asked for green tea. The waiter from room service had served them and discreetly left.

Arbaaz recalled the words of his mentor, Abdul Dada. *Politics is like a stage. Each politician plays his part according to the lines that are given to him. But backstage, the hero and the villain enjoy their drink together.*

Everybody was of the same religion when it came to matters of money.

'How does it feel to be in opposition?' asked Gadgil.

'The questions are the same,' said Arbaaz. 'It's just that *we* get to ask them.'

'And the government gets to come up with ways to avoid answering them,' said Gadgil. Both men laughed.

'One thing that I can say is that this PM has all the right instincts,' said Gadgil. 'I hope that Vajpayee gets a full term.'

'You believe otherwise?' asked Arbaaz.

'Who knows?' said Gadgil. 'He had thirteen days, then thirteen months. He's carrying eighteen alliance partners with him. Difficult to say… animal instincts often win.'

'I can vouch for that,' said Arbaaz. 'I was in Parliament just a day ago and saw the animal instincts at work.'

Gadgil laughed heartily. He then turned serious. 'Why do you think I can help you?' asked Keshav Gadgil.

'Because your party has six seats in Parliament,' said Arbaaz. 'The government of Atal Bihari Vajpayee needs every alliance seat to remain in power.'

'What exactly do you want?' asked Gadgil.

'Simple, really,' said Arbaaz. 'The armed forces will soon buy all-terrain trucks. The specifications are decided by the Ministry of Defence. I simply need you to arrange an introduction with the Defence Secretary.'

'What's in it for the Shiv Sena?' asked Gadgil.

'My eternal gratitude,' said Arbaaz.

'Why do you need the meeting?' asked Gadgil.

'Think about your question carefully, Keshav,' said Arbaaz. 'Would you really like to know? Sometimes isn't it better not to know? Ever seen those spy movies where the hero is interrogated using third-degree methods?'

'By terrorists?' asked Gadgil.

'More likely by NDTV's Arnab Goswami,' joked Arbaaz.

Arvind settled into his business class seat on the Kolkata—Delhi sector flight, relieved to have finally cleared all the security hassles. The security check had taken hours.

The previous year had ended with flight IC-814 en route from Kathmandu to Delhi being hijacked by the Harkat-ul-Mujahideen, a Pakistan-based Islamic extremist group. After touching down in Amritsar, Lahore and Dubai, the hijackers had finally forced the aircraft to land in Taliban-controlled Kandahar. The crisis had lasted for seven days and ended only after India agreed to release three dangerous militants. Ever since that hijacking, security procedures at all Indian airports had become exceptionally strict.

Arvind pulled out the folder from his soft leather briefcase. Opening it, he took out the notification that had been issued by the Prime Minister's Office.

No. 260/31/C/25/2000-E&S1
Government of India
Prime Minister's Office
New Delhi

16 January 2000

NOTIFICATION

Subject: Appointment of a Council on Trade and Industry

The government has decided to constitute a Council on Trade and Industry to the Prime Minister with the following composition:

Members: Mr Arvind Bagadia, Mr Ratan Tata, Mr Mukesh Ambani, Mr Kumar Mangalam Birla, Mr Azim Premji, Mr Nusli Wadia, Mr Rahul Bajaj, Mr Shashi Ruia.

Mr Arvind Bagadia shall be the chairman.

The Economic Advisor to the Prime Minister shall be an ex-officio member. Currently, that position is held by Sardar Harpal Singh.

The Council on Trade and Industry will afford an opportunity for a policy dialogue on important economic issues relevant to trade and industry between the Prime Minister and Members of the Council.

The Council may co-opt or invite such person(s) as it deems appropriate, to participate in any of its sessions as special invitee(s).

The Council shall ordinarily meet once in two months.

The Council will be covered within the definition/explanation of High Level Commissions/ Committees as given in Cabinet Secretariat OM No. 105/1/1/75-CF dated 20.11.'75.

Joint Secretary to Prime Minister

Copy for information to:
Cabinet Secretary

Secretary, Planning Commission
Finance Secretary

Arvind thought about it. Committees never did anything. Someone had remarked that a committee was usually a group of the unwilling chosen from the unfit, to do the unnecessary. But this one was different. It was a chance to do something meaningful for the country.

Arvind smiled to himself. The boy who had started out by scamming people was now a respected businessman officiating as the chairman of the PM's Council on Trade and Industry.

His expression turned serious. He felt like a fraud at times. As though he were impersonating an honourable man. Then he remembered a line that he had read in one of Honore de Balzac's books. *Behind every great fortune there is a crime.*

There was no such thing as an honourable man with a fortune.

The Defence Secretary looked at the sheet that Arbaaz handed over to him. It contained a set of specifications.

Specifications for 8 x 8 High-Mobility Heavy-Duty Universal Cargo/Troop Carrier
Suspension: Independent
Payload: 21,200 kg
Drive: 8 x 8
Power: 300 kW
Engine: 2,200 Nm/1,000 RPM
Transmission: Semiautomatic split, 14-speed
Cab: 1+3 seats, add-on armouring
Wheelbase: 1,955 + 2,865 + 1,455 mm

Gross vehicle weight (max.): 37,000 kg
Payload: 21,100 kg
Top speed: 110 km/h
Superstructure: Cargo body with tarpaulin, foldable benches for 24 troops.

'This is quite similar to the specifications that we already have in place,' said the secretary. 'Why do we need to change them?'

'Because change is the only constant in life,' said Arbaaz, as he handed over a slip containing a Swiss account number to the secretary.

The office located in Trump Tower at 725 Fifth Avenue at the corner of East 56th Street in midtown Manhattan had been done up elegantly in pastel shades. The New York office of PCM-Braid Insurance had been established earlier in the year, upon Vinay completing his MBA from Harvard Business School.

After completing his Bachelor's from Stanford, Vinay had worked for two years with McKinsey & Company. He had joined the consulting firm as a business analyst as part of one of the client-service teams. He had stayed on for two years before moving on to the Harvard MBA.

'*Knowhow* is of little relevance in India,' Arvind had advised his son. '*Know who* is far more relevant. Why are you spending so much time in America? Come back home.'

How was Vinay to tell his father that he was living with a pretty girl called Alisha whose father was someone called Arbaaz Sheikh? The proverbial shit would have hit the fan. Vinay had found ways to delay the inevitable while thinking of reasons that could help defend the indefensible.

While applying for the McKinsey job he had said, 'I need cross-sectoral experience to get into Harvard.'

While applying for an MBA at Harvard he had said, 'I need global acceptability, and a Harvard MBA delivers precisely that.'

After that, he had run out of excuses.

The young man had then come up with yet another plan. He suggested that Braid should open an office in New York City and that he should manage it. This would allow him to be part of Arvind's business empire while continuing to gain a global perspective.

His father had remained unconvinced.

Vinay had performed well in all ten academic units at Harvard. These included accounting, finance, marketing, organizational behaviour, general management, operations management, international economy, entrepreneurial management, negotiation and strategy. However, what he had truly excelled in was accounting, the subject that was hardwired into Marwaris by their munims.

He had approached his professor of accounting, a sixty-two-year-old polka-dot bowtie-wearing wizard who adored him, and told him of his predicament. His professor had thought about it for a day and then called Vinay.

'There is an insurance company here in the United States called Prime Mutual Consolidated, or PMC,' he said. 'I do a significant amount of consulting work for them. The CEO is one of my former students.'

Vinay wondered where the conversation was going.

'The Indian Council on Trade and Industry has opened up the insurance sector this year to private players and has even allowed 26 per cent foreign equity,' said his professor. 'They would be happy to partner with your family to set up an insurance venture provided that you stay on in NYC to tie up the deal.'

Vinay had spoken to his father. This time Arvind was convinced.

'Speak to my friend Sardar Harpal Singh,' said Arvind to Vinay. 'He's the PM's Economic Advisor. He will be able to help get all the clearances sorted out.'

The deal was sewn up a couple of months later.

What tempted Sardar Harpal Singh to assist with the clearances was the fact that it would kick-start the insurance sector reforms that the government had initiated.

What tempted Arvind was that Vinay would have to come to Calcutta—Kolkata after the recent name change—for a week each month.

What tempted Vinay was that he could spend the remaining three weeks each month in NYC with Alisha.

It wasn't just a win-win. It was a win-win-win.

The Prime Minister's guest list for the state banquet in honour of Bill and Hillary Clinton was restricted to a mere 150 names. There was a mad scramble to get on it. Many powerful people were unable to make the list in spite of being powerful. They felt rather miffed at being left out. Arbaaz was among those.

Arvind attended the dinner along with Abhilasha. When Arvind was formally introduced to Bill Clinton as the chairman of one of India's fastest-growing business groups, the American President shook his hand vigorously and said, 'I hope that Indian and American business interests can negotiate a lasting peace.'

'You don't make peace with friends, Mr President,' replied Arvind. 'One only negotiates with enemies. The Americans are our friends.'

A day later, on 22 March 2000, President Clinton addressed a joint sitting of both Houses of Parliament.

'Mr Vice-President, Mr Prime Minister, Mr Speaker, Members of the Lok Sabha and Rajya Sabha, I am privileged to speak to you and, through you, to the people of India. I am honoured to be joined today by members of my Cabinet and staff at the White House, and a very large representation of members of our United States Congress from both political parties. We're all honoured to be here and we thank you for your warm welcome,' began Clinton.

There was applause from the MPs. Clinton then turned to the issue of India—Pakistan relations.

'I share many of your government's concerns about the course Pakistan is taking; your disappointment that past overtures have not always met with success; your outrage over recent violence. But I also believe India has a special opportunity, as a democracy, to show its neighbours that democracy is about dialogue. It does not have to be about friendship, but it is about building working relationships among people who differ. One of the wisest things anyone ever said to me is that you don't make peace with your friends.'

The Council on Trade and Industry met at the Prime Minister's Office at 7 Race Course Road. Both Sardar Harpal Singh and Arvind entered through the main gate facing Rashtrapati Bhavan and walked up the grand staircase. They spoke together as they walked.

'Something has come to my attention that needs your intervention,' said Arvind.

'What?' asked Harpal.

'The Prime Minister is keen to encourage industrial growth in the country but I have with me an example of efforts being made to scuttle domestic producers,' said Arvind.

'I hope that you can back up your claims,' said Harpal.

Arvind passed a single A4 sheet of paper to Harpal. 'This is a set of specifications that the Ministry of Defence has published for the new all-terrain trucks that will be ordered by the army very soon. The bidding process will start in a couple of weeks.'

Harpal studied the sheet. 'It seems straightforward enough. What's the problem?'

'The army regularly places its order on an Indian company operating from Karnataka,' said Arvind. 'These trucks are ideally suited to Indian conditions. The new specifications have been written in a way to prevent them from bidding.'

'What do you mean?' asked Harpal.

'The payload of the trucks currently in use by the army is 21,100 kgs,' said Arvind. 'The specifications now require 21,200 kgs.'

'It could be a simple clerical error,' said Harpal.

'The present engines deliver 2,100 Nm/1,000 RPM. The specifications now require 2,200 Nm/1,000 RPM,' said Arvind.

'Hmm.'

'The present wheelbase is 1,950–2,860-1,450 mm. The specifications now demand 1,955-2,865-1,455 mm,' said Arvind. 'This is a conscious effort to edge out the main player so that someone else can make an entry. You must intervene.'

On Arbaaz's desk was a newspaper that announced that an eighteen-year-old from Bareilly had won the Miss World 2000 title. Her name was Priyanka Chopra—or something like that.

But Arbaaz felt like a loser. 'That Bagadia bastard scuttled my deal,' said Arbaaz to Murali.

Murali kept quiet. *After all, you gypped him in the dotcom deal,* thought Murali to himself. *Why should you expect his undying love?*

'I have to set this right,' said Arbaaz, picking up the phone. He dialled a number in Delhi.

'May I speak to Sardar Harpal Singh?' he asked.

'I must admit that I gently prodded the Defence Secretary to have those technical specifications changed back to the original,' said Sardar Harpal Singh. 'I had no idea that you were an interested party, Arbaaz.'

'Any chance you that you could rescind your instructions?' asked Arbaaz.

'It would be most improper, son,' said Harpal. 'In any case, I am sure you will agree that we should never compromise on the equipment that our jawans use.'

'Oh, absolutely,' said Arbaaz. *I helped you sort out your illegal squatters here in Mumbai thus giving you access to a property worth crores, where's the reciprocity?*

'I'm sure that you must be wondering where the reciprocity comes in,' said Harpal.

'It never entered my mind,' lied Arbaaz. 'What I did for you has nothing to do with this order for trucks.'

'I feel terrible that my intervention has caused you a loss, Arbaaz,' said Sardar Harpal Singh. 'Meet me when you're in Delhi next. I'll give you a little proposal that will make up for it.'

The Kumbh Mela of 2001 was no ordinary mela. The Kumbh occurred every twelve years in Allahabad but this was not only the final one in the usual twelve-year cycle, it was also the final one in twelve cycles—the conclusion of a 144-year cycle, thus making it a Maha Kumbh Mela.

One of the visitors among the seventy million who visited during those forty-four days was Vinay. Vinay's friend from Stanford, Karma Tshering, had decided to join him. Karma was now pursuing a PhD in Alternative Medicine from the Yale School of Medicine. In parallel, he had founded a start-up called Anayasar Research Private Limited. It was entirely focused on healing and longevity research.

Vinay and Karma reached Allahabad and Vinay's mood brightened. 'It is said that bathing at the confluence of the three sacred rivers—the Ganges, Yamuna, and the invisible Saraswati—purifies the body and the soul and liberates one from karma. But I have brought my own karma along with me!' he joked.

The Kumbh Mela was the Festival of the Urn from which one could access *amrit*—the nectar of immortality. A massive temporary city had been created to accommodate the millions of pilgrims who were arriving for the most auspicious bathing days. It was almost like a giant yogi convention, where yogis, sadhus, pilgrims and tourists congregated from all over the world. Many of them came from remote forests and mountain caves in the Himalayas. The most striking among them were the Naga Babas, who spent their entire lives stark naked. They covered their bodies with only holy ash and wore their hair in thick dreadlocks—like Bob Marley. The main bathing day—known as the Shahi Snan—was on 24 January. That was the day of Mauni Amavasya. Fifteen million would take a dip on that day.

Among the first few to take a dip that day had been Mahashiva Baba, followed by Adhyapika Jyoti. Vinay had spotted her from a distance as she retired to her tent. She now sat on the floor facing Mahashiva Baba, the man looking as though he had spent most of his life inside a gym. They were surrounded by disciples. When Vinay peeped into the tent, Adhyapika Jyoti had instantly recognized him and called him in.

'How is your father?' asked Adhyapika Jyoti, affectionately patting Vinay's head.

'He is angry with me for finding excuses to stay on in America,' said Vinay.

'Just keep your love and affection flowing towards him, son,' she said. 'Even the mightiest rocks are unable to withstand the constant pounding of a flowing river.'

Adhyapika Jyoti introduced him to Mahashiva Baba. 'This is Mahashiva Baba,' she said, pointing to the muscular man in her tent. 'He is my guru.'

Vinay touched the holy man's feet. 'I blessed your father when he was a little boy,' said Mahashiva Baba, his prominent jaw breaking into a smile. 'Your grandparents had brought him to the Kurukshetra camp.'

How does the man have such a razor-sharp memory? thought Vinay to himself. But before he could dwell on it further, Mahashiva Baba asked, 'And your friend? Is he enjoying the trip?'

Karma smiled. 'It's an incredible experience,' he said. 'But why does the Kumbh Mela happen in these months, specifically?'

'The time for the Kumbha Mela is determined by the astrological positions of Jupiter and the Sun. In Prayag it takes place when Jupiter is in Taurus and the Sun enters Capricorn,' answered Mahashiva Baba.

'What about the nectar of immortality?' asked Karma.

'That nectar is available to everyone,' said Mahashiva Baba, handing over a small crumpled ball of paper to Karma. 'It's just that many do not see it for what it is. We are so caught up in fighting our battles that it remains hidden even though it's in plain sight.'

'Is that Hindu philosophy?' asked Karma, accepting the little crumpled ball.

'No, it's the Hindu religion,' said Mahashiva Baba.

'What's the difference?' asked Karma.

'Philosophy concerns questions that may never be answered,' said Baba.

'And religion?' asked Karma.

'That's about answers that may never be questioned.'

Alisha had her coffee at her desk at 8 am. The report had to be completed in the next thirty minutes and there was simply no time to go downstairs to the NY Coffee Station. She needed to be out of the office soon in order to review a customer's art collection.

She was dressed in a crisp white blouse and dark-grey conservative business suit that was feminine yet reassuring to the conservative male constituency of Marsh & McLennan. She had finished it off with basic black pumps and an elegant necklace. There was only one word that could describe Alisha. Stunning. Several male colleagues had tried asking her out but she had turned them down gently. She already had her guy.

Alisha had been working in the company for over three years, having joined just after graduating from Stanford. The decision to move to New York City had been a difficult one. She would have preferred to stay in San Francisco or Seattle, but Vinay's decision to pursue an MBA from Harvard had prompted the switch. It was easier to drive three-and-a-half hours to Cambridge from NYC and spend the weekends with him. Of course, it was far easier now given that they both worked in the Big Apple.

Marsh & McLennan were insurance brokers but Alisha wasn't there because of her number-crunching skills. She was there precisely for the opposite reason. Alisha had majored in Art History at Stanford. Art History was a discipline that attempted to understand works of art from a variety of perspectives, including the original context of their making and reception as well as their subsequent circulation, collection, conservation and display.

Valuable possessions, such as fine art or antiques, were afforded only limited financial protection under homeowners' insurance. Marsh had pioneered the idea of a valuable articles policy to be added to homeowners' insurance to provide additional protection. Alisha was the in-house resource for Marsh on art assessment, valuation and coverage.

Alisha clicked the send button on her computer, having attached the final report for her boss. She then picked up her purse, switched off her computer and waited for the elevator down from the 96th floor of the North Tower of the World Trade Centre.

Vinay watched the television in his Trump Towers office, feeling sick to his stomach.

An aircraft had just smashed into the North Tower of the World Trade Centre. He had desperately tried reaching Alisha's mobile—without success. The huge surge in mobile traffic and loss of cellular infrastructure had made most mobile phones unreachable.

Alisha, if something happens to you, I'll kill myself, he thought to himself as he ran out of the office and headed towards the World Trade Centre in his car.

Vinay did not know one important fact. The office of Marsh & McLennan, where Alisha worked on the 96th floor, had been directly hit by American Airlines Flight 11 at 8.46 am.

'Will you always love me?' Alisha had asked him. They had been having dinner at Windows on the World, the restaurant on the 106th floor of the World Trade Centre.

'Nothing can take me away from you,' Vinay had said to her. 'I'm mad about you. And only where there is madness can there be love.'

'What about our parents?' Alisha had asked. 'Your father and mine are old enemies. Also, the religion bit. They'll never agree.'

'Love conquers all,' said Vinay holding her hand. 'They'll come round.'

Vinay found himself paralyzed. His car could not move. New York City was almost entirely locked down, with bridges and tunnels closed to all but emergency vehicles. Public transportation had shut down and traffic snarls that were miles long were visible along all the arterial routes. He tried calling Alisha's number once again from his mobile. No luck.

Inside the North Tower, Alisha had taken the elevator down to the North Tower's 55th floor to meet with her client. The meeting had started at 8.30 am. At 8.46 am, as Alisha was flipping the pages of her presentation folder, the entire building had swayed. Alisha had then heard a loud booming noise outside.

'Earthquake!' someone shouted.

'Everyone, get the hell out of here,' yelled someone else.

Alisha grabbed her purse and followed the crowd down the stairs.

The North Tower was a massive building but its stairwell was small in comparison. The steps were just about wide enough to accommodate two people next to one another. It was now packed like a can of sardines. The descent downwards was painfully slow. *Take a step and wait. Take a step and wait.*

Alisha looked at her phone. She tried calling Vinay but there was no signal. The phone belonging to the man next to her rang. 'Your building has been hit by a plane,' the voice told him. The crowd inside the stairwell assumed that a small private aircraft had strayed off course. People began worrying about the smoke. More flowed in every time a stairwell door was opened.

But in the paralyzed streets of NYC, Vinay was in utter panic. He dialled her mobile for the millionth time that day. He got her voice mail.

As Alisha reached the 20th floor, folks carrying badly injured friends from higher floors caught up with them. Alisha and others moved aside to let them pass. One lady's hair had melted into her face. Her skin had also melted. The woman was sobbing. 'How bad do I look?' she asked.

Alisha lied. 'You're not looking bad, don't worry.'

Then they heard another crash. There was utter silence inside the stairwell as the human beings gathered in the stairwell now realized that this was no accident. Another aircraft had crashed—this time into the South Tower. It was 9.03 am.

Inside the stairwell, the focus was entirely on moving ahead one step at a time. Several people helped others with their inhalers. Fire-fighters with air tanks on their backs passed Alisha, heading towards their own deaths on higher floors. People passed rolls of paper towels and bottled water along the chain. Alisha splashed water on a towel and covered her mouth and nose. She felt nauseated and terribly hot. Perspiration was running down her face and her weary legs shook. She was terrified that she might pass out. She suddenly felt dampness on her feet. Pipes had burst and water was gushing over the steps. The descent had just become even more precarious. Luckily, her pumps had flat rubber soles.

Having reached the bottom, Alisha found herself in water upto her knees. She blankly stared at the utter destruction around her. Elevators had crashed. The ornate marble on the walls had crumbled. Windowpanes lay shattered.

Rescue-workers guided them into the lower mall area, just below the courtyard. Alisha ran up the stationary escalator to the courtyard while policemen yelled, 'Run! Run! Don't look up!'

Oblivious to the danger above, Alisha turned to take a photo of the building on her phone. At that moment there was a monstrous roar as the South Tower came crashing down.

Alisha looked for an escape. The subway entrance was only twenty feet away. Alisha ran in and simply kept running. She could hear her heart thumping as she gasped for oxygen. She was soaked to the skin. But she was alive.

She had to reach Vinay somehow. Then her parents. None of the subway payphones were working. The place was eerily deserted. She got the hell out of there. The North Tower had collapsed too. Hundreds of people covered in a thick layer of soot and dust were wandering about aimlessly.

Alisha requested a woman for the use of her working phone but she adamantly refused. She began walking because there were no taxis, buses or cars. A man placed a flier of the New York City Rescue Mission in her hand. It provided phones, food and water. She reached there, exhausted. She waited an interminable period of time in line for a phone.

She dialled Vinay's number and reached his voice mail. She called again. This time she got through.

The relief that swept over Vinay was palpable in his voice. *I will never let you leave me ever again,* he thought to himself.

'Are you hurt?' he asked, the concern overwhelmingly evident.

'I'm fine, baby,' she said. 'Please get through to my mother. Tell her I'm fine. Just say that you're an office colleague.'

'Alisha,' began Vinay. 'I need to…'

'What?' asked Alisha. The line of people behind her was getting restless.

'I need to marry you, sweetheart,' said Vinay. 'I've just imagined what living without you feels like and I don't ever want to be in that place again.'

'No blood tests, no waiting period, no hassle. Just wham, bam, married, ma'am,' said the hotel concierge to Vinay and Alisha. 'Clark County—the one in which Las Vegas is located—issues more than 80,000 marriage licences each year. I'll organize everything, don't worry.'

Later in the day they appeared before a clerk at the Marriage Licence Bureau. The notice outside was specific:

Your proposed union must include two people who are unrelated and both at least eighteen years old. Proof of name and age will be required. No blood tests are required. You will need a valid driver's licence, passport, military ID card or other government-issued ID card. Even couples from outside the United States can be married in Las Vegas. You should obtain a certified copy of your marriage certificate and an apostille from the Nevada Secretary of State so that your marriage is accepted internationally.

'Congratulations,' said the bored clerk. 'I now pronounce you husband and wife. That'll be sixty dollars, please.'

The concierge who had very kindly agreed to accompany them joked, 'In the long run, getting married may cost you your finances, independence and your sanity. But for now, it will only cost you sixty bucks.'

Vinay spent double of that. One hundred and twenty dollars.

Besides the sixty-dollar licence, the Certified Marriage Certificate cost ten dollars and the Apostille from the Nevada Secretary of State cost twenty dollars. Oh, and there was an added five-dollar service charge for paying by credit card.

And a twenty-five-buck tip for the concierge.

'You did what?' shouted Arvind, spilling his whisky on the file in front of him.

'I got married,' said Vinay. 'And I'm sorry that it's Arbaaz Sheikh's daughter. And I really love you and Mummy. And I hope that both of you can forgive me.' *It was easier to ask for forgiveness than permission,* Vinay had decided.

Vinay knew that he was blabbering. He had never been more nervous. He had timed his visit to Kolkata with the Durga Puja celebrations so that his parents would be in a good mood.

He was wrong.

'You love us?' asked Arvind. 'Then why *this* particular girl? You did this to shame me, your own father, by marrying the daughter of *that* man!'

Abhilasha looked on nervously. There was a part of her that simply wanted to hug her son and tell him that she was fine with whichever girl he chose. There was another part of her that wanted to comfort her husband.

'Your father, my dadaji, chose his own wife and was hated by his family for it,' argued Vinay. 'I hope you will not hate me for the rest of your life.'

Arvind turned around and walked out of the living room. 'As of today, I no longer have a son,' he said.

Abhilasha ran after Arvind after sending sympathetic glances Vinay's way. 'I'll try to bring him round,' she whispered to Vinay. 'You stop worrying.'

Vinay waited in Kolkata for the entire week but his father refused to meet him. His mother nervously informed him that his father was planning to cut him off from the business entirely.

Vinay took the weekend flight back to NYC.

'This is what happens when we allow little girls the freedom to go and study in America,' shouted Arbaaz on the phone. 'They betray their fathers!'

Alisha had thought about it long and hard. Unlike Vinay, she had decided to break the news to her parents on the phone. There was every possibility that if she went back to Mumbai, her father would lock her up in a room.

'Please, Daddy,' pleaded Alisha over the phone. 'It just happened. All I know is that I love him.'

'What about your father?' asked a furious Arbaaz. 'You have no love for your father?'

'Of course she loves you,' interjected Paromita who was listening on the parallel extension. Arbaaz left the phone momentarily to deal with his wife.

'You keep out of this!' yelled Arbaaz. 'I was never in agreement with the idea of sending her abroad on her own.'

He came back on the line. 'Divorce him now! That's my command.'

'I cannot do that, Daddy,' said Alisha.

'Then there is nothing further to discuss,' said Arbaaz.

'I could have died in the attack on the World Trade Centre,' said Alisha. 'Isn't it a blessing that I'm alive and settled with someone I love?'

'For all I care, you could be dead,' said Arbaaz, disconnecting the line.

Vinay sat in the conference room of Prime Consolidated Mutual. He was now directly responsible for overseeing the Indian operations on behalf of PCM. Ever since they had inked the joint venture, the company had been trying to drum up institutional business in India.

The preceding months had been exceptionally difficult. Alisha had been emotionally shattered by her father's anger. Vinay's father was still not talking to him. Vinay had been offered a job by Prime Consolidated Mutual so that he could continue to stay on in NYC. He had gratefully accepted. *Eat with your relatives but do business with strangers,* was the wise rule that most Marwaris broke—sometimes with impunity. It was only now that Vinay was realizing the import of those words.

The managing director of Prime was a rosy-cheeked Texan by the name of Bill Purdy. Besides the slight Texas drawl and his passion for cigars, there was nothing Texan about him. He had spent most of his life in London and NYC.

'The recent earthquake in Goo-jay-rat has made the government realize the necessity of taking out adequate insurance,' said Bill. 'I'm told that the employees of the state governments are underinsured. Our managing director in India says that two states are open to the idea of private insurers managing the gratuity, pension and life coverage of government employees.'

'Which ones?' asked Vinay.

'Goo-jay-rat and Mad-yeah Parade-ish,' said Bill getting the pronunciations of both Gujarat and Madhya Pradesh royally garbled.

'Tell him to set up meetings with the Chief Ministers of both states and I'll make a trip along with him,' suggested Vinay.

'Is it safe to go?' asked Bill. It wasn't an unfair question. India had been in the news for all the wrong reasons. The year 2001 had started with a massive earthquake in Gujarat that killed 20,000 people. By the middle of the year there was a much-hyped Agra summit between Pakistan's President Musharraf and India's PM Atal Bihari Vajpayee that started with a bang and ended with a whimper. The year had concluded with a direct assault of Pakistan-sponsored terrorists on India's Parliament.

'Oh, it's absolutely safe,' said Vinay, who had stopped making his monthly trips owing to the cold war with his father. 'Nothing has been officially denied. When it comes to India, one should never believe anything until it has been officially denied.'

They were back under the beige umbrella in the huge garden of Sardar Harpal Singh's house in Maharani Bagh. Harpal seemed to look younger each time that Arbaaz saw him. They briefly indulged in chatting about the morning news of the bandit queen Phoolan Devi who had been shot down by her old enemies. Then Harpal turned to business.

'I felt terrible for having been unable to help you with those truck specifications,' said Harpal.

'Think no more about it, sir,' said Arbaaz. 'I'm simply happy to have the honour of knowing you.'

'That's kind of you,' said Harpal. 'But the reason that I wanted to see you was something else.'

Arbaaz leaned forward. 'Yes?'

'As you may know, I divide my time between India and Bhutan,' said Harpal. 'I have invested in a Bhutanese start-up. I thought that it would be an interesting proposition for you. I really do wish to repay you in some way, Arbaaz.'

'You are embarrassing me, sir,' said Arbaaz, although he was intently waiting for the Sardar to make an offer.

'The company is incorporated in India and is, as yet, unlisted. It has been founded by a young Bhutanese researcher. The primary research facilities are in Bhutan, the company is called Anayasar Research Private Limited, and they're doing cutting-edge experimentation on human longevity.'

Arbaaz stayed silent and listened. After all, *silent* and *listen* were simply anagrams of one another.

'I currently own 40 per cent of the company,' said Harpal. 'The balance 60 per cent is held by the founder Karma Tshering.'

'How and why did you get in?' asked Arbaaz.

'The Queen of Bhutan, Her Majesty Ashi Dorji Wangmo Wangchuck, suggested that I invest.'

'Did you see a worthwhile opportunity?' asked Arbaaz.

'The present King of Bhutan is credited with many modern reforms in the country,' said Harpal. 'This is a man who has said that he cares less about Gross National Product and more about Gross National Happiness. Issues like environment, health and education are top priorities for him. The royal family is loved by the people because of this. He and his queen see research of this type as vital to the future happiness of their people.'

'Ah,' said Arbaaz, not certain what Harpal was offering him.

'I want to offer you the opportunity to pick up my forty per cent,' said Harpal. 'I will be left with no stake in the company.'

'I'm not sure that I would want to invest,' said Arbaaz. The entire project seemed a tad fanciful to Arbaaz. It was almost as though Harpal were attempting to con him into investing.

'I'm not asking you to invest,' said Harpal. 'I'm simply gifting those shares to you.'

'Why?' asked Arbaaz.

'Because every good deed must be repaid,' said the sardar. 'You got my Mumbai land worth crores cleared. I cannot leave the debt unpaid.'

Vinay emerged from the Gandhinagar office of the Chief Minister feeling a sense of positive energy. The fifty-two-year-old chief minister, a man called Narendra Modi, was shaking up the lethargic administration. It was rumoured that he demanded PowerPoint presentations from the departmental secretaries to monitor progress. He remained accessible at all hours on his mobile phone and expected the same of his ministers. He regularly dropped in at project sites to monitor work progress for himself.

By the time Vinay walked into the CM's office, all the key decision-makers in the government had already assembled and discussed how they could work in partnership with Prime Consolidated Mutual. It was the most professional meeting that Vinay had ever experienced with the Indian bureaucracy. They had quickly plotted the way forward in a series of bulleted action points.

Vinay reached the Cama Hotel on Khanpur Road, went to his room, kicked off his shoes and lay down on the bed. He then called Alisha to find out how she was. They spoke for ten minutes. Then he called it a day.

The next morning, Vinay heard a commotion downstairs. He got up and looked out of the window. A huge mob was making its way along the street below. It was hurling rocks at cars and windows it passed. Vinay quickly put on his shoes and headed downstairs to the lobby but he was intercepted by the manager.

'Go back to your room, sir,' said the frightened man.

'What's happening?' asked Vinay. 'Why is there a mob on the street?'

'Yesterday, the Sabarmati Express that was returning from Ayodhya to Ahmedabad was stopped at Godhra station,' said the manager. 'Many of the passengers were Hindu pilgrims. The train was set on fire. Some fifty-nine people have died. The Hindus of Gujarat are angry. Riots are happening all over the city and in other parts of the state too.'

'How do I get out of here?' asked Vinay.

'You are in the safest place in Gujarat,' said the manager. 'Khanpur Road has not been affected at all. Yes, there is a mob, but they're surrounded by police. In many other areas, the police are entirely absent. But our owner has used his clout to ensure that the cops give adequate security cover to this area.'

'So I'm stuck here?' asked Vinay.

'There are six premier hotels in Ahmedabad,' said the manager. 'Two of them are safe—this one and Le Meridien. The rest of the city has descended into chaos. Your safest bet is to stay in your room. I shall try and make your stay as comfortable as I can.'

'Vinay is in Ahmedabad,' said Abhilasha. 'I'm worried.'

Following the Godhra incident, Gujarat had spiralled into a whirlpool of chaos and brutal violence. Curfew had been imposed in twenty-seven towns and cities across the state. India seemingly lived from one communal riot to another. The years 1905 in Bengal, 1921 in Kerala, 1947 in Punjab, 1984 in Delhi, 1989 in Kashmir… and now 2002 in Ahmedabad had been marked by unspeakable acts of violence. Only the geography and communities varied.

In Gujarat, swords, explosives and gas cylinders were being used to destroy Muslim homes and shops. It was an orgy of violence—murder, arson, looting, rape, acid attacks… even children, mothers-to-be and their foetuses were not spared.

'How do you know?' asked Arvind.

'He spoke to me before leaving from America,' said Abhilasha. 'I'm sorry, but he's my son. You may disown him but he will always be my boy. I have already lost one son. I cannot and will not lose another.'

Then Abhilasha broke down and cried her heart out.

Arvind picked up the phone and dialled the number of the Superintendent of Police, Kalyan Sarkar. 'I need your assistance,' he said. 'Do you know anyone in the Gujarat Police? My son Vinay was on a business trip to Ahmedabad and is holed up at the Cama Hotel. Can you get someone to go there and pull him out?'

Arvind put down the phone. It rang ten minutes later and he answered it. 'Thanks, Kalyan, I appreciate it. Yes, you can ask them to drive him down to Mumbai. How many hours by road? Ten? Isn't it a risk? What if his car is attacked?'

Abhilasha listened to Arvind's side of the conversation nervously, tears continuing to stream down her cheeks.

'Ah, that's a good idea,' said Arvind as he put down the phone once again.

'Save my son,' said Abhilasha to Arvind. 'He's everything to me.'

'He's my son too,' said Arvind. 'Come on, let's get to the airport.'

'Why?' asked Abhilasha.

'We're going to Mumbai,' said Arvind. 'Kalyan has spoken to the police in Gujarat. They've arranged an ambulance that will bring Vinay to Mumbai.'

'Ambulance? What's happened to my son?' wailed Abhilasha frantically.

'Nothing has happened to him, Abhilasha,' said Arvind, getting up and putting his arms around her gently. 'It's safer for him to travel in an ambulance than an ordinary car. There's less chance of being attacked by a mob.'

By the time Vinay reached the Bagadia guest house on Mumbai's Altamount Road, his parents were already waiting for him.

Abhilasha ran outside to hug him as he stepped out of the ambulance. He looked tired and anxious but seemed fine. 'I had mentally promised a darshan and donation to Tirupati Balaji if you came back to me safe,' she whispered in his ear. 'He did not let me down.' Her tears continued to cascade down her face and onto his shirt.

Vinay looked over his mother's shoulder as he continued to be tightly embraced by her. His father was standing on the steps.

There were tears on his face too.

'Yes, sweetheart, I am fine,' said Vinay to Alisha over the phone. 'I have reached Mumbai. Sorry I couldn't reach you earlier but the lines were jammed.'

Vinay disconnected the call. He was seated at the dining table of the guest house. He looked up and saw his father at the entrance to the dining room. His father looked much older than his sixty years. His anger against Vinay had taken its toll on him.

'I forced your mother to take a sleeping pill,' said Arvind, sitting down at the table. 'She had worked herself into a frenzy. She's not been keeping well these days.'

'Why didn't she tell me?'

'She knew that you were dealing with enough stress on account of me,' said Arvind. 'She has persistent stomach pains. Whenever we go to the doctors they tell us that it's a stomach virus, gas, or acidity. We once even rushed her to the hospital thinking that she had appendicitis.'

'Poor Ma,' said Vinay. 'She's worked herself up over this thing between you and me.'

'My fault,' said Arvind. 'I have many of those.'

'I'm sorry, Papa,' said Vinay. 'I know that you are angry with me.'

'Ssh,' said Arvind. He asked the servant for a cup of tea.

'When I heard that you were in Ahmedabad, I realized how foolish I had been,' said Arvind hesitantly. 'I hope that we can put it behind us, beta.'

Vinay got up from his chair, walked up to his father and put his hands on his old man's shoulders. No more words were necessary.

Some months later, Arvind came back to Mumbai to pay his respects at the funeral of Dhirubhai Ambani. Upon returning to Kolkata he dictated a letter to Hilda. When it was ready, he looked at the letter that she had printed on his thick watermarked Royal Executive Bond letterhead and signed it with his usual flourish.

25 July 2002

Hon'ble President of India Shri APJ Abdul Kalam,

Please accept my heartiest congratulations on having been elected to the country's highest constitutional office. I cannot think of any other person who so richly deserves the honour.

India and every Indian is proud to see you as the occupant of Rashtrapati Bhavan.

With respect and regards,
Sincerely,

Arvind Bagadia

The article in the *Hindustan Times* was dated 24 December 2002.

Prime Minister Atal Bihari Vajpayee has said that the launch of the Delhi Metro would help ease traffic congestion in the capital and also check pollution. Inaugurating the Delhi Metro, Vajpayee said running of the underground rail was a long-cherished dream of the people, which had been realized. Vajpayee pressed a button from the dais and unveiled a plaque to mark the inauguration of the Metro.

Deputy Prime Minister Lal Krishna Advani, Urban Development Minister Ananth Kumar, Lieutenant Governor Vijay Kapoor, Chief Minister Sheila Dikshit and Delhi Metro Chairman Madan Lal Khurana also spoke on the occasion.

Before inaugurating the Metro, Vajpayee, along with Advani, also travelled in the train with VIP guests that included Sardar Harpal Singh, the government's Economic Advisor, and business stalwarts such as Arvind Bagadia.

'Will he speak to me?' asked Alisha.

'I've tried everything, Alisha,' said Paromita. 'Your father is as obstinate as a mule. I know he misses you. But his ego gets in the way.'

'Should I come to Mumbai?' asked Alisha.

'I'll let you know when the time's right,' said Paromita.

'It's been three years,' said Alisha. 'I miss you and him.'

'He's suddenly very busy,' said Paromita. 'The recent elections resulted in Sonia Gandhi coming into power. Your father is tipped to be a minister with Cabinet rank in the government. He has gone with Yash Dhar to Delhi.'

Poor Atal Bihari Vajpayee had been advised to call early elections in 2004 because the pollsters were predicting an easy majority for the NDA. The campaign plank had been *India Shining*. The BJP had discovered that much of India felt that India was shining only for a select few. Vajpayee's party received a drubbing at the hustings. The Indian National Congress, which had ruled India for most of the years after Independence, returned to power after an exile of eight years. Rajiv Gandhi's son, Rahul, even won his first general election from the family's constituency of Amethi.

'So Sonia Gandhi will become PM?' asked Alisha.

'She's played the ultimate political card yesterday,' said Paromita. 'She's declined to become the new Prime Minister. She's asked Narasimha Rao's former Finance Minister,

Dr Manmohan Singh, to head the new government.'

Paromita paused. 'How's Vinay?' she asked.

'He's fine,' said Alisha. 'He's gone to Bhutan along with his father for some work.'

'They're getting on fine?' asked Paromita.

'Thank heavens, one father—child relationship is back on track,' said Alisha. *'Mera number kab aayega?'*

Only nine Indian billionaires made it into the international list of *Forbes* in 2004 but that year the magazine also introduced the *Forbes'* list of India's richest. It was the magazine's inaugural list for India, reflective of the fact that India's economic strength was growing. For the first time ever, the magazine had compiled a list of the forty wealthiest Indians.

1. *Lakshmi N. Mittal of Mittal Steel*
2. *Azim Premji of Wipro*
3. *Mukesh and Anil Ambani of Reliance*
4. *Kumar Mangalam Birla of A. V. Birla*
5. *Pallonji Mistry of Tata Sons*
6. *Sunil Mittal of Bharti Group*
7. *Shiv Nadar of HCL*
8. *Adi Godrej of Godrej Industries*
9. *Malvinder and Shivinder Singh of Ranbaxy*
10. *Dilip Shanghvi of Sun Pharma*

Arvind was disappointed to see that he hadn't made it to the top ten of India. He scanned the list further.

11. *Anil Agarwal of Sterlite*
12. *Shashi and Ravi Ruia of Essar*
13. *Om Prakash Jindal of Jindal Group*
14. *Rahul Bajaj of Bajaj Auto*

15. N.R. Narayana Murthy of Infosys
16. Subhash Chandra of Zee Telefilms
17. Yusuf Hamed of Cipla
18. Brijmohan Lal Munjal of Hero Group
19. Habil Khorakiwala of Wockhardt
20. Vivek Burman of Dabur

No luck with the top twenty either. Oh well, there was always next time. He read the rest of the list.

21. Nandan Nilekani of Infosys
22. S. Gopalakrishnan of Infosys
23. N.S. Raghavan of Infosys
24. Narendra Patni of Patni Comp
25. Ajay Piramal of Nicholas Piramal
26. Vijay Mallya of UB Group
27. Arvind Bagadia of Braid

Number 27. Not bad, thought Arvind. If he could keep growing the business, he could easily enter the top ten in a couple of years. He scanned the rest of the list as a matter of general interest.

28. Baba Kalyani of Kalyani Group
29. B. Ramalinga Raju of Satyam
30. Kiran Mazumdar-Shaw of Biocon
31. Karsanbhai Patel of Nirma
32. Arbaaz Sheikh of Dhanda
33. Uday Kotak of Kotak Mahindra
34. S.D. Shibulal of Infosys
35. K. Anji Reddy of Dr Reddy's
36. Narottam Sekhsaria of Gujarat Ambuja
37. Jaiprakash Gaur of Jaiprakash Inds
38. Shyam and Hari Bhartia of Jubilant Organo
39. Keshub Mahindra of M&M
40. Desh Bandhu Gupta of Lupin

It was Number 32 that caught his attention. Arbaaz Sheikh at 32! *The bastard has succeeded in transforming himself from mafia don to respectable businessman by creating an investment company and bank,* thought Arvind. *Why didn't I think of using Deshmukh to get into banking?*

Arvind made up his mind to ensure that he would alter the contours of the *Forbes* list sooner rather than later.

Arvind and Vinay settled into their business class seats on the Kolkata—Delhi sector flight. There would be a short halt in Delhi before they took a flight to Paro in Bhutan. A car would be meeting them at Paro to drive them to Karma's research centre.

The call from Karma had been a heaven-sent opportunity. He was open to bringing new investors into his company. 'Why don't you and your father come to Bhutan?' he had said over the phone.

The Kingdom of Bhutan was a landlocked country bordered to the north by China and to the south, east and west by India. It had been ruled by the Royal House of Wangchuck since 1907.

'Do you think that they could really be onto something?' asked Arvind, scanning the report that Vinay had prepared for his information.

'I believe so,' said Vinay. 'Karma's company, Anayasar Research Private Limited, has been carrying out cutting-edge experiments. It's just that none has caught on as yet.'

'This could be another one of those crazy bubbles,' said Arvind. 'Just look what happened with dotcom valuations. And see what happened with Enron.'

'Anayasar is not a bubble,' said Vinay. 'In fact, hardly anyone knows about the company. It is managed by Karma Tshering, a brilliant scientist who did far-seeing research as a PhD student at Yale Medical School. He was my roommate at Stanford. The company continues to be privately held.'

'Who is funding him?' asked Arvind.

'Sardar Harpal Singh,' replied Vinay. 'He owns 40 per cent of the equity. He bought the stake at a premium in order to provide start-up funding to Karma.'

Arvind allowed the flight attendant to pour some milk into his tea. Taking a sip, he asked, 'If that's the case, Karma will want to retain control with his 60 per cent.'

'It's true that management control lies completely with Karma. He is free to do what he wants and that includes bringing in new investors. He currently holds 60 per cent of the equity, true, but may consider selling some of it to friendly investors because he needs additional funds.'

'How close is he to a breakthrough?' asked Arvind.

'Difficult to say,' replied Vinay. 'Five years, maybe fifteen. What's important is the fact that he is the only one who is approaching the issue of human longevity with an entirely non-Western perspective.'

Karma Tshering's laboratory was unlike any other. From the outside it looked like a monastery—a stunningly beautiful one at that. Located to the north of Paro, it hung on a precipitous cliff around 10,000 feet above sea level. The structure had been built into the rock face and could only be approached by a mule track that passed through a thick pine forest. It usually remained partially hidden by clouds that only served to accentuate its remoteness.

Inside, though, was a modern state-of-the-art laboratory created by constructing a steel and glass inner shell within the old structure. The 11,000-square-foot lab contained row upon rows of gleaming laboratory tables and equipment with twenty-five researchers in white lab coats carrying out an astounding variety of experiments.

Karma was excited to see his Stanford roommate. It had been three years since the Kumbh Mela. They thumped each other's backs as though they were still college kids. Vinay introduced his father to Karma and the three men then headed to a small conference room built on a cantilever that offered a stunning view of a valley and waterfall below. They sat down and a young lady brought in lemon tea and fresh apples.

'Tell me why you decided upon this place for your lab, Karma,' said Arvind.

'Access to many of Bhutan's monasteries was kept deliberately difficult,' replied Karma. 'This was one of the oldest ones, having been built around the seventh century. It was almost entirely destroyed during the Duar War of 1864 when the British invaded. It lay abandoned for many years—crumbling, remote and inaccessible. When I returned to Bhutan and expressed an interest in setting up a laboratory, Her Majesty Ashi Dorji Wangmo Wangchuck suggested that we restore this place and put it to use.'

'Now tell me about your project,' said Arvind.

'It's simple yet complex,' explained Karma. 'How much do you know about Ashoka?'

'The Mauryan emperor?' asked Arvind.

'Yes,' said Karma. 'It is said that during Ashoka's reign, the Mauryan kingdom carried out significant research into the science of longevity. Their quest was to find the nectar of immortality.'

'Why? Was there an immediate imperative?' asked Arvind.

'The Kalinga War,' replied Karma. 'Around 300,000 people died in that bloody war and Ashoka was repentant of the bloodshed. There was probably a part of him that wanted to resurrect the dead. He created a team of researchers who were called the Nine Unknowns.'

'Surely that's fantasy,' scoffed Vinay. A novel called *The Nine Unknown* published in 1923 by the American writer Talbot Mundy had popularized the notion that Ashoka had established a secret society devoted to scientific research.

'Don't be fooled by the conspiracy theory argument,' said Karma. 'Mundy theorized that the nine men were involved in the research of subjects as diverse as propaganda, physiology, microbiology, alchemy, communication, gravity, cosmology, light and sociology. That's nonsense. There were indeed nine men but they were entirely involved in developing eighteen key processes.'

'Processes for?' asked Arvind.

'Processes for attaining human immortality.'

Karma led them out of the conference room and into the lab. At the far end was a giant tank filled with thousands of jellyfish. Karma then provided Arvind and Vinay with special spectacles that magnified their vision.

The jellyfish were bell-shaped creatures around half a centimetre wide. The jelly in the walls of their stomachs was uniformly thin except for some thickening at the apex. The overall distinguishing feature was the large stomach, bright-red in colour, in a cruciform shape. The younger specimens had around eight tentacles but the older ones had ten times the number.

'They're called *Turritopsis dohrnii*,' said Karma pointing to the creatures. 'They're only found in two regions—the Mediterranean Sea and the waters of Japan.'

'What's so special about them?' asked Vinay.

'They're the only species we know to be immortal,' replied Karma.

'Immortal?' asked Vinay in disbelief.

'Have you read the *Epic of Gilgamesh*?' asked Karma in response.

'The flood myth?' asked Arvind, even though he hadn't read it. Karma nodded.

'Don't need to read it,' said Arvind. 'I experienced the Mumbai floods this year when I was there for a meeting. I was stranded for five days! And that was no myth!'

Karma and Vinay laughed. It was easy to laugh after the event was over. The fact was that thousands lost their homes due to floods caused by one of the heaviest downpours on 26 July 2005.

'The *Epic of Gilgamesh* is a poem from ancient Mesopotamia,' said Karma getting back to the ancient flood myth. 'It has been dated to the Third Dynasty of Ur—around 2100 BCE. In that story, Utnapishtim tells Gilgamesh that the secret to immortality lies in a coral found on the ocean floor. As it turns out, he wasn't wrong.'

Vinay's head was spinning. 'How? Please explain, Karma.'

'The discovery was unwittingly made in 1988 by Christian Sommer, a German marine-biology student. He spent his summer in Rapallo, a small city on the Italian Riviera,' said Karma. 'He was conducting research on hydrozoans.

They're small invertebrates that can look like jellyfish or soft coral depending on their stage of life-cycle.'

'What did he find?' asked Arvind.

'Among the hundreds of organisms he collected was an obscure species known as *Turritopsis dohrnii*. Sommer kept them in petri dishes and observed their reproduction habits,' replied Karma. 'What he noticed was that his *Turritopsis dohrnii* refused to die. It appeared to age in reverse, growing younger and younger until it reached its earliest stage of development, at which point it began its life cycle anew.'

'What could explain it?' asked Arvind.

'If a jellyfish is exposed to environmental stress or physical assault, or if it is sick or old, it can revert to the polyp stage, thus forming a new polyp colony,' replied Karma. 'It does this using a process known as trans-differentiation, altering the differentiated state of the cells and transforming them into new types of cells, like stem cells.'

'Reversing age,' murmured Vinay.

'It is the only established case of an animal that is capable of reverting completely to a sexually immature, colonial stage after having attained sexual maturity as a solitary individual,' said Karma. 'Theoretically, this process can go on indefinitely, effectively rendering the jellyfish biologically immortal.'

'Where does Ashoka fit into your jellyfish research?' asked Vinay. Karma didn't answer the question. Instead, he led them to a wall that bore a giant poster. It had been printed on aged paper using vegetable dyes and then sealed off with a massive glass plate.

'Read it,' said Karma. Arvind and Vinay began to read.

The Eighteen Steps of Rasayana

1. *Svedana: Steam mercury with a number of plant substances, some minerals, alkalis and salts.*
2. *Mardana: Rub the steamed mercury in a mortar along with plant and acidic materials.*
3. *Murchana: Triturate the mercury in a mortar with plant extracts until it loses its own character and form.*
4. *Uthapana: Steam the mercury along with alkalis, salts, the three myrobalans and alum. Then rub it in sunlight so that the characteristics of mercury, freed from impurities, are resurrected.*
5. *Patana: Use all three techniques, namely upwards (udhva), downwards (adhah) and sideways (tiryak) to grind mercury with alkalis and salts and subject the product to distillation.*
6. *Rodhana: Mix the distilled mercury with saline water in a closed pot to restore its vigour and potency.*
7. *Niyamana: Continue the process by steaming mercury for three days with plant products, alum, borax and iron sulphate to restrain its motility.*
8. *Sandipana: Steam the product with alum, black pepper, sour gruel, alkali and vegetable substances to increase the mercury's power of assimilation.*
9. *Gaganagrass: Fix and assimilate the essence of mica, gagana, to the desired extent.*
10. *Carana: Boil the product with sour gruel, leaves of certain plants and alum for a week so that the mica is fully assimilated.*
11. *Garbhadruti: Heat and treat the mercury with metals so that the essence of the latter becomes liquefied and the product passes through a piece of cloth.*
12. *Bahyadruti: Obtain essence of minerals or metallic substances externally.*
13. *Jarana: Heat the mercurial product with the desired minerals or metals, alkalis and salts so that they are fully assimilated.*

14. *Ranjana: Treat the mercury with sulphur, gold, silver and copper as well as salts in such a way that the mercury attains colour.*
15. *Sarana: Absorb the mercury with gold or silver in an oil-base to accelerate transformation.*
16. *Kramana: Smear mercury with plant extracts, minerals and milk, and then heat it to activate transmuting powers.*
17. *Vedhana: Rub the resultant mercury with a few select substances including oil so that it acquires transmuting power.*
18. *Bhaksana: Consume the prescribed quality and quantity of the mercurial product which has undergone the foregoing seventeen processes, for rejuvenation, longevity and immortality.*

'I still don't understand,' said Vinay, after reading all eighteen steps. 'What does Ashoka's research have to do with the immortality of jellyfish?'

'Where do jellyfish live?' asked Karma.

'The oceans,' replied Vinay.

'Saltwater fish from the oceans—like tuna, mackerel and shark—sometimes cause problems for the humans who eat them,' said Karma. 'Do you recall what problem that is?'

'Mercury poisoning?' suggested Vinay.

'Right, mercury poisoning,' said Karma. 'You will notice that Ashoka's eighteen steps focus on mercury. It is my hypothesis that the very mercury that can kill us can also produce immortality. It may have done precisely that for jellyfish.'

'So what exactly is the recipe for immortality?' asked Vinay.

'We can't tell as yet,' answered Karma. 'The Chinese believe that the lingzhi mushroom is the Mushroom of Immortality. The alchemists known as the Fangshi were said to have known secret locations on Mount Penglai where lingzhi grew. We have still been unable to find even one of them.'

'Any other possibilities?' asked Vinay.

'Then there's amrit—or *soma*—said to have been derived by churning an ocean of milk. A few years ago, an archaeologist, Viktor Sarianidi, found vessels that were purportedly used for the making of soma at a site in Afghanistan. They contained residues of ephedra, poppy and cannabis. While these would certainly produce a hallucinogenic effect, they would be unable to fight mortality.'

'How does mercury fit in?' asked Vinay.

'There's always been the idea of ingesting liquid metals for longevity,' said Karma. 'That's an old one. Egyptians, Greeks, Romans, Chinese and Indians saw metals as being strong and seemingly indestructible. It followed that whoever ate metal would also imbibe those qualities. The number of people who experienced mortality instead of immortality from those experiments was significant! But now we seem to be finding that mercury does indeed have some interesting properties.'

'What about the West?' asked Vinay. 'Weren't they also involved in this quest for immortality?'

'Of course they were,' said Karma. 'There was the European quest for the Philosopher's Stone and the Elixir of Life. The stone symbolized perfection, enlightenment and bliss. The theory was that earth, air, fire and water were derived from *prima materia* or original matter. Finding prima materia became the route to immortality!'

'Did Ashoka's nine unknown men discover the secret to immortality?' asked Arvind. 'Do we know what happened?'

'Ashoka's edicts are to be found on thirty-three inscriptions on pillars, boulders and caves. These inscriptions are dispersed throughout the areas of modern-day Bangladesh, India, Nepal and Pakistan. There is no reference to the nine men or their research in any of these edicts. This would have been a secret project. It's even possible that the team was disbanded,' said Karma.

'So there is no direct evidence?' asked Vinay.

'No direct evidence,' replied Karma. 'But there is circumstantial evidence.'

'What?' asked Vinay.

'Gold,' answered Karma.

'Gold?' asked Arvind. 'What do you mean?'

'The eleventh-century Persian chemist and physician, Abu Rayhan Biruni, tells us that ancient India practised a science called Rasayana,' replied Karma. 'It was meant to restore the health of those who were ill beyond hope. It was meant to give back youth to old age. In effect, it was concerned with transmuting the human body from mortal to immortal.'

'But what does that have to do with gold?' asked Arvind.

'If one went through the seventeen steps on mercury—before the eighteenth step of ingestion—one would have transformed mercury into gold, together with additional curative powers,' said Karma.

'What's the circumstantial evidence that you talk about?' asked Arvind.

'Indian history,' said Karma.

'Indian history?' asked a puzzled Arvind.

'There have been many periods in Indian history when certain places of worship became fabulously wealthy,' replied Karma. 'Mostly these were by endowments from rulers.'

'I guess it would have been common for rulers to donate gold or jewels to temples,' said Vinay.

'True,' replied Karma. 'But in many instances the contribution was far more than the usual capacity of the king. Samudragupta, Harsha, Nagabhata, Krishnadevaraya, Marthanda Varma and even Maharaja Ranjit Singh were some of the rulers who distributed wealth far in excess of their explained sources.'

'In today's world they would have had problems explaining the source to tax authorities,' joked Arvind.

'Are you saying what I think you are saying?' asked Vinay of Karma.

'I am indeed,' said Karma. 'It is very possible that the Rasayana formula was passed on from one generation to another, being used to manufacture gold.'

'Like from king to crown prince?' asked Vinay.

'No,' said Karma. 'If that had been the case then we would have seen all the gold deposits concentrated in one geographic region of the subcontinent. It seems as though the formula zigzagged across India, crossing boundaries of ancient kingdoms. This leads to the conclusion that the formula would have been passed on from one practitioner to another—not necessarily to blood relatives.'

'If that was the case then why aren't all the dead kings of India alive?' asked Vinay. 'If Rasayana could help attain immortality, then those who practised it should have been living to tell the tale.'

'You are absolutely right,' said Karma. 'My guess is that Ashoka's research was work in progress. It's also possible that some of the knowledge may have gotten diluted down the ages.'

'You think that you can find it?' asked Arvind.

'That's precisely what I'm attempting to find out,' said Karma.

'How?' asked Vinay.

'By working backwards from a species that we know to be immortal,' replied Karma. 'That's why my company's name is Rasayana spelt backwards—Anayasar.'

'How much money do you need?' asked Arvind.

'Around a hundred crore,' said Karma. 'The problem is that we need to set up labs in other countries so that the best researchers from around the world can address this challenge in teams. That's why we envisage a substantial cost. I'm willing to sell 40 per cent in the company and allow myself to be left with just 20 per cent.'

The Honourable Minister of Sports and Youth Affairs sat in his office at Room Number 401 of Shastri Bhavan in New Delhi. *Why has the PM given me this ministry?* he wondered to himself. *Is it a desire to prevent me from making any money?* The truth was that Yash Dhar's stint at the Civil Aviation Ministry had been notorious for corrupt deals. No Prime Minister would want to repeat the mistake.

On the opposite side of his massive teakwood desk sat an array of secretaries—the Sports Secretary, an Additional Secretary, a Joint Secretary, a Deputy Secretary and an Under-Secretary. *With so many secretaries, it's no wonder the government is rarely able to get anything done*, thought Yash Dhar to himself.

Yash was slightly miffed at the fact that his friend, Arbaaz Sheikh, had been given the Railways portfolio. It was a plum job, ripe for pickings. The annual railway expenses the previous year had been 33,000 crore. Anyone could dip their snout in that trough!

'What's our agenda for today?' asked Yash.

The secretary cleared his throat. 'I have made a list of points for you, Minister,' he said, handing it over. Yash looked at it.

1. *Upgrading Nehru Yuva Kendras (NYKS)*
2. *Review of National Service Scheme (NSS)*
3. *Elections of National Sports Federations and Regional Sports Associations*
4. *Reorganization of Sports Authority of India (SAI)*
5. *Upgrade Laxmibai National Institute of Physical Education (LNIPE)*
6. *Review Rajiv Gandhi National Institute of Youth Development (RGNIYD)*
7. *Grants for Creation of Sports Infrastructure*
8. *Grants to Rural Schools for Sports Equipment and Playground*
9. *Grants for Installation of Synthetic Playing Surfaces*
10. *Grants for Promotion of Sports in Universities and Colleges*
11. *Sports Scholarship Scheme*
12. *Arjuna Awards list*
13. *Rajiv Gandhi Khel Ratna Awards list*
14. *Maulana Abdul Kalam Azad Trophy*
15. *Indian Premier League*

His gaze immediately fell on the last point. 'What is this Indian Premier League? I heard that Zee Entertainment was starting the Indian Cricket League,' he said.

'The Board of Control for Cricket in India—the BCCI—and the International Cricket Council did not recognize the ICL,' said the Secretary. 'To prevent players from joining the ICL, the BCCI is planning to launch their own outfit.'

'To what extent do I have a say in the BCCI?' asked Yash.

'It's India's richest sporting body and the richest cricket board in the world,' said the secretary. 'The BCCI's constitution provides for annual elections at its Annual General Meeting. BCCI does not depend on the government for its finances. The board was formed in December 1928 as a society registered under the Tamil Nadu Societies Registration Act. In that sense, you have no say.'

'But?' asked Yash.

'None of the office-bearers of the BCCI want it to be brought under the ambit of the Right To Information Act—the RTI. All of them have hundreds of skeletons lurking in their closets. You could threaten them, saying that you plan to bring the BCCI under RTI.'

The Memorial Sloan Kettering Cancer Centre was located at 1275 York Avenue, between 67th and 68th Streets in Manhattan. Vinay led his parents to the registration desk on the ninth floor. The attendant at the desk gave Abhilasha a bracelet to wear along with a printout of the schedule for the day. It covered appointments with doctors as well as blood and other tests.

A week earlier, Abhilasha had been attending a family wedding along with Arvind. They were forced to return home within ten minutes owing to Abhilasha's acute stomach ache. By the time they reached the hospital, Abhilasha was doubled over in pain. At the hospital, the young doctor recommended that they remove Abhilasha's appendix without any delay. By then, their family physician, Dr Sikdar, arrived. 'She has neither fever nor vomiting,' said Dr Sikdar. 'No surgery should be undertaken without scans.'

Abhilasha was wheeled into the diagnostics section. Arvind, who was standing in the control room, closely observed the technician's face. His expression was grim. When Arvind asked him for a feedback, he seemed shaken and said that he needed to first speak with the Chief GP. Arvind knew in his gut that it was not a good sign.

Arvind walked into the doctor's cabin where Dr Sikdar was talking to the technician and the Chief GP. They stopped talking when he entered. 'Tell me what it is, for heaven's sakes!' thundered Arvind.

Dr Sikdar turned towards Arvind and said, 'Sorry, Arvindji, your wife has a tumour.' Arvind asked if it was malignant. The reply was in the affirmative. Arvind sat down heavily on one of the chairs in the cabin and put his face in his hands. He was a broken man. *How many challenges will you place in my path, oh God?* he asked the old man in the sky despairingly. Arvind was tired. There was a part of him that wanted to lie down and cry until he died.

Arvind pulled himself out of depression the next day and visited the oncologist. He learned that Abhilasha had Stage IV Wilms' tumour and that the tumour had ruptured. It was a condition in which cancerous cells grew in one or both of the kidneys. Stage IV tumours were those that had spread beyond the kidneys into other organs. It was now evident that the intense stomach pain on the previous occasion had been caused by the ruptured tumour bleeding into Abhilasha's abdomen. Dr Sikdar was clear on the course of action. They needed to take her to Sloan Kettering in America.

Vinay had been stunned to hear the news of his mother's condition. He knew that she had been looking unwell on his past few trips but he would have never imagined that she had cancer. He immediately swung into action in New York, setting up meetings with the key doctors at Sloan Kettering and making all the necessary arrangements in anticipation of the arrival of his parents from Calcutta. He had spoken to Karma in Bhutan who had been most helpful, connecting Vinay with all his relevant medical contacts. Alisha stayed by Vinay's side throughout. She knew that hers was the only shoulder that he could cry on.

On the day that Arvind and Abhilasha arrived in NYC, Vinay and Alisha reached JFK airport and waited and waited anxiously to see them. After a thirty-minute wait, Vinay's parents emerged, accompanied by Dr Sikdar. Vinay rushed forward to meet his father and touch his feet. Even in her weakened state, Abhilasha gestured for Alisha to step forward. She lightly pecked her daughter-in-law on both cheeks and hugged her. 'I always missed having a daughter. You've solved that problem for me,' she said, as Alisha escorted her to the waiting car.

They checked into the Pierre on 61st Street and Fifth Avenue and immediately headed to York Avenue for the first of Abhilasha's consultations. The next day, a surgeon from Sloan Kettering conducted exploratory surgery. Due to the rupture, the tumour was dispersed throughout the abdomen. It was like a sheet of paper and could not be removed easily. A tissue sample was collected and Arvind, Vinay and Dr Sikdar had to wait for forty-eight hours for the results.

Two days later, they waited outside the doctor's office to be told whether Abhilasha's tumour was of favourable or unfavourable histology. The report was a good one. Abhilasha's tumour would respond to treatment. The doctors decided to start immediate chemotherapy to shrink the tumour before removing it surgically.

Karma flew to NYC two weeks later when the surgery was performed. The surgeon had been recommended by him as also the consulting hepatologist. During the surgery, the doctor had to remove parts of Abhilasha's liver, diaphragm and kidneys.

One week after surgery, under the supervision of a Sloan Kettering radiation oncologist, Abhilasha began radiation therapy to kill any remaining tumour cells.

Accompanying it was an alternative therapy recommended by Karma.

'What is the ownership structure of Anayasar Research Private Limited as of date?' asked Arvind. Father and son were in the Alipore Road house. Abhilasha was taking a walk on the lawns.

'We hold 40 per cent, Karma holds 20 per cent. The balance 40 per cent is held by Sardar Harpal Singh.'

'Why don't we speak to Sardar Harpal Singh and find out if he would be interested in selling some of his stake to us?' asked Arvind. 'I'm very excited about the brilliant work that Karma is doing.'

'You can do that,' said Vinay. 'I'm heading back to America tonight because Alisha needs me. Also, Karma will be leaving NYC in a couple of days. I need to meet him before he goes back to Bhutan.'

The Bagadia family had been sent back to Kolkata by the doctors. Arvind had been initially hesitant but the Sloan Kettering doctors and Karma had encouraged the move. They were convinced that Abhilasha's condition would greatly improve once she was back in familiar surroundings. She would have to continue Karma's therapy as part of the treatment protocol.

When Karma had broached the idea of supplementing the chemo with his own concoction, Arvind had been sceptical but Karma's arguments had won him over.

'Five thousand years ago, Ayurvedic doctors were treating patients with tumours. The *Charaka Samhita, Sushruta Samhita* as well as the *Ashtanga Hridayam* give detailed descriptions about the treatments,' Karma had explained to Arvind.

'What is the alternative therapy that you want to administer?' Arvind had asked.

'*Selaginella bryopteris*,' said Karma.

'What's that?' asked Arvind.

'A study done by my researchers has found that compounds developed from *Selaginella bryopteris* stopped the growth of cancer cells in the laboratory. It's a traditional Indian herb,' said Karma.

'Does it have a common name?' asked Arvind.

'It's also called *sanjeevani*.'

'How did you zero in on sanjeevani?' asked Arvind.

'You remember the jellyfish that I showed you in my laboratory?' asked Karma. 'Did you notice that jellyfish tend to glow in the dark? This property is known as bioluminescence—the ability of a living organism to produce light.'

'So?' asked Arvind.

'In the *Ramayan* it is mentioned as the herb that Hanuman brought back with him to restore Lakshmana to life after his battle with Indrajit, Ravana's son. In the Valmiki *Ramayan*, Jambavan tells Hanuman: *O Hanuman, you are the only one who can save the lives of the two brothers, as well as the lives of all the* vanaras. *On the Himalayas, between the Kailas and Rishabh mountains, there lies a mountain of life-giving herbs. Go immediately to the golden peak on the mountain called Himavan, which is rich in herbs, and bring back the four magic herbs. The one called sanjeevani will bring the dead back to life… It always emits light.*'

Arvind was silent as he thought about what Karma had just revealed.

'It is evident that both jellyfish and sanjeevani contain something specific that causes bioluminescence and healing,' said Karma.

The Honourable Minister for Railways watched the chaos unfold on his television screen. That day, on 11 July 2006, seven blasts had occurred in a matter of eleven minutes on Mumbai's Suburban Railway network.

'What do we know?' he asked the Secretary, Railways.

'It seems that bombs were set off in pressure cookers on trains plying the Western line,' said the secretary. 'Are you planning to go to Mumbai?'

'No,' said Arbaaz. 'My presence will cause more confusion for the local administration. Let's focus on the things that we need to do and get those done. Do you have a list of the trains that were bombed?'

The secretary passed it to Arbaaz.

1. *Travelling north from Churchgate, blast at Khar Road–Santacruz, First Class Compartment, Time 18.24*
2. *Fast local from Churchgate–Borivali, blast at Bandra–Khar Road, First Class Compartment, Time 18.24*
3. *Slow local from Churchgate–Borivali, blast at Jogeshwari, First Class Compartment, Time 18.25*
4. *Fast local from Churchgate–Borivali, blast at Mahim Junction, First Class Compartment, Time 18.26*
5. *Travelling north from Churchgate, blast at Mira Road–Bhayandar, First Class Compartment, 18.29*
6. *Fast local from Churchgate–Virar, blast at Matunga Road–Mahim Junction, First Class Compartment, 18.30*
7. *Fast local from Churchgate–Virar, blast at Borivali, First Class Compartment, 18.35*

'This was meticulous planning,' said Arbaaz. 'All the bombs were placed at Churchgate and set with timers so that they would explode at specific stations. This is no ordinary attack. The bastards even used pressure cookers to increase the after-burn.'

'Should we announce compensation?' asked the secretary.

Arbaaz flew into a rage. 'You think compensation solves everything? Do we all think that money can solve the loss of a family member? Let's focus on the problem at hand. Compensation is the last item that will be discussed.'

The secretary and all the others in the room stayed quiet. This was not a minister that they could play games with. 'Update me regarding rescue efforts,' said Arbaaz.

'Our initial efforts were hampered by heavy rains and monsoon flooding,' said the duly chastised secretary. 'Luckily, fellow passengers and bystanders began helping victims reach waiting ambulances.'

'At every blast site, I need a team of first-aid providers. Have that done immediately,' said Arbaaz.

Arbaaz then picked up the phone and personally spoke with the administrators of the biggest private hospitals in Mumbai. 'You will not experience the rush of wounded,' he said to them. 'Most of them get taken to government hospitals. I need you to depute teams at the stations so that the wounded can be administered first aid. The government will pick up the entire cost.'

The television was showing visuals, one of which was of a father holding the corpse of his little girl. He was wailing piteously.

'What's the status of the railway lines?' asked Arbaaz, forcing himself to turn to the key issues at hand.

'The western line has been shut down for the time being,' said the secretary.

'Let services resume,' said Arbaaz. 'Ensure that strict security arrangements, including frisking and searching of commuters, are put in place.'

Once again Arbaaz picked up his phone. The call was to Murali in Mumbai. 'Murali, you know the BEST chief? Speak to him. Find out if they can press extra buses into service so that stranded commuters can reach home safely.'

'What about mobile networks? Are they operating?' asked Arbaaz.

'Jammed for the moment,' replied the secretary.

'Speak to the TV channels. Find out if they can run SMS messages from those who wish to contact their families. It may be a few hours before mobile services resume and there can be nothing more terrifying than waiting at home, not knowing whether a loved one is dead or alive.'

The secretary made notes and handed it over to the additional secretary.

'*Now* let's talk about compensation,' said Arbaaz. 'Announce 5,00,000 rupees as compensation and a government job to the next of kin of those killed in the serial blasts.'

'Yes, sir,' said the secretary.

'Now I request to be left alone because I need to make a personal phone call,' said Arbaaz.

Alisha recognized his voice instantly. It was the same voice that had cooed to her when she was a baby. It was the same voice that had played word games with her when she was in school. It was the same voice that had gone ahead with all her childish whims.

'Alisha?' he asked.

His daughter remained silent. Tears were welling up in her eyes.

'Alisha?' asked Arbaaz again.

'Yes, Daddy,' she said, the floodgates now open.

'I love you, sweetheart,' he said. 'I just needed to hear your voice.'

'I love you too, Daddy,' said Alisha. 'I've missed you terribly.'

'I am sorry for having been so harsh,' he said 'We all make mistakes. Can you find it in your heart to forgive me?'

'All I know is that I have my father back,' said Alisha. 'Today, I don't want to spoil my tomorrow because of yesterday.'

The *Forbes* list of India's richest for 2006 ran into forty names. The top twenty names on the list for that year were:

1. *Lakshmi Mittal (Steel)*
2. *Mukesh Ambani (Diversified)*
3. *Anil Ambani (Diversified)*
4. *Azim Premji (Software)*
5. *Kushal Pal Singh (Real estate)*
6. *Sunil Mittal (Telecom)*
7. *Kumar Mangalam Birla (Commodities)*
8. *Tulsi Tanti (Wind energy)*
9. *Ramesh Chandra (Real estate)*
10. *Pallonji Mistry (Construction)*
11. *Anil Agarwal (Mining)*
12. *Shashi & Ravi Ruia (Diversified)*
13. *Adi Godrej (Diversified)*
14. *Shiv Nadar (Technology)*
15. *Indu Jain (Media)*
16. *Dilip Shanghvi (Pharma)*
17. *Rahul Bajaj (Manufacturing)*
18. *Arvind Bagadia (Investments)*
19. *Baba Kalyani (Manufacturing)*
20. *Arbaaz Sheikh (Investments)*

Arvind was happy he had made it to the top twenty but was unhappy to see Arbaaz Sheikh's name also on the list.

Karma walked into Vinay and Alisha's apartment that evening holding a bottle of K5. It was Bhutanese whisky.

'I thought that monks were into a different type of spiritual activity,' joked Vinay as Karma gave Alisha a kiss on the cheek. She was dressed casually in faded jeans and a black kurti, its smartness accentuated by a chunky brass necklace. She looked radiant. It was because of the hour-long conversation that she had had with her father.

Karma smiled. 'After being lost a hundred years, this ancient recipe was discovered in an ancient distillery deep in the Himalayan mountains,' he said. 'This whisky is handcrafted to perfection by master distillers at the Gelephu Distillery in southern Bhutan.'

'Thanks for the commercial break,' joked Vinay. Karma settled into the leather recliner while Alisha sat cross-legged on the sofa. Vinay went to the bar cabinet to pour drinks.

'That sanjeevani thing has got my father all excited,' said Vinay, taking a sip of the K5 that Karma had brought. 'I thought it was just a fanciful story!' Vinay had finally recalled that it was the herb that had been administered by Hanuman to Lakshmana as he lay dying on the battlefield.

'This is the problem with Western-educated minds,' said Karma, conveniently forgetting that he, too, had been educated in the West. 'There are many ancient remedies that we need to rediscover. We are currently conducting research into sanjeevani, *Withania somnifera,* Indian frankincense, mangosteen and pomegranate. All of them have incredible anti-cancer properties.'

'Seriously?' asked Vinay.

'*Withania somnifera* is an Ayurvedic plant,' said Karma. 'In the laboratory, we found that a compound from the herb stopped the growth of some types of breast cancer cells. Similarly, my team also looked at acetyl-11-keto-beta-boswellic acid taken from the gum resin of Indian frankincense. We were actually able to slow the growth of bowel cancer in mice.'

'Incredible,' murmured Vinay. 'Could my mother have been cured without surgery and chemotherapy, Karma?'

'We're not there yet,' said Karma. 'Remember, Vinay, our quest is for longevity, not to find specific cures. It's just that we're discovering new things along the way. For example, the mangosteen fruit has a long history of medicinal use in Chinese and Ayurvedic medicine. We were testing the compound alpha mangosteen taken from the outer layer of the fruit when our team in Japan found that it could slow down the progress of cancer in the lymph nodes.'

'You also mentioned pomegranate,' said Vinay.

'That is regarded as a sacred fruit in several religions,' said Karma. 'Pomegranate extracts seem to have anti-carcinogenic properties that work for prostate, bowel and liver cancers.'

'So immortality is not impossible?' asked Alisha.

'According to the Rig-Veda, amrit is indeed the drink that bestows immortality,' replied Karma. 'In the Rig-Veda, the deities Indra and Agni say: *We have drunk soma and become immortal; we have attained the light, the gods discovered. Now, what may foeman's malice do to harm us? What, O Immortal, mortal man's deception?* Why shouldn't we take that statement at face value and believe that the ancients had a solution?'

'I thought that amrit was simply soma, a hallucinogenic substance,' said Alisha.

'There are multiple references to amrit and soma across Hindu, Zoroastrian, and other Indic texts,' explained Karma. 'Ambrosia, the food of immortality to the Greeks, is similar to amrit. Both words emerge from the same Indo-European root that roughly translates to *non-death*.'

The two men walked together through Lodhi Gardens. The space seemed to come alive in the mornings, with ducks quacking loudly on the lake accompanied by the chirping of birds in the trees.

Arvind had arrived in Delhi the previous night from Kolkata. Sardar Harpal Singh was a regular morning walker and had suggested that Arvind join him. It was the best way to conduct a meeting.

The men indulged in idle chatter for a while. They discussed Benazir Bhutto's assassination in Pakistan. Then they discussed BJP strongman Pramod Mahajan's death at the hands of his own brother in Mumbai. They discussed the choice of Pratibha Patil as the next President of India and the visit of George W. Bush to India. Finally, they discussed the weather. Having run out of further topics to discuss, they got down to business.

'How can I help you, Arvind?' asked Harpal.

'You hold shares in a company called Anayasar Research Private Limited,' said Arvind. 'The founder of the company, Karma Tshering, was a roommate of Vinay's at Stanford. We invested in the company too. We now hold 40 per cent of the shares.'

'That boy is a genius,' said Harpal. The men casually took in the sights of Mohammed Shah's Tomb, Sikander Lodhi's Tomb, Sheesh Gumbad and Bara Gumbad as they walked and talked.

'I agree,' said Arvind. 'The therapy that he administered to Abhilasha when she was convalescing from her surgery enabled her to bounce back quicker than any other patient in Sloan Kettering. I am convinced that he's on to something big.'

The ninety-acre garden—originally called Lady Wellington Park—had been created in 1936 but remodelled in 1968 by American landscape architects Joseph Allen Stein and Garrett Eckbo. It was brimming with early-morning joggers and walkers.

'What exactly do you want from me?' asked Harpal.

'I was wondering whether you would be willing to sell your shares to me?' asked Arvind. 'We would factor in the future prospects of the company while doing a valuation for the shares.'

'I'm afraid I can't help you,' said Harpal. 'You see, I gave away my shares to someone quite a while ago.'

'You are still shown as the shareholder in the register of members,' said Arvind.

'Possibly,' said Harpal. 'Being a closely held company it's possible that there has been some delay in registering the share transfers, but my stake of 40 per cent is now with Arbaaz Sheikh.'

'Arbaaz?' asked Arvind. 'The current Railways Minister?'

'And your business rival,' added Harpal. 'The fact of the matter is that even though both of you hate each other for a variety of reasons, I consider both of you to be my friends.'

'He's an underworld operator!' spluttered Arvind. 'Mafia!'

'All of us are criminals,' said Harpal. 'And remember, in life there are indeed angels with blemishes and devils with beauty.'

'We need to slightly readjust the Dhanda portfolio,' said Murali to Arbaaz. Both the men were in Arbaaz's office.

'Why?' asked Arbaaz.

'We are heavily invested in technology companies,' said Murali. 'I plan to decrease our exposure.'

'Good idea,' said Arbaaz. 'I was in touch with Yash Dhar. His unofficial tip is that Satyam Computer Services will go belly-up in a year or two.'

'Why?' asked Murali. 'Their financial results are excellent.'

'Often, the balance sheet is simply telling you that the balance is shit. Get out of that company yesterday.'

'What's that?' asked Karma.

'Excuse me?' asked Alisha.

Karma pointed to Alisha's wrist. 'What's that?'

Alisha's petite frame and slim hands could carry off anything. She had worn the small copper kada that her father had given her many years ago at the airport.

'It's just a copper bangle, Karma,' said Alisha. 'My dad gave it to me. It has some antique and emotional value. Have never been able to understand what's written on it, though.'

'Could I see it?' asked Karma.

'Sure,' said Alisha, pulling it off her wrist, getting up from the sofa and handing it over to him.

Karma held it carefully in his hands and rotated it slowly. He seemed fascinated, almost transfixed.

'The script is Gurmukhi,' said Karma. 'This kada is from the Punjab. Very similar to the paperweight that I saw in Vinay's office.'

'Really?' asked Alisha. 'I never saw any similarity.'

'Could we see that paperweight tomorrow?' asked Karma. 'I'll drop in at your office.'

'Sure,' said Vinay, taking a sip of his K5 whisky.

'There must be thousands of drinking water wells in Pakistan. What's so important about this one?' asked Alisha.

'It's a place of historical interest,' replied Vinay. 'Two thousand years ago, King Shalivahan was asked by the royal astrologers to leave his son, Puran, cloistered for twelve years. After the twelve years had passed, Puran finally got to meet his father.'

'What happened then?' asked Alisha.

'Puran's stepmother, Luna, accused Puran of trying to molest her. The angry Shalivahan ordered that his son be captured and that his hands and feet be hacked off. After that, his body was dumped in a well.'

Alisha shuddered. *Why are we in the possession of copper wristlets that are associated with such a gruesome place?* she thought to herself.

'Miraculously, Puran remained alive for twelve years inside the well until the great Guru Goraknath reached there. The guru pulled him out and restored his body and health. Prince Puran went on to become a celebrated yogi himself. Since that day, the well has become famous for its curative powers,' said Vinay, bringing the story to a happy ending.

'But why would our fathers have copper wristlets that are from this place?' asked Alisha.

'I have no clue,' shrugged Vinay. 'Karma is attempting to find out.'

Arbaaz looked at the notice once again. When had Arvind Bagadia wrapped his tentacles around Anayasar? Was there nothing in this world that could be achieved without a fight with Bagadia? The worst part of it was that they were now related. Anything that one said or did would now affect the children.

Notice is hereby given that the 7th Annual General Meeting of Anayasar Research Private Limited will be held at the Taj Chambers, Taj Mahal Hotel, Mumbai, on 26 November 2008 at 7 pm to transact the following business:

Ordinary Business

1. *Consider and adopt the Audited Financial Statements (including consolidated financial statements) of the Company for the previous financial year along with the Reports of the Directors and Auditors thereon.*
2. *Confirm the non-payment of any Dividend or Interim-Dividend.*
3. *Re-appoint Mr Karma Tshering who retires by rotation at this meeting and, being eligible, offers himself for re-appointment.*
4. *Appoint Auditors and in this regard to consider and if thought fit, to pass with or without modification, an appropriate resolution to this effect.*

Special Business

5. *Appointment of Mr Arvind Bagadia as Whole-time Director of the Company.*
6. *Appointment of Mr Arbaaz Sheikh as Whole-time Director of the Company.*

The *Forbes* list of India's richest for 2008 ran into forty names. Arvind quickly ran his eyes down the top ten.

1. *Mukesh Ambani*
2. *Lakshmi Mittal*
3. *Anil Ambani*
4. *Sunil Mittal*
5. *Kushal Pal Singh*
6. *Shashi & Ravi Ruia*

7. *Azim Premji*
8. *Arvind Bagadia*
9. *Arbaaz Sheikh*
10. *Kumar Mangalam Birla*

Arvind had made it to the top ten of the Forbes list of richest Indians. He should have been overjoyed but he wasn't. The fact that Arbaaz Sheikh was just below him was niggling him.

Arvind's target was clear. Like that boy Abhinav Bindra who had won a gold medal in shooting for India at the Beijing Olympics a month earlier, he wanted to be Number One.

Both Arvind and Arbaaz had strategies in place for improving their respective rankings. One hoped that Anayasar would help him grow bigger. The other was considering taking up cricket.

'I was waiting for your call,' said Yash. Arbaaz laughed.

'The BCCI has invited bids for eight franchises,' said Arbaaz. 'I want a piece of the action.'

'You want to bid for a team?' asked Yash. 'I doubt you can do that. You are a minister. So am I.'

'Buying a franchise is a foolish way of doing business,' said Arbaaz. 'That is meant for people who want publicity. Neither you nor I need that. We simply want money.'

'What do you want me to do?'

'Speak to them,' said Arbaaz. 'Let them allot the television and media rights to one of our nominee companies.'

'We do not have any infrastructure for broadcasting,' said Yash.

'Who says that we will broadcast anything?' asked Arbaaz.

Vinay and Alisha reached the building at 12 East 65th Street. From the second floor hung a flag of Pakistan. A brass plaque outside the entrance to Number Twelve announced that it was the Pakistan Consulate. They walked in and went up to someone behind a desk labelled 'Information'.

'Yes?' said the individual, looking up from the computer terminal.

'We need to know the requirements for Indian nationals to get visas to visit Pakistan,' said Vinay.

'It's been weeks,' said Vinay on the phone. 'How can a visa application take so much time?'

The official at the other end gave him some mumbo-jumbo about procedures and clearances. 'It's under active consideration,' said the official as he put down the phone.

Vinay knew the drill. His father used to joke that in South Asia, an official saying that a file was 'under consideration' usually meant that he had lost the file while 'under active consideration' meant that he was trying to find it.

Vinay put down the phone, feeling uneasy. A visa would not be forthcoming via usual channels. It would need a push.

He made a call to New Delhi. He waited on the line as the secretary tried to find Sardar Harpal Singh.

'I don't quite understand,' said Sardar Harpal Singh. 'You say that you wish to visit Pakistan on a tourist visa and that you need my assistance in getting the Pakistan Foreign Ministry to process it?'

'Yes,' said Vinay.

'And you do not want your father to know about it?' asked Harpal.

'No,' said Vinay.

'Son, you will have to tell me the reason for all this secrecy,' said Harpal. 'And I do not want any fibbing.'

Vinay fidgeted uncomfortably as he spoke into the phone. 'As you may know, my father was angry with me for marrying a girl without his permission.'

'He did mention it to me,' said Harpal.

'Did he tell you why he was against my marriage?' asked Vinay.

'He just said that she wasn't from the right sort of family,' said Harpal. 'He did not elaborate.'

'I'm married to the daughter of my father's arch rival—Arbaaz Sheikh,' said Vinay.

'Hmm, I see,' said Harpal, stroking his beard in thought. 'I know both men. Your father as well as your father-in-law. I like them both. Pity that they do not get along. That still doesn't explain why you need to go to Pakistan.'

Arbaaz was in his car, on his way to the Taj Mahal Hotel. His mobile phone began to ring. It was Yash Dhar.

'Spoke with the BCCI chaps,' said Yash. 'They are willing to consider allotting media rights to our nominee company if we assure them that the BCCI will not be brought under the ambit of the Right To Information Act.'

'Good,' said Arbaaz. 'Go ahead and sign the contract. Include a clause that requires a payment of 500 crore to surrender the rights should the media rights need to be allotted elsewhere.'

'Ah,' said Yash, realizing what Arbaaz's game plan was.

His strategy was surrender, pure and simple.

The Taj's invitation-only Chambers club consisted of a suite of rooms, a bar, library and dining room. It was a little haven for businessmen to transact deals in an area that was never mentioned in any of the hotel brochures. The annual membership fees were a closely guarded secret. If you had to ask how much, you were obviously not destined for membership. The sole purpose of havens such as the Chambers was to make their billionaire members feel at home, with trained, discreet staff, at hideaway locations within familiar hotels.

Inside one of the meeting rooms, the Annual General Meeting of Anayasar Research Private Limited commenced an hour late. Both the main shareholders purportedly had 'other conflicting engagements'. The truth was that neither man wanted to be there first.

The AGM of Anayasar was probably one of the smallest ever. There were only three shareholders—Arvind, Arbaaz and Karma. The fourth person present at the meeting was the Company Secretary, Mr Kapoor. It was an uncomfortable meeting, punctuated by prolonged periods of silence.

The two rivals glared at each other even though they maintained a veneer of cordiality. Both men knew that

Anayasar was a goldmine—literally. If Karma discovered the elixir of immortality it would be the biggest coup in medical history. Even if he didn't, there was always the possibility that he would discover the formula for manufacturing gold from other metals.

It was a strange situation for Karma. He was a minority shareholder—with a mere 20 per cent—now saddled with two shareholders who hated each other, each holding 40 per cent. He looked at Arvind, with whom he had a closer relationship, for some reassurance. There was none forthcoming. Karma realized that the situation was one of a stalemate, with both men sticking to their guns.

The first few items of the agenda were non-controversial and were passed with unanimous consent, but the last two items involved the appointment of Arvind and Arbaaz as whole-time directors.

'I cannot support the motion,' said Arbaaz as Arvind's name was proposed.

'I will not support such a motion,' said Arvind as Arbaaz's name was proposed.

Both resolutions were passed 60–40 with Karma voting in favour of both men. 'Why can't both of you compromise?' asked Karma.

'Compromise? That's simply both parties getting what neither of them wanted!' said Arvind.

Then the gloves came off.

'You made me lose a ton of money when you pulled the Qurbani scam…'

'You had me raided by the Income Tax and stolen from…'

'You screwed me by stealing Albert Mills…'

'You tried to drive down the price of my company's shares to ruin me…'

'You conned me by not transferring funds in the dotcom deal…'

'You spoilt my defence deal by cancelling the new specifications…'

'Your son trapped my daughter…'

'Your daughter misled my son…'

'Anayasar shares were received first by me; you should exit…'

'Karma is my son's classmate; *you* should exit…'

The two men did not notice Karma getting up and leaving the conference room, utterly disgusted with the predicament that he found himself in. The Company Secretary had already left.

Sardar Harpal Singh was stunned into silence. His face drained of colour as he heard Vinay's words. *This can't be happening. The consequences are simply too terrible to contemplate,* he thought.

Vinay had told him about the two wristlets bearing the names Manjit and Daljit and the fact that each wristlet had originally belonged to Arbaaz and Arvind.

'Are the kadas made of copper?' asked Harpal, his heart beating faster.

'Yes,' replied Vinay.

'Do they have anything else written on them besides the name?' asked Harpal. The thumping in his chest was uncomfortable.

'Both have reference to Puran da Khoo, apparently some well near Sialkot,' said Vinay. 'That's precisely why we wish to go there.'

'Where are Arvind and Arbaaz?' asked Harpal nervously. *Why did I give up the search so quickly? Why didn't I listen to her?*

'There's an AGM of Anayasar being held at the Taj Chambers in Mumbai,' said Vinay. 'Both of them should be there.'

The men were still arguing when they heard a sound. *Ack, ack, ack.*

'That's gunfire,' said Arbaaz.

'Bullshit,' said Arvind.

Ack, ack, ack. This time Arvind realized that Arbaaz was right. It was quite definitely gunfire. The burst came from inside and the shots were reverberating through the hotel.

Then they heard a massive explosion. It felt like it had come from the main lobby. They ran to the reception desk in the Chambers foyer where several other members had also arrived. The club was getting filled up with a ton of guests who were being herded in from other parts of the hotel.

'What's going on?' asked Arbaaz.

'There's a bunch of gunmen downstairs,' stammered a terrified woman. 'One of them just shot down my friend.' She was in tears. One of the other ladies tried to comfort her. More guests trooped in. Arvind noticed that there were several business tycoons, MPs, a high court judge, American investment bankers and a couple of journalists.

Just then another explosion shook the floor and the lights went out. Then they were in complete darkness.

Arbaaz, Arvind, and fifty other guests, barricaded themselves into the Lavender Room as soon as the shots broke out inside the Chambers.

The Lavender Room was located at the far end of a corridor that contained doors to several meeting rooms. Arbaaz broke off the leg of a chair and jammed it through the door handles. Then he pushed a table against the door.

He pressed a speed dial on his phone to reach Raju. 'What's happening outside?' he asked, speaking softly.

'A bunch of terrorists is wreaking havoc in Mumbai,' said Raju. 'They've attacked Leopold Café and CST, the railway station. Do you have access to a television? Are you safe?'

'I'm fine,' said Arbaaz. 'And no, the power's out. If these bastards think that they can get away with this, they need to get their heads examined. Any idea who they are?'

'The residents of Macchimar Nagar say that they came off a boat carrying large bags,' said Raju. 'Cops are tight-lipped but my contacts are telling me that they're Pakistanis. Anything you want me to do?'

'Call up Paromita and tell her I'm fine,' said Arbaaz. 'My phone is running out of juice. Speak to the cops. Tell them that our boys will assist wherever they need. How organized are the cops?'

'They're running around like headless chickens. The National Security Guards have been called in,' said Raju. 'Oh shit!'

'What?' asked Arbaaz.

'On my television I can see that the top floor of the Taj Mahal Hotel is in flames. They've set off an explosion inside the dome.'

Arbaaz's phone went dead. He heard groans. One of the hotel maintenance workers had been shot in the corridor.

A bullet had ripped into his back, tearing out his abdomen as it exited. Arvind had managed to pull him in just as they were closing the doors.

The maintenance worker's white uniform was soaked in blood. Arvind attempted to push the man's intestines back inside him with a towel. Another guest administered painkillers taken from yet another guest.

Arbaaz heard a phone ring. It belonged to the MP inside with them. The idiot was talking into a live newscast. Arbaaz was shocked as he heard the man let the world know that hundreds of people—including CEOs, foreigners, a minister and government officials—were safe inside the Chambers. Arbaaz got up to smash the man's phone but it was too late. The damage had already been done.

Arbaaz signalled to Arvind. They needed to take matters into their own hands.

The two men were alone in the corridor. There were over 200 people inside the Chambers but there was a deathly silence in the corridor. Everyone had locked themselves into the meeting rooms.

Arvind and Arbaaz headed towards the terrace of the Chambers through the library. The fire in the hotel was roaring and if they could find an access down the terrace, they would be able to evacuate the trapped guests to the main road below. Suddenly, another round of firing was heard.

The two crouched behind a table, just a few feet away from the bloodthirsty gunmen. The guns went silent. Both men seemed to have excess adrenaline running through their systems. It was a hyper-aware state in which every smell, sound or sight was amplified and instantly analysed and processed.

Arvind could feel the thumping in his chest as he contemplated what his death would be like. Then his phone rang loudly. Both men froze. It was Abhilasha trying to reach him. The gunmen instantly traced the location of the phone.

A barrage of bullets rained towards them. The sound of gunfire was deafening. Bullets flew and soon the place was laced with broken glass, bullet casings, flesh and blood.

Then there was silence once again.

When the mayhem came to an end almost a week later, the events were pieced together by the authorities. Ten Pakistani members of Lashkar-e-Taiba had carried out twelve coordinated shooting and bombing attacks that went on for four days across Mumbai.

Only one attacker was captured alive. His name was Ajmal Kasab. He later confessed during interrogation that the attacks had been conducted with the active support and guidance of Pakistan's intelligence agency, the Inter-Services Intelligence.

The locations at which the attacks had occurred were Chhatrapati Shivaji Terminus, the Taj Mahal Palace and Tower, the Oberoi Trident, Leopold Café, Cama Hospital, the Nariman House Jewish Community Centre, Metro Cinema, the lane behind the Times of India Group building, St Xavier's College, Mazagaon and Vile Parle.

The attacks had begun on Wednesday, 26 November 2008 and had continued till Saturday, 29 November 2008. It was estimated that 164 people were killed. More than 308 had been injured.

The funerals of Arvind Bagadia and Arbaaz Sheikh were held a day apart in order to provide time to travel from one city to the other to mourners who needed to be present at both men's last rites.

Arbaaz's funeral in Mumbai was attended by his wife Paromita, his daughter Alisha, his son-in-law Vinay, and his trusted lieutenants Raju and Murali. Among the hundreds of important people in business and government were several other known faces including those of Karma Tshering, Sardar Harpal Singh and Adhyapika Jyoti. Yash Dhar had also attended, having carefully cancelled all further nominee bidding plans for the IPL on his way to the funeral. Present also were hundreds of the poor and downtrodden whom Arbaaz had helped in myriad ways over the years. Islam forbade loud wailing and an overt display of grief but no religious law could prevent the tears of Paromita and Alisha.

Softly keening was one more woman.

Arbaaz's corpse had been purified with a ritual bath and then wrapped in a white cloth from head to toe. His *janaaza* had taken several hours to reach the Qabristan in Marine Lines. His grave was sprinkled with perfumed water before his body was lowered into it with his head pointing towards Mecca. It was covered with wooden boards and mourners tossed handfuls of sand over the covering while the maulvi recited *lilaha va inna illaha raziun*. We have come from God and unto him we shall return. Arbaaz had been sixty-six-years old.

Arvind's funeral in Kolkata was attended by his wife Abhilasha, his son Vinay and his daughter-in-law Alisha. Among the hundreds of VIPs who congregated were several other known faces including Kalyan Sarkar, Kishore Deshmukh, Yash Dhar, Karma Tshering, Sardar Harpal Singh, Darius Dastur and Adhyapika Jyoti. Sitting inside a Kolkata prison cell, Satyapal Mittal had thanked God for ridding the world of scum when he read the news. Another man in another prison cell in Mumbai, Devendra Dixit, had also thanked God for his mercy. Abhilasha, who had expected to die first, had been pipped to the post by her husband. Broken and in shock, Abhilasha found that her tears had dried up after crying for several days.

Another woman in that group shared her grief.

Arvind's body had been bathed, clothed and decorated with garlands of flowers before being carried to the cremation ground. Vinay applied ghee at seven auspicious places of his father's body and placed coins on his forehead. Supervised by the priests, he put grains of rice into his father's mouth. Sandalwood was placed all over Arvind's body and ghee was liberally sprinkled. Vinay went around the body seven times with a pot of water before breaking it near the feet of his dead father. He then consigned sixty-six-year-old Arvind's corpse to the fire as the priests continued chanting hymns.

Neither Arvind nor Arbaaz ever made it to the number one position in the *Forbes* list of richest Indians.

They possibly could have if their mortality had not gotten in the way.

ॐ त्रियम्बकं यजामहे

सुगन्धिं पुष्टिवर्धनं ।

1833, Lahore

उर्वारुकमिव बन्धनान्

मृत्योर्मोक्षिय मामृतात् ॥

Poles of gold and silver propped up the scarlet tents. Luxurious shawls from Kashmir lined the interiors while the floors were covered with fine wool and silk carpets. But inside the tent, the diminutive and simply dressed maharaja sat on an ordinary chair that spoke volumes about his personality. This particular king refused to sit on a throne, refused to wear a crown and refused to mint coins in his own name. He was known as Maharaja Ranjit Singh.

The maharaja looked at the architect's drawing with his single good eye. He had contracted smallpox as a child and the virus had blinded him in one eye besides leaving his skin pockmarked. The single eye and pockmarks hadn't prevented him from creating a vast and prosperous empire.

When the king's foreign minister had met the British Governor-General of India, the Englishman had enquired as to which of the maharaja's eyes was without vision. The minister had replied, 'The maharaja is like the sun and the sun has only one eye. The splendour and luminosity of his single eye is so great that I have never dared to look at the other!'

'It has to shine like the sun,' said the maharaja to the architect. 'A symbol of the purity of the region that we call the *Punj-Ab*, or the Land of Five Rivers. I swear by the waters of the Beas, Ravi, Sutlej, Chenab and Jhelum, that the Harmandir Sahib will shine splendidly—like the sun.'

'It shall be done, Sarkar,' replied the architect. 'As you know, the Harmandir Sahib is located within the tank—the pool of the nectar of immortality that we call Amritsar. All of Harmandir Sahib's gilded surfaces will be reflected in the tank's waters.'

The Lion of Punjab looked at the drawing yet again. He was not satisfied. After all, this was a man who had seized Lahore and made it his capital at age nineteen. He had then proceeded to bring the whole of the region from the Sutlej to the Jhelum under his command. This was a king who was used to getting things done.

'Diwan Dinanath, what do you think?' asked the maharaja.

'Your generosity in such matters is without parallel, my lord,' said the finance minister clutching the oilskin-covered folder that never seemed to leave his hands. On the cover was the symbol of a jellyfish. 'Any amount of gold that is needed for such an enterprise shall be made available without question.'

Diwan Dinanath was the son of a Kashmiri Pandit, Bakht Mal. His family had migrated to Delhi in 1815 during the tyrannical rule of Afghan governors in the valley. Dinanath was a man who exemplified merit, honesty, loyalty and strength.

'Will you be able to arrange enough of it?' asked the maharaja. 'I have already expended six quintals of gold on the gilding of the Vishwanath Temple at Varanasi.'

'When it comes to matters of faith, Sarkar, you have never held back,' replied Diwan Dinanath. 'You have made a sizeable offering to the temple of Jwala Mukhi. Eighty bighas of land have also been donated to support the shrine of Ismail alias Wadda near Shalimar Gardens. Fifteen thousand has been spent on the repairs of the mosques in Lahore.'

'Money well spent,' said the maharaja, placing a large paperweight on the drawings. The paperweight was a diamond of 186 carats that had been looted by Nadir Shah in 1739 from the Mughals. It was known as the *Koh-i-Noor*, or the Mountain of Light.

After the assassination of Nadir Shah, the stone had come into the hands of his general, Ahmad Shah Durrani. A descendant of Ahmed Shah, Shah Shuja Durrani had absconded with the stone but Maharaja Ranjit Singh had forced him into surrendering it in return for a peace treaty.

'Moreover, I have signed the treaty with Shah Shuja Durrani,' continued the maharaja.

'That was a masterstroke, Sarkar. We now have control of Peshawar.'

'Yes, but more importantly, Shah Shuja has committed to me that the sandalwood doors—the ones carried away by Mahmud of Ghazni from the Somnath Temple 800 years ago—will be delivered back to us,' said the maharaja. That part of the treaty had meant much more to him than anything else. It was almost like recovering lost honour.

'I am depending on you, Diwan Dinanath,' said the Maharaja Ranjit Singh. 'I hope that you can make my dreams for the Harmandir Sahib possible.'

'It shall be done, your majesty,' replied the Diwan.

In his head Diwan Dinanath started reciting the ancient words. Words that had been passed on in a chain of succession from times that could no longer be remembered.

'Svedana… Mardana… Murchana… Uthapana… Patana… Rodhana… Niyamana… Sandipana…'

Diwan Dinanath looked at the drawings on the table before the monarch as he continued his mental recitation.

'Gaganagrass… Carana… Garbhadruti… Bahyadruti… Jarana… Ranjana… Sarana… Kramana… Vedhana… Bhaksana'

Diwan Dinanath was also getting old. He was happy that he had found a capable successor in Sialkot. Jagat Singh possessed all the qualities that were needed to carry on the legacy.

Book Seven
2010

Karma Tshering's stunningly beautiful monastery-laboratory was humming with activity. The thick pine forest in which it was nestled was covered by clouds that rolled in over the hills. Inside the conference room that offered an awesome view of the valley below were gathered several individuals. The founder, Karma Tshering, sat at the head. Across him at the other end of the table sat Adhyapika Jyoti. Between these two extremities sat Vinay, Alisha, Abhilasha, Paromita and Sardar Harpal Singh.

Seated on Alisha's lap was a bouncing baby boy, two years old. His name was Siddharth. The name was chosen because Siddharth had been the real name of Gautama Buddha. At this moment the boy named after Gautama Buddha was interested only in divine thoughts of toppling over the glass of water in front of Alisha.

'The tenth Annual General Meeting of Anayasar Research Private Limited is called to order,' said Karma. 'I understand that 100 per cent of the company's shareholders are present.'

'With the permission of the Chair, I would like to say something,' said a voice. Everyone turned towards Adhyapika Jyoti. 'May I compliment both Vinay and Alisha for donating the shares held by their fathers to Jeevan

Prakash,' she said. 'I am sure that the 80 per cent shares that we hold will be used for the good of all humanity.'

'I would also like to say something,' said Abhilasha. Karma nodded his assent.

'I just wish to say that I am proud of both these children for taking the decision that they did,' said Abhilasha.

'I second that,' said Paromita. 'I could not have expected differently from either Vinay or Alisha. God bless you both.'

Karma stood up, walked out of the conference room and came back holding a glass box with a highly polished wooden base. He placed it on the conference table. Inside the box were two wristlets, one placed on top of the other. Each wristlet bore a name—Manjit and Daljit. But these were not copper kadas.

They were gold.

Karma lifted the glass box and took out the two kadas. The moment he separated them, they turned to copper. Adhyapika Jyoti smiled. *He is the ideal person to be the Preserver of the Secret,* she thought.

He put them back into the case, touching one another, and the wristlets once again sparkled like gold.

'The wristlets that you see are Rasayana in action,' said Karma. 'It emphasizes the interconnectedness of things. What we perceive to be objects are actually complex relationships—an interplay between elements. It is evidence of the fact that any element can become another. I am happy that Jeevan Prakash and Anayasar will now be working together to attain bigger goals than mere gold.'

'Why do the wristlets change from copper to gold and vice-versa?' asked Vinay.

'Quantum physics reveals a basic oneness of the universe,' said Karma. 'Increasingly, physics now says that we cannot deconstruct the universe into independently existing building blocks. As we dig deeper into matter we realize that what we actually have is a complicated web of relationships between the various parts of the whole. Every element is not an element but a relationship, an interplay.'

'But science tells us that matter is made up of molecules and atoms,' said Vinay. 'Where is the oneness in that?'

'In fact, what science is telling us only now was revealed to us aeons ago by Eastern mystics. The rishis were entirely focused on the awareness of the unity and mutual interrelation of all things and events. All things were seen as interdependent and inseparable parts of the cosmic whole.'

Adhyapika Jyoti nodded. 'We need to understand the oneness of the universe,' she said. 'There is no distinction between the animate and inanimate or between spirit and matter. The cosmos is one indivisible and inseparable reality that is perpetually in motion. The *Upanishads* tell us: *What is soundless, touchless, formless, imperishable; likewise tasteless, constant, odourless; without beginning, without end, higher than the great, stable; by discerning That, one is liberated from the mouth of death.*'

'So the world is actually an illusion—*maya*?' asked Vinay.

'No,' said Adhyapika. 'Maya does not mean that the world is an illusion. The illusion lies in our point of view. If we think that the shapes and structures around us are realities of nature instead of appreciating that they are the products of our measuring and classifying minds then *that* is maya. It's like looking at a map and saying that you know the terrain entirely. The map can never be the terrain! You simply need a third eye that distinguishes between the map and terrain.'

'And how does one activate the third eye?' asked Vinay.

'Through meditation. The Sanskrit word for meditation is *samadhi*. But what does that word mean?' asked Adhyapika. 'It simply means *mental equilibrium*. It describes a balanced and tranquil state of mind in which the basic unity of the universe is experienced.'

'If I can't experience it, I could attempt to observe it,' said Vinay.

'But the observer is part of the process, not separate from it,' said Karma. 'Heisenberg's Uncertainty Principle told us that we can either obtain exact knowledge about a particle's position and remain unaware of its momentum or vice-versa. The observer cannot play the role of a detached observer. In fact, he influences the properties of the perceived objects.'

'So what is the solution?'

'The solution is balance,' said Karma. 'Have you heard of the Chinese concept of *yin* and *yang*?'

'Sure,' answered Vinay.

'The man who wants to travel further and further East will eventually land up in the West. And the man who wants to travel further and further West will eventually land up in the East. In effect, the yang, having reached its climax, retreats in favour of the yin; and the yin after reaching its climax, retreats in favour of the yang.'

'I still do not understand,' said Vinay.

'Rasayana is one of the three elements needed for immortality. The other two also need to be in harmony,' said Adhyapika.

She paused.

There was a reverent silence in the room, except for the gurgling of little Siddharth.

Adhyapika Jyoti spoke. 'Everyone thinks that immortality can be attained in the way that one can transform metals,' she intoned. 'Rasayana tells us that in the seventeenth step, one transforms mercury to gold and by the eighteenth step we ingest it and become immortal. No one bothers to consider the fact that there is a reason why gold is created in the seventeenth step.'

'Why?' asked Vinay.

'It is the ultimate test of the human being,' she explained. 'Most succumb. After they have attained gold, they want more of it. And more. And yet some more. The purpose of life now becomes the accumulation of gold. The quest for immortality is lost.'

Karma nodded in agreement.

'The reason that the Rasayana formula was kept a closely guarded secret was because Ashoka and his men did not want the gold ever to be used for war. It was to be used for the good of mankind,' said Adhyapika Jyoti. 'I have done precisely that. Whatever gold was ever created using the formula was used by me towards creating 2,000 Jeevan Prakash ashrams in 150 countries. Each of these has affiliated schools, hospitals, orphanages, old age homes and universities. Over 100 million people are followers of the programme. I have never broken that rule—except once in 1991.'

'For what?' asked Vinay.

'The government was in deep crisis. The country had no money and the only way to tide over the crisis was by pledging gold.'

'You mean that… you… you?' asked Vinay, flabbergasted.

Adhyapika Jyoti smiled. 'I have been repaid in abundant measure by having the two of you in my life,' she said, looking at Vinay and Alisha.

Vinay and Alisha smiled. The feeling was entirely mutual.

'But what about immortality?' asked Vinay, snapping back to his business avatar.

'I believe that we could attain the eighteenth step of Rasayana by studying jellyfish and sanjeevani—both of which exhibit bioluminescence. While sanjeevani cured Lakshman, it does not seem to have the same curative powers these days. Maybe the reason lies in the humans that we're are trying to heal. Maybe the humans of the *Ramayan* era had qualities that allowed such herbs to work?'

'That is precisely what we are trying to teach through Jeevan Prakash,' said Adhyapika. 'Build the alternative human traits that would allow for immortality. May I suggest that we end this meeting with a short prayer?'

She folded her hands in mental supplication to Shiva and began chanting in Sanskrit.

'Om tryambakam yajaamahe

We worship the three-eyed lord

sugandhim pushti-vardhanam.

who is fragrant and who nourishes and nurtures all beings.

Urvaarukam-iva bandhanaan

As the ripened cucumber is freed from bondage to the creeper by the gardener

mrityormuksheeya maamrataat!

may He liberate us from death for the sake of immortality.'

1947

Epilogue

Constable Sukhbir Singh went inside the death train in Amritsar, calling out to his colleagues for help. He began the process of looking for survivors although his instincts told him that no one had been left alive.

Luckily, Sukhbir Singh's instincts were often wrong.

Within a few minutes he struck gold. What was that sound? Was it sobbing? Sukhbir began shoving aside corpses like a man possessed. If there was even one survivor left on this train, Sukhbir would find him.

A few minutes later, he pulled out a small, frightened boy from underneath a bench seat. The boy's kurta was stained with blood from a corpse that had fallen on him. His cheeks were stained with tears and soot. The boy trembled as Sukhbir reached for him.

'Hush, little one, I'm not going to hurt you,' whispered Sukhbir as he lifted the whimpering boy into his arms. He hugged him gently, attempting to drive away the memories of the demons that the boy had witnessed. Unfortunately, he knew that the demons would plague the boy for the rest of his life.

Drenched in sweat and blood, Sukhbir Singh was about to exit the train with the child when he heard a groan. Were his ears deceiving him? Was it yet another human voice? And then it came again.

Sukhbir called out to his colleague, Chandprakash. 'Chand, I need you to take this boy to the retiring room. Find him something to eat and drink. I need to find the other voice.'

When the train had left Sialkot, the carriages had been overflowing with humanity and hundreds had climbed to the roof in their desperate bid to get to the Indian side. Others were precariously hanging on for dear life from the train's doors and windows.

A sardarni in her mid-twenties with a pair of small boys in tow attempted to board, after leaving behind her house, farmland, livestock and almost everything else that her family owned. She had also left behind her husband—who was probably a corpse by now.

Her family had been threatened that if they did not remove themselves from the freshly carved state of Pakistan, they would be butchered. Truth be told, her husband had sensed trouble when Muslims had begun assembling at the local mosque each day for long meetings. Finally, Muslims from all surrounding areas had banded together and attacked the Sikh village.

Although vastly outnumbered, the Sikhs had managed to hold off the attackers for a few hours with their old rifles and rusting swords. When the mob had finally broken through, they had shown no mercy. The sardarni had seen a thirteen-year-old girl raped. She had seen an old man hacked to pieces with a hatchet. She had seen women throwing themselves into the village well to escape a worse fate. She had seen many things she wished she had never seen.

They had captured her husband, knowing full well that he was the most influential man in the village. He had defended himself valiantly but it had been of no use. The marauders had gleefully hacked off his arms, leaving him incapacitated.

A volley of kicks and punches had followed while he pleaded with his wife to flee with the boys before the plunderers could have their way with her. 'Make sure that they are wearing their kadas,' he pleaded with her. 'There is no other way to continue the legacy.'

She had followed his instructions in a daze. Grabbing the boys, she had fled into the fields that bordered the village. She felt ashamed of herself for leaving him there to die.

She figured that they would navigate a few fields, cross a small river and head to the railway station while avoiding the main road. Before they could cut across the very first farmland, she found herself in the lecherous grip of a stinking rioter who had followed her from the village. The boys had looked on helplessly as the man had pinned her to the ground, preparing to satisfy his lust. He lay atop her and fumbled with his trouser buttons, trying to pull out his manhood.

The boys attempted to pull him off her but he was simply too strong for the five-year-olds. Suddenly, the boys saw his body go limp. It was a miracle! The sardarni extricated herself from under the brute, her kurta covered in his blood. She bent over his lifeless body, rolled it over and pulled out the kirpan from his stomach. She knew that she would possibly need the knife yet again. More than saving herself, it had been a desperate bid to save the lives of the boys.

The scene that followed at Sialkot Junction had been one of frenzied madness. Thousands of helpless souls were frantically clinging on to any and every part of the train.

She was determined to get the boys on board. She pushed both of them into the carriage, a stinking hellhole of sweating bodies and wailing children. She knew that they were small and agile enough to find a gap to cram into. But before she could find a way to board, the locomotive began moving, hissing great clouds of steam accompanied by strenuous huffing and puffing.

The train's impending departure drew a scream of dismay from those who had not been able to board. It was the last train that would ever leave from Sialkot for the Indian side. The sardarni reached out for the handlebar as she ran alongside the iron monster. She managed to touch it. But it was too late. The platform had ended and the train had picked up speed.

'No!' she screamed in mental anguish. Tears flowed down her cheeks as she realized that the children were on a train to Amritsar without her. She fainted on the platform as it dawned on her that she had nothing left to live for.

Railway Constable Chandprakash hurried back to the crowded retiring room from the canteen. He had left the little boy with a young lady wearing a beige cotton saree with a carrot-coloured border. In one hand he held a glass of sweet tea and in the other a paratha. It was all that he had managed to get even after bribing the canteen manager.

All around the station were scenes of destruction and chaos. A permanent smell of acrid smoke permeated the air. It had started with a shoe store being set alight at Farid Chowk. The violence had spread to Chowk Prag Dass where twenty-five Muslims had been butchered. After that an orgy of rioting and killing had followed. Ten thousand houses had been burnt down in Amritsar alone. Amritsar

Junction was fortunately in the control of the army but most of the city's Muslims were desperately finding ways to escape the marauding Hindu and Sikh gangs that roamed the streets.

The little boy had been trembling when Sukhbir had handed him over to Chandprakash. In spite of his best efforts, Chand had been unable to calm the boy. In the crowded retiring room, a young lady clad in a beige cotton saree who spoke Hindi without the slightest trace of a Punjabi accent had stepped forward. She had taken the child into her arms. Cooing softly into his ears and hugging him gently, she had succeeded in calming him somewhat. She was the one who had noticed the copper kada around the boy's right wrist. It bore a name—Daljit.

Chand wondered why his beautiful Punjab was being dismembered so viciously. He quickened his pace as he crossed the crowded platform that separated the canteen from the retiring room. He entered the retiring room and looked around for the beige-saree-with-a-carrot-border-lady.

The room was crowded and noisy. A young man was getting his arm bandaged by a comrade; an old matron was attempting to pacify a wailing baby; an elderly couple was repacking their trunk; an army captain was sitting in a corner, deep in thought; a sadhu was reciting prayers under his breath; a ponytailed girl was sleeping with her head on her mother's lap. A single fan valiantly attempted to circulate the foul air but the smell of death was unassailable.

Chand scanned the room carefully but could not spot either the lady or the boy. He stepped out of the room and visually scoured the platform. She had been wearing a beige saree with a carrot-coloured border. If she were on the platform, he would certainly spot her. Chand continued searching for an hour before giving up.

The sad truth was that there were simply too many helpless souls in Amritsar that day. One missing kid wasn't really that big a deal.

The sardarni, who had left the two boys on the train exiting from Sialkot, sat bewildered on the station platform. What was left to live for? Her husband would be dead by now. Her precious boys were on a train filled with strangers headed to a land that would soon be sealed off from the country that she found herself stranded in.

'Let me help you,' said the voice. It was gentle, yet firm.

She looked up and saw a handsome sardar with blue eyes. He looked to be in his late twenties. 'The gurudwara is in flames,' he said. 'We don't have much time. My family is heading out in a caravan. You want to join us?'

The sardarni gratefully took his hand and got up.

'What's your name?' he asked.

'Parmeet,' she replied. 'And yours?'

'Harpal,' he answered.

'I need to go back to my village to check on my husband. Could you come with me?' she asked.

Harpal looked over her shoulder. The members of the caravan were growing impatient. They had to leave quickly. Then he made up his mind. He walked over to them and told them to proceed. He and the woman would catch up soon.

They crossed the river and fields and reached her village but hardly anything remained of it. The houses had been burnt down and corpses littered the streets. The marauders had left after taking away anything of value. She frantically looked through the mess of what had once been their home and saw her husband, covered in bruises and blood, his arms hacked off. She hugged his body, praying that he would miraculously come alive through her love, but it was not to be.

Harpal gently placed his hand on her shoulder. 'We need to go,' he said to her.

She reluctantly let go of her husband and stood up. 'You go,' she said to Harpal. 'I need to make one more stop.'

'It is not safe,' said Harpal. 'There are bloodthirsty mobs roaming about. We've already lost time.'

'Now that my husband is dead, I cannot leave without visiting Puran da Khoo—the Puran Bhagat well,' she said.

'Why?' asked Harpal, reluctant to leave her.

'It contains the only thing that my husband lived for,' replied Parmeet.

'Come on,' said Harpal urgently. 'Let's go get it and then get out of here.'

After a long trek they reached the well. The land that surrounded it was also littered with corpses. Parmeet ignored the limbs that lay scattered on the ground surrounding it and peered inside the well. She walked a few steps clockwise to peer inside again. Then she saw it. It was a set of stones that were of a slightly different colour about halfway down the well. She pulled up the bucket from the well, removed it and tied the rope around her body. She handed over the other end to Harpal.' You will need to hold my weight, can you manage?'

When she emerged, she was holding a small parcel covered in oilskin that bore a squiggly symbol of a jellyfish. An hour later, they were on their way to Pasrur to meet up with the caravan.

Over the next few weeks they would hide in fields at night with only the clothes on their backs to lie on, while plodding on, hungry and thirsty, during the searing hot day. The one single possession that Parmeet hung on to was the oilskin from the well. She never let that out of her sight.

A military escort of Sikh soldiers from the Punjab Regiment accompanied the caravan. Names of places that had once been familiar now seemed alien—Hundal, Chawinda, Narowal. When they reached Narowal, they waded through knee-deep mud. As they walked, Harpal saw someone pouring water on them from a balcony. He squinted his eyes to look up. The person pouring the water was risking her own life and was hiding behind a curtain to stay invisible. It was a humanitarian gesture, an attempt to quench the thirst of the travellers who were fleeing.

'Don't drink it,' said some of the caravan members. 'It may be poisoned!'

Harpal ignored them. Cupping his hands together, he gratefully drank the water.

Eighteen days after leaving Sialkot, the caravan crossed into Dera Baba Nanak in India. The famished travellers were immediately taken to the gurudwara and fed mounds of yellow rice. Food had never tasted so delicious as it did that day. They slept in the gurudwara at night, weary but secure in the hope that they would live to see another day.

Railway Constable Sukhbir Singh had spent an hour sifting through corpses on the train. He needed to find the second voice. It was getting faint but the whimper was unmistakably that of a child. His efforts were eventually rewarded.

A near-comatose boy, barely five years old, lay sandwiched between the corpses of two burly men. His mouth and nose were squished against the torso of one of the corpses, thus making it nearly impossible for him to breathe. The whimpers that Sukhbir had heard had actually been desperate gasps for breath.

Sukhbir gently extricated the boy from the macabre mess and held him in his strong arms. 'Doctor Saheb,' he yelled out. 'I need help for this boy! We may need to send him to the hospital.'

'Sure, Sukhbir, let me have a look at him,' said the greying army doctor who looked as though he would soon fall down from exhaustion. His name was Dr Murshid Khan. He continued to look after the thousands of Hindu refugees while his own family was under attack in Amritsar. *Was he to pack himself off to Pakistan just because he was Muslim?* Dr Murshid Khan had no intention of running away.

The doctor quickly checked the boy's pulse. Placing his stethoscope against the boy's chest, he tried to fathom his breathing. 'He seems fine,' he said at length. 'Let's not take any chances, though. He seems dehydrated and is running a fever. Let's move him to Victoria Jubilee Hospital and keep him under observation.'

The lady in the beige saree with a carrot-border looked at the boy who lay asleep with his head on her lap. Then she looked at her husband. 'Are you angry with me?' she asked nervously.

They had been married five years and, despite trying every conceivable position and every ridiculous potion, the couple had failed to produce a child. They had been on an extended tour visiting important pilgrimage destinations to seek divine intervention. Amritsar's Golden Temple had been their final stop.

They had just finished their darshan of Harmandir Sahib and were awaiting their train to Ambala when Chandprakash had showed up, holding the little boy. It had seemed like the Almighty had finally heard their prayers.

Her husband looked at her and then at the sleeping boy. These had been the most challenging years of his life. He had gone against his father's wishes by turning down the factory manager's position at the Darjeeling tea estate where his father worked. Shifting to Calcutta and setting up a jute-trading business of his own had also been exhausting. His decision to marry Shakuntala had been the last straw. Shakuntala's caste was lower than that of the Bagadia family and Brijmohanlal's conservative clan had opposed the marriage. Brijmohanlal had gone ahead even though all familial support had been cut off.

'I love you, Shakuntala,' he whispered to her. 'Yes, what you did may be considered wrong, but there were no survivors on that ghastly train.You may even have given this boy a fresh start in life.'

Shakuntala smiled. 'I am so relieved to hear you say that,' she replied. 'I was worried that you were angry with me for stealing the boy. I thought that you would ask me to return him to the police.'

'And what would that achieve?' asked Brijmohan. 'He would have been sent to an orphanage to live a life devoid of care and affection. There is a reason why this boy was handed to you.'

'I quite like the name "Daljit",' said Shakuntala, tenderly holding the boy's wrist that bore the copper kada.

'Well, I suggest that you take off that kada and lock it away,' said Brijmohan. 'It's better that we call him something else. The sooner he is absorbed into our way of life, the quicker he will let go of the nightmare that he has been through.'

'What shall we call him?' asked Shakuntala softly.

'Where does the beautiful lotus flower bloom? In a pool of muck! This boy is our lotus—a lotus that we plucked from the muck. Let's call him "Arvind".'

Victoria Jubilee Hospital was teeming with patients. The riots had resulted in thousands of deaths but an even greater number of wounded.

'Where are the parents?' asked the matron as the boy was handed over by the doctor.

'He has none. The parents are probably dead,' replied the doctor. 'He has a fever. He will need some care until he can be shifted to an orphanage.'

'Doctor Saheb, just look around you,' said the matron. 'We are unable to cope with the hundreds who are critically wounded. Why don't you take him to someone's home instead?'

'My own house lies in ashes,' said the doctor dejectedly. 'My family and I are leaving Amritsar today.'

'For Pakistan?' asked the matron sadly.

'No,' replied Dr Khan, slightly irritated at the assumption. 'I'm taking my family to Bombay. This country has temporarily lost its sanity but I'm sure that the 345 million people of India will eventually find a way to heal their wounds.'

'What about the boy?' asked the matron.

'I'll take him along. I'm sure I'll find someone who will give him the love he deserves.'

'What's that inscribed on the kada on his wrist?' asked the matron, looking at the copper wristlet.

'Probably his name—Manjit,' said Dr Khan, as he walked out of the hospital cradling the little boy in his arms.

Dr Murshid Khan heaved a sigh of relief as their truck pulled into Bombay. It had been a harrowing trip and he couldn't imagine how they would have made it thus far without the help of their truck-driver. There had been instances of looting and wanton violence along the route and a trip that should not have taken more than a few days had ended in taking two weeks.

Their truck was carrying a load of cotton for the textile mills of Bombay and Dr Khan and his wife, daughter, son and little Manjit had spent the better part of the fortnight bouncing on bales of cotton.

'Any specific place in Bombay where you want to be dropped?' asked the driver.

'My cousin lives in Dongri,' answered Dr Khan. 'He's also a doctor.'

'That's perfect,' replied the driver. 'I need to take this stuff to Navroji Mills. Same area. I'll drop you off near the entrance to Mazgaon Dock.'

As they approached the dock, a tanker suddenly overtook their truck. It was a close call.

'Damn fool!' muttered the driver. 'His rash driving will kill some...'

Suddenly, there was an overwhelming explosion. The blast was heard miles away as flames enveloped all the vehicles on the road.

Ayub Sheikh got up from the bench in an instant. He had been taking a bidi-break from his backbreaking work at the docks when he saw the fuel tanker smash into the electrical substation by the side of the road. What followed was the equivalent of a bomb explosion. The tanker self-detonated, shattering windows in the neighbourhood and igniting several others cars and trucks next to it.

Ayub and his friends rushed to the accident spot, pulling out survivors and corpses from the flaming vehicles with their bare hands.

The truck was in flames. The driver had died instantly, dagger-like shards of his windscreen having lodged themselves in his chest. The cotton cargo was ablaze and Ayub could discern several people among the bales who were also on fire. Their screams were gut-wrenching.

At that moment he noticed a body on the road, its small wrist bearing a kada.

The little boy wearing the kada had been thrown off the truck by the explosion and he had landed on a pile of rubbish. The garbage had cushioned the impact of his fall and saved him from any major injury.

Ayub surmised that the boy's entire family had perished on that truck. The boy was now an orphan.

'*Shukran Allah walhamdu lillah,*' muttered Ayub softly to himself as he picked up the boy and held him in his arms.

Ayub and his wife Shabana had lost their own son to a construction accident a couple of years ago. Since then, they had stopped trying for more children. The vacuum in their lives had emptied any wish to refill it.

But at that moment, Ayub made up his mind. Ayub's salary was thirty rupees per month, barely enough to support himself and his wife. But that would not stop Ayub from taking in the little boy.

'You are a survivor, little one,' he murmured into the boy's ears. 'You flew into the air when that truck caught fire. You are no less than a strong eagle. I shall call you "Arbaaz".'

Arriving home, Ayub had silently handed over Arbaaz to Shabana. 'This boy needs a family. I can think of no better family than ours,' he said to his wife. She looked at the darling boy, his face covered in soot from the explosion. Ayub saw his wife smile for the first time in two years.

'He is wearing a kada,' she observed. 'Must be Sikh. What should we do?'

'It's copper. Put it in our drinking water pot,' said Ayub. 'And forget that he is anything but our son.'

The caravan that arrived in Amritsar had been directed to the refugee camp within the Khalsa College premises. It was a vast ocean of humanity, around 25,000 people. The camp kitchen struggled to cope with the flood and local gurudwaras were attempting to supplement the efforts. The camp was filled with the old, infirm, destitute and orphaned. It was a collective of human misery.

Parmeet ate the dry roti that was offered to her. Her eyes were moist with tears. Dry rotis and moist eyes. How could she cope with the loss of Daljit and Manjit? How could she forgive herself for leaving her husband to be killed by the mobs? She felt a hand on her own. It was Harpal's.

'I met the *daroga* of the police station,' said Harpal. 'He says that several thousand women and children are missing. They simply do not have the resources to look for any particular children.'

'In that case, let's go to the railway station,' replied Parmeet. 'It's possible that someone may have seen or heard something. Both boys were wearing identifying copper kadas on their wrists.'

'What was special about those kadas?' asked Harpal.

'The two kadas were identical, having been forged from metal by my husband,' said Parmeet. 'Each kada had a name—"Daljit" and "Manjit"—engraved on it. And each kada had the location of the Puran Bhagat well also inscribed on it.'

'Why?' asked Harpal.

'In the event that none of the elders survived, the boys would still have access to my husband's research,' said Parmeet.

'It's like looking for a needle in a haystack, Parmeet,' replied Harpal. 'Over fifteen million people have fled their homes. The chances of anyone having seen the boys is remote.'

'I don't care,' said Parmeet defiantly. 'Are you coming with me or not?'

Harpal smiled. He knew that nothing would come of her plan. But he also knew that it was the only way in which Parmeet would get closure. 'I'm with you,' he replied to her.

The crowds at Amritsar Junction were overwhelming. That wasn't surprising, given that around five million people were busy boarding trains to new homes in India or Pakistan.

There was complete confusion inside the station. According to the map drawn up by Sir Cyril Radcliffe, around 8,000 kilometres of the Northern Frontier Railway had been lost to Pakistan. The Partition actually cut through many existing railway lines. All of these services had now been disrupted or cancelled. While massacre and genocide prevailed, railway personnel were supposed to focus on divvying up property, tracks, equipment, assets, rolling stock and manpower.

Parmeet and Harpal headed to the station master's office, hoping that he might point them in any direction that would somehow lead to Daljit and Manjit. The station master was a burly Jat with a curled moustache. Hundred of passengers were waiting outside his office hoping that he could wave a miraculous wand to solve their problems. Tears began welling up in Parmeet's eyes once again.

The attendant outside the station master's office noticed Parmeet and motioned her over. 'Why are you crying?' he asked.

'My boys are missing,' explained Parmeet. 'They boarded a train from Sialkot but I was unable to board myself. They should have reached here twenty days ago.'

The attendant remained quiet. He knew which train the lady was referring to. It was the last train that had left Sialkot for Amritsar around three weeks ago. *The train of death.*

'Why are you quiet?' asked Parmeet agitatedly. 'Did you see my boys?' she asked naïvely.

'There were hardly any survivors,' said the attendant gently. 'Maybe you should meet Constable Sukhbir Singh. He's the one who pulled out most of the bodies.'

'Where can we find him?' asked Harpal.

'He's off duty today,' replied the attendant. 'I can give you his residential address. He's a nice man and will help if he can.'

The violence in Amritsar had ebbed but a ghastly air of death and desolation was all-pervading.

A mere thirty-two miles separated Amritsar from Lahore but the thirty-two miles constituted an entire world.

Before Partition, Lahore's quarter-million Hindus and Sikhs made up about a third of the city's population. After Partition, there were virtually no Hindus or Sikhs left in Lahore.

On the other hand, Amritsar's Muslims constituted almost 50 per cent of the city's population of 400,000. Now there were almost no Muslims left in Amritsar.

Mob frenzy had gutted 4,000 houses in Lahore and 10,000 houses in Amritsar. Punjab had been surgically dissected and the wounds would take time to heal, if ever. Parmeet and Harpal reached the address given by the attendant only to find the house gutted.

Please, God, prayed Parmeet fervently. *Give the boys back to me.*

Harpal stopped a passer-by. 'Is this house where Constable Sukhbir Singh stays?' he asked.

'He died,' said the stranger. 'Third-degree burns.'

'But this is a Hindu locality,' sputtered Harpal. 'I thought that it was Muslim homes in Amritsar that were targeted.'

'As also homes of traitors,' replied the man. 'The neighbours found that Sukhbir had given shelter to a Muslim family. His deputy Chandprakash, who was visiting, had also been involved. The house was set alight and when they tried to get out, the mobs pelted them with stones. All of them perished, including two children.'

'How old were the kids?' asked Parmeet frantically. The man looked at her suspiciously.

'How old were they?' she asked again, her voice quavering.

'Around five or six. I never saw them but that's what I heard.'

Harpal attempted to grasp her hand but before he could do so, Parmeet had fallen to the ground, sobbing.

Harpal and Parmeet reached the Kurukshetra camp a week later after hitching rides on buses and trucks. It was said that this camp—being run jointly by the Armed Forces and Mahashiva Baba—was one of the biggest ones. As soon as they entered the camp they saw the enormity of the task that confronted the helpers. Thousands of refugees had to be looked after. Parmeet was in a daze. The fact that she had lost everything that was of value to her, her husband and the boys, made her want to give up on life. It was only Harpal who kept trying to flag her spirits. In addition, another young Sikh woman called Kamaljot became her friend.

Then, one day, she saw Mahashiva Baba. He motioned her to approach him. 'Sometimes, the best way to heal is by helping others heal,' he said to her. Those words had instilled a new zeal in her. She stopped thinking of herself as a refugee and instead started actively helping others in the camp. She would cook food, clean toilets, bandage wounds and wash sheets. She was seemingly indefatigable. At night she would retire with a manuscript that had been left behind at the camp by a young volunteer from England. He worked at a publishing company called George Allen &Unwin. Disputes with the fifty-something author had held up publication and the executive had discarded his copy at the camp before returning to England. It was tentatively titled *The Lord of the Rings*. Parmeet would read a couple of pages each night before falling asleep next to Kamaljot. It was the only reading material that she had been able to find inside the enormous Kurukshetra camp.

She had stayed on at the camp along with Harpal and his kin until 14 December 1950—a day before Sardar Vallabhbhai Patel died. That day Harpal had proposed to her.

'I hope you will not consider it inappropriate, but it has been three years since you lost your family, Parmeet,' he had said hesitantly to her. 'I find myself hopelessly in love with you. Could you see yourself marrying me?'

'Harpal, I also want…' she began but her words were cut off by Mahashiva Baba who appeared from nowhere.

'Did helping others help you?' he asked her, with Harpal looking on.

'Yes, Baba, it did,' she said.

'How would you like to help the whole world? It could be your path to God,' he said to her.

'Yes, Baba, I would like that,' said Parmeet.

'Are you willing to renounce and forsake everything to serve the greater good of humanity?' asked Mahashiva Baba.

Parmeet looked at Harpal, torn between two tantalizing possibilities. Then she looked at Mahashiva Baba. She knelt down before her guru.

'Henceforth, you shall be known as Adhyapika Jyoti,' said Mahashiva Baba, placing his hand on her head in blessing.

Parmeet saw Harpal pack his things as he prepared to leave the camp. She felt the tears well up in her eyes as she saw the man that she had grown to love get ready to leave her.

She was torn between her duty to the world and her love for him. Every fibre of her being wanted him to stay on but she knew that she had no right to ask that of him.

'Where will you go?' she asked him, her voice choked with emotion.

'An uncle runs a general merchandise shop in Thimpu,' he said. 'I will work for him before I venture into a business of my own.'

'Thimpu?' she asked.

'Bhutan,' he replied.

'Will you miss me?' she asked.

'You really want an answer?' asked Harpal. 'Isn't it obvious what my answer would be?'

'You have already done for me more than what was your duty,' said Parmeet. 'Will you do me one last favour?'

'I can never say no to you, Parmeet,' he said.

'Marry Kamaljot,' said Parmeet. 'She will be a good wife.'

Parmeet—now christened Adhyapika Jyoti—sat inside Mahashiva Baba's tent. In front of her was the oilskin parcel. She had opened it and revealed all to Baba.

'This is the Rasayana formula that Ashoka's research team worked on,' said Baba in a whisper He gently turned the pages that had turned yellow with age. 'This paper seems modern enough,' said Baba.

'Each successor in the chain was entrusted with the task of copying the previous papers into new and destroying the old,' replied Parmeet. 'My husband was the final one in the chain. He had been identified as a successor by Jagat Singh who had been chosen by Diwan Dinanath, the finance minister of Maharaja Ranjit Singh. Jagat Singh died young and so my husband had to step in at a rather early age.'

'But your husband must have been training someone to take over and guard the secret?' asked Baba.

'Our son, Manjit, was a playful sort,' said Parmeet. 'My husband knew that he would not be the ideal person to carry the secret. Luckily, the rules did not require the successor to be a blood relative. My husband and I took in Jagat Singh's son after his early death. His name was Daljit. My husband had identified the boy as the next keeper of the secret.'

'So the two boys who left you in Sialkot were not brothers?' asked Baba.

'No, Manjit was my son, Daljit was not,' said Adhyapika Jyoti. 'But I treated both equally. There was never any difference between them as far as my love and affection went.'

'It is important that you become the Preserver of the Secret until such time as you are able to find a worth successor,' said Baba. 'It is vital that the chain is preserved.'

'Why?' asked Adhyapika Jyoti.

'We human beings think that mortality is a natural process,' said Baba. 'It is not. *Immortality* is our natural state. We have interfered with nature and upset that natural state. We need someone to reverse that.'

'What do you mean?' asked Adhyapika.

'Mortality is one of the significant characteristics that separates human beings from God,' said Baba. 'To become immortal one has to become one with God. One has to *be* God. *All* of us are God. We are energy and God is energy. We are made of the same stuff. It's like comparing oceans, rivers, lakes and streams. Different forms, same stuff. The day you can forget your form and recognize your true self—the stuff that you are made of—you will have become God.'

'Are you God?' asked Adhyapika.

'Yes,' answered Baba.

'Of what use is Rasayana to me then?' asked Adhyapika. 'I would rather follow in your footsteps, Baba. It is said that you have been alive for over 300 years!'

'That's true,' said Baba, a faint smile hovering on his face.

'You've been alive since 300 years?' asked Adhyapika Jyoti.

'That's false,' said Baba.

Adhyapika Jyoti looked utterly confused. Mahashiva Baba helped her. 'I have indeed been alive *for* 300 years but not *since* 300 years.'

'What do you mean?' asked Adhyapika Jyoti.

'I have not only been alive for 300 years but also for 3,000 years. Also for 4,000, 5,000, 6,000 and 7,000 years!'

Adhyapika Jyoti looked terrified. 'Who are you?' she whispered.

'I am Hanuman,' said Mahashiva Baba simply, as his muscles rippled and his prominent jaw broke into a smile.

Adhyapika Jyoti trembled as she asked her next question. 'Didn't the events of the *Ramayan* happen thousands of years ago?'

'Yes,' replied Mahashiva Baba. 'Lord Rama was born when the sun was in Aries, Saturn was in Libra, Jupiter was in Cancer, Venus was in Pisces and Mars was in Capricorn. It was the lunar month of *Chaitra*, the ninth day after the new moon and the moon was near *Punarvasu Nakshatra*. Cancer was the *lagna* and Jupiter was above the horizon.'

'What does that mean?' asked Adhyapika Jyoti.

'It means that Rama was born on 10 January in 5114 BCE at precisely 12.30 pm.'

'And you lived on?' asked Adhyapika.

'Lord Rama offered me *moksha*—liberation from the cycle of birth, death and rebirth—but I shunned it,' replied Baba. 'I requested that I be allowed to remain on earth for as long as Rama continues to be venerated by people. I am a *Chiranjeevi*.'

'Chiranjeevi?' asked Adhyapika.

'The term Chiranjeevi is a combination of *chiram*—which means permanent—and *jeevi*—which means living being. In effect, it refers to immortals.'

'So you would have seen it all,' murmured Adhyapika Jyoti.

'Indeed I have. In fact I even saw the Rasayana formula being handed over for safekeeping to Kalapasika by Ashoka,' said Baba.

'You were there?' asked Adhyapika Jyoti incredulously.

'Who were the Nine Special Men of Ashoka?' asked Mahashiva Baba.

'Scientists and researchers?' asked Adhyapika tentatively.

'One of them—the first Preserver of the Secret—Kalapasika was indeed a scientist. But the other eight were not.'

'Who were they?' asked Adhyapika.

'The *Ashta Chiranjeevi*,' replied Mahashiva Baba. 'The Eight Immortals, including me.'

Adhyapika Jyoti's head was spinning. She didn't know what to believe anymore.

'Who are the Eight Immortals?' asked Adhyapika.

'One of them is Ashwatthama, the son of guru Drona. He was given immortality not as a boon but as a curse for his misdeeds. Then there's Vyasa, the sage who narrated the *Mahabharata*. He was born in Tretayug, lived through Dwaparyug and Kalyug. Also there is the Asura King Bali whose pious deeds on earth provided him with the boon of being able to visit his subjects once a year during Onam.'

'That's only three,' said Adhyapika.

'Well, the fourth is Vibhishana, Ravana's brother. He was made immortal in order to maintain morality and righteousness in Lanka. Fifth, there's Kripa, the *kulguru* of the Kurus. His impartiality towards all of his students was the reason for his immortality. And sixth, Parshurama, the master of *astras*, *shastras* and celestial weapons. He is waiting for Kalki, the final avatar of Vishnu, to appear so that he may train him in warfare. Seventh is Markendeya, a devotee of Shiva who was granted immortality by him when Shiva and Yama fought each other. Finally, there's me, the eighth.'

'But why were all of you in Ashoka's kingdom at the same time?'

'After the Kalinga War ended, Ashoka devoted much of his kingdom's resources towards tracing us. Ashoka sent missionaries to many places. One of the reasons for sending travellers to far-flung places was to find us. He then had to convince each of us that the research was being carried out for the good of mankind, not for his own personal gain.'

'In that case, why leave the secret with Kalapasika?' asked Adhyapika. 'Why not leave the Rasayana formula with one of the eight immortals?'

'Because Kalapasika's research was work in progress,' answered Mahashiva Baba. 'We are immortals but Kalapasika was not. He used the eight of us—along with other materials such as jellyfish and sanjeevani—as his test subjects. He succeeded in the penultimate step of Rasayana—converting mercury to gold—but not in converting mortal to immortal. It was believed that some time in the future, the research would yield results and hence the need for a chain of researchers who would continue the work.'

'But all eight of you became immortal without Rasayana,' said Adhyapika Jyoti.

'It is now being proved by science that through various yogic practices, amrit can be released from the pituitary gland during deep meditation. It happened for me. You do not need to synthesize it through Rasayana.'

'But why is the Rasayana formula not working any more?' she asked. 'Why are the very Preservers of the Secret turning out to be mortal? Why has Rasayana simply become alchemy to create gold for kings who can then endow places of worship?'

'Because of the missing third eye,' said Baba.

'The third eye?' asked Adhyapika.

'The third eye—as on Shiva's forehead—is the spiritual eye or *ajna chakra*. It symbolizes higher consciousness and allows us to understand that we are only seeing a map. The map is a representation of an actual terrain but seeing the map is not the same as seeing the terrain. Every person possesses a third eye but it can be activated only after years of meditation. It's the reason why we pray to Shiva for immortality. *Om tryambakam yajaamahe, sugandhim pushti-vardhanam, Urvaarukam-iva bandhanaan, mrityormuksheeya maamrataat!* We worship the three-eyed lord who is fragrant and who nourishes and nurtures all beings. As the ripened cucumber is freed from its bondage to the creeper by the gardener, may He liberate us from death for the sake of immortality.'

Baba opened the oilskin folder once again and turned to the last page. He read out the words in Prakrit on the last page:

All that is gold does not glitter,
Not all those who wander are lost.
Food that is sweet can be bitter
Eyes meant to see can be glossed.
Seeing eyes are children two,
But the discerning eye is the mother.
Potions and chants, it is true,
Are complemented by another.

'Everything in the universe can be attained through a combination of three processes,' said Baba. '*Mantra, tantra* and *yantra*. These three processes are similar to the Taoist philosophy of the three treasures—*ching, qi* and *shen*.'

Adhyapika Jyoti remained silent.

'Immortality requires all three processes to be perfectly balanced. Mantra is the use of one's mind—or *man*. Rishis who sit in meditation for years are said to use mantra. Reciting the Mahamrityunjaya Mantra is thus the first element.'

'What is the second?' asked Adhyapika Jyoti.

'The second element is tantra,' said Baba. 'It's the use of one's body—or *tan*—to achieve something. Yogic *asana*s, for example, are tantra. The alchemical potions created by Rasayana are also tantra.'

'The third element is yantra,' said Baba. 'It's related to the third eye—the one that separates illusion from reality. It's the use of one's consciousness, one's spirit, one's soul. The three elements—mantra, tantra and yantra—are about the equilibrium of mind, body and consciousness. *Seeing eyes are children two, but the discerning eye is the mother. Potions and chants, it is true, are complemented by another.*'

Mahashiva Baba gave a small ball of crumpled paper to Adhyapika Jyoti. 'What is it?' she asked.

'Sanjeevani,' replied Baba. 'The very same one that I brought back for Lakshmana. It will work provided that all three elements are balanced. It's easy to master mantra and tantra but very few are able to activate their third eye.'

'And if the three are balanced?' asked Adhyapika.

'One lives forever,' said Baba.

'But if we can turn ordinary metals into gold, why can't we turn mortal to immortal?

'What does the *Brihadaranyaka Upanishad* say?' asked Baba. '*Asato mā sad gamaya, tamaso mā jyotir gamaya, mrtyor māmrtam gamaya.* From the unreal lead me to the real, from darkness lead me to light, from death lead me to immortality.'

'Yes,' said Adhyapika hesitantly. 'And?'

'Before you can go from mortal to immortal, you have to be able to distinguish real from unreal. One doesn't need gold or a crown to be a master. The third eye is what one needs.'

Adhyapika Jyoti prostrated herself before Mahashiva Baba. In her mind, she recalled a passage from the manuscript of *The Lord of the Rings*:

All that is gold does not glitter,
Not all those who wander are lost;
The old that is strong does not wither,
Deep roots are not reached by the frost.
From the ashes a fire shall be woken,
A light from the shadows shall spring;
Renewed shall be blade that was broken,
The crownless again shall be king.

Bibliography & Notes

I have always held the view that a book should be a starting point into a deeper exploration of the subject. In keeping with the tradition established in my previous novels, here's a list of books, in alphabetical order, that I referred to extensively while penning this novel. You may wish to consider reading some of these wonderful books.

1. *96 Great Questions to Ask Before You Hire,* by Paul Falcone, Amacom
2. *Ageless Body, Timeless Mind: The Quantum Alternative to Growing Old,* by Deepak Chopra, Harmony
3. *Alchemy and Alchemists,* by C. J. S. Thompson, Dover Publications
4. *Ambani & Sons,* by Hamish McDonald, Roli Books
5. *Ancient Indian System of Rasayana Suvarnatantra: A Treatise on Alchemy/ Rasayana,* by Chittrabrata Palit and Nupur Dasgupta
6. *A Random Walk Down Wall Street,* by Burton G Malkiel, W. W. Norton & Company
7. *Bombay to Mumbai: Changing Perspectives,* by P. Rohatgi, Pheroza J. Godrej, R. Mehrotra, Marg Foundation
8. *Brain, Mind, Cosmos: The Nature of Our Existence and the Universe,* edited by Deepak Chopra, Kindle Edition
9. *Business Legends,* by Gita Piramal, Penguin India
10. *Business Maharajas,* by Gita Piramal, Penguin India
11. *Dongri to Dubai: Six Decades of the Mumbai Mafia,* by Hussain Zaidi, Roli Books
12. *Einstein for Everyone,* by Robert L. Piccioni, Jaico Publishing
13. *India After Gandhi: The History of the World's Largest Democracy,* by Ramachandra Guha, Harper Perennial
14. *India After Independence 1947-2000,* by Bipan Chandra, Penguin
15. *India's Ancient Past,* by R. S. Sharma, Oxford
16. *Information Science,* by David G. Luenberger, Princeton University Press

17. *Ramayana,* by C. Rajagopalachari, Bharatiya Vidya Bhavan
18. *Rasayana & Ageing,* by Dr Sujata Yadav, Delhi Chaukhambha Orientalia
19. *The Alchemical Body: Siddha Traditions in Medieval India,* by David Gordon White, University of Chicago Press
20. *The Big Con: The Story of the Confidence Man,* by David Maurer, Anchor
21. *The Book of Immortality: The Science, Belief and Magic Behind Living Forever,* by Adam Leith Gollner, Scribner
22. *The Dancing Wu Li Masters: An Overview of the New Physics,* by Gary Zukav, Harper One
23. *The Early History and Growth of Calcutta,* by Binaya Krishna Deb, Nabu Press
24. *The Elixir of Immortality: A Modern-Day Alchemist's Discovery of the Philosopher's Stone,* by Robert E. Cox, Inner Traditions
25. *The Great Indian Scam—Story of the Missing Rs 4,000 crore,* by SK Barua, Vision Books
26. *The Great Partition: The Making of India and Pakistan,* by Yasmin Khan, Penguin Books India
27. *The Marwaris: From Jagat Seth to the Birlas,* by Thomas A. Timberg, Penguin
28. *The Mouse Merchant: Money in Ancient India,* by Arshia Sattar
29. *The Nine Unknown,* by Talbot Mundy, Wildside Press
30. *The Polyester Prince: The Rise of Dhirubhai Ambani,* by Hamish McDonald, Allen & Unwin
31. *The Seven Immortals of Indian Mythology,* by Sunita Puroshothaman, Priority Publications
32. *The Silk Road Journey With Xuanzang,* by Sally Wriggins, Westview Press
33. *The Tao of Physics: An Exploration of the Parallels between Modern Physics and Eastern Mysticism,* by Fritjof Capra, Shambhala Press
34. *The Wonder That Was India,* by A. L. Basham, Picador
35. *The Wonder That Was India Vol. 2,* by S. Rizvi, Picador
36. *Titan: The Life of John D. Rockefeller,* by Ron Chernow, RHUS

37. *When the Dot-Com Boom Went Bust,* New York Times, Amazon Kindle Edition

Like in my previous title, Chanakya's Chant, some lines used within the text by characters in this novel are variations or adaptations of popular statements. These are listed below for your reference:

1. "All that is gold does not glitter, Not all those who wander are lost..." is from JRR Tolkien's first volume of the Lord of the Rings.
2. "Yesterday is history, tomorrow is a mystery, and today is a gift; that's why they call it the present."—Eleanor Roosevelt
3. "You don't get anything clean without getting something else dirty." —Cecil Baxter
4. "Business is the art of extracting money from another man's pocket without resorting to violence."—Max Amsterdam
5. "You kill my dog, you better hide your cat."—Muhammad Ali
6. "The golden rule is that those who have the gold make the rules."—Wizard of Id
7. "When I was young I thought that money was the most important thing in life; now that I am old I know that it is."—Oscar Wilde
8. "Many marriages are simply working partnerships between businessmen and housekeepers."—Mignon McLaughlin
9. "The young man knows the rules but the old man knows the exceptions."—Oliver Wendell
10. "When it's a question of money everybody is of the same religion."—Voltaire
11. "Everybody's got to believe in something. I believe I'll have another beer."—W.C. Fields
12. "We should always tell the press freely and frankly anything that they could easily find out some other way."—Yes Minister
13. "I've learned that life is like a roll of toilet paper. The closer it gets to the end, the faster it goes."—Andy Rooney
14. "Be fearful when others are greedy and greedy when others are fearful."—Warren Buffet

15. "There are three rules for writing a novel. Unfortunately, no one knows what they are." —W. Somerset Maugham
16. "A civil servant is sometimes like a broken cannon - it won't work and you can't fire it." —George S. Patton
17. "He that would keep a secret must keep it secret that he hath a secret to keep." —Jonathan Lynn & Antony Jay
18. "I believe in God; I just don't trust anyone who works for him." —Unknown
19. "A moment of time cannot be bought by an inch of gold." —Chinese proverb
20. "Philosophy is questions that may never be answered. Religion is answers that may never be questioned." —Unknown
21. "A little lie is like a little pregnancy it doesn't take long before everyone knows." —C.S. Lewis
22. "You can get more with a kind word and a gun than you can with a kind word alone." —Al Capone
23. "Rule No.1: Never lose money. Rule No.2: Never forget rule No.1." —Warren Buffet

The inspiration for some of the ideas and themes in this book emerged from the real world as well as popular culture. Here's a list so that you may go back and visit, watch or read some of them:

1. Business rivalry: This theme has been at the core of many Bollywood movies including *Deewar* (1975), *Guru* (2007) and *Kalyug* (1981) as well as Hollywood films such as *Trading Places* (1983) and *Pirates of Silicon Valley* (1999). My primary inspiration for this theme though was a novel called *The Immigrants* (1977) by Howard Fast and *The Polyester Prince: The Rise of Dhirubhai Ambani* (1998).

2. Mafia and underworld: Even though the mafia has been depicted in various ways in America through movies like the *Godfather* (1972), *Goodfellas* (1990) and *The Untouchables* (1987); and in India through movies like *Company* (2002) and *Sarkar* (2005) my primary inspiration for some of the characters in this book were Karim Lala, Dawood Ibrahim and Varadarajan Mudaliar. Please refer to the bibliography for books that were used as research material.

3. Rags to riches: We all root for the underdog, the one who manages to become something bigger than he was. It is a recurring theme in movies such as *Boiler Room* (2000) and *Wall Street* (1987) and novels such as *Master of the Game* (1982) by Sidney Sheldon. The inspiration for characters and events in this book, however, came from real life examples of individuals such as Dhirubhai Ambani and John D. Rockefeller. In particular the book *Titan: The Life of John D. Rockefeller* (2007) by Ron Chernow.

4. Children of business rivals in love: This theme has been repeated endlessly in popular culture including Bollywood movies like *Qayamat Se Qayamat Tak* (1988) and books like *Kane & Abel* (1979) by Jeffrey Archer. In fact this theme also shows up in the book *The Immigrants.* But all of these were possibly inspired in part by *Romeo & Juliet* that depicted two warring factions (Montague and Capulet) and two children from these factions (Juliet and Romeo) who are in love.

5. Pump-and-dump scam: Pump and dump scams have been described in Hollywood movies such as *Boiler Room* and the popular television series *Hustle* (2004). It is a common fraud in which the price of a worthless company is artificially inflated by rumours, insider trading, fraudulent stock tips and inflated price transactions. The rise of Harshad Mehta and his ability to inflate prices, the Enron scandal and, in particular, the case of Langbar International were real life instances that influenced this book. Langbar International was created in 2003 and a director (Steve Pearson) was brought on board to "sell" the company to other unsuspecting investors. He was left as a patsy to be subsequently prosecuted.

6. Get-rich-quick scam: The fraud involves selling something worthless to a bunch of unsuspecting people. These were popularised in shows, books and movies such as *Hustle, The Brothers Bloom* (2008), *If Tomorrow Comes* (1985) by Sidney Sheldon, *The Sting* (1973), and *The Art of the Steal* (2013). My primary inspiration came from a book, *The Big Con* (1999), which is considered to be the bible on this topic.

7. Oil-in-water scam: The idea for this emerged from the Salad Oil Scandal. The scandal involved the company Allied

Crude Vegetable Oil in New Jersey, led by Tino De Angelis, which discovered that it could obtain loans based upon the inflated inventory of its salad oil inside the tanks of its cargo ships.

8. Melt-value of coinage: The inspiration for this idea came from a real incident in 2011 in Delhi where a team was found to be collecting coins from Chandni Chowk and then melting those coins down into slabs because the intrinsic value of the metal was higher than that of the coins.

9. Fool-half-the-people-all-the-time: The modern version of this scam is the email stock tip but the basic concept comes from the book *A Random Walk Down Wall Street* by Burton Malkiel. Essentially, you can create a segment of individuals who believe that you are always right through segmenting and targeting.

10. Salting mines: Salting is the process of adding gold to an ore sample to change the value of the ore.An example of salting is the former Canadian gold company Bre-X, which salted its drill samples, leading investors to believe that they were in possession of one of the largest gold reserves ever discovered. This was shown subsequently in the television documentary *Masterminds—Fool's Gold* (2004). I have adapted the idea of salting to simply convincing others that gold is indeed present.

11. Fictitious companies web: The direct inspiration for this story is from the year 1982 when 11 non-resident companies invested in shares of Reliance Industries. The announcement of the companies' names included odd names such as Crocodile Investments and Fiasco Investments. I have built on the same idea.

12. Scam income tax raid: Even though this event has been popularised in the Bollywood movie *Special 26* (2013) that particular movie actually draws inspiration from a real event that happened in Mumbai and came to be known as the 1987 Opera House Heist. A bunch of men posing as Income Tax officers robbed a jewellery store. This event was the inspiration behind the fraudulent raid shown in the book.

13. Fake stamp paper scam: The direct inspiration for this was the Telgi Scam in which Abdul Karim Telgi allegedly earned millions for himself and possible political masters by printing and selling counterfeit stamp paper all over India. A film called *Mudrank* (2008) based on the Telgi story was also made.
14. Matka betting: The inspiration for this element came from two real world examples. The first was Kalyanji Bhagat who started the Worli Matka in 1962 and the second was Rattan Khatri who ran the New Worli Matka from 1964 onwards. The Bollywood film *Dharmatma* (1975) was based on Rattan Khatri.
15. Switch-the-horse scam: Although some of the intricacies of race track betting are depicted in *The Killing,* a 1956 Hollywood movie, the actual idea of switching horses to scam someone came from the Australian Fine Cotton Scandal in which white paint, peroxide and brown hair dye was employed to mask the true markings of Bold Personality as it edged out Harbour Gold at Brisbane's Eagle Farm in August of 1984.
16. Sell me this pen: People tend to associate this line with the movie *Wolf on Wall Street* (2013), the fact of the matter is that the routine was always used very regularly in sales training programs well before the film came out. Scores of sales training books such as *Sales Training* by Darin George (2008), *96 Great Questions to Ask Before You Hire* by Paul Falcone (2008), *The Complete Idiot's Guide to the Perfect Job Interview* by Marc Dorio (2009) and countless others describe the concept. I personally experienced it during a sales training conference in my business days also. There is no clear "right" answer to the question so I took liberties in developing the conversation that ensued.
17. Unknown deposits in bank account: The idea emerged from a scam in the US called the Deposit Slip Scam. The scammer would leave blank deposit slips imprinted with his account number in the bank and unsuspecting customers would use these slips to deposit money in their own accounts, not realizing that it would end up in the scammers account. This book uses a variation of that theme by actually depositing money into an unsuspecting politician's account.

18. Value of information: The notion that information and timing of information has value was best depicted in the Hollywood movie, *Trading Places* as well as the movie *Wall Street* but for this book the primary inspiration was a book called *Information Science* by David G. Luenberger.

19. Parsi properties: It is a fact that the largest landholdings in Mumbai are those of Parsis but a case in 2014 of a caretaker who showed that his wealthy Parsi employer had left a will in his favour became the inspiration for the idea that lonely widows could be scammed into parting with valuable properties.

20. Dotcom scam: The Dotcom Bust of 2000 was the primary source of the idea. Several companies were being floated and they were generating fictitious revenue in order to prop up valuations. An interesting documentary on the topic is entitled *The dot.com Bubble* (2011). Another valuable resource was *When the Dot-Com Boom Went Bust* (2014) a compilation of articles by the New York Times regarding the companies and shenanigans of that time.

21. Municipal plans scam: The genesis of this idea was in the Mumbai Mantralaya Fire of 2012. The conspiracy theory doing the rounds was that important BMC files had allegedly been destroyed in the fire and that "uncomfortable" files had been lost. The fraud described in this book is a variation of that.

22. Short selling cartel: The incident of Dhirubhai Ambani fighting off the Kolkata Bear Cartel is beautifully detailed in SK Barua and JR Varma's *The Great Indian Scam—Story of the Missing Rs 4,000 crore* as well as in the book *Ambani & Sons*. This incident was the primary inspiration for the short-selling idea in which the promoter turns the tables on the cartel.

23. Aircraft purchase scam: A 2003 article in the *Economist* was the primary source of information for aircraft purchase bribery. This particular article detailed the methods used to channel money as well as the involvement of aircraft suppliers in the same.